THE BLACKENED BLADE

THE BLACKENED BLADE SERIES

ISLA DAVON

First edit by Moon and Bloom editing.

Second Edit by Lunar Rose Services.

AUTHORS NOTE

This book is written in British-English.

While my editor and I have gone over this book multiple times trying to find and correct any typos that may have occurred, some may have slipped through the cracks. If you spot any please don't report it and instead email me at the below address so I can promptly fix it.
Thank you.

Author.IslaDavon@gmail.com

CONTENT WARNING

This book contains scenes of blood and violence, bad language and adult content, as well as bullying and attempted assault. Please read at your own discretion.

For my Family,
Who have always supported me through even my most
difficult of times. Words cannot describe or measure my
gratitude or love to you all.

To my sister S. Thank you for putting up with me.

And finally, to all the readers who love getting lost in pages,
and laughing and crying with the friends we call book
characters...I hope you enjoy each page, each moment and
each new friend.

CHAPTER ONE

I always wished this hellhole of a prison would burn, to watch it crumble and fall to ash...I just didn't think I'd be in it when it happened.

I watch on through the small bars on the door, only as wide and as long as my hand, as the smoke slowly billows through the halls. The smell of burning cinders and ash seeps into my tiny room as screams pour out from the cells around me. Other prisoners beg and plead to be released, to not be left to burn...for someone to save them.

But no help would come here, at least not for us.

This was the solitary floor. A dark basement made of thick solid concrete on all sides with only a large metal door breaking it up. The only company down here was the cold and damp, or the yells from other prisoners who were too deranged and broken to even form a proper sentence anymore.

This was The Facility.

A prison made for the supernatural by those who

despise our kind. They weren't prejudiced in their selection. Witches, warlocks, shifters, seers, demons, elves, fae, all types of supes...we were all regarded with disgust and hatred. No one knew *who* headed this group or how they came to be, just that they existed in the shadows.

Some call them *hunters,* others call them *heroes,* but they were so far from that. The very beings that call themselves human were the least humane.

I used to think they were a tale parents told their children so they would behave. Tales told to place fear in little children's minds so they would be obedient. To have them listen and do their schoolwork and control their abilities in public lest they be taken and locked away, never seeing their families or the light of day again.

I was a witch from a prominent clan. But one with no power of my own. And for that lack of power, I was isolated, ridiculed, and tormented by my own kind. I was an outcast and pariah, almost human in my own kind's eyes.

But even that pain and isolation would not have prepared me for *this.*

Over these past six years in The Facility...I've been beaten until bloody and broken. I've fought against creatures and beasts for their 'tests' and amusement. I've been starved until it almost drove me mad with hunger. I've been physically and mentally tortured in ways I never imagined were possible, but for what, I still don't know.

Smoke quickly pours in through the bars and through the cracks around the door. Each breath I take pulls the deathly fumes into my lungs.

This can't be my end. I'd survived all this time in this

hellhole, fought through every torture session and experiment. I couldn't die now. Not here and not like this.

I decided after the first few months here and a particularly bad 'session' that I wasn't going to let them break me. That my spirit was my most powerful strength. They could break everything else, but not that. That part of me remained untouched, unbroken, and still searching for her freedom.

I wasted too much of my life hiding away. I was too timid, too scared to fight for myself.

I used to think I wasn't worthy of help. That there was a reason for my torment. Never realising I could fight for myself until I *had* to here.

I narrow my eyes at the large metal door, its thick grey bars and rusted paint chips blurring slightly with the smoke slowly filling the small cell.

I wouldn't go down without a fight.

I throw myself at the door, pushing my full weight against it as I clash with the cold metal. I hear a crack followed by a pain that sears through my left shoulder and down my arm, but the door doesn't budge an inch. I push the pain to the back of my mind as I try again; I'd been through worse anyway.

Thrashing against the door, I join the voices around me to scream.

I wouldn't beg or cry for help, but I'll make sure I'm heard, even if it's just by the helpless and broken inmates trapped around me.

My lungs begin to burn, my throat dry and hoarse as my vision starts to blur slightly.

Was the smoke blurring my view? Or did I inhale too much of the fumes?

I place my hands against the metal door, unwilling to give up or give in to the fatigue slowly pulling at me. I drag my aching limbs up and push against the door again, pushing every last drop of strength into my arms. I continue until my head falls onto the thick, cold metal before it.

All my life I gave up or gave in to others. I was always trying to please anyone who was even a little nice to me. I had hoped that if I did that, I'd receive some of their affection in return. I allowed myself and my worth to mean nothing to others, to be seen as a pushover, to be hit and hurt and laughed at.

A small chuckle leaves my lips, not an ounce of humour laced in its hoarse tone.

For the majority of my life, I was abandoned or neglected by those I loved, not worthy or powerful enough to receive their affection.

I became broken. An isolated shell of a girl who was beaten and bullied throughout her school years, *a different kind of hell in my youth.*

I was betrayed by the people I held the dearest; all their sweet whispers were just bitter lies. And then I was brought here. *To wither and slowly rot.*

But I survived.

I had survived through all of it.

Even at my bloodiest, I still pushed forward. I learned quickly in this pit of hell that I could never give up on myself again.

I slam my hand against the door once again, but my

legs suddenly give way, hitting the hard floor as my knees buckle. My cheek scrapes off the metal door as I fall downward, and a warm trickle makes its way down my face as small black spots appear in my eyes.

My hands fall limply to my sides, too weak and heavy to lift again.

I tilt my head to look down at the scars, both new and old, covering every finger and every inch of skin. Just above that, on my wrist, a thick silver and black metal band the size of a sleeve cuff sits against my skin. It was a shackle placed there by The Facility.

I wasn't sure exactly what it was made of, just that it always felt cold against my skin and that it made me weak. It also made me slow and my body groggy and unable to move properly or recover quickly. It was as if there were a permanent weight on me so heavy my body couldn't function properly, draining me of even the tiniest slither of strength. They had only removed it when I was being sent for testing.

If only this wasn't here. If only I'd known sooner that I wasn't as weak as I had thought. If I'd known before what I was capable of, my life would have been different, and *they* wouldn't have been able to take me. Nobody would have.

I shake my head, pulling for any last drop of strength left in me as I shakily turn and reach for the door.

I scrape and scratch at the thick metal as my breathing becomes thinner and raspy with each inhale. The smoke and fumes were clawing their way through my lungs, making each breath heavy and painful.

All I can see and taste are the fumes, the smell of

smoke and ash surrounding me as I feel the warm embrace of death quickly circling me.

A sharp pain flares from each finger as I continue to scratch and scrape at the thick grey door, followed by a warm trickle. Small red marks cover the door as I try to cling to a sliver of hope.

I couldn't stop now, I wouldn't.

I had to do all I could and what I should have done years ago.

I'll fight until my last breath leaves this scarred body.

I wouldn't cry for help or beg or plead. It gets you nowhere.

There is no knight in shining armour coming for me and no saviour ready to rescue me. Long gone are the hopes for a hero.

My sight is darkening, colours dimming around me as sounds fade into the distance.

My hands drop to the ground once again. This time, I can't muster any strength to pull them back up.

I try to pull some air into my smoke-filled lungs, my mind hazing in and out of consciousness as I try to battle fate and will my body to continue to function...*to live.*

My mouth opens and closes as I feel my body tremble slightly. My vision further darkens as my body slumps limply to the side, the solid feel of concrete behind me as I shakily turn one final time toward the blood-stained prison door.

My greatest regret in this life, *and I have many,* is not living freely. Not believing I was worthy enough to defend myself.

That I took every hit, every hard word, and every cold

look as if it was what I deserved. That I believed every sweet whisper and fake smile and questioned nothing, and that I held onto hope in relationships when there was none there to begin with.

My life was painful, and even in these short twenty-seven years, they felt like an eternity of misery.

I deserved better.

The *younger* me deserved better.

I should have bitten the hands that swung toward me, even with no strength back then.

I should have made the bruises that marred my body during my academy years the wounds of my tormentors, not mine.

I should have grown and not allowed myself to be locked in a cage believing only her sweet words and their scathing looks.

To all those who made my life miserable...I wouldn't be so forgiving.

I would fight to be free not just from this prison but from the rules and thoughts of others.

I would be *me* unapologetically.

Darkness completely overtakes my sight, my last breath seeping from my lips. The only sound being the last thump of my heart as the black void consumes me.

CHAPTER TWO

$\mathcal{M}$y fingers brush against a softness—a gentle, warm feeling shifting beneath me as I move, almost like a cloud.

The Facility only gave clothes for their prisoners with fabric like a burlap sack. No blankets or pillows sparred for dirty supes in their prison.

So, what was this?

Did I truly die and was this heaven or some sort of paradise? Hell couldn't feel *this* good.

My body feels *light*.

There's no pain or heaviness in my chest, no stinging feeling from my fingers, and no smoky taste or scent surrounding me. And although I still feel a little weak, it's nothing compared to before. It's as if something has been lifted from me, a weight removed, and with it gone all the aches and pains that pulled at me and held me down each day.

I take a deep breath; the air is light and plentiful as I inhale and exhale. I take a moment to just breathe and enjoy the peace that I haven't been able to in over six years.

Whatever this was, or whatever afterlife I had entered, it was warmer and more welcoming than anything I had felt in a very long time.

I slowly open my eyes, a brightness hitting me instantly, so I quickly close them again.

Bright lights were undoubtedly a heavenly thing, right?

I mean, it wasn't a far stretch for me to think I'd make it here. I wasn't a bad person, and I never hurt anyone... anyone innocent, anyway.

Guards and beasts that wanted to kill me don't count.

Also, I had suffered a lot in that life.

Over six years imprisoned in a place that could give hell a run for its money, and even before that, I was bruised and beaten down in the mini hell called Wensridge Academy.

It was a private supernatural academy for the elite filled mainly with malicious, entitled spawns from prestigious and power-mad supernaturals—ones who tried to break my spirit long before The Facility.

I open my eyes again slowly, squinting as I raise my hand to block the light.

I wondered what heaven would look like. My idea of paradise would be lots of hot food and some clouds to relax on.

Oh, and television.

Six years was a long time to be without Netflix and chocolate. *I have a lot of catching up to do.*

My eyes adjust to the light as I slowly glance down

my body. There are no scars or burn marks covering my skin.

My fingers stroke the soft flesh on my arm. They weren't as thin anymore, and there was even a soft glow to my skin that I hadn't seen since my younger years.

My fingers freeze as I turn my arm over.

There's a large purple bruise down the side of my arm, surrounded by a few smaller ones in shades of yellow and brown.

I look at my other arm, twisting it back and forth, finding more bruises.

My body definitely looks better than before, although why would I have bruises in heaven?

I go to move, realising the soft 'cloud' underneath me is a bed.

A cream cotton blanket is draped over my legs with a fluffy matching pillow behind me. I pull myself further up and glance around.

Looking around the space I'm now in, my eyes now fully adjusted, as I gaze around a familiar room.

A room I hadn't seen in over seven years after having graduated from the academy.

The small bed I'm lying in is made of old chestnut wood with a worn headboard and scratched legs. An even older wooden desk sits across from it, and to the left of that is a large old pinewood dresser and matching wardrobe. Their wood is worn with tiny cracks and scrapes, something I'm sure was second-hand or to be thrown out before it found its place here.

The walls around the room are painted a drab beige with a few water stains dripping from the ceiling in certain corners and small splotches of mould in the others.

Frail fabric lines the curtain poles beside a small window near the wardrobe with light cream curtains that are dusty and fraying at their hems.

I turn to my right, noticing a familiar white door beside me. It's been left somewhat ajar, showing a discoloured tiled floor and a small dingy sink.

I turn back around. The room looks old and empty and void of any colour or life. Just how I remembered it from seven years ago when I had to spend my last three academy years in it.

So, instead of heaven, it looks like I was sent to hell.

I guess thoughts *do* carry weight because there's no way that paradise is the place where I spent five years being tormented and isolated.

I push the blankets from me and climb from the bed.

Everything felt so *real*.

The feel of the cold floor beneath my toes, the air sweeping in through the old and draughty window to my left, and the noise of voices and people moving from the door furthest to my right.

Wait...*Voices?*

Why would there be any voices here?

I make my way to the door and quickly pull it open.

I'm met with three pairs of eyes as they pass me, a glare set on one as the two others giggle and sneer beside her.

"Going for a walk in your *jammies*?" a blonde girl jeers as they pass.

The middle one spins back around, her glaring eyes

meeting mine as she spits the word '*Pathetic*' before they head down the dormitory stairway.

I watch as they disappear down the stairs and to the floor below.

What is happening? Why am I seeing all this, experiencing all this *again*?

I mean, I know I said my academy years were my mini hell, but was I really going through this again as my *actual* hell?

Or was this some sort of illusion or nightmare?

Because this wasn't the worst part of my life.

The Facility held the first spot on that one. So, wouldn't *that* be what hell would want me to experience if I had to suffer?

I shake my head.

What was happening here?

Why was I here?

I pinch the bruised skin on my arm, my nose scrunching at the slight ache forming there.

Probably not the best test for this.

I look back at my arm and down to my fingers. They were completely free of any scars or calluses.

I flex my fingers, feeling no pain from the once broken and torn tissue. There is now only the feeling of soft and young skin.

Was this a dream?

But I definitely died.

I'd been on the cusp of death many times, especially after their specialised 'tests', so I know that I took my final breath in that cell.

A slight pang lances through my chest with the thought.

All those years of fighting, and I'm done in by a fire and trapped in that horrible fucking cell.

I guess the only relief would be that The Facility itself burned too.

Hopefully to ashes.

I slowly head back into the room, closing the door as I approach the bathroom and mirror.

My breath leaves me as I gaze at the reflection of a young girl.

A girl with familiar blue eyes stares back at me. Her long rose gold hair falls down her slender shoulders in light waves. Her fair skin is bright and unblemished, with two parted, full, rosy lips. There are no scars coating her skin, no cuts or burns, only some light bruising here or there. Nothing like before.

This was a different me.

A *younger* me.

One before The Facility.

What was the point of showing me this?

Of what I had been before? Of a younger and brighter me?

And of one who knew only the agony and taunts from kids her age but who didn't yet know *true* pain and horror.

I place my hands on the sink, tightly gripping the edge while staring into the narrowed eyes gazing back at me.

Why did this feel so real?

Why did everything feel as if it wasn't a dream, as if it wasn't some illusion made up to make me suffer?

Why did every moment I stand here breathing and moving feel as if this is *actually* real?

My eyes catch on the corner of the mirror, the edge broken and jagged.

Taking my finger, I slide it slowly over the sharp edge. A minor ache instantly flares from the cut as a trickle of blood falls from the small wound.

I flick my gaze between the cut and the mirror's reflection.

What kind of illusion, dream, or nightmare felt this real?

And if it wasn't one of those, then was all this some-how...*real*?

If it wasn't some sort of hell or punishment, then was I supposed to believe that I was brought back from dying or being dead...and back to the past?

Time travel wasn't even possible.

There weren't any *Back to the Future* possibilities. No supernatural had that ability; it would go against nature and its balance. And miracles...if they were real, I should have been saved years ago from *everything*.

I make my way out of the bathroom and toward the window, pushing the curtains to the side. I look out to the familiar courtyard in front of the girl's dormitory and toward the trio of girls from before.

They're surrounded by at least seven or eight boys, all talking and laughing as other students pass them, heading to or from different buildings around the dormitory courtyard.

Behind them sits the forest treeline where I can see squirrels flitting about the trees and birds flocking above.

Was it really possible? A second chance?

Did God pity my miserable life, or had he messed up somewhere and wanted to rectify that shit?

A small dark chuckle leaves my lips before I freeze the air pulled from my body in one quick breath.

My eyes catch on her long sunshine blonde hair, petite nose, and delicate pink lips as they curve up in laughter.

My heart races in my chest as I watch her make her way through the courtyard and toward the main building, surrounded by her usual entourage.

Seria.

My half-sister.

And the one who betrayed me and left me broken even before The Facility took me.

For years, I believed her sweet whispers, her *'encouraging'* words. Only it was all fake, all orchestrated lies.

She was the reason for my agony and misery in the academy.

The match to the flame that slowly burnt me from the inside out.

She made me believe I was weak, keeping me where she wanted me so she could reign queen surrounded by her lackeys and pawns.

Her laughter fades into the distance as bells ring, pulling me from my thoughts.

Fine.

Illusion, dream, miracle, or hellish curse, I'll take it.

If this is a chance to relive the life that had been taken

from me, then I'll live it and take both my freedom and revenge.

An image of the last time I saw her flashes in my mind.

She stands over me as I kneel on the ground, tears streaming down my cheeks as she bends down and cups my face in her soft hand.

She brushes a tear away as she leans in closer, calling my name tenderly before slowly whispering gently in my ear words I had never thought would come from her lips.

"Poor, Micai, always so pitiful...and pathetic. *What did you think was going to happen here?"*

My breath freezes in my lungs as she continues telling me everything I had believed was a lie. She tells me how she always despised me and how she tried at every chance she could to make my life miserable. That every one of my most painful moments over the years was orchestrated by some plot of hers for her own amusement and my punishment. That something like me shouldn't even exist, something so weak, magicless, and pathetic. That I was a stain and a blemish to the Bane family name and should have been snuffed out the moment I took my own mother's life at birth.

Something cracks inside me with her final words, a little voice in the back of my head telling me she's right. That I shouldn't be here. That if I wasn't here, then maybe the one person who could've loved me would have still been alive. That my father would have been happy and not lost his mate.

I was an abomination.

Born from a powerful magical clan with not a lick of power. I was worthless. My father knew it, the family knew it, all the students in the academy knew it, and Seria...

She pulls back, lacing her tiny fingers around my chin before clutching it with a bruising grip. Her blue eyes meet mine, a look so unfamiliar and dark I couldn't recognise her.

A slow, twisted grin pulls at her lips as she smiles a look of genuine glee twinkling in her eyes as she gazes at my face.

"Now it's all mine." Her grip becomes tighter and more painful, "As it always should have been."

She shoves me back, and I hit the ground hard, my head spinning and pain slicing through me before everything goes dark around me, only the fading sound of Seria's heels moving further away from where I lie.

I loosen my grip on the windowsill, my knuckles white with my hold on it.

I gaze once again toward the main academy building, a small grin pulling at my lips.

"Enjoy it while you can because this time...I'll be the one to give you all a taste of real misery."

CHAPTER THREE

I don the traditional navy and black uniform, brushing my hand down over the gold embroidered academy crest of the fitted blazer and toward its matching pleated skirt. Fixing my white shirt collar, I take the red tie from on top of the dresser. It was a helpful indication of what year I was in, at least.

The academy was broken up into five years; from the ages of fifteen and sixteen to twenty and twenty-one. It was supposed to be for supernaturals to learn how to control their abilities and powers better and to learn about the world and its history on a grander scale.

But mainly, it was just a hierarchical breeding ground for students to form connections that they would later benefit from after the academy.

Prestige and power were everything, even in the supernatural community.

Who you were and what family you came from was what determined your position. Whether you were feared, admired, or an outcast, it was all decided by your blood or supernatural abilities.

Unfortunately for me, even though I had come from a powerful clan, *one of the oldest clans in the Realm,* my lack of power left me a pariah even in my own family.

Which made me an easy target.

I grab the tie and loop it around my neck, securing the crimson knot.

The academy had a colour system for each year: Ivory for the First years, Emerald for the Second years, Crimson for the Third years, Navy for the Fourth years, Black for the Fifth years and a Light golden-colour for the Sixth years.

Thankfully, with this, I was able to figure out that I was in my third year. Which meant I was either seventeen or eighteen years old, depending on the month.

My hand stills as I'm smoothing out my tie. *I had gone back almost ten years.*

I shake my head before adjusting my white shirt collar once again. Brushing my fingers through my long, rosy strands, it felt soft and smooth to the touch, so different from the tight cut they had given me for years at The Facility.

My fingers catch on a small knot at the end of my long strands. I wasn't used to taking care of such long hair. As pretty as it was, it would still be difficult to maintain. I'd have to do something about it later.

I take one final look in the small mirror on the dresser and brush my fingers over the reflection I see there, a small smile embracing my lips as I make my way to the door.

No matter what happens from now on, I will be free. Freer than I ever was before.

I would choose my own path no matter what that meant or where it would lead me.

I'll fight for the second chance I've been given.

I go down the dormitory stairs as another loud bell rings from the main academy building, signalling the start of school.

From what I remember, classes would start about ten minutes later.

I open the door and take a step out of the dormitory building. The sun shines brightly in the sky as the scents of pinewood and wildflowers drift from the forest to me. A light breeze brushes through my hair as it properly hits me.

I was free.

Physically *free*.

How long had it been since I had seen the sun in the sky or smelled fresh air? How long had it been since I was able to move around as I pleased, and outside at that?

My breath catches in my chest as a realisation dawns on me.

I could never have this taken from me again. This freedom.

There would be no dark and damp cells in my future and no cage of any kind imprisoning me ever again. *Never*.

This was my second chance, my second life, and I will never again let someone take it from me.

I slowly make my way to the main building where

classes are held, enjoying the scents and scenery around me.

The main academy building stood three stories tall, with grey bricks spread throughout its exterior. Light layers of ivy sprawled up its old walls hiding some of its gothic-inspired arched and ornate stained-glass windows.

Its main entrance was a feature by itself framed by two large grey marbled gryphons and a large eight-foot black mahogany door adorned with intricate details and carvings.

I walk through the massive, ornate doors and toward the main reception.

After a few minutes of pretending to have lost my class schedule and with a few annoyed sighs and narrow looks from the secretary, I now hold it in my hands.

It also came with the date. Looks like I was back in early October. So, I was still seventeen since my birthday wasn't until November.

I glance at my schedule as I make my way through the hall. I had 'World History' right now on the second floor.

I make my way up the stairway and head into the class, following a group of boys already heading in.

I scan the room full of students and walk toward an empty seat in the middle section.

Just as I'm about to sit down, I hear a nasal voice call out from behind me. "...*Bane...Ms. Micai Bane.*"

I turn in the direction of the voice and am met with two narrowed grey eyes.

The charcoal grey-haired man taps his pen impatiently on the desk in front of him as he raises a brow.

The class falls silent, all eyes flickering between me and the annoyed teacher with slight amusement.

"You're late, Ms. Bane, and I believe I've made it very clear on what my policy is for tardiness."

I glance toward the boys I entered the class with. Some turned away uninterested, a couple of them smile, patronizingly. One even winked, but none were being stopped or called out to.

So why me?

And then it hit me *who* this teacher was: *Mr. Finch.*

He was a man who, in my previous life, I had felt intimidated by. He would try at any chance he could get to degrade and humiliate the students he deemed unworthy of the academy's education and of his time.

Unfortunately for the old me, I had been frequently humiliated by the asshat of a teacher. He had made the younger me, with already a small sense of worth, feel even smaller.

"Are you listening, Ms. Bane?" He sighs, brushing a hand down his olive-green silk tie, annoyance synching his brows together.

"Since you seem to lack focus as well as basic awareness, then maybe standing for a while will help you remember better."

He points to the wall beside the steps as giggles ring out around the class.

"Stand there and don't cause any more problems for the class, Ms. Bane." He twists around and starts preparing for his lesson.

How did I ever fear this man? His ego was evidently bigger than his five-foot-eight-inch frame. I'd met more terrifying guards almost twice his height with glares so dark and chilling they would make you tremble with just one look.

He begins the lesson in his poorly fitted brown blazer with its small check patches around his elbows and all I could see now was a weak and pathetic man. One who tried to get his kicks from demeaning kids a fraction of his age.

I take a step toward the wall and lean against it as he turns back to meet my eyes.

"I don't remember telling you to get comfortable there, Ms. Bane. This is a punishment."

His gaze hardens as he points to me again. "Fix your posture and stand properly."

Did he think I would listen and apologise, complying quietly like the girl of yesterday?

Well, unfortunately for him, she's no longer here and he's stuck with me. *They all are.*

"You told me to stand, and last time I checked..." I glance down at the ground and back to his slightly widened eyes, "I'm standing."

Pin-drop silence fills the classroom as the rest of the students watch on, their gazes filled with either shock or agitation at my quick retort. Some mouths part or eyes widen while others openly mock or glare at me. A student even kicks over the chair of the seat I had been heading to, a sneer stretching the boy's lips as he and those around him chuckle and ignore my gaze.

Mr. Finch clears his throat, steering my attention back to him as he schools his surprised expression and replaces it with one of anger regarding my defiance.

"You will get yourself into a lot of trouble, Ms. Bane."

"For what?" I slightly tilt my head, a mocking smile lacing my lips.

His nostrils flare and his eyes narrow. "For being disruptive-"

"Disruptive? In what way?" I ask.

"In the way you're behaving right now and interrupting the lesson."

"I've done as you've asked. You're the one preventing the class from continuing."

His glare darkens, his lips pinching together as he squares his stance.

How did I ever find such a weak man intimidating?

I match his stare, adding a little of the glare I used to give the guards from The Facility on testing days.

He flinches, his face falling slightly at whatever he sees in my expression.

Just as he opens his mouth, the classroom door flings open, and in walks a very tall guy. His uniform is messy and loose, with an oversized leather jacket instead of the academy blazer. He wears multiple piercings in his ears and an expression that screams 'Don't fuck with me'.

It seems that everyone got the message because they scattered from the seats at the back of the room, with the rest of the class not even daring to look his way.

Who was this boy, and why had I never noticed him before?

The boy makes his way to the back of the class, a giant yawn stretching his lips as he passes me.

I glance back toward Mr. Finch, his eyes twitching as he watches the boy's back from the front of the class.

A small smile stretches my lips as I call, "Aren't you going to ask him to stand too, Mr. Finch?"

The boy turns back before taking his seat, his eyes narrowing toward Mr. Finch.

"Don't you have a policy to uphold?" I ask mockingly.

The boy's gaze flickers from me to Mr. Finch as the teacher begins to visibly sweat.

"N–no. No need. I've made my point; you can take your seat, Ms. Bane."

The boy takes his seat, resting his head on the desk, no longer interested.

"What was the point again?" I question, pulling myself up straighter.

Did he think we were finished here? That he could try to humiliate me and drop it when and as he pleases? *Fuck that.*

"Ms. Bane-"

"I mean, what point was there in singling me out specifically? Because I was a couple of minutes late?" I give him a knowing stare. "I wasn't the only late person though, so why me?"

He smooths his tie down his chest again with a disinterested look on his face.

"Ms. Bane, I already-" He starts, before I cut him off.

"Yes, I guess someone with *issues* like yours wouldn't need a real reason to behave the way you do," I add with a smile as Mr. Finch's face flushes red. His eyes turn to pinpricks as the wrinkles around his lips grow.

"Listen here, Ms. Bane-" He grits out before I cut him off again.

"I have. I heard you. Loud. And. Clear."

His eyes meet mine, the words drying up in his throat, and a crease grows deeper in his brows the longer he stares at me.

I slowly turn around and make my way toward the only available seats at the back of the class. The students were originally there, having taken all the middle section spaces.

Surprised looks and whispers ring out as I take the nearest available seat beside Mr. Tall, Dark, and Broody himself.

It was the only available space, and he was asleep anyway, so who cared?

Apparently him.

He sits up, noticing my presence, a brow raised as our eyes meet. His head slightly tilts to the right, his loose brown hair falling to the side with the small movement and showing off the dark ink crawling up his neck. His piercing blue eyes trail down my body and back up a crease now furrowing his dark brows.

He takes a small object from his pocket, flicking it back and forth as he watches me before leaning toward me.

"That's my seat." His voice is gruff and husky with a dark, threatening undertone.

He clearly didn't like company, but I had already put up with one asshole for today.

I meet his cold gaze before glancing toward the seat he's sitting on.

"Looks like you already have one."

His brows raise, his eyes slightly widening as a dark smile stretches his perfectly full lips.

He continues to flick what I now can see is a very sharp pocket-knife.

"They're all mine, sweetheart. You see, I like my space. I don't share."

He gives me a grin that would have Mr. Finch peeing himself.

"I like to stretch," he flicks his blade out further and closer toward me. "And I would *hate* for one of my blades to hit you." His expression begs to differ.

I glance around the room pointing toward an ample open space on the floor to the front of the class.

"There's lots of space for you to *stretch* down there."

He glances toward the area before a chuckle falls from his lips, one so dark and deranged it has Mr. Finch flinching at the front of the class and other students huddling closer to their desks.

His grin widens, his teeth glistening as his stare grows feral.

He shifts quickly, darting his hand toward me, and before I know it, there's the sharp tip of a blade touching the skin on my cheek. The cold metal presses against me further as he leans in closer, his breath tickling across my face as he opens his mouth.

"Don't you know who you're fucking with?" His words are cold, reflecting the dark threat in his eyes, one promising pain. A deranged look that you would only see in a wild animal, having been backed into a corner one too many times. One that's been pushed to its limits and now reflects only the darkness and brutality it's seen and been shown time and time again.

"Enlighten me." I stare into his piercing blue eyes and

lean closer to him, my gaze unwavering as the blade slightly grazes my cheek.

Whatever pain he could inflict on me would never be as bad as what I'd already been through.

His eyes widen as a small wet trickle falls down my cheek and a single red droplet makes its way onto the floor between us.

I lean in closer to him, just a fraction of space between us now, as our noses almost touch. "Or get used to sharing."

I pull back, straightening myself in my seat as Mr. Finch writes something on the board.

A loud, husky laugh rings out beside me, the whole class falling silent, with Mr. Finch dropping his marker and stumbling to pick it up again.

The boy stares at me, his gaze a little less cutting as he wipes his eyes.

He takes the blade, placing it to his lips as he licks the tiny droplets of blood away, his gaze never leaving mine as his look becomes more curious than cold.

Then, he places the small blade back into his pocket.

"It's been a while since I've had anything fun to play with." A wicked smile spreads across his lips, "And just when I was getting bored, too."

His eyes trail down my frame before flickering back toward my gaze.

He slowly leans back down on the desk, resting his head on his arms, his gaze unflinching as he watches me.

He gives me one last crazed grin before slowly closing his eyes again.

Other than a few quick, curious glances and some

light whispers, the rest of the class continues without a problem. Mr. Finch continues his lesson a little more nervous than when it began, and I get to enjoy over an hour and a half of 'World History' in all its boring glory. Another thing I hated about my previous life, *the classes.*

I yawn, stretching a little as I lift myself up with the ring of the class bell and make my way to the door.

I grab the sheet with my schedule on it as I make my way outside and freeze at the words listing my next class; 'Music of the Arts'.

It wasn't the class I had the problem with but the words following this particular lesson; 'Group class; 2nd, 3rd and 4th years.'

My half-sister Seria was a year behind me, so thankfully, we didn't have many chances to meet during class times. Except this one.

Every second class, every Monday for an entire year, I would have to see her. This time knowing her smiles and sweet words were all fake. A show or performance to make herself seem innocent and kind to others, hiding her dark malice under a gentle mask.

I head to the class a few doors down and stop just feet from the classroom. A tinkling laughter filters out through the door, and I freeze.

Her voice used to constantly remind me of a fairy or what I'd imagine a mermaid or siren would sound like. So sweet, so angelic.

I truly loved my sister. She had joined our family late, when I was fourteen, and she was just thirteen. I had longed for affection and had hoped we would bond as sisters.

I never understood why the few friends I had around me left me after she came, or why their gazes toward me turned cold. *Now I do.*

Most of the miserable moments I suffered and tears I shed had been some orchestrated scheme or manipulation of hers. She had happily admitted at least that much herself the last time I had seen her before The Facility.

I take a step toward the room, my gaze hardening toward the door as my rage begins to build.

A hard shove slams into my shoulder making me stumble to the side as the group of male students chuckles echo around the corridor as they leave.

My anger gets pushed to the back of me as I realise where I am and that the girl through those doors didn't know I knew she was a fake, evil bitch who deserved every drop of misery she had served me on a platter and then the whole buffet to follow.

I take a slow breath, calming my anger.

Now wasn't the time.

I wasn't strong enough to take her and her lackeys on. I couldn't even manage to hold my own and not fumble when that group pushed me. There was no way to protect myself from what would come if I took her on now. I was physically too weak.

I had to train first. I had the time now, plenty, in fact.

One moment of pain would never make up for what she's done to me over the years anyway, and for what I've suffered because of her.

The deadliest predator is the one you don't even see coming.

It'll make it all the sweeter when I come for her, for all of them.

I take another step toward the door, this time much calmer, when suddenly I'm knocked to the side and sent slamming into the wall beside me.

Pain slices through my right shoulder and back, a heavy ache growing in my head from the impact. It dulls my senses as a figure looms over me.

"What do you think you were doing standing in everyone's way?" A tall blonde boy towers over me, a scowl stretching his features as he glares down at me. He's flanked on both sides by two brawny boys.

The boy with mousy brown hair gives me a twisted grin.

"Maybe she forgot her place...in the gutters." He sneers, a dark chuckle leaving his lips.

The blonde I now remember was Jeremy Colton, and the mousy-haired boy beside him was Jake Andrews. Both of them are wolf shifters and were constant tormentors throughout my academy years.

Jeremy joins Jake in his joke, laughing as the third and most familiar boy just stares at me.

Kane was my childhood friend. He was also a shifter and a jock, part of the school's football team with the other two asses.

We were childhood friends, but that was *before* Seria.

His cold, icy stare seems to agree with me.

A face that once held so much warmth and affection was now wearing a mask of indifference while watching others torment and physically assault me.

Kane turns away and heads toward the class, making

his way to Seria and the other three boys I used to call childhood friends.

I turn and watch him leave, wondering if the memories I had of my young childhood were all lies and illusions.

The memories of the five of us flash in mind as I watch him make his way to stand beside Xander, one of the five of us playing hide and seek in the forest behind our homes, one of building our own small forts and playing by the lake, and one of smiles and tears and promises of eternal love and friendship.

They had pulled me through a dismal youth and given me some resemblance of a childhood, knowing all too well what my home and family life were like. They were a hope of a better world to a younger me...but not now.

That was before Seria, before the academy, and before The Facility.

A hand slams into the wall beside my face, just barely missing me by mere millimetres.

"What are you glaring at, Pleb?" I turn back toward Jeremy and Jake, both towering over me, their eyes slowly creeping up my exposed legs from the fall.

What I wouldn't do to slap the scum off their faces.

I ball my hands into fists but quickly realise I'm not strong enough.

This body is physically too weak to take on two normal boys, let alone two athletic shifters.

My younger self had no scars or broken bones, but she had no physical strength or training, either.

My mind is as sharp as a twenty-seven-year-old with

years of experience fighting and surviving assholes, but this seventeen-year-old body is weak even by human standards.

I needed time to become stronger.

Sure, I could inflict some well-deserved pain, but it would be fleeting for a shifter who would heal quickly. But for me, I'd have some unnecessary broken or fractured bones that would take time I didn't have to heal.

Jeremy bends down toward me, "Maybe I should teach you your place in a more *memorable* way?"

I clench my fists. What's a few broken bones anyway? He deserved everything I'd give him. Even with this weak body, I'd make sure I would inflict as much pain as I could.

His grin widens, his eyes gleaming with some disgusting thought as he leans closer.

Except he quickly freezes, and the grin stretching his lips fades as he gazes at my face.

"Try..." I grit out, "And you'll regret the thought ever having crossed your mind."

His eyes slightly widen before quickly curving upwards, a heavy and mocking laugh falling from his lips with his two lackeys joining in.

"You're serious? You think you're something now?" Chuckles Jake.

"Who the hell put that thought in your head?" Jeremy pulls himself straight, a mocking smile stretching his lips. "You're pathetic and weak and can't do anything for yourself."

He jabs his meaty finger into my shoulder, a sharp sting searing from it and from the hit just moments ago.

"Fuck, Micai, you don't even have a drop of magic in you, do you?" He shakes his head and shrugs, "What the hell could *you* do to anyone? I'm sure even a *human* could knock you over with ease."

Jake steps closer. "You're nothing. Don't forget that. We tolerate you, that's all. But if you step out of line, well..." His grin falls, his eyes hardening, "I wouldn't want to waste my time having to deal with you, but I will if I have to."

Such dark threats from such small boys. I'd seen and fought bigger beasts that would have them wet their pants and leave them balled up in a fetal position.

I try to pull myself up, ignoring the pain searing down my back and shoulder as I stand up straight, my gaze never leaving Jeremy and Jake.

Jake pulls Jeremy's shoulder, "Let me handle her–"

His words are cut short as a stream of cold liquid and lumpy clumps of brown are poured over my head.

The brown liquid falls down my hair, trickling onto my face and down my uniform until it reaches the floor. The lumps and chunks roll beside it and down my face and clothes. It leaves a trail of rotten sludge down my uniform and a smell so foul and rotten that Jake and Jeremy have to step back and as far away from me as possible to avoid it.

A laugh rings out beside me before a small carton hits the top of my head and then tumbles toward the floor. More snickers and chuckles resound around me as Jake and Jeremy join in with the new group that's arrived. Their laughter echoes around the corridor as a voice giggles from beside me.

"I kept that *just* for you, Micai. Aren't you grateful?" The petite redhead smiles mockingly at me as a group of boys surround her.

"It's chocolate milk, don't you like it?" She laughs, as more droplets and chunks of the spoiled milk fall down my face while the boys around her chuckle and sneer at me.

The redhead is Ivy Harris, a classmate of Seria's and her easily manipulated pawn.

This tiny green-eyed witch relished male attention and wore way too much makeup, *trying* and failing to cover up the hatred she had for her natural freckles. Her small stature and heavy hand with dark eyeshadow and eyeliner always reminded me of a particular dumpster-diving pest. Well, I guess the boys around her *were* trash.

I brush my hand through my now wet and stench-ridden strands, pushing them back as a smile stretches my lips with the thought.

"What are you smiling at?" Ivy sneers, her petite face quickly twisting with her fiery temper. "Did your lonely, pathetic life drive you crazy already?" She begins to laugh again but soon stops.

"Maybe."

I couldn't really call myself 'sane' anymore, not with what I had been through, and crap like this was juvenile to me now, almost *cute* even. Not that it meant I would take it all lying down anymore.

"So maybe you should be more careful from now on, Ivy." I meet her gaze as the laughing around us fades. An incredulous look contorts Ivy's face and wrinkles her brow, a huff of air falling from her lips before they open again. "Who do you–"

The bell rings above us, signalling the start of class.

Ivy's eyes flick toward the classroom and then back to me before tightening at their corners.

"This isn't over." She bumps into my shoulder as she passes me, heading into the classroom with the group of boys trailing after her.

I try to roll my shoulder out, the pain making me slightly wince. I'd had worse, but hopefully, it would heal quickly. It looked like she wouldn't be leaving me alone anytime soon, and if I remember correctly, none of them had the personality to drop something when it came to messing with me.

I'd have to train and get stronger fast.

A throat clears behind me, pulling me from my thoughts.

A blonde woman stands behind me with a stack of papers in her hand pressed against her floral print dress.

She struggles to adjust her glasses as she gazes toward me. When she finishes fixing them, her eyes scan down my hair to my uniform. Her nose scrunches slightly, and she has a look of pity in her eyes as she shakes her head.

"You can take the rest of the class off and clean up, Micai. I'll give notes from this lesson to another student to pass on later." She gives me a nod and a small pat on my uninjured shoulder before heading into the class.

This teacher was either utterly naive or oblivious. I wouldn't be getting any notes, but I could still appreciate the reprieve she was giving me. I didn't want to give those assholes the satisfaction of me walking in there covered in whatever this crap was.

Mrs. Fleur was the Music of the Arts teacher, and from what I remember, she was always very messy and unorganised yet had more warmth to her than the rest of the faculty. She never treated me badly anyway.

I head down the stairway and out of the main building, heading toward the girls' dormitory.

I needed a hot shower, and fast, the sickly smell and spoiled liquid becoming sticky against my skin.

Days like these were tame compared to what they threw at me in my second year, *dull,* even if I remember correctly. *Not that any of that could hold a candle to what I'd survived in The Facility.*

Either way, one thing was for sure: I wasn't as strong as I needed to be to handle all the malice and attacks that would be directed at me.

And I had to be stronger so I could not only stop the hit coming toward me but break the hand throwing it.

Students here needed to know I wouldn't take anything lying down anymore.

There were consequences for touching me.

And sooner or later, I would have them all pay in full.

CHAPTER FOUR

I make my way under the flowing heat, the warm water pouring down my face and purifying me of the sickly smell and chunks of rotten liquid one I now recognise as spoiled chocolate milk.

I had peeled off my soaked and ruined uniform the moment I reached my room and found the sticky substance stuck to my neck and chest.

I stand below the gentle spray, a slight sting on my face with the water's contact reminding me of the boy from earlier and the small cut there.

Who was he? Why hadn't I ever seen him before, especially if everyone was so terrified of him?

Was I so immersed in my own miserable thoughts that I didn't see anyone else?

I slide my hands down my face and hair, trying to wash away any residue and all the annoyance from this morning with it.

A sharp pain slices through my shoulder with the motion.

I rub a hand along my shoulder and down my arm, my fingertips sliding gently across the soft and smooth skin, and a strange feeling bubbles up from deep inside me.

There were really no scars anymore.

No evidence or proof that I had suffered for more than half a decade in what could only be described as hell on earth.

Without the shackles on me, I could heal. But, with it, it could take days to heal wounds or bigger cuts with broken or fractured bones never mending properly.

It was also why I was so severely scarred. Why every part of my body held hideous scars and disfigured lines of skin from my neck to my toes.

I hated how I looked, trying and failing to cover as much of myself as I could.

Each scar would remind me of what The Facility had done and what they were taking from me. That even if by some miracle I got out of there, I would always be reminded of my torment by my own body...that I could never escape what had happened.

My eyes wander down my arms and chest toward my legs and feet as a warm trickle falls down my cheeks and joins the flow of water to the drain.

They were gone.

My skin was soft, young, and unblemished. Unmarked or tainted by years of torment and pain.

A shaky breath leaves my lips.

I was really free...and my body was now no longer a reminder or something I had to turn away from.

I slowly reach for the soap and try to scrub all the

emotions of the day and the past away, taking a peaceful moment for myself.

After a few minutes I drag myself from the shower and dry off. And just as I make my way out of the bathroom, I glance in the mirror noticing a strange, shaped bruise on my right hip and another forming on my left.

I brush my finger across the small, darkened skin on my right noticing the colour quickly turning to a deep black shade, almost as if the shape was being tattooed on my skin. It becomes darker and darker, with the one on my left hip taking on the same hue.

The shapes begin to take on form, almost creating a long line before twisting into an elongated backward 's' shape. It's slightly thicker on one end and bleeds into a thinner tip at the other with two small sharp curves also slowly appearing there.

I stroke the skin once the mark has finished forming on both of my hips.

They certainly weren't bruises, and I could sense something about the marks. A strange familiarity or deja vu feeling washes over me as I stare at them, but I can't ever recall seeing something like them in this life or my previous one. So why were they appearing now?

Could they have some connection as to why I was still alive or why I was brought back almost a decade into my past?

What did the shapes mean, and why did they appear on my hips?

My brows scrunch together, too many questions flitting through my mind as I stare at the marks on my skin.

Where would I even begin to look to find what they were or what they meant?

It's not like I could just go around flashing my hips, asking other students or teachers if they knew what it was.

No. Something in me tells me that's the exact thing I shouldn't do.

For some reason, I felt that these tattoos or marks or whatever they were might be something bigger.

I think they might be a small thread connecting to the reason why I'm here now.

And magic able to surpass the bounds of nature and balance was not something I should be discussing around here especially in a place filled only with enemies and unknowns.

Whatever they were, I didn't feel anything sinister coming from them.

Honestly, they looked kind of cool, but it was probably best to keep them covered and from prying eyes.

I'm pulled from my wandering thoughts as a bell rings in the distance. I walk out of the bathroom and toward the dresser and throw on fresh clothes. A white tee and grey sweats. I grab a brush from the drawer since my fingers are not enough to tame these long locks.

A small bracelet falls from the drawer as I take the brush out.

I bend to pick it up, taking the small silver and black metal chain in my hands as a familiar cold shiver runs down my spine.

My eyes narrow at the small chain, a letter 'M' charm falling from its black and silver loops.

It had been a gift from Seria, one she had given me the first week we met. She had said she had a matching 'S' one and wanted us to share something as sisters.

From then on, I wore it every day, but now the small chain holds a strange cognition, more than just a memory or memento of my younger years.

Something niggles at the back of my mind, an eerie familiarity from the cold metal. Another shiver runs through me, sending goosebumps up my arm as something whispers in my ears, telling me to throw it away.

I twist the bracelet in my hand, wondering why I had such a strong aversion to a charm I'd worn every day before I was taken by The Facility.

And that's when it hits me.

I drop the small chain to the floor as a tremor works its way through me.

How did I not realise straight away?

The same cold feeling that would run from my wrists and into my bones. The same thin black and silver metal that encased my wrists every day in that hellhole.

The shackles, the thick metal cuff. *The Facility.*

I shakily take the bracelet up from the floor and inspect it more carefully. There was no doubt.

They may be smaller and designed differently, but there's no way I'd mistake it for something else.

I wouldn't forget the cold, bone-chilling feeling they left me with. The same feeling I have now holding this bracelet, although slightly smaller in effect.

A shaky breath leaves my lips as I twist around, searching the room as if someone from The Facility would jump out at me any minute.

I shake my head.

No, they weren't here. It wasn't possible.

This was Wensridge Academy, one of the oldest and most prestigious institutions in the supernatural world.

But then *how* was this here?

I grip the metal chain, the 'M' letter digging into my skin and reminding me of the small letter charm.

A charm I was given as a gift...*by Seria.*

But why did she have this? How did she get it? Did she even know what this was? How could she have something like this, and why did she give it to me? Or was it all a coincidence–

No...it couldn't be.

If there's anything I've learnt about Seria, it's that you can't trust anything she shows you. There's a vindictive malice behind those eyes.

Forget a wolf; she's a snake in sheep's clothing.

One who would slowly poison you bit by bit so she could watch you writhe and suffer slowly before her, all while smiling and feigning innocence.

Was this the reason why I had become so physically weak?

I never had power or any magical aptitude when I was younger, but it was only when I was fourteen or fifteen did my body become so fragile.

It left me unable to even participate in some of the classes due to my weakened state.

I was also sick a fair bit, and it made it easy for the assholes in this school to keep coming back, knowing I wouldn't be able to put up much of a fight.

Had she known? Was she the reason why I didn't have

the strength all these years that later grew in The Facility when my shackles were off?

A dark chuckle leaves my lips.

I always thought that it was because of The Facility. That maybe they brought out my abilities. I never even questioned why I didn't have the strength I did there in my academy years.

My grip tightens on the bracelet before I fling it into the drawer. My breath comes out in short spurts as rage begins to fester and boil inside me.

How? Why? Just why?! Why did she hate me so much? What did I ever do to deserve such manipulation and betrayal?

How could she hate me when she took everything from me and I still loved her?!

She had everything I ever wanted: our father's love, our bloodlines, powerful magic abilities, the admiration of everyone who met her, and the love and affection of the four boys whom I used to call friends.

I clung to her, believing in the fake affection she showed me.

I thought she was the only one who truly loved me when everyone else had turned away from me.

She would tell me that even without any magic, she loved me, that we would always be sisters, and that she would always be on my side.

Was that it?

Was this all a punishment for being so stupid for voluntarily stepping into her vicious web, blinded by the only affection I was being shown?

Did I bring this on myself?

Was it my fault all this happened–

No, I couldn't go there, I couldn't think like that.

The younger me was lonely and starved for affection, the only love taken by Seria after she came along with everything else. I craved a bond, a connection, a love of any kind from anyone.

Unfortunately, the people who usually give such things unconditionally did not exist in my life. And that wasn't my fault, it was *theirs*.

Now, long gone has the desire for their affection dried up in me.

I'm no longer blind. It just took six years in Hell and death to truly open my eyes, but I'll never close them again.

The only darkness I'll see is the one I willingly walk toward.

I push an old shirt over the bracelet and close the drawer.

I'd have to look into how Seria got something like that and what connection she had to The Facility soon.

I had been buried for too long under years of lies and insecurities, except I was no longer that little girl, and it was time to show that.

I head to the bathroom and take scissors from the tiny cabinet below the sink. I gaze into the mirror and begin snipping away.

The ignorant and cynical students and teachers here, my old childhood friends, Seria's pawns, and the witch herself, along with The Facility. I would make them regret ever looking my way.

Bit by bit, I'll take my revenge and show them they should never have fucked with me.

A few snips later, I stare into the mirror.

My wavy rose gold hair falls just above my shoulders, a brighter look reflected in the blue eyes gazing back at me and a lighter feel to my body than I've ever felt before.

There were no cages or shackles or guards here...not yet.

In this life, I had time to train, and with that *'bracelet'* gone, my body should slowly be able to build its strength and heal again.

I peer down at my thin arms and soft hands.

I would need to train and build my strength and my abilities would soon follow.

I was quick to adjust as I learnt in The Facility, quickly adapting to any fight and creature they put me against. They would bring in bigger and stronger beasts each time to see how long I could last and how bloody I could become.

If it weren't for those stupid shackles, my weakened body, and The Facility keeping me in a constant survival state, I would have ripped through every guard and creature there. Nothing would have kept me caged.

I make my way out of the bathroom and toward the window. The sky slowly begins to dim, and I welcome the early night.

I look toward the forest treeline.

I'd need a quiet and secluded place where no one would go and I could train unseen.

My gaze narrows at the slowly darkening forest.

There was no better place than a restricted forest, right?

I go to my wardrobe and pull out an oversized grey hoodie and old trainers, and place them on the bed.

I'd wait until dark and then begin. The cover of night would keep prying eyes away while I train.

Little by little, I would build it all back again and then some, and when I do...I'll make them all slowly suffer.

CHAPTER FIVE

I pull the grey hoodie over me, shrouding my face in darkness as I slowly walk through the silent dormitory and toward the back door.

I had forgotten how little my existence meant to the people in this academy.

No one came to get me or scold me for not attending the rest of my classes, but I guess that in itself was a benefit.

I slip past the small lounge where our dorm mother, Ms. Klein, sits watching an old black and white movie, drinking something that vaguely smells like brandy from a small pumpkin-shaped mug.

Her laugh covers the sound of the door latching and clicking shut as I slowly make my way out the back door of the dormitory.

I quickly slink over to the benches using the night to stay in the shadows as I approach the forest's treeline.

Hearing footsteps and voices getting nearer I dash to

the trees carefully ducking behind one as a group passes by the bench where I had just been.

They're tall, most likely all boys by their frames. They're dressed in dark clothing and too sticking to the shadows, so I can't make out their faces.

Probably a group sneaking out to the town a few miles away. It wasn't uncommon.

One of them suddenly kicks at the stone bench, the force of it making the thick, heavy brick shake before a corner begins to crumble.

Another boy beside him tugs at his arm, telling him to '*Come on*' before walking toward the third and final boy. They slowly pass the bulletin board in the courtyard and down the path leading toward the academy's main gate.

Wensridge Academy had a huge campus surrounded by hundreds of acres of forest. The nearest town was around ten miles east.

A great location for training young supernaturals and keeping their privacy, but not so great for the bored, entitled students looking for entertainment.

The town itself was small, with only several local boutiques and cafes for socialising. Most of the places were older than the residents who managed them and usually needed some renovation or at least a new slap of paint.

I wait until they're entirely out of sight before I head deeper into the forest, sticking to the trees as I make my way further from the academy.

I walk for at least twenty minutes, the academy falling behind me and no longer in my sight. There's nothing but the forest trees surrounding me as I search for a small area to train.

A small brook trickles in the distance, leaves rustle around me with the autumn wind, and small forest creatures begin to prepare for sleep as others start to wake.

A squirrel scrambles up a tree beside me and climbs into a small hole while an owl passes by, its eyes glowing in the dark as it glances toward the tree.

The forest creatures move and scatter around me, with nature's nightlife falling and awakening as I slowly move through the area.

I turn toward the sky, the stars now beginning to shine above me as the moon gently forms its soft light, showing me more of the darkened forest's features.

I felt no fear in the dark, only a pure sense of freedom and enjoyment at taking in the beauty of a free world surrounding me and in doing what I couldn't for six long years.

I take a deep breath and continue to soak in my surroundings for another moment before looking around me.

This area was restricted by the academy.

The further you go, the more chances you could meet with some wild, magical beast or lose your footing and fall into a ditch or off a steep cliff. But that's what made it perfect.

It was secluded from the rest of the academy, and there were no prying eyes out this far.

If I met some creature...well, I guess I'd be getting some hands-on experience, hopefully resulting in some physical improvement. *And not end in my death.*

I release a cold breath. It takes on a small smoky form leaving my lips, the air becoming even more icy as I head deeper into the forest.

The snapping of a twig in the distance pulls my attention, followed by the crunching sound of leaves beneath feet making its way closer.

I crouch down beside a large fallen tree trunk, hiding in its shadow and behind its moss-covered bark.

The figure moves closer, a hooded dark jumper covering its face. The person sighs, their cold breath forming like my own into smoke with the colder air here.

Their large frame and physique tell me it's either a man or a tall boy.

His shoulders are stiff, his back rigid as he looks out into the darker end of the forest.

What was he even doing out here? Was he a student, or maybe a teacher on patrol?

But to be this far out?

He moves forward toward the eerier side of the woods, when a small trickle of moonlight catches on to his hood, making a little strand of silvery-white hair visible in the light.

I wait, watching on as he slowly disappears into the right side of the woods before I pull myself up and head toward the opposite area, the one with more moonlight covering its forest floor. After a few more minutes of walking, I find a small clearing with trees surrounding it on all sides, giving me great cover from prying eyes.

I listen for any noises of footsteps around me before I head in.

But there's only the scattering of leaves with the wind and some small animals scurrying about.

I pull off my hoodie and step into the clearing, stretching the tiredness from my limbs as I make my way into the centre.

I roll my shoulders out and take my stance, remembering the movement and training I had picked up in The Facility when fighting.

Even in my most weakened state, I tried to train my body.

Every day that I could move in that cell, I trained. Even if I couldn't throw a proper punch or could only complete ten push-ups, I'd still keep moving to strengthen my body.

Even if I didn't have the strength or agility right now, I had my memories, and the mind was a powerful thing.

I raise my fists, putting as much strength into them as possible as I throw out a jab-cross combo, building my pace quickly before switching to a lead and rear hook. I snap back, quickly changing my stance as I lightly bounce on my feet, a rhythm taking place as I bring my hands and fists to my head. I pivot my hips and foot, twisting into a strong roundhouse kick. I repeat it over and over, alternating between each leg and then turning into another jab-cross combo while pivoting into a side step.

I let my body relax into the movements, letting my old routine play out over and over until I lose track of time and all I can feel is the physical burn from my body and the sound of my own racing heart and heavy breathing in my ears.

After a while, I swipe away the sweat dripping down my face and chest as I take a minute to calm down.

I was much more out of breath and tired than I'd hoped.

It seems it might take a bit longer to get to where I needed to be. I'd have to train every night.

I grab my hoodie from the ground and throw it on quickly, the icy air catching me.

Soon it will be winter, and with it will come a few *'fun'* events. Only this time I wouldn't be sitting still.

I make my way out of the small clearing and back toward the academy, listening as I move through the dark forest for any footsteps or voices.

I didn't want to bump into the strange guy from before.

After a few minutes of walking, the trees break, and I make out the familiar shape of the academy and the dormitory building.

I quickly slink into the courtyard's shadows and approach the dorm's back door.

I gently pull the door, only to be met with resistance.

It was locked.

Ms. Klein must have made her way to bed. *I guess I had spent longer training than I had thought.*

I sigh, pulling a small safety pin from my hoodie pocket and gently pushing it into the door's keyhole. I twist and turn the small metal pin until I hear a click.

A grin stretches my lips as the door slowly creaks open and I enter.

The moon shone through the old dorm's windows,

continuing to light my way and guiding me until I reached my room.

I creep inside and flop down onto the welcoming bed, the old and worn wood creaking underneath me as my body reaches its limits for the night.

Darkness begins to take me again, this time a gentle and calming kind, and one I welcome.

My eyes begin to close with the soft warmth surrounding me, and the last words filling my head are of a familiar, sweet, gravelly voice calling my name.

'*Micai*'.

CHAPTER SIX

$\mathcal{T}$he sound of voices and laughter pulls me from my slumber. I open my eyes, narrowing them toward the door separating my room from the corridor where the voices persist. I roll over, my muscles screaming for me to lay still and go back to sleep. But the ache thrumming through my body is a welcome one.

It's proof of my hard work. Of the progress I'm slowly making, and of the new journey in this life I've decided to fight for. An ache I'll happily accept and get used to with time.

The laughter begins to slowly fade as I drag a tired hand down my face and make my way up and toward the shower. I open the bathroom door and listen to the old wood screech and creak as I enter.

I hadn't always been in this old room, but after a few *'pranks'* had gone wrong the school grew tired of the clean-up and decided to move me here.

The girl's dorm had undergone renovations over the summer break, updating old plumbing and modernising the rooms, making them more luxurious. But my room had been left untouched, the bathroom fixtures still their original brass, complete with rust and all. The mirror was broken at its corners and the sink held a few hairline cracks.

Although I guess I could understand why my room was the only one left untouched. Over the years, my tormentors had taken it upon themselves to destroy my property; that included uniforms, my pyjamas, my school books, and *my room*.

In my first year, they had stripped my room bare. No bed or furniture, just a single box placed in the centre of the room with all my shredded clothes and books.

In my second year, they covered my walls and floor with pig's blood and left dead pigeon feathers all over my bed and bathroom. And how did I know they were dead? Because I found their carcasses under my duvet cover and pillows.

But that wasn't what finally prompted the school to move me here to this dinky old space. It was only at the beginning of my third year, just a couple of months ago, when they let a *vasbeer* into my room.

The tiny magical rodent goes feral in enclosed spaces and '*marks its territory*' quite fervently. Unfortunately for me, the creature's feces were laced with toxins and the minute number of possessions I had had to be thrown away.

The room also had to be completely wiped and detoxified, the process apparently taking weeks. And, in the meantime, I was brought here. To a room that quite literally just last year was being used for storage. It's also less than half the size of the other girls' rooms and filled only with second-hand furniture that was scratched.

The room wasn't really the issue. It was my possessions, or what little I had of them. A few pressed flowers kept from childhood, a couple of my favourite books brought from home, and a photo of my deceased mother. It was the only one I had of her, and it had been burnt during the 'cleaning process'. The school had told me there could be no exceptions *everything* had to be destroyed. *But it was all I had of her.*

I twist the old rusting shower tap, pulling myself from my thoughts as a decent enough spray of water spurts from its head. I guess I should be glad it's working and with warm water too, a luxury compared to The Facility.

I take a step under it and let the water flow down my body, taking the edge off the ache in my muscles and washing away the sweat and dirt I didn't have the strength to last night.

After a few minutes and some heavy scrubbing, I step out and dry off, brushing my now shorter and easier-to-manage strands. Then I throw on my uniform.

I look at my reflection in the mirror as I leave the bathroom, enjoying the new look I'd given myself.

Grabbing my bag, I head out of my room and down to the first floor.

A gurgling sound rolls from my stomach, a new sort of ache taking over. Right, this body was used to more than just one stale meal a day.

I make my way to the back of the main building, where the cafeteria sits.

This building is by far the most modernised out of the whole academy.

With a wide-open room painted in white and dove-grey tones. There were enormous white and black tables and seats placed around the space, and a large marble serving stand at the top of the room. Servers in uniforms stand behind the table, dishing out fresh food and drinks.

I make my way through the doors, the smell of fresh bread, bacon, and pancakes hitting me instantly, and I am all but drooling.

I walk past a few tables, heading toward the food as the room falls quiet. I peer around to find the few small groups of students in the room looking at me, some wearing surprised looks while others openly glaring and scowling.

Ignoring them all, I make my way over to the food, every prisoner's wet dream and more being served: fresh summer fruit platters, flaky croissants, crispy bacon, eggs Benedict, and fluffy pancakes served with an extra helping of syrup and cream. And they were all plated by servers wearing matching black and grey uniforms.

The weary smile plastered on their faces already tells me they are sick of dealing with the ungrateful, pompous students at this school.

I ask for the croissant, an extra serving of bacon, and a fluffy pancake with an extra dollop of cream, 'cause why not? Giving my thanks to the server his eyes slightly widen before he nods and hands me an orange juice.

Making my way over to an empty table in the corner, I put my tray down. A few annoyed murmurs sounded at my presence, with some pointed glares also thrown my way. The rest openly ignore my existence continuing whatever conversations they were having before I came.

I take my seat and begin digging in. I block them out, the fresh and delicious meal before me begging for my attention as I take my first bite. I have to suppress the loud moan that wants to leave my lips as the flaky goodness meets my tastebuds.

Whoever said you couldn't experience heaven clearly hadn't tasted these croissants; they were pure bundles of baked joy.

How long has it been since I had something so good and so *fresh*?

Six years?

Or was it even longer than that?

I don't think I truly ever enjoyed food like this, but you never truly appreciate something until it's no longer there or taken from you.

Every meal was precious, even the tiny stale crumbs given.

In The Facility, I'd gone days without food and had been pushed to my limits to see how long I could last. It was just minor amusement for the guards, but every day without food was an agony I never wanted to experience again.

I zone everything else out slowly, enjoying every morsel of the food in front of me, savouring every crumb as if it were my last meal.

Finishing the last of my orange juice down to its final drop, I glance around the slowly filling room. The stereotypical school cliques were already forming, but the ratio of boys to girls was almost seven to one in the supernatural world, so there was always one or two girls surrounded by a larger group of boys.

A group of varsity boys pull two large tables together, loud and boisterous voices laughing and ringing out from their group as they gain the attention of two girls joining them.

At another table, a small group of three girls float mirrors above their small salad plates as they fix their hair.

Witches, always so prim and proper. *And power-obsessed.*

They, along with the warlocks and shifters, comprised almost eighty percent of the supernatural population. Which also gave them an attitude of '*The majority rules*'.

I take notice of a few of the smaller groups divided up around the room, talking more quietly or eating peacefully among themselves and ignoring the noise of the athletes in the centre. Their hair colours were more vibrant, their postures more elegant, and they seemed utterly uninterested in everyone else surrounding them. They were more than likely types of fae, seers, or elves who preferred their own company.

More and more students filtered into the room, taking up the remaining seats, but all steering clear of me and my table.

I take my tray back to the servers and glance to the table in the corner where I just ate.

There didn't seem to be anything visibly wrong with that space, so why did everyone seem to be avoiding it? Was there something I didn't know?

And then it hits me. *The cafeteria. The other students here. The isolation and bullying.*

In the past I avoided the cafeteria in my second and third year like the plague, opting for a cold sandwich in the dorms or some fruit instead. Anything to avoid *them*.

To avoid the cutting looks, cold words, them kicking the chairs from below me, pouring drinks on me and lacing my meals with laxatives or potions they wanted to 'test' out.

The cafeteria was a place of pure misery in my past, but now, with all this hot and delicious food, there's no way *anyone* could keep me away.

I make my way out of the cafeteria and toward my first class of the day. Maybe if I was early enough, I could grab a quick nap. The late-night training had meant less sleep, and this seventeen-year-old body was not accustomed to that. Even so, the training had been worth it. Even through the aches, I felt different. Though small, I felt a slight change in me. A strength that was growing inside, just waiting to expand and flourish.

Perhaps not wearing that bracelet for just a couple of days was already showing results. Maybe it had been stunting my physical strength and weakening me this whole time.

I grit my teeth, clenching my fists as I walk through the corridor to class.

I'll never be that weak and naive girl again.

I'll train every night, make my muscles and body scream with the burn until I'm brimming with the strength and power I should have always had.

A few days pass with the same routine: wake, shower, eat, go to my classes, eat again because—*meals are essential and heavenly*—train until I collapse into bed, and then sleep again.

Other than a few snide jokes about my shorter hair and a few people trying to trip me up or kick my chair from under me, it was relatively peaceful. The majority opting to ignore me.

The classes were even longer and more boring than I remembered, especially *Spells, Illusions and Curses.*

Mrs. Brunswick was a teacher who believed in status and tradition like the rest of the student body, so my being a powerless witch with no proper backing left me at the bottom of her concern with only scathing looks given to me throughout the lesson. Even then, I guess that was better than the students around her who preferred to pretend I didn't exist at all.

I attended every class this week except for the Defence class, which I had missed when I slept in both on Monday, and then again on Wednesday. I had a particularly gruelling training session on Tuesday night when I'd switched up my routine and added a few laps around the clearing. I couldn't pull myself up in time for breakfast, let alone class.

I hadn't attended the Defence class in my previous life, having been too physically weak and opting for a less active class. Except this time, I was genuinely looking forward to it.

The teacher, Mr. Valor, was known to have a reputation for his profound teaching and strong fighting skills. He had only joined the faculty this year and was a master of weaponry and battle strategy. And apparently, he treated everyone fairly equally and disciplined, regardless of status or strength.

Making my way through the cafeteria doors, I head straight toward the food.

I made it my routine as much as possible to get a delicious breakfast and dinner here. Staying on guard with my food and learning from my previous life, I did not let my meals out of my sight for even a second. And so far, so good.

The smell of cheese hits my nose. There was freshly made lasagne, vegetable risotto, and beef Wellington on the dinner menu tonight.

The server gives me a small smile as I almost foam at the mouth over the delicious-looking food.

"What will it be tonight, Micai?" Finn grinned, a friendly strawberry-blonde-haired server. His bright blue eyes curve into crescents as my eyes flicker back and forth between the beef Wellington and lasagne.

Finn and a few of the other servers had gotten used to my presence over the past few days. We'd even gotten into the habit of greeting and chatting from time to time. I think we bonded over our dislike of the pompous students and their snobbery in this school. That and they always gave me extra food.

I can't not like people who feed me.

"The cheesy lasagne, please."

He chuckles and cuts me an extra-large piece, handing me a bottle of water as he leans in a little closer.

"I'll save you some Wellington if there's any spare." He gives me a wink and goes to serve another student behind me.

I'd been training every night, strengthening my muscles and body, and I needed all the extra calories I could get. So, it definitely helped to have connections in the kitchen.

I make my way over to my usual spot, the table always being empty. And just the way I liked it.

I don't usually like to stay too long during dinner time, it always becomes too crowded and too noisy. But today, that cheesy lasagne was calling to me, and you can't rush a meal like that.

Digging straight into the extra-large portion of lasagne as the room became noisier, I glanced up, watching the tables fill up with students as classes finished for the day.

Taking another big bite of my meal, the soft and creamy pasta and tender meat pull all my attention back to the plate in front of me.

I take a few more delicious bites, enjoying every morsel. The lasagne is only half eaten when suddenly a bright purple liquid is poured all over my plate, drenching my lasagne in the watery substance.

"You're finished now, right?" a familiar high-pitched voice calls. "So move."

Ivy drops an empty can beside my plate and raises a brow. A beat of silence passes as I stare at my tainted meal.

"What? Are you deaf, as well as ugly *and* stupid?" The group of boys around her laugh as they look down at me.

I look back down at my drenched plate, my meal now soggy and soiled by what smells faintly of grape juice.

My hand slightly shakes as I clench the fork, only seeming to incite more laughter from the group surrounding my table.

"Or did you want to continue your meal?" A mocking grin laces Ivy's lips as she leans closer, her eyes flickering from me to the messy food in front of me.

"After all, we shouldn't waste food, should we, Micai?" She gives a person now standing behind me a nod.

A rough hand pushes my shoulder forward, a brown-haired boy nodding toward the tainted lasagne with a dark smirk on his lips. "Eat."

He pushes my shoulder again, trying to edge me closer down toward the sloppy plate, while another boy with a blonde mohawk comes to the other side of me.

"Make sure she eats all of it since she's so eager to stay." He sneers.

Ivy laughs, the sound of it grating on my ears as the boys around her join in.

I look up into Ivy's curved green eyes. It wasn't their taunts that bothered me or even what they had done to me here before. But to ruin the meal that just a moment ago I had been happily enjoying was *intolerable*. Another 'lesson' I learned in The Facility...that every piece of food given was precious.

I grab the dripping, messy plate as they continue to chuckle and, in one swift move, drive it into the closest face to me.

Ivy's.

The boys surrounding us all freeze, their eyes open

wide as they watch the plate fall to the floor with a clatter. The remaining lasagne and grape juice slowly drip down Ivy's horrified face and down her newly stained uniform.

The already quiet room falls into a pin-drop silence. Only a couple of whispers and stifled chuckles across the room can be heard as I pull myself up and slowly straighten myself. I brush tiny droplets from my blazer as I glance toward Ivy.

"Since you didn't want me to waste anything, it's better to share, right?" I flick my gaze to the boys around me and Ivy. "Or should I have put it with the rest of the *trash*?" A slight grin stretches my lips as Ivy wipes her face, her cheeks almost tomato red. Or maybe that was the sauce still dripping from her skin?

Her eyes tighten into slits as her voice reaches a pitch that would make dogs whimper.

"What is *wrong* with you?! Did you really go insane?!" she screeches, her small, freckled nose scrunching as her face twists into an ugly scowl. One of the boys beside her tries to peel a piece of pasta off her cheek, but she slaps his hand away, giving him a foul glare before turning back toward me.

"Maybe?" I look at the splattered lasagne remains on the floor as a hand tries to grab me from behind. I shirk the hand off and sidestep another coming toward me, quickly pushing past the two bodies around me until I'm standing beside them.

Ivy's eyes widen before quickly curving up into crescents, her lips twisting into a mocking grin as she wipes her face.

"Is *any attention better than none,* Micai? Are you that

deprived of it, you'll do whatever you can to get even a slither now?" She wipes more sauce from her face, her nose slowly tilting upwards as her lips stretch wider. "Have you finally realised how pathetic your life is and gone deranged from how hated you are by everyone here...and at *home*?" Chuckles and snickering rings out from around the room and from the boys around Ivy.

The old me would have shrunk back and curled into a small ball with just the mention of *home*. She would have walked away and never spoken back, shedding a few quiet tears while trying to clean herself up in her room alone. But, unfortunately for these assholes, I had no problem hitting back. I'd even bite if she wanted it so badly.

"If I'm so *pathetic* and *deranged,* then maybe you should be a little worried, Ivy." I take a step closer, her face still dripping with red and white sauce. "Because if I really have no one, then I have nothing to lose."

I lift a piece of pasta from her blazer, dropping it to the floor as it makes a light splatter noise.

"Having nothing and no one can really do something to someone's mentality." Meeting Ivy's gaze again, I give her a smirk, one that has her slightly flinching and taking a subconscious step back before I continue. "Even someone small or weak can light a match that would burn an entire house down to ashes."

There's a moment of silence before one of the morons around Ivy barks out laughing, and then another, until they're all clutching their stomachs and wiping their eyes.

"As if *you* could do anything." Laughs the brown-haired ass who had pushed me toward the spoiled lasagne. "What are you gonna do, *bite us*?"

"Or curse us?" the blonde boy sneers, wiping his eyes. "You've got to have talent and ability for that or at least some sort of magic...which you don't."

"Of course, she doesn't." Ivy scoffs before chanting something under her breath, and within just a moment, all the mess over her face and hair is wiped clean. Her uniform pristine once again. The only evidence of what happened between us being the plate and mess still splattered on the floor below us.

"I guess that was your attempt at payback?" She grins, a dark glint in her eyes. "Only it's futile. You can't touch us. To do that, you'd have to have power or be someone. And you're nothing."

Her lip curls up. "And now I'm going to make sure you suffer heavily for it, for even *thinking* you could stand up to me." She leans toward me as she whispers. "Whatever little hope you've clung to, I'll break it like I broke you before, except this time you won't be getting back up. You'll wish you had stayed buried in your own misery... I'll make you wish you never even made this little *attempt*."

The gaze she gives me reminds me of one I'd seen before, a look that's filled with twisted excitement. A sadistic gaze, as if she was looking at some easy prey.

Of course, that's what she thought, what they all thought.

Does she think I'd back down with her words begging for forgiveness?

A laugh so gravelly and humourless peels from my lips and has all their annoying voices falling silent.

"Payback?" Another dark chuckle falls from my throat as I stare down at the mess and then back to Ivy. "Do you feel like you've paid for everything you've done to me over the years?" I shake my head. "No. How could something so miniscule be payback? It's not even the beginning."

Ivy scoffs and rolls her eyes. "And what exactly do you think *you* can do? You don't have magic, Micai, or friends. Your own family doesn't even care about what happens to you." She pokes a bony finger into my chest and sneers. "There's no one who would help you or stand up for you, or they would have done it already. Years of humiliation and misery, why do you still put up with it all? Why exist where you're not wanted? Where there's not even one person who wants you around?" She places her hand on her chest, a mocking smile stretching her lips as the boys around her snicker. "Even *I* think that's sad."

Her words ring out in my head, feelings from years before trying to claw their way through my chest, old wounds trying to open and break free. The loneliness, the fear, the pain of being unwanted and feeling worthless and empty.

No.

I shake my head. I had survived and lived through worse things than *Ivy fucking Harris*.

This was my second chance, and I would have them pay for all they've done to me and more.

I open my mouth to speak, when suddenly a hand

grabs me from behind. An icy shiver works its way through my body with the contact.

A stream of blonde hair flows in front of me as a familiar voice calls, "What's happening here?" She flicks her gaze to Ivy and then to me. "Micai?" Seria's blue eyes meet my stare as a gentle smile curves her lips. "Is everything okay here, Micai?"

A feeling like ants burrowing under my skin stretches across my body, with how my name falls from those small pink lips.

She gazes back and forth between Ivy and me, waiting for my usual quick reply. And the longer I wait, the more I see what I never had.

The expression on her face appears so sweet and warm, yet that smile never really reaches her eyes. Something darker moves about behind them, something scheming and calculating that sits waiting and watching.

There's a little tick in her jaw, a tight clench as she waits impatiently for my usual compliant answer, her grin slightly faltering on her lips before she schools it again into its usual soft smile.

How was I ever so blind? How did I not see it before? And what else will I notice now that I'm not completely oblivious?

She shakes her head, a gentle sigh leaving her lips as she turns back to Ivy. "Whatever has happened here, I'm sure we can resolve it amicably, right?"

Ivy gives her a small smile and a nod. "Of course, Seria. Micai and I just had a little disagreement. But we're all good and clear now, right, Micai?"

"Disagreement?" Seria cants her head slightly, a brow

raised as she looks toward the plate and the mess on the floor.

"Micai got a little upset when I tried to explain something," Ivy answers, a fake frown lacing her lips. "And she...threw her food at me."

Seria's eyes widen, flicking quickly back to me as I watch on taking in their annoying little charade.

"I don't know what happened here, but violence is never the way. Ivy is a classmate of mine, and an underclassman to you, Micai. You should lead by example, not take your anger out on her because of whatever was said." She continues to drone on, spewing crap about 'keeping the peace' and 'school etiquette' as Ivy and the boys around her grin and sneer at me.

Bile rises in my throat with the anger at just having to listen to their nonsense.

I'd rather listen to a monkey screeching while scraping a chalkboard all day than hear another word of bullshit from their mouths.

Why was it that even though all this wasn't my fault, everyone seemed to be so okay with blaming me?

What had I ever done wrong to the students in this school? Was pedigree and power really everything in this academy, *this world*?

The funny thing is when you're locked in a cell to rot, none of it matters. Not power, not prestige, not wealth... we all die the same.

I open my mouth, ready to put both of them in their place, when the cafeteria door swings open with a bang and in they walk.

My four old childhood friends. The ones who left me for Seria.

Xander, Kane, Anders, and Knox shift their stance to us, their gazes instantly hardening as they see the scene around us. Then, they walk straight over and place themselves around Seria in a protective stance.

These cold looks used to pierce me. They would hurt more than the dark words and whispers of others, or the physical hits thrown at me. I used to shrink into a shell, unable to stand their cold gazes.

The younger me had wanted the love and affection that they had shown me when we were kids...but not anymore. I didn't need them or their affection.

I meet each set of eyes with a steady and cold look of my own; these faces are now all strangers to me after years apart.

Kane glances at Ivy, then towards Seria, who's now sporting a frown, before turning back to me.

"What did you do?" he grits out.

I sigh, drained from all the drama. I ignore him and walk past them and towards the door.

"Micai!" Kane yells as everyone's eyes fall on me.

I stop at the door, twisting back toward him with a small, tight smile tilting my lips as I meet his cold eyes.

"What's the point in talking to you? You've already made up your mind." I turn away, ignoring the noise behind me as I make my way out of the cafeteria.

How did I never see the bullshit right in front of my face?

Why did I ever want the love of such cold idiots? And

why did I ever let Ivy and those assholes have a hold over my life? Why did I never fight back?

Sure, I wasn't physically strong, *but still*...I could have done something, *anything.* Something other than allowing them to get their claws in me, allowing them to break the younger me into small pieces, crushing her to a point she felt she couldn't even talk back.

One thing was definite now...there would be no holding back. Even if it hurts, even if I bleed, I'll pay them all back for everything they've done to me.

CHAPTER SEVEN

I walk in the direction of the main academy building and to my first class. A whole week had already gone by since I came back.

The weekend had passed quickly after Friday's little incident.

Thankfully, the majority of the students here went home during that time, what with having no classes and nothing better to do here or in town. They would travel home on Friday evenings, arriving back late on Sunday before classes start back up again on Monday.

And for the few who stayed, they would spend it studying in the library or working out on the training grounds.

I spent most of the weekend training or cleaning up after some petty low-grade bullying from Friday; my uniform was torn and ripped in my locker, my books were burnt in the courtyard and my dormitory door was painted with the slur words *'pathetic whore'* in black paint.

Scrubbing it away didn't work with whatever paint or

liquid they used, *they might have even spelled it*. So, I painted over it and now it's completely black. And honestly, I kind of like it.

I took the rest of the two days to train and rest properly. I'm not where I need to be just yet, but I could feel myself getting stronger. Each training session lasted longer without me out of breath and each move had slightly more strength in it than before.

I'd also been healing. Any small scratches or bruises would heal quickly, and my ability to recover from training and the muscle pain from it was much faster as well.

I had never even considered the possibility of that stupid charm bracelet being something so malicious. It definitely contributed to my lack of strength and inability to recover.

Another way for Seria to keep me under her shoe and physically unable to fight back.

That was another thing. Retribution for Friday's little incident would come harder in one form or another. The minor petty pranks or cutting glares and words were too trivial for them.

Both Ivy and Seria wouldn't let me off so easily. Although at least with Ivy she would try to take me head-on, enjoying the attention from whatever scene she causes.

Whereas Seria would work in the shadows and through other people, pitting them against me. Her schemes ran deep, like thin black threads spread throughout the academy. You never knew what was going on behind that fake smile or what malicious plots she planned.

Either way, whether it's Seria, Ivy, or even Kane, I'm sure they'll make a move soon enough, but this time, I'll be ready.

I make my way toward the history classroom with even a few minutes to spare.

I watch Mr. Finch's expression as I pass him and head up to a seat at the back of the room. He *really* doesn't like me. His lips are pursed and his posture slightly rigid, his gaze dripping with contempt before he turns away to give out sheets to each student slowly filtering into the room and taking their seats.

There are a few more empty spaces than last week, meaning I have a few extra spaces between me and the rest of the class.

I also notice the blue-eyed stabby guy isn't here either.

Other than a few glares from some of the students and a couple more disgruntled looks from Mr. Finch, everything goes by normally.

The bell rings ending, the class and I get up slowly, making my way toward the next class before pausing as I realise what it is. *Music of the Arts.*

And Monday's lesson meant a shared class with the second, third, and fourth years.

Which meant Ivy.

And Seria.

And Kane, Xander, Knox and Anders. *Fun.*

I head to the class, stopping before making my way into the room, and that's when I see them.

Knox's light brown hair falls to one side, his other completely shaved as he leans back on his seat with his feet resting on the nearest desk.

Anders creeps up beside him, a wicked grin on his lips and a gleam in his green eyes as he pushes Knox forward, almost toppling him over. His blonde shoulder-length hair sways side to side as he chuckles at a narrow-eyed Knox.

Knox shakes his head, catching Anders in a choke-hold as they both laugh and play together. That playful nature of theirs and warm smiles once made me feel safe and at peace and a part of something when I had nothing and no one.

Kane and Xander stand to the left of them, watching on and cheering. Their backs are to the door, but there's no mistaking Kane's athletic build and brown wavy hair or Xander's brawny stature and tight-cut black hairstyle.

I'm hit by a short memory from our younger days, one before Seria's arrival.

Large tears trickle from my small eyes as I crouch down further, curling into a small ball as I clutch my knees closer. Another sniffle sounds out around me as I wipe away more tears.

I didn't like this day. Each year, it always felt too long and the looks from Father and all the other adults...a cold shiver runs up my bent back.

They didn't like me normally and usually just ignored me, doing the bare minimum for me to exist. But on this day, every year, I could feel the anger and hate in their gazes.

The day of my birth was the day I took my mother from my father.

I killed her...that's what the servants all tell me each year. That's why father can't bear to look at me or be around me for long...because I remind him of what I took from him. His mate.

A mate was something precious, something you only get once they say...and I killed her by being born.

Every year on this day, I learnt it was best to hide, to find somewhere far away from everyone's gazes and words. I couldn't take the look on their faces when they saw me, and with each year I grew older they grew angrier.

My stomach rumbles as I wipe another tear away, a familiar ache rolling through me as I move. I rub the empty spot, hoping the hunger pain will soon pass.

Normally, someone would make me a small breakfast or snack, some porridge, or a small apple. They would take it to my room and tell me to eat quietly and not bother Father.

But on this day, with their angry expressions, they would whisper hurtful words if I asked for anything.

'Food? Isn't it nice to be alive and able to eat? Something your poor mother can't do anymore.'

'All you do is take, take, take. The master doesn't deserve such a selfish brat.'

'Food for you? I think you've taken enough from the master, don't you?'

'You're hungry? You won't die from not eating for a day or two, will you?'

'Don't ask for anything today, not so much as a crumb. Something like you should live like a dead rat—'

I close my eyes tight, trying to push away the memories and cold words, just as I hear a familiar voice calling my name.

"Micai?" Knox crawls in through our secret hiding spots entrance; a small man-made hole big enough for a dog or a few small kids. It's our little haven away from everyone, hidden by a cluster of old trees wrapped around each other and giving us cover from the rest of the forest and world.

"Are you okay, M?" Calls Anders as his blonde hair pops up behind Knox's shoulder, followed quickly by Kane and Xander.

"What's wrong?" Kane asks, his brows pinching together as he watches me wipe my tears away. "Was it those stupid servants again?"

Xander pushes past Kane and Anders as Knox takes the space beside me, his hand rubbing my back gently as he gives me a warm smile.

"Tell me who," Xander kneels to my other side, "And I'll make them pay." His hand reaches toward my cheek, brushing the wet from there away. "No one gets to make you cry, Micai."

"Yeah, we'll beat 'em all up." Anders laughs. "No matter what the adults or anyone say to you, M, you're one of us."

"And ours," Kane adds, a slight tint to his cheeks as he flickers his gaze to the floor.

The matching smiles and agreed hums they all gave me had butterflies taking over from the hunger pains and had me grinning back at them.

"There's the Micai we know," Knox grins, brushing a strand of hair from my face, his brown eyes twinkling. He slowly takes something from his other hand, one I didn't even notice was behind his back, and gives it to me.

"Happy birthday, Micai." My little heart beats faster as I take the small bunch of purple flowers from him, Violets, and a *small blush reddens his cheeks. "They're almost as bright and as beautiful as you are."*

"No fair, man," Anders groans as he pushes in closer to me, handing me another small bunch of flowers, Bluebells this time. "I wanted to give mine first."

He stares at me, his grin growing, "Happy B-day, M."

"Yeah, yeah, nobody agreed to that." Kane sits down beside Anders, one hand behind his back as his eyes flit between mine and the forest floor.

"We all picked them out with you in mind." He pulls out his flowers, a bunch of Baby's Breath. He hands them over gently, my bouquet growing bigger as his brown eyes meet mine again. "Thank you for being born, Micai."

My eyes start to tear up again, warmth trickling down my cheeks with his words. Only this time, it's from a feeling of happiness from the warmth and comfort they always give me and make me feel. An unconditional love from the boys who always pull me from any darkness trying to suffocate me back home.

"You made her cry, Kane!" Anders growls as he swats Kane on his shoulder. Kane quickly whips around and places Anders in a playful chokehold.

A giggle bubbles up my throat as I watch them play.

Knox bumps me on my shoulder, his eyes flitting to Xander as he edges closer. He gently takes out his flowers, a bunch of yellow Primroses, and hands them to me.

A warm smile stretches his lips. "We'll always be your family and will always protect you, Micai."

I'm yanked from my memory as Kane shifts to the side, reaching for Anders as Knox gets the better of him. And there, in between him and Xander, sits *Seria.*

A soft smirk spreads across her lips as the boys around her talk and laugh. Other boys try to catch her attention in the seats around her as Xander and Kane give them cutting glares.

Her long blonde hair falls on the desk as she turns toward Knox, fluttering her lashes as she runs a hand down his arm and pulls him to sit beside her.

Nobody else from the second-year class would sit in the seats allocated for the third years in the centre of the room. But rules were meant to be bent for her, right?

The music teacher, Ms. Fleur was quite relaxed about seating anyway, so I guess that would also work in my favour too.

I make my way into the room and toward the fourth-year seats.

They were on the opposite side and near the windows.

The laughter in the class stops, a colder atmosphere filling the room along with a heavy silence as I find an empty seat at the back and sit down.

I get a few narrowed gazes and some pointed glances before a few giggles and chuckles ring out on the opposite side of the room and by the second-year seats.

I sigh, glancing toward the echoing laughs and whispers.

Ivy Harris sits with two other girls and five boys, all blatantly staring my way while grinning and chuckling.

"Seems like she's scared," the petite blonde to the right of Ivy sneers.

Scared of catching fleas, maybe.

Ivy smirks, an expression across her face as if knowing something that everyone else doesn't.

She brushes a hand through her ginger hair, her gaze focused fully on me as she opens her mouth.

"That little outburst on Friday was a little out of character for you, Micai...has something been bothering you lately?" Her brows scrunch together as stifled chuckles fall from behind her. "Have you been having friend troubles?" Her eyes widen mockingly as she bites back her chuckle. "Sorry, for a second I forgot, you don't have any friends." She shakes her head before tapping a manicured finger on her lips. "I meant any *boy* troubles?"

"*Boys*? What boys would want to be near *her*?" Laughs a girl with a black bob to Ivy's other side. "What sane person would want to be around someone so pathetic and weak?"

I roll my eyes. Is this the best they could do?

Just as I'm about to ignore it and turn away, Ivy opens her mouth again.

"Or is it your *daddy* issues? Having problems at home, are we, Micai?"

"Hey–" a voice shouts from the front row before quickly cutting off. "Ivy." Seria stands up, her lips pinched as she gazes toward the students around Ivy. "Don't mention my father." Her gaze narrows as she meets Ivy. "Remember who you're dealing with. The Bane clan is not one you want to mess with."

The room falls into a pin-drop silence as Seria speaks, their gazes flickering between Ivy and her as they look at one another.

Ivy's complexion turns ashen. "I didn't mean any disrespect, Seria. I–I would never–"

"Don't use my father's name in the future, Ivy," Seria warns again, her expression calm yet her tone cutting. "I won't allow it."

Ivy nods repeatedly, "Of course. The Bane Clan is one of the founding nine families. I would never disrespect you or your father, *ever*." At this, Seria's eyes seem to glimmer with pride at the praise.

A bitter grin stretches my lips at her words. Because I, unlike Seria, don't have my father or the backing of my family. So that made me fair game, right?

Seria gives her a small smile and nod as Ivy breathes a sigh of relief.

She takes her seat again as Xander stands beside her. He looks down at her, his hand brushing against her cheek gently as she smiles and calls his name sweetly.

A long time ago, something like that would have bothered me. It would have tugged painfully at a part of me that still had hope for the love and friendships we used to have. The younger me would have turned away, too hurt by the picture-perfect image in front of her. Watching the boys she used to love, give their hearts wholly to her younger sister.

But thankfully, none of that affected me now. The love I once had for them had withered quickly with each day I spent in captivity.

I realised I had been holding onto something that was never really there to begin with.

If they loved me like they told me when we were

younger, they would never have left me so easily for Seria.

They never would have turned away and grown cold. To allow the torment and abuse I suffered at the hands of students in the academy to go on and just watch or walk away from me with ease as if all the years we spent together never existed.

Even with Seria's schemes and sweet words, loyalty and love came hand in hand. If they believed her over me, whom they had known for years, then I couldn't have meant much to them to begin with.

With years imprisoned to think, I learnt that love couldn't be extinguished so effortlessly if it's *true.*

If it's real, nobody can take it away, not even time or death itself. You'll cling to it with everything you have, because to lose it would be to lose a part of yourself.

"We'll talk again another time, Micai," Ivy calls, jerking me from my thoughts as she goes to take her seat.

Another time?

I sigh, glancing toward Ivy. "You clearly have more issues to worry about than I do, so maybe you should focus on your own shit instead of mine."

Ivy freezes, silence falling around her with only the fourth-years near me murmuring and whispering.

"What was that–" Ivy begins to stand up again before quickly being cut off.

"Your voice is grating on everyone's ears, Ivy," a girl at the back of the second-year area calls. Her tone is sharp as she flips her long, silky black hair over her shoulder while the two enormous boys beside her narrow their eyes at Ivy's group. "Why don't you keep the drama for another day and not give the rest of us a headache?" She raises a brow, giving Ivy and her entourage a pointed look.

Ivy scoffs, opening her mouth before flitting her eyes around the room, with the majority of the class shifting away from her gaze. Her face scrunches up, her mouth closing as her lips pinch together.

She spins away, not even glancing back at the raven-haired girl as she quickly takes her seat. Then she starts chatting to the boys and two girls beside her as if nothing happened. The only indication of her annoyance being the red tinge tinting her cheeks and the slight tick to her jaw.

I turn back toward the front of the class, a few more chuckles ringing out on the other side of the room before a grunt follows, cutting it off.

My brows raise in surprise as I meet the two sets of eyes whose laughs are being suppressed. Knox rubs his side while Anders rubs his head, as Xander and Kane stand next to them, scowling.

"It was funny, though," Anders mutters before turning away.

Knox flicks his gaze to the floor before returning to Seria. Her gaze is slightly darker, her smile tight as she stares at me.

I feel another icy gaze on me from beside her and am soon met by Xander's blue eyes glaring me down.

A small hand tugs at his side, returning his attention to her. A look of pure adoration and love fills them again quickly as he gazes at her.

Something pulls at me, an ache building in my chest.

But not from watching them, not from any want of affection of *theirs.*

I had a taste of true love once. And even behind a cement walk with a gravelly voice, I knew it was real.

It blew everything I ever felt before away, completing me in ways I never thought possible. It wrapped itself around the lonely child within me and warmed the parts of my soul that had become cold and stiff. It pushed me to survive and fight on days when all I wanted was to give up. It gave me hope when there was none, and comfort when all I could feel was pain.

A small, shaky smile stretches my lips, an ache beginning to grow in my chest before I shake my head and will it away. *Now was not the time.*

I feel a chill on my neck, twisting to meet Kane's narrowed gaze.

What was wrong with him now? Did I breathe too much and suck up some of Seria's private oxygen?

He was always the stubborn, grumpy one, and stupidly, I used to think that was cute. His now permanently scowling face just looked like he had swallowed a bag of bitter dicks.

Was that a wolf-shifter thing, or did he reserve that expression just for me?

I raise my hand in a wave, his eyes further narrowing on it before I swiftly spin around while giving him the middle finger and my best smile.

His eyes widen, but Mrs. Fleur scurries into the classroom before he can properly react.

She's wearing a floral pastel dress; her long blonde

hair is tangled messily into a bun on her head, with her hands clutching a hefty bundle of papers.

She makes it to the desk just as the bundle topples.

She grabs the papers, trying to slide them off her table in one quick move, a giant smile stretching her lips with a swift save.

"Hello students," she beams, nodding for students to take their seats. "Apologies for my tardiness. I was making some printouts for everyone as part of the lesson for today." She takes a large pile of sheets and hands them out to each student. "As you all know from our last lesson, you will have regular assessments throughout the year. However, your solo singing assessments will be held in this group class on Mondays." She gives me a slight nod as she hands me a sheet and then heads to the front of the class. "We'll be commencing the solo assessments next week at the end of each class and will do two at a time." Her following smile is bright and enthusiastic as she continues. "We'll go alphabetically to make it fair, and you can even choose your own song."

She gives everyone a huge smile as if she's holding in a squeal and bounces enthusiastically to her seat.

My frustration grows as the rest of the class begins to whisper excitedly.

She hushes them and begins the lesson as my irritation reaches its peak.

I had forgotten about this part of it.

'Music of the Arts'. It's in the name, so how could I have forgotten?

I have to *sing.*

I never enjoyed this class, although it was one of the

few available that didn't require magic or any physical activity, so it was an easy decision.

My previous life's music lessons and assessments involved me shakily singing, too low and nervous for anyone to hear properly, but then with all the snickering and whispers, it would have been hard for even a stronger singer.

It didn't help that Seria had the voice of an opera house angel. Her soft and soothing voice made everyone fall silent in awe when she stood up and sang.

My voice, on the other hand, was too weak and would crack from nerves, yet Seria would still persuade me to continue. And back then, I thought it was her showing her support and affection.

I grip the worksheet in my hand, scrunching its paper.

Back then, I hated singing and the sound of my own voice as it left my lips.

I *used* to hate it...until *he* taught me how freeing it could be. How something as small as humming and singing in that cold cell could pull me from the pain and to a different place away from it all...to somewhere that the two of us only existed.

He's also the reason why I'll never sing to another person again.

I rub the centre of my chest, a familiar ache building again with the thought of him. He was my only warmth and comfort there, the balm to my lifeless soul, and the only shred of hope I had in that hell...*Zrael*.

His rough, gravelly voice calls to me, my name on his lips the last word I hear when I close my eyes every night, and his husky, soulful voice singing to me to wake up each morning.

Whatever they had done to him in The Facility had damaged his vocal cords. His voice had a rough sound like gravel scraping down his throat. It sounded as if he was in pain with each syllable. It was only when he sang that his voice was legible, the magic laced in his melodies allowing him a freedom his broken voice wouldn't allow anymore.

And his voice...*Gods* could he sing.

If Seria was an angel, then Zrael was the devil himself, seducing me to join him in Hell. And with his husky timber and smooth-like-silk tones I'd willingly give my soul over for a few minutes more of basking in his voice.

He showed me the true beauty of singing, and together, we created our own small freedom away from The Facility, away from our cells, and the hell we faced each day.

He was my strength, my safe haven, my home...but *he, too,* was taken from me.

The class bell rings just in time, dragging me from my darkening thoughts.

I peer around the room as the other students begin to pack up and slowly leave.

They make their way out of the classroom in small groups, talking and laughing together as if nothing else mattered, even time.

Time.

Right, I am *here* now. I had time. I could do something before the wheels begin to move.

I watch as Knox turns and glances back at me. He opens his mouth before quickly closing it again. His brows slightly pinch together with an unreadable look in his eyes. He meets my gaze once more, slowly opening his lips before his name is called from outside. He gives me one last strange look before turning toward the voice and quickly leaving the classroom.

What could he have possibly wanted to say? Was he going to tell me to stay away and not cause trouble?

I shake my head. I wouldn't cause any trouble or come for Seria...*yet.*

I pull out my class schedule and see there is an hour before lunch and then Physical Defence class.

Just what I needed: something to eat and somewhere to blow off steam.

CHAPTER EIGHT

I finished the last of the ham and cheese baguette I grabbed from the girl's dormitory kitchen.

It wasn't nearly as good or as fresh as the cafeteria food, but it would do for now. It also gave me more time to change for the Physical Defence class.

I throw on the academy's training gear: a matching pair of marl grey sweats with a navy, silk embroidered crest on the chest. The grey sweatshirt had a long zip down the centre, and you could choose white or black vest tops for underneath. I went with black, it was better for stains, *or blood.*

I make my way outside and toward the training grounds. That was where most of the Physical Defence classes were held, even in cold or rainy weather.

The grounds were located to the far left of the main academy building and spanned the length and width of around three football pitches.

The only thing bigger than the training grounds was the forest surrounding it and the academy on all sides.

I see the training grounds in the distance. It was a bit of a walk from the dormitories, but I was excited to finally join a class that might benefit me.

I had only heard rumours about the instructor, Mr. Valor. He was a high, pure-blood elf whose reputation on the battlefield made him someone even the academy's dean fought to get his hands on.

From the snippet of whispers I heard from the other female students, he was also apparently the most attractive among the faculty. But with a glare so icy you couldn't keep your gaze on him for long. *Not that I cared.*

I walk past a row of wooden benches, the training ground now in sight, as I notice a group of boys approaching me.

Their eyes harden when they meet my gaze, though they turn and continue chatting and chuckling to each other as they get closer to me.

I watch from my peripheral view as they near me, my guard up and hands balled into fists and ready for any sort of shift or attack.

They continue to laugh and talk as if I don't exist, my fists clenched and shoulders stiff as we stroll past each other.

My body begins to relax as they leave in the opposite direction, my shoulders slightly dropping as I make my way toward the training grounds again.

I guess with all the other incidents I've been a little paranoid lately.

Suddenly, a hand wraps around my mouth from

behind, with an arm joining it around my waist. They pull me into the shadows behind a nearby building and out of sight. It's so fast that I don't even get the time to react or fight back before I'm thrown hard against the building's stone wall.

Pain slices up my back as three massive figures stand towering over me.

The three boys from moments ago.

They sneer down at me, their eyes dark and leery as they watch me.

"What do you think you're doing?" My back hits the wall as I watch them, cursing the slight tremor working its way down my legs from the hit. If I had been stronger, I would've brushed something like that off with ease.

A boy in the centre, with sandy-brown hair and dark brown eyes, bends down toward me. His hand extends and reaches for me. I slap it away as the two boys beside him chuckle.

I could tell by their expressions that they meant business. And that whatever they had planned for me was not something I would be walking away from with just a few broken bones.

"It's better if she fights a little," a boy sneers with beady grey eyes and murky moss-green hair. His eyes narrow, pulling at a small, thick scar above his brows as a slight glow of silver slices through his iris'. *A shifter, then.* And by the colour of it and his hair, he was more than likely a type of reptilian.

"She'll learn soon enough how things will work." His eyes roam up my legs as his grin grows darker.

His look mirrors one I've seen hundreds of times

before, one that without fail makes my skin crawl and screams for me to gouge out the eyes giving it.

A foul feeling slithers up my back, knowing what will come, questioning whether I can do what I have to. If this body can truly fight back like I need it to and if it can find the strength it needs to defend itself against not one, but *three* shifters.

Unfortunately for me, shifters usually group together, and by their bulkier frames and the little *grab* from a moment ago, that seems to be what I'm facing.

Either way, I'll have to fight.

"Are you sure we'll be alright here, Dean?" a blonde boy calls to my right, as his green eyes flicker back toward the pathway. "What if someone comes? We *are* pretty close to the cafeteria."

"It'll be fine." *Dean,* the boy directly in front of me, stands back up and straightens himself.

"Even if someone does come..." He stares down at me, meeting my eyes as a mocking grin stretches his lips. "Nobody would care if it's *her* anyway."

The two boys around him chuckle as he continues.

"We *could* also do this in a much easier way..." His eyes trail down my body. "Where we *all* could have a little fun–"

"That's not what we agreed on, Dean!" The Joker wannabe scowls, cutting off *Dean's* sick proposition.

"She needs to be taught a lesson and be put in her place." He spits his words, a vitriol of hate swirling in his murky eyes as they meet mine again. "Something so worthless only deserves to be used and discarded like the little whore she–"

THE BLACKENED BLADE | 95

Before he can finish his useless little speech, I kick my foot out, slamming it into his leg and causing him to stumble forward. My best bet was to catch them off guard and move swiftly.

I clench my fist as tight as possible and throw it forward, aiming for his head. Only before the hit can land, it's caught by another bulky hand from beside me.

Dean's.

He yanks me up with ease before throwing me back into the stone wall behind me. I hear something crack as pain splinters through me, slicing down my back and shoulders as my body slides down the wall.

"I guess that's what I get for trying to be nice." Dean pushes his fingers through my hair before roughly grabbing it and pulling me closer to face him. Every strand on my head burns with his grip, as if each one is going to be yanked out by the force of his grasp on me.

"We could have done this the easy way." He sighs while using his other hand to loosen his trouser belt. "...But I guess I wouldn't have been gentle either way." Slowly, he begins to undo his top trouser button as a slight moment of panic courses through my body. Memories and flashes of the first few weeks in The Facility and the constant threat of the guards hit me.

I pull myself back just as quick, taking a breath and pushing the memories and my panic back down. I bury them deep in the place where I put all the pain and fear I've carried over the years.

If I could fight and survive back then, I could do it here and now. I didn't have strength then either, but I was still able to protect myself.

A low chuckle rings out from beside Dean.

"About fucking time." The green-haired ass grins as he pushes in closer beside him and sneers down at me. His eyes ogle my chest as his hand reaches toward me. And just as he leans closer, I spit directly in his face.

"That's the only thing you'll be getting from me."

He reels back, a look of pure shock taking over his expression before turning to rage.

He tries to grab me, but Dean elbows him, pushing him back again. "Patience, Leon, you'll get your turn with her. And then you can do *whatever* you want."

"As if I'll—"

My words are cut off as my head is yanked back harder, with Dean chuckling. He pulls his trouser zipper down just as I try to throw my knee out toward his crotch. But it's quickly caught by Leon, who also catches the fist aiming for his face. *Fucking shifter speed.*

The grip on my hair falls away as I'm shoved backwards and slammed into the bricks behind me again. *And hard.*

I quickly scramble to straighten myself, but suddenly, my head is whipped sideways, my vision sporting tiny black spots as I try to steady myself and take in what's happened.

He hit me.

The asshole had slapped me hard enough to make my head spin, and my teeth chatter with its force.

The pain works its way from my stinging cheek into my head. A throbbing pain hammers its way through my skull while I try to pull myself quickly back together.

I stumble sideways, my hand falling on the wall behind me as muffled voices ring out around me.

"You should have done that from the start," Leon chuckles. "Then she wouldn't have acted so stupid."

"I didn't want her face bruised or swollen...it's a turn-off," Dean answers nonchalantly as my vision begins to clear.

"I couldn't care less. It's not her face I'll be having fun with." Leon's eyes leer down at my thighs and then back up to my chest. "Besides, you can always take her from behind." A low snicker leaves his throat as a dark, twisted grin stretches his lips.

"Fuck yo—"

A hand grips my shoulder roughly, pulling me up straight and cutting me off before slamming me against the wall again.

The back of my skull hits the cold bricks as my head spins and my vision blurs. A sharp pain sears down my back.

Something was definitely broken or fractured.

A tremor works its way through me as I feel a large hand roughly grasp my throat and shift my face upwards, followed by the feel of bodies crowding closer to me.

I try to throw myself forward, but a hand grips my wrist on each side of me and slams them both into the wall above me with a bruising grip.

A feeling of uselessness tries to seep its way into my mind as I struggle and thrash against their holds to no avail. I couldn't let them do this, *I wouldn't*.

A hand tugs at my sweatshirt before I feel cold air on

my chest, followed by a rough hand grasping and groping my breasts. I hear a low hum and a muffled voice.

"...*Not bad.*"

A couple of chuckles follow as bile burns the back of my throat, held back only by the hand forcefully clutching my neck. I continue to thrash and fight, trying to break free from their grip on me. Even in my past life they didn't go this far. I had been locked up, bullied mentally and emotionally, and beaten black and blue, but *this*...

The fingers flex around my throat as my blurred vision becomes clearer, and I see Dean holding my neck. But before I can push myself forward to fight, his other hand grabs my left leg and forces it to one side. His hand around my throat snakes up to my face as he wraps his long fingers around my mouth, pushing me further into the stone wall behind me as he covers my lips.

His other hand hurriedly moves up my thigh, his shifter strength not giving me much room to thrash anymore as he pushes himself flush against my body.

He leans into my ear, "You can cry and scream if you want, but no one will save you. Hell, they would probably sit back and watch the show...or even *help*."

A disgusting hard bulge forms against my thighs as a low growl leaves his lips. His eyes begin to glow gold, and his fangs descend as he leans in closer. *Bastard wolf shifter.*

His breath brushes across my neck, "You should have stayed the same quiet little *bitch* everyone tolerated...but I guess this works better for us."

Leon chuckles, his face contorted in a sick smirk as the grip on my breast tightens painfully. "Make sure to be quick so we can all get a turn." My left wrist is yanked up higher, pain searing through my shoulder and arm with its force.

"Make sure you hold her tight, Cole," orders Leon to the blonde boy on my left.

"Can't have her lashing out again while Dean's having his fun." The hand holding my right wrist tightens as Dean pulls slightly back, releasing his grip on my mouth and leg as he adjusts his trousers. His eyes glow a darker shade of gold as they turn to meet mine again, a sick smirk lacing his lips. He leans back in, reaching for my trousers, and manages to slide them down just a fraction before his hand quickly falls away.

He stumbles backward, his eyes dazed and face scrunched in pain as he falls back on his feet and then to the ground, a red mark already forming on his forehead.

I lift my head, ignoring the searing pain from the hit I'd just delivered Dean.

A warm trickle follows the throbbing down my face, but I ignore it. There was no time to dwell on it. I needed to move.

Any damage I incurred now would be worth it as long as I fought back and gave my all.

I use everything and anything around me to inflict as much pain on them as I can: my hands, my feet, my nails and teeth, and anything else I could find.

In the split second of chaos and confusion, I make my move.

Using all my strength, I yank my wrists free from the hands holding them and fall to the ground. My knees hit the cement hard, probably drawing blood, but I pull myself up as fast as I can. And just in time too as a set of hands try to grab me from my side with another moving toward Dean. I twist around, dodging Leon's hands, and with the full force of my strength, I kick my feet out, knocking his legs from under him.

He goes down with a loud smash, crashing into a metal bin behind him and sending it rolling down onto the pathway, leaving a trail of trash in its wake.

I turn back quickly, hearing shuffling from behind me, but I'm a moment too late as two sets of hands are on me before I can fully pull myself back up.

Dean and Cole snatch me from the ground as I thrash against their hold.

Shoving me back against the wall, Dean pushes Cole's hands away, clutching both my wrists above me with a bruising grip.

His eyes are a bright gold, his wolf nearing the surface as he gets in my face.

"For pulling that little stunt, I'll make sure that when we're done here with you, you'll be so broken and bruised you'll wish you had just let me fuck you fast from the start." His spit hits my face as he continues, vitriol and hate seeping from his eyes. "You'll have to *crawl* back when we're done with you." A smile so disgusting and vile twists his lips, his eyes lost in his contorted thoughts as his hand reaches for his trousers again, all the while keeping his head a safe distance from my own.

His words run through my mind, time slightly slowing with my thoughts, "*You'll be so broken and bruised... you'll have to crawl back...*"

Crawling...haven't I done enough of that throughout

my life? Of crouching smaller for others, of giving into demands and orders easily? Of pretending to be blind and deaf to my own pain while silently praying for peace and relief from it every day?

Even now, my body just wants to stop, to give up, to curl into a ball in some hidden space where no one can reach me anymore...to where I don't have to feel the pain that comes with just breathing and existing.

And as for being '*broken and bruised,*'...there aren't enough pores on my body or blood in my veins to measure the number of times I've been *broken and bruised.* I've experienced more pain in my twenty-seven years than every last one of these horrid pricks combined and then some. And now they want to add *more*?

No.

No more.

Even something as small and as helpless as a mouse has teeth, and as long as I can breathe, I can continue to fight.

"I thought the others were disgusting trash."

Dean stills his movements, his eyes meeting mine as I continue. "But you three take being *scum* to a whole new level."

He moves his hand from his trousers and grabs my face, roughly clutching my cheeks and chin in his hand as he gets into my face.

"You think talking shit is going to help you? Whores like you never shut up unless there's something shoved down your throat to keep you quiet." He gives me a dark grin before twisting his head to Cole and Leon.

"I think one of you should keep her mouth preoccupied while I fu–"

His words are cut off, the air pouring from his lungs as his eyes widen.

Shifters are a hard bunch to go against, especially with superhuman strength, speed, and a more rapid recovery than others. However, there's one place that's a weak spot for all men, even supernaturals.

"Dean?" Cole calls, his brows furrowing as he watches his friend bend forward before falling to the ground, a low whimper leaving his lips as his hands cup his crotch.

"What the fuck?!" Barks Leon.

Cole crouches beside Dean as Leon reaches for me.

I let him grab me, his grip bruising on my shoulders as his face gets closer to mine. That's when I rear back slightly and throw my head toward his, watching on through my own pain as he lets go and stumbles backward.

You think they would have learnt the first time around.

I slide a hand through my hair, pushing it back and finding my fingers now coated in a familiar crimson liquid.

"Leon!" shouts Cole. "You're fucking crazy! Do you know what you've just done?! You're fucked now!" Cole glares as he pulls himself up and takes a step away from Dean and toward me.

He moves forward as I slowly take a step backward and in the direction of the bin that Leon knocked over just moments ago. Thankfully, some handy items, including a dark, empty glass bottle, tumbled from the metal bin when he crashed into it.

Before Cole can reach me, I grab the glass, brandishing it between my fingers as he stands just feet from me.

My gaze flickers to Dean, still whimpering on the ground behind Cole, and then to Leon, one hand on his head as he tries to steady himself. *Best make this quick, then.*

"What do you think you're gonna do with that?" Cole's lip curls up as his eyes glow gold, taking another step closer as he continues. "We both know you won't do anything. You're too weak, and we're all shifters anyway." He shrugs, a taunting smile stretching his lips. "We *heal...* but *you* won't."

He tries to take another stride forward, but I move quickly, smashing the bottle on the wall nearest me and twisting the bottle around toward him.

"Of course, shifters heal, but the real question is...*how fast,*" I take a step closer to Cole as his eyes flicker between my face and the broken and jagged bottle.

"You think you can get me with that? I'm faster and stronger than you, Micai." He scoffs.

"But I can still do damage, Cole. Who knows, maybe I'll get lucky and hit an artery?"

His smug grin falls, his brows furrowed, and his eyes focused more intently on my expression and the thick, sharp glass pointing toward him.

I take another step toward him as his eyes meet mine again, a more cautious look in them as he watches me.

"And after I'm done with you, I'll take my time with him." I point the broken bottle toward Dean on the ground. "What was it he said? Oh yeah...I'll make it so he'll have to *crawl back* when I'm done with him...that's if he's still breathing, I guess." I shrug, twisting the bottle round playfully. "And unlike you scumbags, I'm in no rush. There'll be no *quickie* here." I chuckle darkly. "I'll take my time and test out just how much a shifter can heal from."

His eyes widen with my words, never leaving my face. Whatever he sees has him taking a small step back as I take my next step.

"You really have gone fucking crazy, haven't you?" He glances back at Dean, just a few feet behind him now.

"Maybe I was crazy *before*. For putting up with everything, for taking it all and staying quiet." I stare at Leon shaking his head and taking a shaky stride toward Cole.

Cole leans down to Dean and wraps an arm around him, pulling him up.

"Now I'm going to return all the *pleasantries* I've gotten the last couple of years." I grip the bottle in my hand, veering it toward the three of them.

"*Fucking bitch—*" Leon slurs, as he tries to head toward me. Except Cole kicks a leg out toward him, pushing him back and sending him stumbling again.

"Not now," Cole calls.

"*Not ever again,*" I call, my voice low and emotionless. "If you, or *they*, come at me like this again, Cole...I promise you, *crawling away* won't even be an option."

He wraps Dean's arm around his shoulder and calls for Leon, whose eyes are still dazed and unfocused.

I watch on, unmoving from the spot I'm standing. Not even dropping the broken bottle I'm holding until they're completely gone and out of sight.

A heavy breath falls from my lips as a slight tremor works its way down my hands and through my body.

I drop the broken bottle and listen to its glass shattering as my vision begins to sway and spin again, with the throbbing in my head working its way down my neck and back. Aches and pains scream from areas all over my body as I begin to slowly relax. It was a miracle I had kept so steady. I guess I have six long years of guard harassment to thank for that.

I hear a bell ring in the distance.

Pulling myself up, I wince with the pain, every inch of my body screaming at me to sit down and stay still. But I wouldn't.

Defence class would be starting soon, and I was adamant that I wouldn't be missing it this time.

CHAPTER NINE

*A*fter removing the blood from my face and hands and tidying up the best I can, I make my way onto the training grounds. The area is almost like a giant football field with large open spaces and obstacle course equipment spread out around the large area. There are low-lying metal barriers separating it from the immense forest around it. There's also a small grey building that sits off to the side where weapons and training equipment are kept locked away for classes, only the instructors having access to it.

I make my way over to the group of thirty or so students already training in the centre of the grounds, when suddenly my name is called from the side.

A man over six feet tall with a face that could make even the most spinsterish of women swoon calls to me.

I freeze for just a moment as I'm met with two deep green eyes. My breath catches in my throat, lost to his bewitching features and a face that even an angel would envy.

His light golden hair sways with the breeze and brushes across his shoulders while the muscles in his arms pull and stretch at the fabric of his cream shirt. He narrows his deep green eyes toward me as I approach.

I continue to walk, picking up my pace as his lips pinch into a slight frown and I realise who it is that I'm staring at.

I guess those rumours about the new Defence teacher were true after all.

There's a slight tick to Mr. Valor's jaw as he watches me and stands at the front of the class, his gaze becoming colder and more cutting the closer I get.

"Three laps around the training ground for being late, Ms. Bane." He shifts his attention back to the class as chuckles fall from the group, then instantly stop with his glare.

I guess with the attack and then tidying up, I *was* late by a few minutes.

I glance around the grounds. It had to be at least three average football pitches long and at least two pitches wide. *This would take a while.*

I begin to stretch out, momentarily forgetting my pain, as a sharp sting moves up my spine and into my shoulders. I wince with the pain just as a familiar voice speaks up from the group.

"Aren't three laps a bit much?"

All eyes turn toward the voice, my own turning toward the familiar, brown-eyed boy.

Knox looks at Mr. Valor as Kane and Xander stare daggers into the back of him.

Anders looks around the training grounds, a low

whistle falling from his lips as he shakes his head. "That is *a lot* for someone like her to cover. I mean, she doesn't even have any physical strength, let alone magi–*ugh*–" Knox elbows him in the side, his eyes narrowed at his friend, before Anders' gaze flickers to me. His creased brow eases out as his eyes slightly widen, and he quickly mouths a '*Sorry*'.

Knox glances back toward me, his mouth open before he freezes. His brows crease deeper the longer he stares, his gaze quickly skimming down toward my clothes. His eyes widen slightly when he reaches my trousers.

I peer down and notice the stains on my knees. There were a few scrapes from the fight earlier and it looks like a little bit of blood seeped through.

I glance back up toward Knox as his gaze meets mine, an unreadable look in his eyes as he tries to take a step toward me. But Xander reaches his hand out, pulling Knox back before cutting me an icy glare.

To them, I was some weak and pathetic memory of the past. An annoyance to share space with now.

I take off my grey zip hoodie, throwing it to the ground before I take off in a slow sprint, putting distance between me and the voices calling out behind me.

I was no longer the weak girl they knew. I may not be the fastest or strongest, but my mentality was no longer the same. I know my worth now and that I deserve more from this life than what I've always been shown by those around me. This second chance, this new life...I won't waste any more of it on them.

The wind whips through my hair and past my face as I build myself up into a run. Something thrums through me as I pick up my pace. Even with my body sore and aching with pain from the attack, I felt a power and strength gradually building in me. This was *freedom*.

Too many days, weeks, and years were wasted rotting away in a small prison cell or a suffocating cage called *Wensridge Academy*. Too many small and mundane moments were taken from me, and too much of my blood and tears were shed in these prisons.

The pain and fear I felt in The Facility, and the years of torment in the academy before that had taken parts of me that I didn't even realise were gone. They left me alone and broken, believing I was unworthy of a good life, *or a life at all*.

I pass by the group finishing my first lap, feeling their eyes on me, and Mr. Valor's voice yelling for their attention as I continue the pace I've set.

None of them could ever understand how this felt. The aches and the pain, I'd embrace them all and let them slowly strengthen me.

This was a small taste of the freedom I now have, of the fresh air surrounding me with no shackles or cage binding me. Nothing was chasing me; there was only an endless path in front of me, with myself making the choice of where to go and how far.

The nightly training had clearly helped in some way, maybe building my stamina up, because even after another lap I'm still staying strong and moving steadily.

I keep my pace, my breathing slightly heavier on my final lap. A small trickle of sweat drips down my face and chest as I see the group in my sight and push myself harder.

I reach Mr. Valor, placing my hands on my knees as I calm my breathing and racing heart.

Mr. Valor shouts for the class to continue as I lift my head up and into two captivating green eyes. The sun catches his white gold strands as he leans down, handing me a cold bottle of water. There's a slight glint in his eyes, his gaze still a little stony and guarded but less cutting now than before.

I straighten myself and take it from his hand, quickly pulling myself from my daze.

I give him my thanks as I gulp the water down in seconds. The cold liquid rapidly cooling and reviving me.

"Join the others, Ms. Bane." He returns to the class and calls for their attention as I make my way over.

I get a few pointed looks but also some curious stares as I head to the back of the group, where I find an empty space.

"We'll start the stance again since the majority of you seem to be having issues." Mr. Valor's lips straighten into a grim line as he looks around the group, a frustrated tone in his voice as a few students avoid his gaze.

He takes a stance in front of the group, his body slightly bent forward as he holds a wooden-tipped blade in his hand.

His muscles bunch in his arms as he flicks the wooden blade outward before throwing the blade upwards in a dummy move meant to distract. He twists his body around, catching the blade to the back of his imaginary opponent, and slashes outward quickly, aiming for a vital point, essentially incapacitating or killing his invisible target.

I watch his posture, remembering the stance and moving easily as he straightens up. It's a simple technique meant to distract, then incapacitate or maim.

How was anyone struggling with this move? How was *this* so hard for them?

"Depending on the wielder of the weapon, and if properly executed," He glanced coldly at a couple of boys whispering to a girl beside them, "It could catch your opponent off guard and disable them. Pair up and practice." He makes his way over to them as they fall silent, shrinking in on themselves as he nears.

Pairs. Great.

There were, unfortunately, a lot more boys than girls in this class. I was actually one of only three here, and they seemed more interested in Mr. Valor than the actual class.

Glancing around the field, I notice the girls are already paired up with boys who immediately jumped toward them at the mention of practising together.

My eyes meet two sets of familiar faces watching me curiously. *Knox and Anders.*

They whisper to each other before Knox takes a step in my direction, only he freezes as a hand grabs his shoulder. Xander's brows are pulled downward, his glare cutting as he flicks his gaze from Knox to me. His lip curls upward as he speaks to Knox and Anders in hushed tones.

I turn my gaze away. Whatever was going on had nothing to do with me anymore.

And maybe if I was lucky, I was the odd number out and could practise by myself.

Mr. Valor approaches me and hands me a small wooden practice dagger. He glances around the field before calling someone over for me to pair up with.

A scowling Kane slowly walks over and stands beside Mr. Valor just before he is called by another teacher across the field.

Kane's scowl looks permanently etched on his face, like a disgruntled pug. *Minus the cuteness.*

I sigh. Of all the assholes I could have been paired with, it had to be *this* one.

"Don't think that I want to be paired with you," he bites out through gritted teeth. "Even being near you makes me cringe."

I wonder what it was that made him turn into such a cold ass. What made a grumpy boy who used to chase after me and cry when I was hurt, turn into someone completely cold and unrecognisable?

I guess whatever it was had nothing to do with me anymore. I also didn't have to take their shitty words or cutting glares sitting down, either. They've made it crystal clear how they feel. Now it's my turn.

"Then just imagine how much shittier it is for me to have to be beside *you*."

Kane freezes, his eyes slightly widening as his mouth opens before it hastily closes again.

Students near us fall silent, a few brows furrow while questioning glances are thrown my way.

Right. The younger me wouldn't ever have talked back or spoken her mind.

"I don't know what crawled up your ass or what broke your little shifter brain into thinking I'd want to be paired with you, but let's be clear...I would rather be alone than spend *one minute longer* in your presence." A humourless chuckle leaves my lips. "I think it's been made *crystal clear* what you all think of me, and any affection we shared is long burned out with all your shit."

His brows scrunch, his lips pinched together as he opens his mouth, but I cut him off.

Narrowing my gaze, I slow my voice so he knows I mean each and every word as I continue. "I don't want to be around you, *any of you*, more than I have to be. So, let's make this as painless as possible."

I take the stance shown earlier as I grip the wooden blade. "Let's get on with it."

Kane's frozen face flares into something else, contorting into something dark and cold as he glares at me. "Of course. This is the *real* you..." He scans me up and down, a hardened expression pulling at his features as he slowly takes the stance, gripping his own blade tightly in his hands. "A manipulative *bitch*."

Before I know it, I'm heading for him, my reaction too quick, catching him off guard and too late for him to dodge.

I replicate Mr. Valor's move, though instead of throwing the blade and twisting to the back, I drop it then catch it with my other hand and thrust it into Kane's front.

I push every last ounce of strength I can into my shoulder and hand, pain slicing up my back with the movement as I flip the blade to its hilt and slam it into his solar plexus. Even for a shifter, that shit should hurt.

A grunt falls from his lips, his eyes widening before scrunching together in a look of pain. He bends forward, kneeling and hitting the grass below us.

I crouch down, placing a hand on his shoulder as I lean my weight on him, pushing him further into the ground.

"*Manipulative?*" I scoff, looking him dead in his eyes. "Who have I got around me to *manipulate*, Kane? You all left *me*, remember?" I shake my head. "Probably the best thing you all ever did, though. Showing me who you really were. *All fake lying assholes.*" I feel my expression harden as he opens his mouth, a slight twitch in his eyes as he watches me.

Pulling myself up straight, I cut off any words he has when he opens his mouth.

"And don't delude yourself, you know nothing about me, Kane. *Nothing.*"

A bell rings out in the distance as I hear Xander and Anders call for Kane.

I make my way through the group and over to Mr. Valor, handing him the wooden blade as he glances back to Kane and the growing crowd.

He looks at the wooden blade and then back over to Kane, a brow raised as he watches me, his lips slightly tilted before he quickly schools it.

"I had heard you had no magical attributes. I guess you've made up for that in other ways." He twirls the blade between his fingers like it weighs nothing before throwing it toward a pole a few metres away, hitting it dead centre. "Don't be late again, Ms. Bane. Your time is better spent learning."

"*Micai,*" I shout as he turns around, a brow raised in question.

"My name's Micai. *Ms. Bane* doesn't really suit me." I grew tired of hearing it. The same surname as *her* and the old memories that came with it. A powerful and prestigious family name that I didn't need anymore.

An unreadable look forms on his face as he slowly nods and then leaves for Kane and the crowd.

"Class is over. Can someone help Mr. Fields up so he can walk it off? You're a shifter..." He pats him on the back, an apathetic look on his face. "You should be able to handle one hit, Mr. Fields." He turns back toward me. "Even if it was a pretty impressive one."

He goes around taking all the wooden weapons back as my eyes meet Knox's. He's standing beside Anders and Xander, who are helping Kane up. His brows scrunch together, his mouth opening slightly before I turn away and head back toward the dormitory, ignoring any noise around me.

Was he planning to complain about me hitting Kane?

He would need to get over it.

It was a Defence class, and there would be plenty more bruises in the future, *especially if any of them were paired with me.*

I leave the grounds and walk in the direction of the dorms, grabbing something quick to eat and showering.

When night falls, I'll slip back into the forest's shadows and train. I'll go over what we learnt today and add my own variations.

If today has shown me anything, it's that I'm getting stronger. My body was still in pain and sore from the attack earlier, but I was healing, my body recovering quicker than it had before. By nightfall, I might even be fully healed.

Maybe I couldn't take a shifter out just yet with my strength, but I was able to hold my own, and soon I would be able to do much more.

CHAPTER TEN

I feel the sweat pour down my back as I push myself harder, twisting and bending, pivoting my body as I shift from one stance to another until it all flows into one. Almost as if I'm dancing.

It was becoming easier to train, my moves quicker and seamless, my body shifting naturally even before my mind could decide what to do next.

I was also lasting much longer. If that little 'punishment' of laps from earlier was any indicator, my endurance was improving too.

I let my body take over as I close my eyes. Opening my senses, I take a breath, moving with the sway of the wind and leaves around me, listening to the nature surrounding me and the nocturnal creatures awakening to the night.

I hear the bristling of the leaves in the trees, the fluttering of wings above me, and in the distance, a low hoot in the trees to my right, followed by the pitter-patter of a small creature's feet scurrying along the forest floor bed to my left.

A small smile curves my lips as my movements come to a finish, sweat dripping down my face as my heart thrums in my chest.

I slowly open my eyes, focusing fully on any other movements around my small clearing in the forest.

I'd claimed the area as my own every night and had watched carefully for anyone entering the forest.

I'd seen the silver-haired guy from the previous time again, just a few nights ago. Thankfully, though, he always seemed to head into the darkest part of the forest, where there were more wild magical beasts.

Was he training too? And against magical beasts?

I shake my head.

It wasn't my business what anyone else did. As long as they stayed away from me and my little area, I could train in peace, and that's all that mattered.

I watch on from the clearing as a small squirrel makes its way up a large pine tree, a grey owl watching on as it hovers from above.

My brows scrunch together.

From where I was standing, they were as clear as day and as detailed, almost as if they were just in front of me. Except they stood at least thirty metres in the distance.

It seemed like my senses, as well as my physical strength, were growing stronger by the day. They were developing beyond even *my* expectations.

Taking a deep breath, I relish in the gentle cool of the breeze brushing past me and the peace of the forest at night.

I roll my shoulders out, basking in the moon's soft light, when suddenly, a loud roar bellows from my right. It shakes the surrounding trees, scattering the birds and creatures around there and sending them scurrying along the forest floor.

I turn towards the loud rumble, my eyes searching the dark forest for whatever creature let out such a bone-chilling noise.

Whatever it was had to be massive.

Maybe a bear, or some sort of wild magical creature?

I had seen animal tracks the further in the forest I travelled. There were definitely wild animals around this forest, but I had only seen trails of maybe a wild boar, a wolf, or a large bobcat. Nothing big enough to make that noise, and thankfully nothing of the magical kind.

A shiver runs down my back.

I grab my hoodie and zip it up to my chin, the frigid Autumn air hitting my sweat and making me shiver.

Or was it the creature's howl giving me goosebumps?

I had fought all sorts of creatures in The Facility to 'test' my strength, although they were usually mutations of whatever wild magical creatures the guards could catch or breed.

I had learnt, with time, to push past any feelings of fear I had. Survival had become my priority, even against the most terrifying or disgusting of creatures I had always fought and lived.

I edge closer to the direction of where the roar sounded from, keeping close to the trees and shadows and listening for any unusual noises as I go deeper.

It could just be a trapped animal or one beast fighting another for territory.

However the forest was restricted and off-bounds to students in the academy for a reason. Wild beasts and magical creatures being the number one issue, so it wouldn't be that far-fetched to have a few around, especially the deeper you go.

I could high-tail it out of there if I saw anything I couldn't handle, but first, I needed to see if it could be a threat to me and my little training area.

I wouldn't feel secure knowing there was some large predator lurking in the area where I train every night.

This area, the darkest part of the forest, was the most restricted. That meant that wild magical beasts roamed freely here, and attacks had occurred when students or even teachers had crossed onto the path.

The further I walk, the more eerie and dark it feels.

A colder chill laces the air as a creepy silence surrounds me, not even the wind wanting to blow through the trees in these parts of the woods.

The ground is uneven and dark; even the soil seems cold and dead. The trees surrounding me flow up and toward the sky, their dark leaves and branches blocking out even the slightest bit of light from the moon shining above.

I push past a large bristly branch and stumble on a mass of tree roots below my feet. I grab onto a nearby branch, trying to steady myself, but my foot catches again. This time, I'm unable to balance myself and fall, tumbling down a steep incline.

I cut my hand and scrape my arms as I continue to

fall, my hands unable to grasp a hold of anything as I descend to the dark forest area below.

I suddenly stop the moment I smack into something soft, grateful for whatever bush or shrub broke my fall.

I try to pull myself up, only pushing further into the soft shrubbery.

That's when I feel it.

A *warmth.*

Something that didn't feel like leaves or a bush...it felt like *fur.*

I brush my hand against it. It was so soft and...*shaggy.*

I struggle to untangle myself and pull away from whatever creature this was before it woke up and retaliated, but I only end up slipping on something below my feet as soon as I stand up.

Falling back down to where I was before, I now feel wet and coated in whatever was covering the ground.

The creature still hadn't woken up or even moved.

I place a hesitant hand back onto its soft fur, waiting for some type of movement or noise.

Only nothing happens.

I bend in closer, leaning my ear against the shaggy fur.

One second goes by, then ten, then thirty...Nothing.

There's no heartbeat.

Whatever animal it was, was dead now.

I slowly drag myself up again, steadying myself using the creature's body below me.

A break in the clouds and trees above me allows for a small trickle of light from the moon to filter through and onto the area around me, and I immediately freeze.

The forest around me is destroyed; trees are uprooted, bark is splintered and strewn across the forest floor, and chunks of tree roots are upheaved with no clear definition of what lay there before. It's pure carnage.

But the most disturbing thing was the body of the animal before me, the body of a huge brown grizzly bear.

Or what remained of it.

Its corpse lay in a mangled heap, or at least most of it. Its limbs had been ripped off and lay in different sections of the clearing around us.

I swallow the bile trying to escape my throat as I stare into the lifeless eyes of the creature's severed head. It's sitting nestled between two woven trees on the opposite side of the area where I'm standing, with crimson liquid slowly dripping from its open jaw.

Gaping into its empty black eyes, another shiver runs down my back before I turn away.

What had taken down such a massive and ferocious animal? What beast or monster managed to rip through such an animal so easily and lay waste to the area around it?

I quickly look around me, my eyes scanning each direction for anything lurking in the distance.

A minute goes by, and then another.

Except there's nothing. *Thankfully.*

I keep my senses about me as I twist back to the partial corpse.

Maybe there was some kind of clue left as to what creature did this?

Granted, this was a far bit away from my little clearing, but who could say the creature wouldn't find me or come looking for a little snack?

More light trickles in around me and down onto the body before me.

Even with just its torso and no limbs or head, it looks to be almost seven feet long.

This bear must have been enormous.

I brush a hand down its fur, looking for any claw marks or bites I can recognise, when I unexpectedly realise my hands don't feel wet anymore, they are sticky.

Wouldn't mud have dried up or turned gritty, not sticky?

I place my hands out toward the small rays of light over the bear's corpse, and now realise they're coated in a familiar crimson liquid.

And it's not just my hands, I was covered from head to toe.

I'm guessing it wasn't mud that I had slipped on earlier, either.

A pool of red liquid trickles beneath my feet from the body beside me.

A heavy sigh leaves my lips as I turn my eyes to the darkened sky, contemplating my luck.

Had I burned through all my good luck when I went back in time?

I shake my thoughts off and take a better look at the corpse. I shouldn't stay out here any longer than necessary.

The body was more like a mass of ripped flesh and meat on its front side, its torso mangled and torn to shreds, with no identifiable claw or bite marks, even from a magical beast.

I make my way around the body, continuing my search as a dark thought hits me.

This wasn't about food.

Even though the body was shredded, there were no bite marks and too much meat and flesh left for anything to have been eaten.

Was this creature primal and protecting its domain, or taking over a new one?

Or was this something else, something much more sinister? Was it for the hunt, the kill, or for *fun*?

A cold chill runs down my spine as I turn around, gazing into the dark forest around me.

Whatever it was...it could still be out there or nearby.

The light fades from the sky, the woods darkening eerily again as an icy mist forms on the forest floor.

I hear a crunch of leaves in the distance, and something shouts in my head, telling me to get out of there and run.

I turn and dash through the forest as fast as my legs will take me.

Whatever it was, it had to be pretty powerful to be able to take on a brown grizzly and make mincemeat out of it.

I had fought a lot of crazy creatures in The Facility, too many to count, but my instinct was telling me that this was something else.

Something that I would be no match for with the strength I had right now.

I run through the forest, ignoring everything else

around me and only slowing when I see the academy building in sight.

I make a quick beeline toward the girl's dormitory and make quick work of the back door lock.

I take my bloodied shoes off and rush quickly up to my room, discarding my clothes on the bathroom floor and jumping straight into the shower. I turn the water on full blast, hoping to cleanse myself of both the blood and the chill running through me.

Sooner or later, I'd have to come face to face with whatever was lurking in that forest, especially if it was expanding its territory, but tonight wasn't the night. I didn't have the strength or agility to take on something that enormous this early.

I'll retreat for now, but I won't next time.

If there's anything I've learnt, it's that even the largest of predators can become prey.

CHAPTER ELEVEN

y stomach growls as I make my way
toward the cafeteria.

I had forgone breakfast to rush to '*Modern Language
and Ideology class*'. Basically, it's a fancy way of saying
Modern English.

Ms. Cheron was a nice teacher, but you knew not to
be late to class or mess with her. Even with her petite 5'2'
frame, she was a small force to be reckoned with.

I yawn as I make my way through the corridor,
another growl following soon after.

Unfortunately, there was no break in between the
next class, '*Spells, Illusions and Curses*' with Ms. Brunswick.
And she would love any excuse to throw me out of her
boring class.

I had arrived on time and smiled brightly just to spite
the old hag. Though unfortunately for my stomach, every
second she drawled on felt like an endless eternity.
Maybe I should have let her throw me out of class...no,
her permanent scowl was *priceless*.

Another rumble from my stomach jerks me from my thoughts just as the scent of bacon hits me.

Pushing through the cafeteria doors, I head straight toward the food, ignoring any of the typical whispers or glares around the room.

A freshly made club sandwich in a thickly sliced brioche bun and a side of fries catches my eye, making my mouth water.

I point to the sandwich and quickly take it from the server, eliciting a small chuckle. Grabbing some juice, I quickly head to my usual morning spot.

Thankfully, not many people seemed to sit there.

I'm making my way over when a bony shoulder knocks into me. I stumble slightly but manage to keep a hold of my tray and food. I look back as two girls wearing emerald ties laugh while taking their seats.

Placing my tray down, I see them glancing back and forth at me from their table, their voices raised as they loudly make snide comments.

"She must really enjoy her food."

"It shows...on her hips."

"Gods, how can she eat all that?"

"Who does she think she is even being in here? Doesn't she know her place?"

"And where does she think she's sitting? I can't wait for her to be put in her place."

The last one has my brows furrowing and my mind questioning my chosen space. What significance does this table hold? I hadn't ever seen anyone near this table, let alone sit and eat. I guess that in itself was a bit strange...Or was this some way to make me move or leave the cafeteria? Another way of removing my existence from their presence?

I lift my gaze toward the voices and narrow my eyes at the group of girls laughing in my direction.

Ignoring them, I turn back to my sandwich and take a bite just as they all fall silent.

What now? Were they going to comment on how I eat, or how much food I can fit in my mouth?

I glance up toward them, their faces paling as they stare toward the food queue. Then they quickly return to their rabbit food, their laughter and voices now utterly quiet.

What? Did the appearance of some crispy bacon terrify them into silence? There were many reasons I loved food. *A very long list, in fact.* Now, silencing those rabid hyenas would be added to it.

I take another bite of my club sandwich, holding back the hum wanting to leave my throat at its delicious flavours melting in my mouth. Then another large bite as a shadow falls over me. I grip my sandwich and pull my plate closer as a dark voice bites out.

"You're sitting in my space. Move."

I drag my stare up the towering dark silhouette before me, slowly following the tattoos across his arms and up to his neck, where a crimson red tie hangs loosely. His sleeves are rolled up and proudly display the black skull and snakes running down his hands, with tattoos lacing each knuckle and finger.

His fists clench into balls and my eyes quickly flick to his face. A *familiar* face.

Even in anger, it appeared almost godly. Such an

inhumanely beautiful face that if it wasn't for all the dark tattoos and piercings, *and the murderous aura,* you would think he was some heavenly being.

His dark hair falls onto his face as he moves closer. He brushes it away, freeing his piercing blue eyes as he grits out *'Move'* once more.

I take another slow bite of my sandwich as he pulls out, what I assume is his pocketknife, and glares down at me.

"Haven't we already been through this?" I meet his eyes just as they narrow at me. "Do you own every seat in this school...?" A glint of recognition sparks in his eyes as his hand freezes. "Or do you just like the ones I sit on?"

His eyes widen a fraction before a slow grin stretches his lips.

"Right, the crazy chick from English."

My eyes widen slightly. Who was he to be calling *me* crazy? I wasn't the one whipping a blade out over seating arrangements. Also, it was World History, not English.

His hand flicks his blade away and places it in his back pocket.

Guess he isn't feeling stabby today.

He pulls the seat out in front of me and sits down. "And it's the opposite, Little Red. You're the one in *my* space."

Little Red? Was he calling *me* that?

I take another bite of my sandwich, finishing it, before I speak.

"I don't see your name here."

His grin turns into something almost deranged, his

teeth glistening as he raises a brow. "That so? I'll have to fix that."

He taps his long fingers on the table, his eyes watching my every move as if seeing something interesting and fun.

I take a crispy fry from my plate and continue eating. I'd get nothing from talking to someone so half-baked.

Just as I'm biting into another fry, his hand reaches toward my plate and fries. My own hand automatically darts forward. His large hand freezes, the small metal fork a mere millimetre from his fingertips.

I narrow my gaze toward his fingers.

"*Get your own.*" His eyes widen for a brief second before he breaks out laughing.

His laugh is deep and husky, sending a slight shiver down my spine with the timbre of it. It puts me in a daze for a moment as the rest of the room falls silent.

His laugh dies off as he shifts back toward me, a glint in his eye as our gaze meets again. The grin spreading across his lips has my toes curling and something warming down my lower spine.

He bends in closer, his smoky scent hitting me. "Don't like sharing, Red?"

His words tug me out of whatever trance I'm in, as I shake my head. "Not my food."

"So, crazy *and* possessive. Not qualities most normies want in their partners, Red." He shakes his head, leaning in toward me. "Personally, though, I think a little crazy every now and then is healthy. And being possessive..." His eyes gloss over a little as he bites down on his bottom lip, "It's sexy as fuck having a woman stake her claim on shit, especially if it gets bloody."

A tray from a server falls to the floor behind the food table. It has the both of us turning around and pulling us from our own little world.

I sigh. What was I even doing listening to this guy? He was clearly more than a little crazy and volatile, whipping out blades and barking orders for someone sitting in a seat.

So why was I staying and listening?

Why didn't I take my food and just leave? Was it because I was stubborn and liked my spot? Or because the only conversations I had with other people were ones insulting or humiliating me?

Or was I craving communication to the point that I was actually *enjoying* his company?

While I'm lost in my own thoughts, his hand suddenly flicks forward so quickly that I miss the movement altogether.

He gives me a wicked grin as he takes a bite of the crispy stolen fry, a playful hum leaving his lips as he watches me.

"Some things taste so much better when shared...*or stolen*, Red."

I grip my fork before pointing it toward the half-eaten fry in his mouth. "Enjoy that, because you won't be getting another one."

His eyes turn into crescents as his grin grows bigger. "Somebody starve you or somethin', Red?" He chuckles, licking the fry crumbs from his fingers.

A beat of silence drums between us as his chuckling abruptly stops.

A cold chill runs up my back as I watch his playful eyes slowly turn into something darker. And I now recognise that what he's shown me so far has been a contained version of himself. That something darker readily lurks beneath the surface, just waiting to pounce.

He gives me a look so dark, so deep, and almost feral that I can't reply. He watches me, and I can tell he's seeing more of me with those piercing blue eyes than I want, something *no one should see.*

I open my mouth to deny it, to playfully laugh it off. I hadn't suffered any of that in this life anyway. Only just as I'm about to talk, he shakes his head and stands up.

The table shakes, my fries tumbling from their plate as he gets up and makes his way out of the cafeteria, not a word more and gone just as quickly as he came.

Silence fills the room as everyone watches him leave. Then they begin chatting and laughing again, their voices now louder that he's gone.

An annoying giggle starts up again.

"Even he *can't stand to be near her."*

"Of course, he would find her repulsive. Just look at her."

"She probably tried to bait him with her bullshit."

"Do you think maybe she smells as well?" The group of salad-eating hyenas snicker.

My gaze flicks to the small group of girls, all wearing matching pin-straight hairstyles and manicured nails.

Their words mean nothing to me, although their loud voices are giving me a headache. And after the confusing and strange moment I'd just shared with a crazy guy, I simply wasn't in the mood for them.

"I bet she doesn't even have anyone for the Halloween Dance. Honestly, who would even ask her?"

"That's so sad. I mean, I have three partners already and another waiting for my reply, and she can't even get one? That's pathetic."

"But who would really want someone like her?" They all turn to me, mocking pouts coating their overly glossed stained lips.

I roll my eyes, scoffing as I pull myself up and away from my table.

"I didn't think anything could turn me off from eating..." I look toward them, meeting each set of raised brows. "But I guess it depends on the surrounding company."

Their faces scrunch up as I make my way past their table.

"Your voices are nauseating. It's almost a talent to make someone feel so disgusted just by listening to them...*Almost.*"

I walk out of the cafeteria, a symphony of screeching sounds falling behind me as I make my way into the corridor and bump straight into something solid.

A hand reaches out to steady me yet quickly pulls back as if burned.

I look up into a set of familiar brown eyes.

Knox is frozen, his gaze slightly wide and awkward as he flickers it between his hands and me.

I hear laughing from behind him and Anders' voice.

"What's the hold-up, man? I'm hungry–" His words

freeze in his mouth when he spots me on the other side of Knox. "Oh."

"Anders, what are you doing? You're in the way," Kane says before his eyes fall on me, his habitual scowl taking over his expression.

I push past Knox and Anders. Kane is the only giant jackass now left in my way of exiting the building. He stands almost a foot above my five-foot-seven-inch frame.

"Move," I seethe. I wasn't in the mood for his bullshit. I'd been given enough of a headache with the hyenas from earlier.

His eyes narrow before something sparks in them.

"Ask nicely."

"Kane," Knox calls with a slight warning to his tone. *But who needed his help?*

I take a step closer to Kane, our toes touching as I glare up into his smug eyes.

"Did you not learn your lesson the last time we spoke?" My eyes narrow as he opens his mouth, but I cut him off before he even has a chance to speak. "You used to be such a stubborn grump when we were kids, all dark clouds and thorny stems. I used to even *like* that about you."

He flinches, his scowl slightly wavering as his eyes soften just a fraction.

"It's a pity that you grew into such a cold dick who only knows how to growl or bark." I thrust my shoulder into his side, forcing him out of my way, and head out of the building, ignoring the voices behind me.

I'll leave those emotions and memories where they belong. In the past.

I no longer know the boys before me—the childhood friends who I once had disappeared with my broken youth and memories a long time ago.

Sentiment wasn't going to prolong my life or help me have it any easier in the academy. It did nothing in my previous life. Nobody stepped up to help me, or to stop the torment or trauma that was inflicted on me. And nobody lent a hand when I was down.

No, they just kicked me further into the abyss that was my own desolation.

The hope of the past is burnt to its wick, and you can no longer make something from nothing.

I make my way toward the girl's dormitory and head to my room.

There is only the future in my mind now, and the past is just a painful memory of mistakes from which to learn.

CHAPTER TWELVE

The week passed by in a flash. I had been training every night and had become much faster and stronger. Except I realised that I had reached a bottleneck. Doing the same routine now wasn't yielding many results, and I was limited on what I could do by myself.

In The Facility, I had been forced to fight whether it was beasts or mutated creatures. It pushed me beyond my limits, survival being the only thing that mattered.

It wasn't something I wanted to go through again, but I needed to do *something* that would push me further and help me grow more.

I had kept to my little clearing while training at night, but I could feel a shift in the air in the forest lately. Fewer animals were moving about, and there was an eerie feeling from the forest and near where I trained.

Maybe the beast that had killed the bear was hunting closer to my little training spot.

And with most of the students having left earlier that day for their weekend, now was the perfect time to find out.

I stealthily make my way past the courtyard and into the forest. I head in the opposite direction of my little clearing and move deeper into it, the glow from the setting sun still lighting my way and giving the eerie forest a less horror-movie vibe.

I watch my footing as I make my way over the uneven forest floor.

Twisted tree roots sprawl under my feet, thick pointed branches lacking foliage jut out from the surrounding trees. Nature itself telling trespassers to keep away.

The further I walk, the more complex the terrain becomes, and with the sunlight now quickly fading to night, a cool mist begins to seep in around the forest surrounding me.

An eerie silence fills the area; not even the wind is willing to blow through here.

Suddenly, I catch my palm on a sharp piece of bark jutting from a tree to my right.

Stopping to check the small wound, I hear a sound rustling to my left.

I turn around quickly, grabbing the dagger I'd sneakily taken from the training grounds locker. The small metal blade gleamed as I gripped it.

It wasn't the best weapon against a beast, especially a large one, but it was better than the small metal forks in the cafeteria.

A feral growl falls from the bushes as I take a defensive stance, my heartbeat kicking up a notch as I imagine all the creatures it could be.

I grip the dagger tightly as the creature pounces from the bushes and bares its fangs just a few feet from me. Its greenish-gold eyes are gleaming and narrowed in my direction.

The thrum of my heart calms at the sight of the animal. A mountain lion.

It had to be the biggest I'd ever seen, stretching out at seven feet long, but I'd fought bigger and worse. A mountain lion I could take easily.

I pull my body lower and into a crouching position as I flip the dagger in my hand.

By the looks of the animal's eyes, it wasn't planning on letting me leave without a taste.

It growls again, slowly stepping closer as its eyes watch my movements.

I twist the blade in my hand, preparing for the attack that's soon to come, when suddenly, the lion freezes.

It makes a shaky retreat and then turns and runs away swiftly.

I watch as it dashes through the forest, never once turning back my way.

Pulling myself up straight, my mind works to understand what just happened. There's no way such a large mountain lion was afraid of the flicker of a dagger.

My brows scrunch together as I look back toward the forest, the mountain lion now completely gone from sight.

A small sigh leaves my lips. It would have been an excellent way to push my training up a notch.

Nothing beats training like trying to survive an animal that wants to eat you.

I turn around to make my way to my little training area to workout instead. All at once, I freeze, the air draining from my lungs.

Two dark, ice-blue eyes stare at me from the treeline opposite from where I stand. Too large to be human or any natural animal of the forest.

The night's dark sky and dim lighting make it difficult to determine what kind of magical beast it is.

It's covered by the shadows and trees around it, yet the shiver coursing its way over my skin tells me it's something I should be running from.

It takes a measured step forward, its eyes focused entirely on me as its enormous body shakes the trees around it with the slight movement.

My breath catches in my throat with the sheer size of the beast. Even walking on all fours, it must be over eight feet tall. Its fur is as black as night, tipped with white and blue strands that seem almost like ice, and the landscape around it seems to freeze up or shrivel with just its appearance.

A cool mist surrounds the ground around it, but I can make out four huge paws, all tipped with razor-sharp claws and a sizeable bristly tail. The beast reminds me of something similar to a wolf shifter or a hellhound but stands three times their size. And with a power so dark and murderous, it emanates from its every pore.

A low growl vibrates from its large mouth, shaking the trees beside it with its vibration.

It takes another step, stalking closer to me.

Every fibre of my being screams for me to run, to turn away and flee. Whatever this beast is, it has the look of a predator who always gets its prey, and tonight, that was me.

Another shiver runs up my spine as the beast stalks closer, my body frozen in place as its eyes stay fixated solely on me.

I bite the inside of my lip, tasting the coppery blood that trickles from it. It helps to drag me from my frozen state and pull me back together.

My eyes close in on the beast.

Never again would I run away.

Never again would I give up without a fight.

If I ran from this beast now, it would surely follow me. Plus, with its sheer size alone, it could easily catch me in seconds.

I needed to fight.

I grip the dagger in my hand and bend lower, preparing for attack.

I had gotten stronger and faster with my training, and I wouldn't be giving this life to anyone, *or anything*, this time around.

I had to survive this. *I would.*

And whatever this beast was, I would beat it.

I watch as it stalks nearer to me, now just a few feet away, as a deep growl falls from its lips and it bares its sharp fangs at me. Its lips spread, almost as if the beast was grinning as it watched me.

Suddenly, the beast leaps forward, its claws extended as it reaches for me.

I dodge, rolling to my left and down into an open

area. I twist and flip, pulling myself onto my feet as the beast dashes toward me. The tree that stood behind me just moments ago now lies shredded at the beast's feet with chunks of bark torn to splinters.

And by the looks of it this was the beast that ripped the brown grizzly bear to pieces. *Literally.*

I clutch the dagger in my hand, the shape of its hilt now embedded into my skin with my tightened grip.

Observing the beast's movements, I wait for it to come to me, slowing my heavy breathing and my beating heart. I won't fall here.

I died once before, but I won't let it happen a second time.

I lift my hands slightly, the blade flipped in my right hand as I narrow my gaze at the beast approaching me.

It charges again, and this time, I meet it halfway in my own run toward it.

It lashes out at me, but I dodge, sliding under its extended claws and beneath its large body.

Slashing the blade outwards and along the beast's side, I catch it before it manoeuvres away from me. I flip out of the way just as its large fangs gnash down just inches from my face.

I'm crouched on the forest floor, blade at the ready, waiting for its next attack, when suddenly the beast bends down, its body almost imitating my own.

Another shudder runs across my skin as its dark eyes gleam, watching mine.

Those weren't the eyes of some wild, mindless beast; they were bloodthirsty, alright, but somehow also *calculating.*

This beast held an intelligence like no other magical creature I'd seen before. Its movements alone proved that.

Its icy blue eyes glowed as the moon trickled down on us, its dark fur bristling with the cold mist surrounding its body.

Everything quickly fell into darkness as clouds covered the last remaining light from the moon, almost like a signal for the beast to attack again.

Its body veers toward me before it swiftly shifts to the right just as I'm swiping my foot out to unsteady it. It leaps into the air, anticipating my move, and uses a large oak tree as leverage to jump.

It twists mid-air before I can land a blow, knocking me across the floor and slamming me into a twisted and torn tree trunk.

The bark slices into my side, drawing blood.

The beast rushes toward me as I back up further into the broken trunk, pulling my knees up under me.

The wound on my side widens, and I wince with pain but lean back further into the tree, using it as leverage as the beast makes its way nearer.

It's on me in seconds, its teeth too close for comfort as I make my move, pushing every ounce of strength I have into my legs, towards the beast's giant face.

It buys me only a moment.

I flip the dagger still gripped in my hand and thrust it into the beast's side, trying but failing to catch its neck.

The beast knocks me backward, smacking my head against the thick wood as a deep guttural snarl pours from its throat.

My head aches with the hit, but as I try to turn and get away, the beast growls. Its breath brushes across the side of my face as it stands over me.

Its teeth are bared, each point sharp and glistening. Its icy eyes narrowed toward me as my movements stilled, my mind falling blank on how to escape this ferocious creature.

Its cold breath sweeps over my skin, chills running down every part of my body as I see the only weapon I have laying too far from reach across the clearing with the beast's blood coating its metal blade.

Another snarl pulls me back to its glowing blue eyes.

Its lips pull back, a strange sound unlike the growls and snarls before, almost like a chuffing noise, as if the beast was laughing.

Its cold breath brushes past my face with the noise. It's so close to me that the fur from its face touches my skin.

My heart races in my chest as I hold my breath.

Was this my end? To be eaten by a beast? To die in the cold woods, once again alone and unknown to anyone?

No...I couldn't die like this. Not again.

I don't know why I was given this second chance, but I doubt I would get a third.

Clenching my fist, I ignore the pain slicing up my side and thrumming through my head.

I didn't go quietly the first time, even locked away and burning in that hell alone. And this time, I was free. There are no shackles, just an oversized mutt who needed leashing.

I watch the beast as it watches me.

"Take a bite..." An unfamiliar, gravelly voice flows from my lips as I allow all my anger to surface with each word. "But I won't go down easy."

A strange noise rolls up its throat, a blue gleam growing brighter in its eyes as it watches me. But before I can make a move, a large gust of cold wind blows around us. The mist covers us completely, along with the surrounding area. It forces my eyes to close from the icy chill lashing against my face.

I quickly force them open again and watch as the icy white mist blankets the area around us. My vision is over-taken and clouded before the mist slowly recedes back into the forest. The large beast follows it, disappearing into the distance with only one final glance back at me with its hauntingly bright blue eyes.

When it and the strange mist is gone, I flick my eyes around the woods, heightening my sight to scan every inch to see where the creature went.

He couldn't hide a body like that so easily.

What was going on?

Was he planning to jump out and kill me when I thought I was safe?

My eyes find nothing, and my ears also pick up no other noise than some small creatures moving in the distance.

It was gone. But why?

It had me where it wanted me. Why would it leave?

My shoulders sag as I lean back onto the broken tree trunk behind me.

A bitter chuckle leaves my lips. *Round one to you then beast...*

I wanted to be pushed harder but not die.

But now was not my time.

I had to get stronger.

This wasn't nearly enough.

I sit there, watching until all the mist has faded from the distance and I hear nothing moving around me.

Slowly, I pull myself up, pain searing up my side and my head throbbing with each move I make. I slowly drag myself through the forest and watch for movement as I make my way back toward the academy.

Placing my hand on my side where my wound sits, the cut is still bleeding and the pain is still sharp, but I can feel it slowly healing and mending itself.

There were definitely some broken or fractured bones there as well from the hit, and it will probably take all night before those fully healed.

After what feels like hours, I finally see the dormitory in the distance. Then, just as I'm about to make my way out of the treeline, I hear voices.

I duck back behind the trees, my body screaming from the sudden movement.

I wait until the voices pass and fade further into the distance, adding another couple of minutes before I pull myself up again.

It wasn't unusual for some students to sneak out or break curfew, so long as you didn't get caught, it went overlooked by the faculty.

I slink from shadow to shadow at an annoyingly slow pace until I'm back in the dorms and in my room.

I fall on top of the bed, the room around me slowly

darkening with the pull of sleep, the aches and wounds slowly healing as my body relaxes.

Aching and exhausted from the night, I drift off to sleep, my last thoughts of needing to become stronger. And find a way to win round two with the beast.

CHAPTER THIRTEEN

unning through an endless darkness, I'm unsure of whether I'm awake, asleep, or dead and whether what I had seen before at the academy was all an illusion.

Or is this an illusion?

I hear noises around me; muffled voices getting closer, sounds of voices shouting and yelling, only I can't make out the words.

I don't know where I'm going or what I'm running for, just that I shouldn't stop. I needed to keep moving forward.

Something grabs my left arm and tries to pull me back. It feels tight and heavy against my skin. I pull at it, trying to release my hand, but then it latches onto my right arm, stopping me from feeling what it is or from pulling it off of me.

Then, as if the ground itself wants to hold me in place, my legs become encased in whatever is below me, stopping me from moving even a step further.

Something begins to slither up my legs and back, coating

me in something thick and heavy as it makes its way toward my neck.

The voices around me become louder, still muffled, and difficult to make out, yet they sound as if they're calling to me.

Images begin to flash around me, blurred and faded, though I can make out people fighting.

I hear the sounds of metal clashing together, of people running and shouting at one another as they move.

The area is still dark, the people faded and blurry as if I were watching an old movie but up close.

They move around me, past me, and through me.

So this wasn't real.

It was an illusion or dream, a memory of sorts.

Memory?

No, I don't remember anything like this.

This was a battle, a fight of some sort.

The image shifts to more fighting and muffled voices, except I can make out a few more apparent shapes this time.

Two people hold a black metal sword and spear as they fight off a larger group. The weapons are pure black from top to bottom. They move as if they're an extension of the person holding them, cutting everything and everyone that comes remotely close to them down with ease. And as if in some sort of trance, I can't take my eyes from them. My hands try to move with the sight of them, the feeling of wanting to hold the dark metal in my palms taking over my thoughts completely.

The image shifts again; just one person in the distance.

They're running from something or someone this time while holding a similar weapon in their hands.

I'm wondering when all this will end when suddenly our eyes meet.

Dark blue eyes gaze back at me from a distance, the tall, dark figure cloaked in the darkness as he watches on.

I flinch as it narrows its eyes at me, raising its blurry arm to throw its weapon toward me.

Even if this is a dream or illusion, I didn't want to take any chances.

I try to move, to thrash against whatever heavy rock or weight holds me in place. I struggle and fight against the heavy restraints, pulling until I feel my arms and legs begin to move a little.

I promised myself I would never be caged again, and even in my dreams, I wouldn't allow it.

I push myself forward with every ounce of strength in me, just as the blade crashes into me.

It hits me right in the chest, the black blade embedding itself in my skin.

I wait for the pain to strike and when I feel none, I remember that this is an illusion.

Is that why I felt nothing?

The blade seeps deeper into me, burying itself in my chest and slowly disappearing into my body.

You would think something like that would send me into a panic, even in a dream, but instead, I felt calm. A faint feeling of warmth spreading through me as it seeped deeper into my body.

Suddenly, the weight and heaviness holding my limbs faded.

My body now free from whatever was holding me in place.

The darkness around me begins to tremble, the ground beneath me quaking with the shift.

Cracks begin to form in the dark, a blinding light pouring through its gaps as the area around me quickly disappears.

I pull my hand over my eyes as the light shines through my window and forces me to wake. The images from the dream still playing out in my mind as I lay in bed listening to the birds and rustling of leaves in the distance.

There were so many questions running through my mind.

What kind of dream was that? What were those black blades that seemed to place me in a trance? Why did my fingertips and palms tingle just thinking about them? And who did those blue glaring eyes belong to?

So many questions spin around my head, and for a dream that could simply be just that, a weird dream and figment of my imagination or deeper consciousness.

I shake my head, a sigh falling from my lips as I stretch out my limbs.

My body feels more rested and energised. And after last night's fight, I thought it would be the opposite.

I glance down to where my wound is, only torn, muddy clothes covering my now fully healed skin.

If not for the mess my clothes and hair are in right now and the dried blood on my side, I'd have thought last night was also a dream.

I drag myself from my warm and cosy bed, pulling the now stained blanket with me and throwing it on the floor.

I'd have to wash that soon, but first, a hot shower.

Peeling off my dirty and ripped clothes, I discard them on the bathroom floor and make my way into the shower. I turn the temperature up to its highest, which unfortunately wasn't as hot as I'd like with its old plumbing and allow the water to cleanse me of the remnants of last night's fight. I let the water trickle down my face, the warmth like a soothing balm to my constantly racing thoughts. I move to turn the tap off and end my relaxing shower before remembering it was Saturday, which meant no classes and no need to rush.

Leaving the shower on, I enjoy a few more minutes of peace and take my time scrubbing before I turn it off and dry myself. I brush my fingers over the tattoo-like mark on my right hip and then my left, before I quickly freeze, looking toward my feet.

There, on my ankles, sit a small curved black line with a small crescent shape above them. Bending down, I trace each one with my finger. The colour is the same as the ones on my hips, but the mark is only half the size. I look back and forth between my right and left ankles, both bearing the same black tattoo-like marks.

What did they mean? Why were they showing up now? Were there going to be more in the future?

I didn't have them in my previous life, so maybe they really were a small piece of the puzzle of why or how I was here now.

I brush my fingers slowly over each mark on my ankles and then my hips. I didn't feel worried or anxious when I looked at them. I felt...some sort of familiarity with them, some genuine connection like they were always meant to be there.

When the words fill my mind, a feeling of rightness fills me. As if there was always a blank part of me waiting for them.

I touch the black marks more fondly before noticing a small patch of dried blood on my neck in the bathroom mirror. I must have missed it while enjoying my shower.

Turning the hot water tap on, the old tap splutters to life before soon turning into a small trickle with barely any lukewarm water falling from its faucet.

I roll my eyes. These old 'features' were getting on my nerves.

I didn't need any pampering or luxury items, but a proper water flow would be nice.

I go to turn the old tap off after cleaning the bit of blood away when suddenly the metal head snaps off in my hand, the water now spraying from the broken faucet and onto the bathroom floor.

Thankfully, it wasn't a colossal amount with the old plumbing.

Still clutching the tap's metal head, I shove it onto the broken faucet, trying to somehow stop the water flow.

Giving it a hard push, I watch as the top melds into the broken metal below it, forcing the flowing water into a more minor trickle. It seeps into the sink, the flow now only a minor dribble and more manageable to clean up.

My gaze flickers between my hand and the newly shaped tap.

I knew my strength had improved, but being able to

bend metal so effortlessly wasn't possible. Or was it that the taps were just really that old, or maybe cheap?

I glance back at the twisted metal, still dripping a small stream of water into the sink.

Even if it was old or cheap, it never felt *that* weak before.

Shaking my head, I walk toward the wardrobe, throwing on a pair of navy sweats and a white t-shirt.

My strength couldn't have just sky-rocketed overnight, right?

I turn toward my window, gazing at the forest in the distance.

I guess there was one way to test it out.

Getting myself ready, I throw on a matching navy hoody and quickly make my way into the forest.

I walk toward my small clearing, the forest taking on a different atmosphere during the day.

The trees and grass are beautiful, rich green tones, nature at its finest as the sun shines above, with small birds fluttering in and out through the trees chasing one another.

Closing my eyes, I listen to the peaceful sounds surrounding me as I take a slow breath in.

There was a small trickle of water running in the distance, the sound of small animals scurrying about the forest and if I focused hard enough, I could hear a few sparse voices in the distance in the academy.

Opening my eyes, I head to a large, sturdy tree on the opposite side of the clearing. One I had used before when testing the strength of my punches that left *me* with more cuts and bruises than I had given *it*.

154 | ISLA DAVON

Let's see if anything has changed.

Tightening my fist, I pull my shoulder back and position myself in front of the thick tree. I push forward in one quick jab, throwing as much strength as possible into the hit. Splinters fly in the air from the bark as my fist makes contact with the tree.

I pull my fist back out with a few splinters and cuts in my skin, but my healing is already closing up the wounds and working quicker than ever before.

My eyes flicker back and forth between my hand and the tree, a vast hole and fist print now embedded all the way to its centre.

A shaky breath leaves my lips.

How was this possible?

It had felt as if the bark was a sheet of cardboard rather than a half a metre thick tree trunk.

I take a step back, my eyes widening at the damage my one punch had caused. I look back down at my hand, all of the cuts and scrapes now completely healed. A small disbelieving chuckle leaves my lips as my eyes flick back and forth between the tree and my fist.

It seemed my healing had also jumped up a few notches. Before, it would have taken at least an hour for those minor abrasions to heal, whereas now they were gone in less than a minute.

Was this because of last night? Did the fight with the beast push me past what I needed to reach a new level?

But to be this strong after one night...?

I shake my head, my eyes falling to my feet.

Or was this something else?

Was it related to the new little marks sitting on my

ankles? Or something to do with why I felt so refreshed this morning after that weird dream?

There were just too many unanswered questions. I didn't even know how or why I was brought back here and to ten years in the past. Why *now?*

I'm grateful and all, second chances or miracles like this don't happen, *ever.* But why me?

Is this just another thing I should be thankful for and not question?

A vivid image of glaring blue eyes comes to mind as my own eyes thin toward the tree. Black blades and strange images. Black markings appearing on me that I never had in my previous life. And now, I have strength and healing that surpasses anything I could have imagined at such a young age.

Maybe I need to start looking into things. I need to learn more about myself and what this strength is. I always thought I was a witch with no power, but now I think I was never one to begin with.

Witches and warlocks didn't have physical strength like this, and I certainly wasn't a shifter.

I'm pretty sure I'd remember turning into an animal.

Maybe I don't take after my parents...but then what was I, and where did this power come from?

I look toward the sky, large grey clouds floating around the sun and dimming its light as I sigh.

I'd have to tackle one thing at a time.

Time.

It was something I now had a lot of, my only ally here. And with it, I would collect every puzzle piece and place everything together until the picture was whole again.

I'll deal with whatever comes, one day at a time.

Right now, I should train.

I'll work out until I'm dripping with sweat and feel every inch of me burn and ache. And all the questions twisting around in my head can be pushed to the back, and no longer a worry for today.

I head off into a run, the Autumn wind whipping past me as my surroundings quickly blur with my pace.

A small smile stretches my lips. *I guess I had gotten faster too.*

CHAPTER FOURTEEN

I walk into the cafeteria and straight towards the cheesy omelette calling my name.

I had trained for the entire weekend, even waking up on Sunday for a six am run and covering fifteen miles with ease. My senses had grown to new heights too, my hearing reaching much further distances and my sight giving even a shifter a run for their money.

I trained both days from dawn till dusk, and again later until the owls stopped hunting and went to sleep. There wasn't really much else to do here at the weekends anyway. Even the cafeteria was closed, so all my meals were either cold baguettes or a quick cup of noodles from the kitchen in the girl's dormitory.

My mouth waters, a hum leaving my lips as I take my omelette from Finn and grab some water to go.

I head directly for my favourite breakfast spot, but I notice something on my seat just before I sit down. There are letters that weren't there before.

The writing is messy and hard to see, but I make out:

A-N-N-E-X.

Annex, what's that?

I grab my napkin and try to rub out whatever this was, from whichever moron wrote it, but soon stop.

I brush my fingers over the letters.

They weren't written, they were *carved* into the seat.

My seat.

I glance around the room. Which asshole was trying to start crap with me now?

What was this anyway, some kind of curse word or hex?

The writing looked horrendous, almost as if some creature had written it rather than an actual intelligent life form.

Who scribbled crap like this, and so openly in the cafeteria? Who would defy school regulations and deface academy property just to bother me?

Not that I can't see any of them doing it–*since they've done worse*–but the academy took that stuff seriously, probably one of the only things they did.

Oh, you could torment each other, teachers could discriminate against students, but *Gods forbid* anyone touches their property.

I narrow my eyes at the messy scratches before sitting on top of it.

Some child's writing wasn't going to stop me from sitting here and enjoying my meal.

I place my omelette on the table and start to dig in.

After a few moments and a few large bites, I pick up my plate and hand it to a server before heading towards Mr. Finch's class.

After the little standoff we had a while back, he hasn't tried to mess with me again. Not that I would take it sitting down anyway. He just gives me a narrowed look and pinched lip most days, or a raised brow like today.

Giving him a little grin, I look at the clock above him. '09:29 am', with even a minute to spare.

I make my way to an empty seat in the middle section, as most of the seats in the back have already been taken.

I settle in as the class starts, but only a few minutes into the lesson and my eyelids begin to droop. A yawn stretches my lips as Mr. Finch drones on in his monotonous voice when the door abruptly flings open.

Mr. Finch turns around, a scowl on his face as his mouth opens before he freezes. His eyes widen and slightly tremble as the tall, dark figure makes his way into the room and up the stairs.

"...F-find a seat, Mr. Portor." Mr. Finch nods shakily before quickly spinning back to the board. There's a slight tremble in his hand as he picks up his marker and continues the lesson.

The tall boy–I now recognise as the stabby guy from before–starts to make his way up the stairs.

The group in the seats at the back begin to scurry like mice, grabbing their bags and fleeing across the room. One of the boys even takes the seat next to me in his rush to get away.

The boy is almost a third of the way up the stairs when our eyes meet. I quickly turn back toward Mr. Finch, my brows furrowing as I question why I turned away in the first place.

A moment later, a large shadow falls over me.

"Move." The familiar deep voice is darker and cutting, and I feel a chill roll down my spine with his cold tone.

Lifting my head, my eyes quickly trail up his large frame and toward his ruffled hair. It's falling onto his face and covering a part of his eyes. But even then, I could still feel the murderous glare he was wearing.

Was he going to do this with every seat I sat on? I was also in the middle section today, so why would he want it?

Just as I open my mouth to tell him to '*get his own*', the boy beside me jerks my attention away as he falls over his own feet trying to get up. He stumbles, grabbing his bag and rushing toward an empty seat across the room.

What–

A tired sigh pours from the lips of the tall, moody boy as he lazily flops in the newly vacated seat beside me. He places his arms down on the desk before leaning his head on them like a pillow.

I glance toward the top of the class and all the empty seats up there, and then back to the boy sitting beside me.

His dark brown hair falls onto his arms and hands, which are covered in black swirls of ink all the way down to his fingertips. He wears a silver skull on his thumb and several black snake rings on his other fingers. There's a heavy leather jacket draped over his shoulders, clearly a favourite of his if the wear and tear on the cuffs and hem are any indication. The leather collar covers most of his neck, with only a tiny part of the ink visible there.

A little dot behind his ear catches my attention, and his hair is parted so I can make out the small freckle or birthmark. More dark swirls of ink surround it, only separated by a silver metal piercing hanging from his ear.

The small metal glistens against the classroom light, dragging me in for a closer look.

On his ear sits a small dangling metal dagger falling from a short black chain. It's decorated with a black handle and...a ruby-red droplet falling from the blade's tip.

I guess calling him 'stabby' was an appropriate nickname.

The small earring begins to move, and I'm met with two piercing blue eyes just inches from my face. I pull back, not realising I had gotten so close.

A grin spreads across his face as he turns his head entirely around to watch me.

"Have you eaten breakfast yet, Red?"

My brows furrow with his question. Why would he care if I ate?

And was this *'Red'* nickname a permanent thing now?

I nod anyway, a larger grin stretching his lips as his eyes light up.

"And I suppose you sat in my seat?"

This again. He really had an issue with this, didn't he? Like some sort of toddler who licks all his food before eating so he doesn't have to share. But I had been using that table for a fair amount of time now, and not once had he, or anyone else, been around to tell me otherwise.

I sigh, "It's not yours, it's-"

"But it's got my name on it." His eyes curve up in a crescent shape, a mischievous gleam in them as he continues. "Didn't you see it?"

My brows scrunch together before quickly widening. *ANNEX.*

It wasn't a new curse word or hex.

A smile the Joker would be proud of now stretches his cheeks as he watches me.

The psycho had actually *carved* his name onto the seat to claim it indefinitely as his own and make his point.

I shake my head as a small scoff leaves my lips. His name on the seat or even the table wouldn't stop me from sitting there.

I mean, what other options were there? To sit at someone else's table? And next to people that openly scowl and glare at me? I'd take my chances with this psycho, blade-happy...Annex.

"*Annex*." The word rolls off my tongue in a small whisper, still sounding like some sort of curse or Wiccan hex to me.

"Yes?" The light humorous timbre of his voice has me turning to meet his gaze again. There's a softer look in them as they trail from my lips to slowly meet my stare.

Suddenly, he shifts forward, his face only a couple of inches from mine as he leans in.

"You're really not scared, are you?" His gaze flickers back and forth, searching my eyes for something. "I can't see even a lick of fear in you, Red. Not a drop. Why is that?"

My brows pinch together. Why would I be scared of him?

He pulls back slightly, his eyes never leaving mine as he continues his perusal of my face.

"Every pleb in this school turns tail when they see me. They know not to breathe in my direction, let alone look. Like they can almost *smell* the blood and death that surrounds me. But *you*..." His grin reappears, stretching his cheeks again. "You're either completely stupid and blind, or you don't care."

Why would I care about what everyone else thinks of him? I knew to believe only by seeing something for myself. Lies were easy to make and spread as quickly as the air itself. And with what they say and how they treat me here, I wouldn't have listened anyway.

But how did I not know of Annex before in my previous life? Even his name stands out, let alone how he looks. So how did I never see him, or hear anything about him?

A slight frown tugs at my lips as I become lost in my own thoughts.

But he only continues to watch me, waiting for something, and when I don't react, he smiles. A real, genuine one this time. One that lights up his whole face, changing his dark and murderous looks into something so bright and breathtaking, it pulls the air softly from my lungs.

He chuckles, "See." He shakes his head, his grin widening. "You're not one of the sheep here, Red. Maybe not quite a wolf yet either...but you're still different."

His blue eyes twinkle as he talks, a darker shade of blue swirling in them as I gaze almost as if in a trance. They flit to my lips before meeting my eyes again, something darker growing in them as a beat of silence passes between us.

Whispering from a few feet away pulls my attention back. Two girls flicker their gaze back and forth between me and Annex. Their brows knit together, and their lips are pinched as they watch us.

I feel movement beside me, and the two girls flinch. They swiftly turn around with a slight tremor to their shoulders as they sit with their gazes now glued to the front of the class.

"Seems like I'm not the only reason people don't sit beside you." He glances around at the empty seats near us. "They're keeping their distance and not just 'cause of me. What did you do, Red? Kill one of the preppy bastard's ponies or somethin'?"

I look around the room, observing the narrowed glances and glares aimed my way before they hastily turn away, fearful of the person beside me.

"I guess I'm not the only one oblivious to the rumours–" I begin before he cuts me off.

"I don't listen to shit like that, Red." He shakes his head. "*Petty gossip?*" He scoffs. "I couldn't give two fucks. The only thing that interests me is blood, blades, and my brothers."

His brows scrunch together as he glares at a group glancing in our direction before turning back toward me, the creases in his eyes relaxing a little.

"You're not like the other wimps here anyway, Red. They're too afraid to move, to bleed, to be free. They're only worried about shitty names and what they can get. Where's the fun in living like that?" He leans in closer again, this time only a breath between us as he continues. "Sometimes freedom means being the bad guy. Sometimes, you gotta embrace the darkness they create in you and make it your own. Don't be consumed by the shit they throw at you or inflict. Instead, let the dark little soul in you break free and make 'em all bleed."

His eyes gloss over, the slightest of frowns tugging at his lips as a wistful expression takes over his face for the briefest of moments.

"Words can hurt, wounds can fester, but even the most broken of bones can heal again, Red."

Ah, and there it is. The reason I feel drawn to him and why I listen intently while he talks. Why a part of me finds some slither of comfort in his company. Why, *unlike all the others here,* I feel no judgement and maybe even some semblance of a connection.

Something pushed him beyond his limits, *broke* him. And he pieced himself back together, cracks and all. He accepts it, welcomes it, and allows it to create a new him.

Someone who doesn't break, who won't fall easily, and who will continue to get back up, grinning even when bloodied and beaten beyond repair.

I'm not sure what he's been through or what he's seen, but something tells me he went through hell just like me. And he survived it, creating the boy with these piercing blue eyes before me. The one who seems deranged and unhinged yet shelters something a little lost or broken deeper inside.

My breath catches in my throat with the realisation that Annex reminds me of myself.

I see a small reflection in his eyes of all the broken and bent parts of myself that I've tried to bury deep within me. Years of pain and torture that I pushed into a deep hole, only using it to fuel my anger and force myself to continue moving forward. Trying to exist in a world where I've only ever been dealt the worst hand.

I shake my head, trying to pull myself from my spiralling thoughts.

This life was my second chance, and this time, I wouldn't suffer like before. Even Annex himself was proof I had already changed my future because he was never a part of my past.

I gaze at the vibrant blue eyes watching me, something dark and unreadable forming in them before he, too, shakes himself free of it.

"Just live the way you want, Red. Whether you're the good guy or the bad guy in someone else's story, everyone becomes a villain at some point. It's only a difference in perspective." He shrugs, leaning back in his chair and stretching his feet out in front of him. "Not that I don't deserve the fear or title," he grins, "I do. And I embrace that shit fully. I own it. Being the unhinged one at times has its benefits."

He stretches his arms out above him sending all the students near us shaking and leaning in the opposite direction.

Why was everyone so afraid of him? What kind of reputation did he have? *Other than being a bit crazy or deranged.*

And why was I the exception?

Why did everything that came out of his mouth sound like he was comforting me? And why did I genuinely feel some sort of comfort from them?

His words from a moment ago replay in my head as I open my mouth.

"So, who's *bad guy* are you?"

Suddenly his heavenly look turns devilish, something wicked forming in his gaze as his eyes grow more intense. "Hopefully, everyone's."

The bell rings around us signalling the end of class and pulling us from our own little world.

Everyone begins to shuffle out of the room as I shift away from Annex. Then suddenly, his hand darts out, grabbing me and pulling me down toward him.

"Always give more than you get, Red. If they knock you down once, get back up and bury them." He gives me a wicked smirk, pulling himself up and brushing against me as he passes.

"I might even lend a hand. I enjoy a good bloodbath from time to time." He passes Mr. Finch, whose eyes widen as his body shakes. "I hear it's good for the skin," he calls over his shoulder, chuckling as he exits the room.

I pull myself up straight as a slightly lighter feeling envelops me. And then I still my movements, my brows furrowing with the strange sensation.

I look toward the now empty doorway.

It had been a long time since someone had tried to comfort me, let alone offer to *help* me.

I guess even if he was deranged, psychotic, or someone's *bad guy*, he was at least better than all the others here.

Annex. A small grin stretches my lips. It still sounded like some kind of curse word to me.

But I guess it suited him.

CHAPTER FIFTEEN

I make my way to my next class after Mr. Finch clears his throat loudly, his brow raised with an annoyed expression plastered on his face. *A look I take great joy in creating on that man's face.*

I head past the groups in the corridor and make it to the music room, anticipating more frustration and drama from the lesson.

Pushing the classroom door open, I make my way to the fourth-year seats in the room and take my place in a space beside the window.

Looking out toward the yellow and red tones of the leaves falling from the trees outside, I remember back to The Facility when even a window would have been an impossible luxury.

The sound of a chair scraping off the ground pulls my attention, drawing me toward the seat in front of me.

I'm met with two bright turquoise eyes that look as if they have tiny flecks of lilac running through them. Either I was seeing things, or he was part Fae or Elf. Their appearance was always the most alluring and mesmerising in the supernatural community.

They curve upwards as a wavy brown and lilac strand tumbles down onto them.

The boy pushes his hair back as a slow smile spreads across his full lips. It pulls at his almost golden skin and perfectly sculpted features, making him look even more breathtaking.

A navy tie hangs loosely around his neck as he casts me a knowing look. He gives me a quick wink before spinning and taking the seat to the front of me.

Did he not know who I was? Or not hear the crap they all spread about me?

My brows pinch together. *A navy tie.*

Or was it because he was a fourth-year? I didn't have many interactions with the years above me. I had hardly even seen any of the fifth or sixth years since I returned, either. Maybe they hadn't heard? Or just didn't care?

A small group of girls across the room squeal, pulling me from my thoughts. Their eyes are glued to the boy in front of me and almost in a daze as he gives them a small smile and wave. Their cheeks flush bright red as they giggle, their voices becoming louder and shriller with the minute piece of attention.

"Ezra!" yells a raven-haired girl from the back of the second-year seats. Her voice sounds cold and discontent. She sits between two tall boys; one gives her a small chuckle while the other raises a brow.

"Yes, Morgan?" The boy, *Ezra*, gives her a playful smile, eliciting more noise from the girls in the front seats of the second-year area.

Morgan rolls her eyes before narrowing them at Ezra.

"Don't make them louder than they already are." She glares toward the group of girls, a few of them cringing at her expression. "It's *annoying*."

One of the girls, a petite blonde I've seen with Ivy's group before, steps forward.

"Annoying?" She scoffs, her small, freckled nose scrunching upward. "Why are you even talking? Nobody asked for your opinion *or wants it*."

Morgan chuckles, but there's no humour in it, only an icy bite that sends a shiver down my back as the room's atmosphere turns cold.

Her laugh fades as she tilts back in her chair, a calm grin stretching her lips.

"It's *pathetic* watching you all cling to some false hope and think you've got a chance..." Morgan looks the blonde up and down, her grin quickly disappearing. "When you don't."

The blonde's eyes widen before she quickly schools it, even as the blush reddening her cheeks remains. "Who do you think you are? You're not even–"

"I'm not, what?" Morgan flicks her raven hair off her shoulder, revealing her smooth porcelain skin, bright amber eyes, and sculpted features. She has the face of a model yet the poise of a viper.

The blonde furrows her brows, her frustration boiling over as she opens her mouth to speak again.

"Be careful," warns Morgan, cutting her off before she can talk. "Don't say something you'll regret...or I'll *make* you regret saying it."

Jake Andrews steps forward and places himself in front of the blonde.

"Tandy's right, no one asked," the asshole shifter snarks with a glare set on Morgan. "Why even get involved? Just stay in your own corner. And stay quiet."

The room falls silent as the two boys beside Morgan stand up, their glares focused fully on Jake and the small group now forming around him.

A mocking chuckle falls from the tall brown-haired boy to the other side of Morgan.

"No one asked for a headache from all the noise either or to be surrounded by annoying flies, but unfortunately, we share a class." He shrugs, a nonchalant look on his face as he grins. "And as for staying *quiet*," his grin grows dark and menacing, "if you want peace, I'll happily send you somewhere you can permanently get some."

Both groups look at each other like they will shift any minute. Tandy and the girls beside her take a couple of steps back in anticipation of some kind of clash.

Morgan looks eerily calm during all this, her eyes roving over the group a few feet away before they take on a strange shimmering hue.

"Hey, hey. Let's calm down here, guys." Ezra steps forward, glancing between the two groups. His hands are up in the air in a pacifying manner as he takes another couple of slow steps toward them.

He smiles, trying to pull all the attention in the room back to him.

"There's no need for anything to break out. Let's keep it peaceful. I'm sure no one wants to do anything messy like fighting. Right?" He flicks his gaze between the two groups of boys and then toward the petite blonde. She blushes as soon as their eyes meet, a small giggle falling from her lips before she looks toward her friends again.

There's a slight tick in his jaw as he smiles and a stiffness to his posture as he watches the other girls talk and giggle in hushed tones. Completely uncaring of the conflict around them anymore.

"I think it's best if everyone just takes a seat. Class will start soon anyway." He flicks his gaze from the boys around Morgan to Jake and his group.

Their eyes meet, and Jake scoffs. "I don't care if things get *messy*. Maybe if you put a leash on–" He points to Morgan, but before he can finish his words, two growls fall from the boys surrounding her before they both start forward toward Jake's group.

"*Jake.*" The word flows from Ezra's lips and, instantly, everyone freezes.

The name falling from his lips sounded almost lyrical but so cold and cutting it sends a shiver down my spine and goosebumps forming on my arms. He still wears a playful smile as he takes another step forward, but it never reaches his eyes, a darker gaze now narrowed at Jake and his group.

Jake flinches slightly with the look.

"Morgan is family. And *no one* disrespects family." Ezra's grin grows. Except it looks less playful as he continues, making his way over to Jake. "So, watch your words. Or did you forget who I am since I'm usually smiling?" He now stands in front of Jake and leans in closer. He then whispers something I can't make out, but from Jake's pale expression I'm presuming he's gotten whatever threat or message Ezra was giving.

Jake then gives Ezra a shaky nod as Ezra slides a hand over his shoulder, flicking away some invisible lint there. Jake stands as if frozen to the spot, his eyes unmoving from Ezra and his jaw taut.

"Then we're all good?" He shifts his attention to each boy around Jake, who now all wear pallid expressions and give consenting nods.

"Morgan?" He turns his stare to her and the boys around her.

"Another time," she says, a dark grin stretching her lips as she gives the group one final glare. A promise I'm sure she'll keep by the looks of her expression.

Ezra gives her a nod, a softer smile embracing his lips as she concedes.

The two boys near her give Jake and his group one last cutting glare before slowly taking their seats beside her. Morgan turns her full attention toward them as they begin talking, falling into their own world again and ignoring everyone else in the room.

Tandy takes a step toward Ezra, a broad, triumphant smile on her lips as if it were her victory. Just as she's nearing him, a pink blush tints her cheeks and she opens her mouth, "Thank you, I-"

"Let's all get along." Ezra cuts her off with a tight smile, quickly turning away and returning to his seat. She quickly closes her mouth, a slight pout shaping her lips as her gaze lingers on Ezra's back before slowly turning back toward Jake and his group.

A low sigh falls from the chair in front of me as Ezra

takes his seat, his shoulders slightly sagging. He looks out the window and away from everyone's gazes, the girls across the room still trying to steal glances.

I guess all that would be very annoying and frustrating to deal with, even if he did *at first*, seem like he enjoyed the attention.

He leans further back in his seat, his scent wafting toward me with the small movement.

A fresh and calming scent tickles my nose. Like lavender and something else, something familiar but nothing that I could place.

Mrs. Fleur then enters the classroom, pulling me from my thoughts. The door bounces off the wall as she enters in a hurry, late once again. She addresses the class and quickly begins the lesson, and I notice the few empty seats in the centre of the room.

Seria, Xander, Knox, Kane, and Anders aren't here.

If they all weren't here, then they must be skipping or something.

And here I was, wondering why it had been so peaceful.

I look toward the teacher who's rambling about *'baritone and sopranos'* as I lean back in my chair. I guess it'll be a peaceful class today.

And a slight reprieve from all the usual drama.

CHAPTER SIXTEEN

I stretch out my legs and warm up for Defence class. I was a little early for the lesson, having finished my lunch a little too fast worrying I would be late again.

And now I was full and ready to tackle whatever came with this lesson; drills, sparring, or a crazy obstacle course, bring it on.

I realised it had been a mistake in my previous life not to attend this class.

Even if I *was* weaker, to miss out on these lessons was a waste. Even the younger me, in her weakened state, would have enjoyed and benefited from it to some extent.

In each class, I learned new techniques to attack and defend during a fight. It also pushed my physical stamina through sparring and running and allowed me to build my strength at a quicker pace than if I was alone. I also enjoyed putting to practise what I had learnt each night during my own training and training until I had it all memorised and perfected.

I also learned that the Defence teacher, Mr. Valor, wasn't as cold or as stern as the rumours had led me to believe. He was strict when it came to training or being late, yet he was also a very fair teacher. He didn't discriminate and treated everyone equally regardless of status or power.

He gave proper lessons and advice and took the time to repeatedly show even the simplest of stances to students who struggled with their form and positioning. He was only stern or cold towards those who were not taking the lessons seriously.

'*One wrong move or mistake would cost you or your comrades their life during battle*', he would call towards boys or girls giggling or messing while we were sparring.

Two girls had to transfer to a different class last week after being unable to stick to the training. They would complain and whine at the back of the group during drills and giggle and mess around during sparring, focusing more on the boys around them instead of the lesson itself.

I think they only joined because of Mr. Valor, hoping to catch his attention. Unfortunately for them, the attention he gave them wasn't the kind they were looking for. He would glare at them and make them run laps when they would disrupt the class.

With them now gone though, it meant I was the only female student in the third-year defence class and have since felt the brunt of the harassment from the other boys here more.

They've tried to trip me up when we run laps, shoulder me in passing, and have been attempting to enter the girls' locker rooms after class. Thankfully, I shower and change in my room.

They do all of this when Mr. Valor isn't around or is distracted by another student.

And when Mr. Valor *is* around, they ignore me completely as if I don't exist.

And I was getting tired of it all.

I stretch out my shoulders and arms as a snicker from behind pulls my attention.

Three stocky boys stand behind me: Jeremy to the centre, Jake to his right, and an unfamiliar ginger-haired boy to his left.

I glimpse around for the other asshole usually with them, and then remember that Kane–along with the rest of the Scooby gang– skipped Music class. So, they probably wouldn't turn up for this one either.

Jeremy narrows his eyes at me, a leeriness in them as Jake whispers in his ear. Both rake their eyes up and down my body, blatantly stopping to stare at my chest.

Thank God I wore my hoodie. *Creepy assholes.*

"Is there something you need?" I ask, flicking my gaze between Jeremy and Jake with a short glance toward the new boy behind them.

Jake leans into Jeremy's side, whispering something again before a vile grin spreads on both of their faces.

Jeremy stalks forward as Jake chuckles.

"Need? What could you possibly have that I'd need, Micai?" His eyes travel back and forth as he begins to circle around me, a group now forming from the rest of the boys in the class that are here. "Or are you offering something?"

A few other students laugh and whistle as Jeremy stops in front of me.

"I wouldn't turn down a quick taste." He licks his lips, his eyes trailing back up my body as a sick smile forms, "...just because it's *cheap*."

The boys nod and chuckle, a darker atmosphere flooding the air as they take a step closer.

I feel boxed in, a slight suffocation and panic trying to pull at me before I push it down and look around me. Their laughter and jeering fades to white noise as I stare at each boy. Each dark and leery gaze, the dirt and filth showing through each smile and stare.

And something almost like a switch flipped inside me.

Hadn't I done this already? Hadn't I dealt with this enough times? These dark, disgusting looks and vile grins that make my skin crawl. Why was I restraining myself after all they had done to me? *All they keep doing.*

Why was I giving them all the benefit of the doubt when they never gave me any? When they've shown me over and over again that they don't deserve it.

They deserve the bruises, the blood, and the broken bones I should have given them from the start and from the moment they threw the first hit.

Why should I worry about repercussions? They and this school's system are already twisted and tainted anyway. Why should I follow the rules when they've created their own?

I've held back and restrained myself enough. Even after the attack with Dean and those vile pricks, I swallowed it all. More worried about what Mr. Valor would do if I was caught fighting back. I enjoyed this class and respected Mr. Valor–the only real fair teacher here. However, it's not enough to take their brutality. Not anymore.

A heavy sigh escapes my lips, a weight lifted from my shoulders as it leaves me.

The laughter around me dies off as Jeremy pokes a meaty finger into my shoulder.

"What are you smiling about?" he sneers as Jake and the ginger boy step closer to him.

"You assholes are all the same..." I slide a hand through my hair, pushing it off my face, and gazing directly into his malicious eyes. "Thinking with only your tiny dicks, and even tinier brains." The area falls silent.

"The fuck did you say bitch?" Jake barks, moving toward me before Jeremy places his arm out to stop him.

He meets my gaze before scoffing. "Micai...do you really think that's wise?"

He tilts his head, a dark smirk growing on his lips. "Look around you. You're surrounded by groups of boys. Ones who despise you and have no problem over-powering a weak little girl and taking what they want. We have power and strength...that you don't."

He takes a step closer, and I can feel his rancid breath brush across my face as a mocking smirk pulls at his lips. "You can't win against us." His grin fades into a dark sneer as he meets my eyes, "You're *nothing*. So why don't you behave and put that mouth of yours to better use...*on your knees.*" He chuckles, joining in on the jeering and laughter around us again.

There are a lot of things I'm sure they have that I

don't. Such as a lack of brain cells, a few genital diseases, and a sadistic tendency that's probably created more than just a few victims, *but power and strength...*I have my own.

My fist meets his face before he can move or dodge, my speed now rivalling that of a shifter's with ease. I feel something crack beneath my knuckles before liquid trickles down my fist, red droplets spraying out onto my face as a loud howl falls from his throat.

His friends run toward me as I pull his head down and slam my knee into his face, silencing his wailing. He flops to the ground, his eyes rolling to the back of his head as I hear shuffling around me.

I turn quickly, twisting away from the large fist coming for me from the side and throw a quick kick out. It lands straight into Jake's stomach, stopping him in his tracks and winding the asshole. He bends over wide-eyed as a grunt leaves his lips. *I guess he wasn't expecting the hit to be that strong.*

The ginger-haired boy lashes out toward me, more wary of my movements than the previous two. He pushes his meaty fist toward me, and it's quicker and with more precision, but still too slow for me.

His eyes flicker behind me and I catch the movement, twisting to the side as a couple of hands try to reach for me. *I guess the rest of the group wanted to get involved too.*

I duck and dodge all the hands aiming for me, punching a few faces that come too near. They shout out in pain, their faces now bloody as they stumble away. The other boys in the group fall back, more cautious of me now.

"Just grab her!" shouts the ginger boy to the rest of the crowd as he balls his fists and comes at me again.

His fist misses my face by millimetres, but mine connects beautifully with his torso. He tilts forward, gritting his teeth, but doesn't go down. He tries to grab me even as I push his hands away and swing my head back, smacking him right in the face.

His eyes gloss over before he stumbles backward then drops to his knees before landing in the grass behind him. He's out cold with the brutal hit to the head just as Jake catches his breath a little.

"Stupid...bitch." He wheezes, his hands gripping his stomach where, hopefully, there's a nice heavy mark of my shoe print. He pulls himself up, his eyes narrowing on me as he takes a shaky step toward me.

Suddenly, he freezes, his eyes going wide as he stares past me.

My brows furrow, my gaze focused entirely on him even through the slight throbbing in my head. As if I would fall for the ole 'look behind you' trick.

I clench my fists, readying for whatever pathetic attack he wanted to play out.

"It seems like you've started the lesson without me," A cold silky voice rings out from behind me.

I twist toward the familiar tone and look straight into Mr. Valor's green eyes. They flicker between the two boys on the ground and then to the crowd surrounding us.

"It was her," grits out Jake as he clutches his stomach and points at me. "She started all of this."

I turn back toward the accusing asshole, his finger

slightly shaking while aimed at me. *From this distance, I could probably break it.*

"I think she broke Jeremy's nose, and Kayden..." He glances toward Jeremy on the ground and then the ginger-haired boy, before looking back at me.

"She should be expelled. Doesn't the school have a no-violence policy?"

I almost laugh. No violence? So, all the harassment and crap I've had to endure is acceptable, but a few broken bones isn't?

They were shifters; they would be fine and back to their horrible selves after just a couple of days' rest anyway. But if the old me had taken a proper hit, she would be out for weeks, or more.

"That's right," Mr. Valor answers as Jake sneers at me.

He couldn't be serious.

I know Mr. Valor was strict about lessons and all, though shouldn't he at least listen to my side?

Or was he just like everyone else in this academy?

"Unless it's during Defence class." Mr. Valor glances at his watch. "Which started five minutes ago."

A small smile pulls at my lips as I meet his green eyes again.

"And since it was supposed to be a sparring class, I see no fault in Ms. Bane practising with her fellow classmates while I ran late."

Jake's eyes go wide. "That's not fair, she–"

"*Fair?*" Mr. Valor's tone darkens, his eyes narrowing as the boy swallows the rest of his words. He takes a step past me, closing the distance between them.

"Is three against one *fair*, Mr. Andrews?" Jake begins

to tremble with whatever he sees in Mr. Valor's face. "Your lack of awareness and ability is baffling. Or was it that you realised just one or two of you weren't capable of being her opponent?" He takes a step towards the two boys still lying on the ground and prods them with the toe of his boot.

One of them groans, and I have to school the grin, trying to stretch my cheeks as he continues.

"It seems I also haven't taught you three well enough. But don't worry, I'll be giving you all *extra* attention from now on."

Jake's eyes tremble as his mouth slowly opens and closes.

Mr. Valor spins toward the rest of the class gathered around us. He narrows his eyes at each boy in the crowd, a darker expression growing in them as each of them shifts away from his gaze.

"You two." His tone is curt as he points to a couple of the boys nearest him. The ones with minor injuries from coming too close to me. "Bring the dead weight to the infirmary and get yourselves patched up." The boys slowly make their way toward Jeremy and Kayden. "And when you come back, you can both join Mr. Andrews who will be enjoying the scenery and fresh air as he runs ten laps around the training grounds."

Both boys go pale but give him a shaky nod before taking the *deadweights* and leaving.

"Ten, but that's impossible--"

"You want more?" Mr. Valor cuts Jake a glare and he quickly shuts his mouth.

Jake grits his teeth as he glances my way and clenches

his fist, his lips curling up before Mr. Valor steps in front of me, blocking Jake's view. He points to the vast open field. *"Begin."*

Jake gives him a shaky nod before taking off in a slow jog. He's still clutching his waist when Mr. Valor shouts '*Run*', and he drops his hand, grunts, and picks up his pace.

Ten laps.

I bite my lip and try to conceal my smile. Most of the class would be bent over and out of breath after three or four, even the shifters finding it difficult.

I watch as he stumbles while trying to run and clutch his waist. It was a fair punishment from Mr. Valor. *But this was far from over between us.*

"We'll continue our lesson at obstacle course number three instead today," Mr. Valor states, yanking me from my thoughts.

A few gripes and groans are heard from the group as we approach the most challenging obstacle course on the training grounds.

It's off to the side of the grounds and nearer the forest, needing its own space as it would span the length of one football field all by itself. It would give even the human military courses a run for their money.

It looks hellish, with poles reaching as high as the forest's pine trees, a mud crawl with metal wiring, and a man-made ditch with icy water, to name but a few things in it.

So why do I feel so excited?

Mr. Valor brings us to the starting point and whips

out a small metal stopwatch. He gazes at each one of us before clicking it. And we begin.

The rest of the class passes by swiftly as I run through the obstacle course a total of three times, others barely completing it twice. By the time the last bell rings, we're all sweaty and out of breath–none more than Jake, though.

Just as I'm leaving, Mr. Valor calls me over. I had hoped to escape any sort of scolding or punishment, though I guess I should be grateful that he waited until after class.

"Who taught you how to fight?" he asks as we make our way through the training grounds.

My brows synch together as I gaze into his curious green eyes.

"No one. I taught myself." It's not a lie. In The Facility, I had to keep moving to survive. I had to be strategic against whatever beast they would put me up against and learn quickly from each fight on what worked and what didn't. Over time, it became easier. My body learned quickly and took to each new *movement* naturally, having memorised it with ease.

His brows pinch together, a slow moment passing as he gazes at me before he gives me a small nod.

"Taking on three shifters without a weapon and getting the better of them is impressive." He takes a few steps forward before turning back toward me, the sun setting in the sky and illuminating his golden white strands, making them glisten as a small grin tilts his lips.

"I'm looking forward to seeing what else you're capable of."

CHAPTER SEVENTEEN

I head toward the dormitory and pass a group of boys and girls in the courtyard. They're placing orange and black streamers and large dark-shaped cutouts over the boards, dormitory walls, and windows.

One group of boys take giant white and orange pumpkins carved with exaggerated expressions and begin placing them around the area.

A group of girls giggle while floating large black crystal beads. They hover over another group of boys who place a large black banner on the academy's grey brick wall.

The boys laugh while placing a lopsided black and purple banner on the academy's wall. It spells out *'Halloween Dance: Night of the Damned'* in shimmering black letters.

"I can't wait." One of the girls with brown hair giggles.

"It's finally this Friday!" a jade-haired girl beside her adds enthusiastically.

"I hope Daniel asks me tonight," adds the third, a small strawberry blonde-haired girl who twirls a lock of hair between two fingers. Her eyes flicker to one of the boys placing the large banner up, a slight blush tinting her cheeks when their eyes meet.

"You've already got Mike, Robbie, and Cole." Laughs the brunette.

"But Daniel is more my type...That, and I like even numbers." Adds the strawberry blonde before they all break out laughing.

I roll my eyes. These girls knew nothing about *real* connections. Just because there was a higher ratio of men to women in the supernatural world, didn't mean that you should treat them as a number or commodity. I would take that one *true* connection over a horde of men.

I rub my chest as an ache begins to build with the thought.

Shaking my head, I work to shield myself from those painful memories. Now was not the time.

I twist away from the bustling groups and make my way toward the dormitory entrance but smack straight into a passing boy carrying a large pumpkin lantern. It hits the ground, smashing open.

A strange shimmering gold glow seeps from the cracks with the mess now pouring from the broken squash.

The small golden lights float up toward me and slowly fade just as a memory flashes in my mind.

Music thrums around the room, a buzz of magic in the air as students wearing costumes of all shapes, sizes and colours dance and grind with one another across the large ballroom.

Golden lights from magical flares float around the room, adding to the opulent party atmosphere. Black shimmering skeleton decorations hang from the walls around the room, their eyes glowing white and their limbs shaking as people pass them.

Large ornate crystal pumpkins sit on each table and at every door and window in the vast room. Every table is covered in black silk with white glittering spiderwebbed fabric on top. Each has tiny obsidian spiders hanging from each hem. There's a sparkling starlight sky cast above the room, with each star twinkling brighter than the ones outside.

I glance around the large ballroom, dazed slightly by all the beautiful decorations and everyone dancing and talking.

Adam's arm wraps around my waist, pulling me against him as we move toward the dance floor.

Adam was one of Seria's classmates and an underclassman.

A few days before the dance, he asked if I would be his partner, saying he knew Seria and that she told him that I hadn't found a date yet.

He was different from the other boys in my year as well. Who preferred to either ignore me or take any chance they could to insult and humiliate me. Adam didn't seem like that. He seemed nice.

"Let's find a space just for us." He pulls me to the back of the dancefloor as the music thrums through the room. Bodies sway together as we make our way to a small spot with dimmer lighting.

Adam pulls me flush against him, his hands sliding down my back as he sways to the music.

A hard knot forms in my throat, a sickly feeling as his hands glide lower, inching quickly toward my backside.

"Adam?" I call, trying to get his attention over the loud music playing around us.

He pulls back a fraction, his eyes meeting mine, his brows drawn together before he schools it and smiles. "Yes, Micai? Is there something wrong?" His hands fall on my hips, brushing up and down my sides, as I try to swallow and think up anything to stop this uncomfortable feeling.

"Food," I blurt out. "Why don't we get something to eat? The food looked great." His hands halt on my sides, the trace of a frown shadowing his lips before it turns into a slow grin.

"How about a drink instead?" His gaze slides down my front. "I would hate for you to get anything on that dress." He bites his lip into his mouth, a strange look forming in his eyes as they trail back up to meet my gaze.

A strange feeling forms in my chest, almost like a knot, as my throat begins to dry. I shake my head. I was probably just nervous. It was my first proper dance and the first time a boy asked me, too.

I give him a small nod and he grins.

"I'll be just a minute. Stay right here." And then he's gone, pushing through the swaying bodies and back toward where we came from.

I brush a hand down my dress, giving the hem a slight tug and try to cover as much of my thighs with the scant black fabric as possible.

Adam had suggested matching vampire costumes, and he seemed so excited, so I agreed. But I didn't think mine would be so...little.

The thin black fabric fits tightly around my waist and

hips, and even tighter around my chest. A thin strip of lace covers my cleavage and neck before flowing out into sleeves and covering my arms. It doesn't leave much to the imagination; if I'm completely honest, it's not something I would have picked.

Adam's costume looks much sleeker: an all-black tailcoat tuxedo with his hair slicked back. He looked like a man from a gothic 1920s movie. Pity I felt like the cheap harlot in the background.

I shake my head again. He had tried his best. We both had matching fangs, bat jewellery, and tiny droplets of blood trailing our necks. And most boys didn't understand girls' fashion anyway.

I give my dress another tug as I try to search for Adam. Maybe it was busy at the drinks table?

Should I go look for him? But he had told me to stay here.

I'm glancing around for any sign of him when suddenly something slams into me, making me stumble sideways and fall to the dance floor. Giggling and chuckling ring out around me as I turn to meet multiple sets of glaring expressions.

I pick myself up, but another shoulder smacks into me from a passing couple, knocking me forward as they laugh. I stumble again while managing to steady myself before falling. I twist around quickly, pushing through the group and dancing couples to break free of the dance floor. It would be better to go find Adam.

I spot him over by the food table. He's talking to a group of boys who all turn to me as I head over. A chuckle leaves their lips as they rake their eyes over my body before patting Adam's back and telling him to 'have fun' before they quickly leave.

Adam nods before handing me a dark purple glass with a bright green liquid in it.

"It tastes better than it looks, Micai." He holds up his purple glass, the same liquid in his, and takes a sip. "Trust me, you'll like it."

I lift the glass to my lips, hesitating for a moment with the expression on his face. His eyes seem strangely fixated on the glass.

"Micai? Something wrong? You don't like what I got you?" He nods to the drink. "You should at least take a proper drink before you judge it, don't you think?" He raises a brow, a slight frustration bleeding through his gaze. I nod, not wanting to ruin the night. Why was I even hesitating?

I take a sip, and Adam grins, "Wasn't so bad, was it, Micai?"

The taste hits the back of my throat; a hit of blackberries and something bitter leaves a strange, grainy aftertaste on my tongue.

He clinks our glass in cheers, and as I take another sip, he tips my glass back further. Most of the cold liquid hits the back of my throat instantly and I struggle to swallow it all at once.

Adam chuckles, "Let's have a lot of fun tonight...just you and me."

He takes the glass from me and places it down on the table beside us. He places a hand around my shoulder, his grey eyes meeting mine as a softer grin spreads on his lips.

"How about we get some fresh air and talk, just us? I want to know more about you, Micai."

I give him another nod, a small smile growing on my lips. I knew Adam was a good guy. And maybe we could be more than just friends if we got to know each other.

We take two steps before Adam's name is called, and a pair of boys approach him. He sighs before asking them 'if it could wait' glancing toward me. Both boys smirk but reply, 'It'll only take a minute.' He turns to me, a frown pulling at his lips.

"I'll just be two minutes with the boys, Micai." He takes a step forward before spinning back toward me. His brows draw together, a colder gaze in his eyes as a stern tone laces his voice, "Don't go anywhere."

I stand off to the side near the food table catching glimpses of Adam with a bigger group of boys in the corner chuckling. He glances over, giving me a grin and wave. He shouldn't be too long now.

I sway slightly on my feet, a little lightheaded and feeling more out of place as people come and go from the table, glaring and scowling when they see me. It's always like this.

I watch the groups move on the dance floor and twist at hearing a familiar laugh, the voice almost like the sound of tinkling bells.

Seria dances in the centre of the room surrounded by Knox and Anders, her hand trailing down Knox's side as she dances between the two. Their eyes are hooded and consumed by her presence between them. She pulls them in closer as they grind against each other, lost to the slow rhythm of the music. Her red slip of a dress hikes up higher as Anders' hand slides up her thigh. She pulls her gaze from them to a spot across the room where Xander and Kane stand. Their eyes are fixated solely on her and filled with a heated look.

And they're not the only ones.

Most of the guys in the room glance back and forth, watching her with a slightly wistful look.

I turn away, a thick knot in my throat and a heavy ache burning in my chest. My gaze meets a pair of blue eyes, her red lips curving up into a sweet crescent as she smiles at me. She leans back into Knox's embrace as she pulls Anders closer again. Their lips gently graze one another before they deepen the kiss.

I'm frozen to the spot as I watch her move from Anders to Knox, and I feel as if the air has been knocked from my lungs in one swift punch.

I close my eyes tight.

Knox and Anders, Kane and Xander...they weren't mine anymore. What we had or were as kids was gone. It was different now. They were with Seria. They chose her.

And why wouldn't they? She was amazing in every way: smart, talented, kind, and beautiful. And...she would take over the family line, too. She was the most powerful witch in our clan. Even if she was younger, with her power, she would become the head in the future.

And me...I had nothing.

No power, no talent...she even resembled Father more, taking on his bright blue eyes and golden blonde locks. Whereas I looked...like this.

I brush a hand across my long, curly, rose-gold strands before my shoulders drop.

Suddenly, the room tilts, and I have to catch myself on the table beside me, knocking over a small web-shaped candy bowl. My head spins as I try to steady myself again.

Maybe I hadn't eaten enough today? Or maybe there wasn't enough air in here. It sure felt like it.

I unsteadily make my way toward the door. I know Adam said to stay there but we were planning on going outside anyway. And with how dizzy I am feeling, the fresh air would help.

I head outside, the cold air instantly hitting me and is a nice respite from my spinning head and turbulent thoughts. There's a small crowd formed at the bottom of the steps, whispering and pointing toward the forest treeline in the distance. I squint, trying to see what they're all looking at and make out a smaller group of people who look like a few of the faculty members.

They're surrounding something on the ground...a student, I think.

I shakily make my way down the steps, holding onto the wall nearest me and make my way through the crowd until I'm able to see a bit better.

A loud gasp rings from beside me. The student near me– dressed as a sexy devil–points a shaky hand toward the forest line and the faculty members there.

One of the teachers had shifted around the student. A girl with raven black hair lays on the ground unmoving, her hair sprawled out around her head as blood pools around her body. My breath gets caught in my chest at the scene.

Who was she? Was she alive? Who or what had hurt her like this?

The doors burst open behind me as the large crowd dancing inside makes their way out.

I get jostled and shoved as they move forward, making their way closer to the accident.

Suddenly, a large magical barrier is erected over the area and near the forest, one of the teachers' voices booming above us and around the academy.

"Make your way back to your dormitories and rooms!"

Groans and shouts ring out around the crowd.

The teacher sends a loud alarm throughout the area, demanding students follow orders, or the alarm won't stop. Its volume rises higher and higher as I cover my ears and try to make my way toward the girl's dormitory.

As I cover my ears, another bout of dizziness hits me, and I almost fall forward. But the crowd pushes me onward and, thankfully, toward the dorms.

I turn back, hoping to spot Adam in the crowd, but instead, I catch another glimpse of the raven-haired girl in the distance.

The forest was a restricted zone in the academy. And there were wild, magical beasts the further in you went. But it wasn't unusual for students to hang out around the treeline, especially on nights like these. But for an attack to happen...it was unheard of.

Whoever she was...I hope she's okay.

My vision begins to blur and dim as I slowly walk to my room, everything darkening before I make it to my bed.

A loud laugh from a group of boys in the courtyard pulls me from the memory and back to the present.

Adam had drugged me. The asshole had spiked my drink.

Back then, I hadn't realised, but after a few rumours at the end of the year about how he had assaulted a first-year girl, I pieced it all together.

I was lucky I had gotten away. I was too naive and stupid in falling for his tricks. I should have grasped instantly when he gave out to me the next day for not staying put. And then joined in on humiliating me with the other boys for the rest of the year.

I quickly head up to my room and take off my hoodie.

I pull off my shoes and change, remembering the rumours of the injured girl. They said her face and body had been badly maimed by some wild beast in the forest. She left the academy that night and never came back. Rumours say she passed away later that year.

I stare out to the forest in the distance from my window.

Was it the beast I had fought? Did he attack that girl?

I narrow my eyes at the shadowy treeline. I won't let that happen this time. I won't let another person get hurt or die.

No Adam Manser, no drugging, and no deaths.

The only attack would be me against the beast, and this time I wouldn't lose.

I clench my fist. I had grown stronger and quicker, so what better way to test my growth?

I look back at the stars rising in the sky...I'll need a strong weapon.

A dark grin stretches my lips as I gaze toward the training ground in the distance.

And I've already seen the perfect pair.

CHAPTER EIGHTEEN

I flip the glistening elven daggers back and forth between my hands. The silver metal feels light to the touch, but its blades are sharp to the tip. The two daggers are covered in ornate elven letters. What they mean, I'm not sure. Typically with elves, though, it's a blessing on the weapon. Which means they were a well-made and loved piece.

I hold the dark grey metal hilt in my hands, the cool material feeling smooth against my skin.

Elven weapons were known for their intricate designs and perfect functionality, yet they were scarce to find and expensive when one did.

I had snuck into the weapons shed on the training ground and jimmied the lock.

Thankfully, there were only a few protection spells on the door, ones that would flare when magic was used, but not against some blunt force.

I guess the other Defence Instructor, Mr. Hampton,

didn't think much of a student breaking into his weapons shed and borrowing them.

Well, that may have something to do with him being almost seven feet tall and built like a tank. And usually, you wouldn't cross a black bear shifter. They were known for their short tempers and protective tendencies.

I twist the delicate metal in my hands.

These must belong to Mr. Valor. He was, after all, an elf. He must have left them there by mistake. I'll return them straight after I deal with the beast.

I swing forward, thrusting one blade out to my right. It slices through the tree I'm standing beside, flowing through the bark like a knife would through butter.

I look down at the glistening daggers in my hand.

They felt cool against my palms, the blades so light in my grasp.

Maybe he wouldn't notice they were missing.

Who am I kidding? You can't forget these beauties.

I headed deeper into the forest, the music and laughing voices from the dance fading in the distance the further I crept.

I had been searching through the forest as soon as it had gotten dark enough to go unnoticed.

Placing the elven daggers into the black straps on my hips and pulling the tight black hood over my hair, I quickly fasten my black face mask behind my ears.

The one good thing about a Halloween Dance was that no one looked twice at a girl dressed entirely in black combat attire and looking like some assassin or ninja.

I halt, hearing the rustle of leaves. I crouch down in preparation for some beast or attack, reaching for the daggers on my hips when suddenly a squirrel pops out of the bush a couple of metres from in front of me.

It scurries past me, holding what looks like a chocolate bar in its tiny paws, before dashing up the nearest tree.

My brows raise with the small forest creatures' cartoon-like antics. It seemed *almost* as comical as my week. Taking third place, at least.

First, was Annex turning up to *'World History class'* in the last few minutes and making Mr. Finch almost wet himself for suggesting he *'Try to arrive a little earlier'.*

In fairness, it was a look that promised more than just a little pain.

Mr. Finch didn't utter a word for the rest of the class and just stared at the board the whole time.

The second–*annoying as much as it was comical*–was when Adam came to me and asked me to go with him to the dance. *Like he had in my previous life.*

And exactly as he did before, he told me how he knew Seria and how she told him I had no partner for the dance yet. He had laid it on thick about how he didn't want me to be alone or miss out on important memories that we could make together with everyone else.

Even before I had the chance to reply, he gave me a huge grin and told me he would pick me up on the night. As if there wasn't even the slightest possibility of me rejecting him.

I'm not sure how I managed to keep a straight expression, let alone not sock him square in his slimy, smug face. How had I fallen so easily for this crap before?

I clench my fists, pushing down the itch growing

there with the feeling of wanting to wipe away the pompous smirk he wore that day. Except it would have ruined the plans I had for him.

The music changes in the distance, a quicker-paced song playing as the lights shine from the direction of the academy.

A dance Adam couldn't possibly be attending in his current *condition*.

Since he enjoyed drugging other people's drinks so much, I took a page from his book and added an extra *ingredient* to his drink this morning. It was a little tasteless concoction that mixed seamlessly into his favourite protein shake.

It was a handy little herb mix that would make his lower parts swollen before growing murky green welts that would itch and leak with pus when touched.

After a few days–*and a few potent medical spells*–the welts and swelling would slowly heal, but without the proper antidote to the herbs, he would be left *permanently* limp.

A small chuckle leaves my lips at the thought of his frustration and discomfort. I hope he thoroughly enjoys his night of scratching.

A groan from the area to my left pulls my attention.

I grab my daggers and stealthily make my way through the dark forest and towards the noise. It becomes louder, almost like a pained grunt.

I push through the trees and bushes and freeze.

On the forest floor lay two boys, both dressed in what I think are supposed to be angel costumes. Their large fake wings lay broken beneath their large and limp frames.

I edge nearer, noticing their pained groans and erratic breathing. Sheathing my daggers, I rush over to the nearest body. I flip him over, my new strength making nimble work of moving his huge frame.

His ash-grey eyes meet mine, a slight tremble in them as my brows scrunch together. His face seemed slightly familiar.

Was he in one of my classes?

His eyes flutter again, and I could see he was trying to keep them open.

His lips open slightly, a mumbled, incoherent sound falling from them, "...Mmm...mmgg...nn."

I shake my head as he tries again, making the same jumbled sounds.

"Sorry. I don't know what you're trying to say."

His eyes slightly shake as they search mine for something. And I could tell that whatever he was trying to say was important. His body stiffens, his jaw tightening as his eyelids begin to flicker, seeming as if he is fighting to stay conscious.

My eyes narrow toward his lips as a white liquid trickles from the corner of his mouth as he tries again to speak.

"Mm...gg...nnn," he slurs, trying to form words as I lean in closer.

I place my hand on his arm, his pulse abnormally quick but slowly steadying more and more as I listen.

His eyes meet mine again with a more exhausted and

desperate look in them. What could he be trying to tell me?

I look around the area and toward the other body across from us.

He's lying face down, and if not for the slight tremor in his hands, I would *almost* think he was dead.

I take a breath and focus, and using my heightened senses, I zone in on his chest and quickly listen for the sound of a heartbeat. His chest rises and falls with the beat of his heart growing louder in my ears, though like his friend beside me, at a slightly abnormal pace.

But thankfully, they weren't in any immediate danger and were fighting whatever was in their systems by themselves.

I peer around the area as the boy below me grunts again. There were a couple of large whiskey and vodka bottles, the expensive stuff, too.

Is it alcohol poisoning? No, the bottles aren't even half gone. They sit on a stump in between the bodies of the two boys, with a few other small items and three red plastic cups.

Three?

Then I see them...a pair of white high heels and a small white feathered clutch.

I shift my attention back toward the boy, his eyes fighting to stay open as his fingers slightly twitch.

"A girl?" I call, and his eyes whip toward me. Just then, a scream rings out from the distance. I let go of his arm and stand up, closing my eyes to allow my senses to take over and listen fully to my surroundings. Music plays in the distance, students chatting and laughing around the academy, animals moving around the forest...and light footsteps sprinting with a *much* heavier footfall chasing behind them.

They sounded like they were heading toward the boys' dormitory.

The body below me grunts and shakes as the one across from us joins him. They wanted to move, to save her.

Their fingers shake, their voices and groans grow louder and clearer with each movement, and their eyes flicker open a little wider each time they try.

Another shout peels out in the distance, pulling my attention back to her.

I had to hurry. She might not have long, especially since she's all alone.

"They're nearing the boys' dorm. Head there when you're both able." I pull the daggers from the straps on my hips, a sharp *'shing'* sound falling from the blades as they're pulled from their sheaths. "I'll help her in the meantime."

Ash-grey eyes widen as I rush off, following her footsteps and laboured breathing, her movements slowing the longer she runs. *I had to move faster.*

Another shout rings out in the distance as I push into a faster run, the forest becoming a blur around me as I try to reach her a second sooner.

She wouldn't die this time; she wouldn't be maimed.

This time, I'll change both our fates.

I was given a second chance, so I'll give one back.

I break through the forest and straight out into a small area just metres from the boys' dormitory. I watch, just a mere few metres away in the treeline, as a familiar raven-haired girl stumbles while running, and falls onto the academy's gravel.

Morgan.

She crawls toward the dormitory, her face pale and her arms and legs covered in cuts and scratches.

Her white, silky dress is ripped and tattered in dirt and small bits of blood as she tries to make her way to safety.

A growl jerks both our attention as the creature stalks from the forest and prowls towards her.

The huge beast looks like some sort of chimaera hybrid. Its head looked like the mix of a lion and snake, scales dripping down its head and out into a solid-looking mane. It has black fur covering its torso and flowing all the way to its feet, with large black horns adorning its colossal head. A long serpent-like tail whips out as it stalks forward. Its tip looks razor-sharp, like a blade, as it moves back and forth.

It lashes out again and slices at the ground around it, doing more damage than I like.

Morgan's pale face scrunches up, her eyes crinkling to slits toward the creature. Then they flicker open wide, a shimmering colour appearing and fading just as quickly as it came. She grits her teeth, her chest rising and falling rapidly as she keeps her gaze on the beast in front of her.

"You wanna kill me...*eat* me?" She chuckles darkly, a slight grin spreading on her face.

"This isn't my first time being hunted by some *disgusting monster*..." Her hand grabs a sharp rock on the gravel below her, her fingers shaking slightly as she points it toward the creature. "Don't think I'll give up that easily."

She clutches her small weapon. And even in the face of such a huge creature, she doesn't back down.

My gaze drifts between Morgan and her unsteady hands.

I had heard she had a defence ability, a barrier of some sort, and quite a strong one at that. So why is she not using her power?

With her personality, it didn't make sense for her to run away like this.

Then it hits me...the boys on the ground trembling and trying to stay conscious, and her strange movements from earlier...What if she *can't* fight? What if she too had taken or been given something?

A loud roar bellows from the beast as I glance back at Morgan, noticing her scraped and bloodied legs.

I focus in on her eyes and notice a similar hazy gaze and a slight trickle of blood and something white on her chin. Almost like the boy in the forest.

The beast roars again and lunges toward her.

I grip my daggers and dash toward the creature, reaching it just as it comes a few inches from Morgan's body. The metal of my blades slices through the dark scales along the side of its face.

It pulls back as dark navy blood pours down its scales and onto the gravel below us.

A roar more thunderous than before pierces the air as the creature howls.

I hear a groan from behind me, remembering

Morgan, and quickly glance her way before turning back toward the beast.

"Get out of here," I call back to her. "Hide somewhere safe...I'll deal with this." I flip the daggers in my hands as a pained voice behind me tries to speak.

"Can't move...any...more..."

Like the boys in the forest.

Then, I would have to lure the creature away somehow. I narrow my eyes toward the ugly-looking beast, meeting two silver slits, its gaze now entirely focused on me as I position myself in front of Morgan.

It flits its eyes between me and her, a mixture of a growl and hiss rolling from its blackened mouth.

Why was it still interested in Morgan?

Did she or her blood smell good to it? And why was something like this even here to begin with, and so close to the academy?

It bares its sharp black teeth toward us, saliva dripping from its maw.

I had dealt with all sorts of creatures in The Facility before, all kinds of mutated or butt ugly beasts, however this one had to be top three for sure.

A slow grin stretches across my lips covered by my black mask.

The creature before me was big and strong, but compared to the beast I had met in the forest before, this one was basic. An easier prey to test out my strength and agility on.

I close my eyes for just a brief second, taking a breath and allowing my senses to take over as all the sounds and scents surround me: Morgan's weakened breath and pained gasps, the music still playing, and the oblivious students laughing in the distance. And of the creature just feet from me, ready to make its move.

I flip one dagger in my hand, not willing to let it take one step closer towards Morgan with her frail and limp body behind me. I hear it nearing and open my eyes just as the creature dashes in my direction, its mouth open wide and claws extended toward my head.

Its movements slow as I race forward, my speed taking over as I quickly manoeuvre into a slide beneath the creature. Thrusting my blades up into its belly, I drag them the length of its torso.

The beast screams, lashing out as I pull myself up behind it. Its sharpened tail crashes, trying to hit me, but I twist beneath it and catch it with my dagger, digging the blade into its flesh to hold it in place.

It roars and flails, seeking to catch me from behind, only its movements only cause the large wound on its stomach to open more, its navy blood pouring out on its black claws.

I hold onto the dagger embedded in its tail and move quickly with the creature's movements. If I let it go, it would probably catch me or Morgan while thrashing about.

Its strength begins to wane with the more blood it loses, unable to fight me in this new position.

Grabbing its tail, I shove the dagger in further and twist it until the blade slides out the other end, the large chunk of tail falling to the ground with the quick movement. Another roar and pained howl bellow from the beast's mouth.

Time to put it out of its misery.

I grab its flailing appendage, seeping its thick navy blood, and wrench the creature backwards with my full strength. The beast stumbles back and falls, now wholly off balance and losing blood at a faster rate. Grabbing my daggers in both hands, I jump toward the beast's unguarded back. It roars as I land on it, sinking my daggers deep into its neck. Pushing them in further and holding my grip as the creature thrashes, its roar begins to wane and weaken until it becomes a low, muffled growl.

After another minute or so, the fight seeps from it as it stops moving and sluggishly sinks to the ground beneath us. Navy blood trickles out from the beast and coats the ground and gravel below us as the creature's final breath falls from its now gaping mouth.

Pulling my daggers out, I tumble from its back as its body slumps onto the gravel behind me. I put my daggers back into my hip straps and turn back to Morgan. I go to reach for her when suddenly I hear a voice shouting her name from the distance and multiple footsteps heading this way.

Turning around, I see four dark figures rushing toward us in the distance as a strange black smoke forms around us.

I glance back at Morgan, her chest rising and falling slowly.

She was alive. That's all that mattered.

The black smoke seems to rush for me with the voices nearing us. I push through it, the feeling almost like something solid beneath me, before I dash for the forest treeline.

I pick up speed once I hit the forest, the area blurring as I run and listen for anyone following.

After a few moments, and once I'm sure I've not been followed, I take off my black mask and pull down my hood to take a deep breath. I gaze at the moon shining above me, the cold air crisp on its last Autumn night, as a light feeling fills my chest.

I saved her.

I *changed* her fate.

And if I could change hers, then I would definitely change my own.

Creeds POV

I hold Morgan's unconscious body in my arms as the others search the area. Placing my forehead against hers, I listen to the sounds of her inhaling and exhaling weakly.

Whoever did this to her would pay.

I would burn this academy down with everyone inside it for my sister's pain.

I look at the scratches and cuts trailing up her legs, blood and dirt still fresh and wet on her silky white angel costume.

A heavy sigh leaves my rising chest as a tremor works its way into my hands.

A voice in my head screams for retribution, for blood for hurting one of mine. *My little sister.*

Morgan always thought I was overprotective. Well, she's seen nothing yet. I won't let her leave my sight after this.

We'd already lost enough. I won't lose her too.

I glance up towards the figure dragging his already bloody blade along the corpse of the beast beside us.

If it wasn't for Annex insisting we come here, we never would have known Morgan was in danger. He'd harped on and on about seeing what *'Red'* looked like and insisted we come to the dance—even opting out on another fight in the ring for it, which for Annex was big. Missing out on the chance to get bloody and break a few bones? This *Red* must be either as crazy as him, or powerful enough to withstand his blows. Because Annex wasn't interested in *normal.* He was a wild card, purely psychotic and deranged.

Fuck, even his face right now was sprayed with blood from the fight he had in the ring just before we arrived. And yet, he looked like he wanted to resurrect the dead beast in front of him to go another round. *For fun.*

Either way, I'm grateful for his new interest. We wouldn't have come here, otherwise.

I clutch Morgan closer as Mallyn and Ezra make their way back from the forest.

They'd run after the figure we had seen standing over Morgan before we got here.

None of us had gotten the best view of the guy other than that he was smaller than us, wearing all black and clutching two very strangely shaped blades.

The blade marks on the beast tell me he was the one that took it down, except why was it here in the first place? And why had Morgan been dragged into it? Why was she left in this state, and why didn't she use her ability?

I peer around me, dark shadows moving around the boys' dormitory building as the night drifts on. Unsuspecting laughter and music play out in the distance.

Whatever the reason or whoever did this to her, they would pay. I would personally rip them to pieces and show them pain even Annex hadn't thought of.

I gently wrap Morgan in my arms as I pull us both up.

I had promised myself she would have a better life and that no one would ever hurt her again.

A small whimper falls from her pale lips, and I have to grind my teeth to stop from roaring.

Never again.

I would never allow anyone to come this close again.

Mallyn and Ezra make their way over to us, each carrying a familiar figure on their back.

Ash and Grey, Morgan's partners.

My gaze hardens toward them. Their eyes widen as their shaky gazes fall on Morgan.

"Mor...ann." Their voices try to call her, yet their words fall short. They struggle and shake, trying to reach for her, but their arms fall limply to their sides.

What the fuck?

Another small whimper leaves Morgan's lips and I shake my head.

No. It doesn't matter what happened. They should have protected her. If they couldn't, then they wouldn't be around for long. She didn't need anyone weak beside her. I would make sure to deal with them later myself.

"Where's the little ninja gone?" Annex grins as he prods the shaking body draped over Ezra's shoulder.

"Careful, you're too close to my face, man." Ezra smacks the blade away, placing Ash down gently on the ground.

"Right, we wouldn't wanna accidentally leave a mark on that pretty skin," smirks the deranged bastard.

"They were too quick." Mallyn dumps Grey on the ground like unwanted trash, a pained grunt leaving the shifter as he hits the floor. Mal wasn't one for physical contact. "There was no trace, not even a trail or scent, to track. Whoever it was, they were quick and skilled, maybe even trained."

These boys were like my brothers. If blood was thicker than water, then these boys were my bones. And *nobody* could match or rival their skills or power.

If they say this person was able to get past them, then they must be on a whole different level.

I look back at the beast. Makes sense if he was able to take that on by himself. And thankfully, those with power like that have a following, so finding him shouldn't be so hard for our network. I'll get Ezra on it later.

I look to Mallyn, his brows furrowed and eyes darkening.

I'd have to check in on him later. I didn't like the look in his eyes, but right now, I had to focus on Morgan.

I cradle her in my arms, holding her gently as I make my way past the dead beast, taking one last glance at its huge body.

I send out a wave of my power, the black smoke flowing out quickly like a small tsunami and consuming the corpse. The body soon disintegrates until only tiny black specks and scorch-like marks are left in its wake.

Nobody needed to know what happened here but us. The academy trying to get involved would only be a hindrance.

We would handle this ourselves. And whoever did this...would pay in blood.

If they were able to target Morgan and her partners on the academy's grounds, then they must have some connection to the school or the people in it.

I look back toward the academy building, music still blaring and voices talking and laughing, wholly unaware of what's just happened.

Or the consequences that will fall on this school for fucking with my family.

I make my way out past the gates and towards my car.

I place Morgan in carefully before turning back toward the boys.

"Get your uniforms ready..." Annex, Mallyn, and Ezra turn to me. "We'll be attending the academy full-time from now on."

Mallyn gives me a small nod, but the look in his eyes and the tick in his jaw tells me he wants to do anything but that.

"I was already showing up from time to time." Ezra shrugs. "All the better for me to collect what we need."

"Perfect. I'll get to see more of Red, then." Annex hums, and the grin stretching his lips tells me he's talking about the unfortunate soul who caught his eye recently.

I get in the car and take off.

I'll start my search for the black-clothed figure first. If they were involved in this, or dragged Morgan into their shit, then I'll make them pay a hundred times what she's suffered tonight.

CHAPTER NINETEEN

ANNEX

I stretch out my shoulders, a deep yawn pulling at my lips as I make my way through the old building.

Creed had us spend the entire weekend searching the forest area around the academy for the masked ninja we saw Friday night. Sadly, that meant no more time in the ring.

My bet was on it being a chick. With that small frame, it had to be.

The others thought it was a guy, though I knew better. Knowing where to hit and stab and cause the most damage was my specialty. So, knowing anatomy and body proportions was a must. Even with the dark lighting, I could see those curves.

But fuck she was fast. Even outrunning Mal and Ez. And those blades...I wouldn't mind a one-on-one with those sharp fuckers.

I wonder if she knows how to properly use them. I guess if I find her, I'll be able to find out.

It'd be a nice change from all the weak assholes in the ring. None of them were lasting as long anymore, but some things are better than nothing, right?

My fists itched to break some bones and to feel the crimson liquid drip through my fingers. To see the tremor in my opponent's eyes as they meet my own and to hear that sweet symphony of agony. *Just. For. Me.*

And Morgan had been fine. Bar a couple of papercuts and getting spiked, she had no lasting problems.

Unfortunate. 'Cause Creed had looked like he wanted to raze the academy and watch it burn. What a pretty show it would've been.

I wouldn't wish pain on Morg. She was Creed's sis and practically family, *whatever that meant*, but still...such a pity.

I make my way through the hallway. Faces are downcast, with bodies shifting to the side.

Everyone in this shitty school bored the fuck out of me. I whip out my blade, sliding my finger across the tip as a couple of gasps ring out to the side of me.

Wimps.

They were all complete pussies in this school, all scared of a bit of blood.

The bell rings, and I watch as the plebs scurry their way to class.

When they're all gone, I slowly head to the stairway.

I hated classes. So boring and annoying, but Creed wants us all to search for the ninja chick. He says she might have answers to questions he wanted to know.

Creed. Such a controlling dickhead, but well, every group needed at least *one,* didn't they?

He even told me I could 'play' with her if she didn't talk. And I don't discriminate.

Doesn't matter to me if you've got a dick and balls, or pussy. Torture is my playtime, and I'm all for equality.

I'm heading up the stairway but freeze when I hear a familiar voice on the staircase above me. I lean a little further out, following the ballsy voice.

Red.

She stands tall, her little blue eyes narrowed, and plump rosy lips set in a straight line.

Fuck, what I wouldn't give for a bite of them. I don't think I've ever seen someone being pissed off look so hot.

Her hair flutters on her little shoulders as the breeze flows in from the windows around her. My fingers itch at my sides, wanting to fist it in my hand and give it a hard yank.

I bet she'd even like it.

"That right?" Her tone is cutting, her gaze growing colder toward whatever asshole is beside her.

Oh little Red was pissed alright. I could tell because she'd given *me* that sexy tone before.

I lean further out, trying to watch the show I'm sure she'd give me.

"You're lucky I was even willing to take a bitch like you out."

A low voice barks at her, another chuckling beside her.

I grip the railing and stare at the dickhead who's trying to get in little Red's face.

The stupid dick has dark brown greasy hair and an ugly face. One I'm gonna help him reconstruct *very* soon.

The prick sneers at her while the other asshole begins pacing around then he stops behind her.

Now I'm no gentleman, far from it, in fact, and I usually couldn't give two fucks about the shit others did around me, but something about those two pricks surrounding her made the dark little voice in my head scream *murder.*

I grab the railing with my other hand, ready to jump up the one floor in one swift move and take some sweet retribution, when suddenly I hear a crash and hard grunt.

I freeze and glance up.

The sneering prick is no longer smiling; he's bent over, gasping for air, his eyes wide and face pale.

The other asshole grabs Red from behind, but in one quick move she thrusts her head back and slams it into his nose. *Beautiful.*

Blood splatters down his face as he falls back and wails in pain. *Little bitch.*

I watch on as Red crouches over dickhead number one, who's still gasping on the floor.

"You think you can do whatever you want, don't you?" She grabs him by the chin, forcing him to meet her face. "Well, not anymore."

She grips him tighter, her voice almost a low growl. "That little *ruse* of yours stops now. Or the only drinks you'll be sipping, will be through a straw. *Permanently.* Am I clear?"

He whimpers, nodding his head. And I have to bite back the small groan wanting to leave my lips. I shift to the side and adjust the growing boner in my pants.

Red was *seriously* hot when she was angry. And *fuck* I wasn't into S&M, but the thought of those narrowed eyes and plump lips uttering orders, or those tiny hands scraping across my chest drawing blood...*yep*, I was hard.

Shuffling and groans from above me pull me back from my thoughts just in time to hear a door close.

"Fucking whore." Prick number two bites out while holding his bloody nose.

Or should I call him *unlucky number two*? 'Cause neither of these dickheads were walking out of this hallway without their bones broken or blood seeping from every pore.

I saunter up the steps, a dark grin stretching my lips.

"What do we have here?"

They must know shits about to happen 'cause when they see my face, they both go pale and silent. The little whites of their eyes begin to shake as I close in on them.

I look at prick number two's hands, the ones he used to grab Red.

Well, *they're* gonna have to be broken.

Who the fuck did he think he was to be touching her in the first place?

"Unfortunately for you boys," I crack my knuckles as they both gulp, "you fucked with the wrooong one today."

They open their mouths to protest just as I lunge toward them, slamming my fist from face to face. Everything blurs around me as their blood coats my hands.

Seems school wouldn't be as boring as I thought. *Especially with Red around to play with.*

CHAPTER TWENTY

MICAI

*A*fter the dance on Friday, everything went back to normal. Most of the students went home late after the dance and arrived back on Sunday evening for our classes today. Nobody even mentioned a beast attack.

I head toward Mr. Finch's classroom after having just dealt with two blockheads trying to corner me in the stairway. It seems Adam wasn't too happy with being stood up.

Funny how he still tried to go in that condition. Or was it all just talk, trying to make me feel some sort of guilt toward him? *A wasted effort.*

His face was twisted in frustration as he talked, his complexion pale with black bags under his eyes, probably from lack of sleep, *or scratching.*

He rambled on about me 'owing him' and how I ruined his night. That I should have been grateful he was even willing to take someone so pathetic with such a bad reputation.

His leery eyes regarded me in the sleaziest of ways

while he talked, like I was some object or piece of meat for amusement. And when he and his friend cornered me, telling me I should *'pay'* for what he had lost out on, they flipped a switch they shouldn't have.

I decided to give him a piece of what he was *owed*–my knee connecting with his balls.

The pained grunt and gasp for air that followed made it worth having the disgusting creep near me. *Even though he deserved so much worse.*

His friend deserved the same, although a broken nose would do for now.

If they hadn't learnt their lesson to stay away from that, then I would have no problem teaching them more thoroughly a second time. However, they won't be walking away with just a broken nose or some badly bruised balls...*or walking at all.*

I find an empty spot at the top of the classroom.

Annex had taken to sitting near me during classes, which meant that in any seat I chose, the rest of the students gave the space around me a wide berth.

I settle in, getting comfortable as class starts. Even with the little stairway hold-up, I was still on time.

Other students in the class sit in their usual little groups, ordinarily consisting of one or two girls surrounded by six or seven guys, or sometimes even more.

I catch some of their whispers, mostly about people hooking up at the dance or how great it was or so and so's costume being ugly.

There was no mention of Adam, other than his lack of attendance. And nothing about anyone being hurt or assaulted this time, either. Nobody even mentioned the beast or an attack of any sort. Its corpse had also disappeared the next morning with only a few black marks left in its place.

The teachers had put it down to students playing with flame magic and the excitement from the night. Nothing else was said or done.

The academy must have covered it up.

But if they weren't bothered with looking into it more, then I would have to do it myself.

How had that beast gotten so close to the academy? We had barriers set in place, so it shouldn't have been that easy, or at the very least, the faculty should have been alerted to its presence. Except there had been no one there that night to help Morgan.

Also, why was it so intent on chasing her? There had been two passed-out bodies in the forest if it wanted a quick meal, so why her?

And *why* had they been so weak? What had they taken or been given to become like that?

There were just too many unanswered questions, and the more time passed, the more questions I had. Like the marks appearing on my body and my new strength and abilities. Or the bracelet Seria gave me that seems suspiciously like the shackles in The Facility. And now this beast has appeared on academy grounds, intent on attacking a student with no one around from the faculty to help. How–

My thoughts are interrupted when the door flings open and in walks Annex. He's wearing a smirk the devil himself would be proud of, with tiny flecks of dark red drops coating his face. The same red liquid drips from his fists as he saunters up the stairs toward me and plants himself in the empty seat next to me.

Mr. Finch clears his throat, breaking the silence the class had fallen into with his arrival. His eyes flicker once to Annex before quickly turning away. He continues the lesson, albeit a bit more shakily.

I try to remember my thoughts before being interrupted but feel a burning stare watching me from the side. I turn towards Annex.

"What?"

His eyes widen slightly in mock surprise. "I didn't say anything."

"But you were staring–"

"And how would you know that?" He cuts me off, a twinkle gleaming in his blue eyes as a mischievous look takes over his expression.

"I could feel your eyes on me," I reply as a slow grin stretches his cheeks.

"You could *feel* it, could you?" A hum falls from his lips. "Are you normally so conscious of others sitting beside you? Or is that reserved solely for me?"

"I'd say more vigilant or watchful. Because you never know when some *maniac* is going to pull out a blade and start swinging it about." I give him a deadpan stare as his grin widens, a small chuckle leaving his lips.

He shakes his head before leaning in closer.

"Where have you been all this time, Red? Hidden under some rock or locked away in a cage? Almost three years in this shitty school, and we only meet now? How the hell did I not know you before?" A strange, soft look forms in his gaze. "Would've been more interesting with you around."

My brows draw together with his words. How *did* we not meet before? How had I gone this long in my previous life and never met Annex? With the way he looks and acts, how had I at least not known of him before? Was I so lost in my own little world and misery that I never took the time to see anything or anyone else around me?

He pulls his bottom lip into his mouth, his eyes curving into soft crescents as he watches me. "But I guess you're here now."

He was right, only in a different way than he intended. I was back and experiencing all new things with each passing day. This second chance wasn't just about revenge anymore, but about living the life I should've always had. One where I choose for myself and live each day without regrets. Where I can experience things I never had a chance to or was denied.

A smile stretches my cheeks before my gaze narrows on the red flecks on Annex's face and his hands.

Unless he was painting moments before he came, that dried liquid eerily resembles blood.

I grab his hand, pulling it toward me, trying to find the wound or cut it's seeping from.

"Not my blood, Red." He smirks, wiping a few flecks from his face with his free hand.

"What happened?" I brush my fingers along his knuckles, not trusting his words as I continue to check for minor cuts. He didn't seem like the type to care, even if he *was* hurt.

A small shiver runs up his hand with the slight touch. He clears his throat, his brows furrowing as he watches me.

"Just teaching some pathetic meat sacks their place."

"Meat sacks?" Do I even want to know? I shake my head. "So, none of this is yours?"

"As if it'd be that easy, Red. I'm practically indestructible, you know. Not many get to make me bleed, and if they do, they usually end up being hauled away moments later in bloody pieces." He chuckles, hitching a thumb behind him.

"Why do you think all these wusses are so scared? I'm not that easy, Red. And either way, I won't die from some measly cuts or bruises."

I guess I shouldn't have gotten worried anyway, it *was* Annex. It was probably the 'meat sacks' that needed the most help in that kind of situation.

I nod, letting go of his fingers. But as I slowly pull my hand back, he takes it in his, his fingers twisting around mine.

His gaze is fixated on our interlocking fingers as he opens his mouth again to talk.

"You've such small hands, Red." His lips pinch into a straight line. "How can something so small and soft…" He mumbles, his words trailing off as he slowly pulls his hand back and gazes at it. Then he shifts his attention back to me.

The creases in his eyes smooth out, the shadow of a frown tracing his lips replaced by a slight grin. "Those eyes…" He leans in further, something more profound and intense growing in his gaze. "Never lose that, Red.

That fight in you...Never let anyone take it away. With it, you can do almost anything."

His sincere expression catches me off guard, his words hitting deeper than I thought as a lump forms in my throat. Annex hadn't even known me for long, and yet he saw something in me, something no one else did. Even with this *magicless body* and these 'soft hands', he could see strength in me.

I shake off the emotion trying to well up inside me.

"Even kick your ass?" I ask as I try to reel my emotions back in.

A soft chuckle escapes his stretched lips as he leans back in his seat.

"We'd have to test that one out."

Instantly, his grin fades, a more serious expression taking over his face–*or his version of one*–as he looks to the board while straightening himself.

"You should really stop distracting me with all this flirting, though, Red. Some of us are here to learn. You should pay attention instead of hitting on me." He glances at me, a shadow of a grin lacing his lips before he schools it. His eyes are then entirely focused on Mr. Finch.

I almost choke on the laugh wanting to spill from my lips. *Flirting* with him?

"If by hitting on you, you mean *actually* wanting to hit you, then yeah, I've got it *baaad* for you."

He shifts in his seat before glancing at me, a slight tilt to his lips as he bends closer.

"Let's keep the foreplay for later, Red." He pulls himself up a little straighter. "I don't mind an audience, but," he side-eyes the rest of the room, "I'd much rather play when it's just you and me." The grin he gives me is downright sinful, a promise in his darkening gaze that sends a slight shiver down my back.

I swallow, trying not to read too much into his idea of *playing* together.

He was clearly insane. So why would I even care?

His idea of fun probably involved a pickaxe, a dark forest, and prey that could talk.

He was a walking, talking horror movie and obviously the antagonist. The type that would poke the bear for a reaction and then have the beast running from his deranged grin.

His gaze flickers between my eyes and lips as a dark smirk pulls at his cheeks.

Why would he think I'd even *want* to play with him? No matter how godly his appearance, clearly, there were more than just a few screws and bolts that went missing when he was created.

I shake my head. Why was I even thinking about this and him? I had enough on my plate, and something like *this*, whatever it was, wasn't possible for me anymore.

His piercing blue eyes meet mine, something deeper in them, something pushing me closer and niggling at me.

When all too quickly he pulls away again, taking all those strange thoughts and feelings with him as he looks toward the board once again.

"Red, you're disturbing my lesson." He shakes his head, a small playful smile tilting his lips as he continues to pretend to pay attention.

A grin stretches my lips as I follow his gaze, deciding to play along.

"I didn't know you were so studious. Especially since you haven't shown up to most of the classes."

He freezes, a slow, wicked smirk taking over his face and pulling at his cheeks.

"Missed me, did you?" He glances back toward me. "Well, don't worry, I'll make sure you don't feel lonely from now on."

My brows scrunch together. What did that mean?

"What—"

Suddenly his phone rings, and the class goes quiet as he pulls it out from his back pocket. He glares at them and gives Mr. Finch a menacing scowl before answering.

Mr. Finch continues his lesson more quietly as Annex frowns at whatever he hears on the other end.

"Fine. I'll be there soon." He grits out.

He stands up, making his way past me before turning back quickly for one last glance.

"We'll play later, Red." With that, he heads down the stairs and leaves the room, slamming the door as he goes.

What did he mean by what he said? Was he going to attend all of his classes now?

A visible sigh of relief spreads quickly across the rest of the room with his absence.

I glance around the room, already missing their anxious or panicked expressions.

Maybe having Annex around more wouldn't be so bad after all.

CHAPTER TWENTY-ONE

I make my way to Music class, wondering if Morgan will be there after the attack on Friday.

Thankfully, she hadn't been badly hurt like in my previous life, but the attack had still happened and something she drank or ate had made her unable to fight back.

Someone in this life and my last had planned this. They wanted to hurt Morgan or, even worse, kill her. But why?

And who?

Who was capable of bringing a beast onto academy grounds? Who had that kind of ability or connections?

I head into the room with more questions building in my mind. My gaze then falls toward the seats she and her two partners always occupy.

They were empty.

Maybe she needed more time to rest? Or more time to clear her system of whatever they used?

I don't even know much about her, but we both lost our lives unjustly once. Maybe that's why I find my thoughts wandering to her, feeling some sort of connection. Either way, I hope we both get to live the lives we should have always had.

I'm making my way across the room and toward my seat when a hand slides out and grabs me from the side. The petite, manicured hand halts me in my tracks as I twist and stare at the bright blue eyes it belongs to.

Seria.

"Why weren't you at the dance on Friday, Micai?" The room around us falls quiet, all eyes drawn to Seria as she continues. "Did Adam and you have a fight or something?" She pauses, her eyes scanning mine for some kind of answer or reaction. A look carrying more than the fake sympathy she's showing outside. She was pushing for answers, but for what? And why?

What game or ploy was she playing now? Especially if she herself was stepping up to the stage to perform.

But I can also ask questions and play along too.

I take a small breath, my brows furrowing as she watches me.

"How did you know Adam had asked me?" He has mentioned her before, and I swiftly realise that she's the connecting factor in his decision to choose me that night. Everyone else had given me a wide berth, so why not Adam?

And why did he also choose me that night?

Because of *Seria.*

She had sent the bastard to me, knowing he would

attempt something vile. It was how she worked. In the shadows, pulling strings and whispering sweet words.

And with her social network, there was no way she didn't know about his *tendencies*. I'm sure he had a past long before he came to the academy, and finding that out would be as easy as breathing for her.

She smiles, her whole face lighting up.

"I'm sure you told me at some point, Micai." Her blue eyes curve upwards, her smile soft and playful as she gazes at me.

My look turns questioning, my brows pinching together as I gaze back at her.

"But I didn't tell anyone?"

A gentle sigh leaves her lips. "I'm sure you've just forgotten–"

"Why would I forget when I never planned on going with him?" I step away from her, her blue eyes darkening a fraction as her expression stiffens.

She gives her head a slight shake, "No, you must–"

"Ah! Or did you hear that from Adam?" I cut her off, a tiny grin pulling at my lips realising she didn't want any connection to the sleazeball. That's why she mentioned my telling her instead of him. She was trying to keep a distance from the sleazy dickhead, knowing what would come out in the future.

Useless strings had to be clipped and there couldn't be any connection when things went awry.

"I guess that makes sense. He *did* mention you." I nod, continuing, "But he didn't exactly wait for an answer when he asked me to go. I guess he just assumed I would." I shrug, before my eyes meet hers again.

"Though I didn't know you two were friends. I would have been clearer about not going if I had known."

Her smile has grown smaller and straighter, as if she's struggling to keep it in place. Something I wouldn't have noticed or simply brushed away before.

Her eyes grow dark and narrow just a fraction before they widen, a contemplative look taking over her expression before she shakes her head.

"We are classmates, but..." Her brows furrow, a slight frown stretching her lips. "We don't really talk much. I'm more surprised he even mentioned me." Her gaze turns back to me, her smile broadening gently again. "And maybe you're right. Maybe I overheard him talking during class about it instead?"

Her words made me chuckle. There's always a way to twist and manipulate one's words with Seria. It almost seemed like a game—some fun and natural ability to mould and shape other words and thoughts to suit her own agenda.

A small smile appears on Seria's lips, her expression soft and tender. The look of complete warmth and affection as she gazes at me. One I wouldn't have doubted before as genuine, yet now I can see the dark glint burning deeper within them.

"But why didn't you go to the dance, Micai?" Her expression turns somewhat worried as she reaches for my hand and takes it in her own. A cold shiver works its way through my body with her touch, and I have to talk myself out of ripping my hand back from her clutches.

"If you didn't like Adam, you could have just come with us."

My mind is wrenched from the cold feeling creeping up my skin and back from her last few words. *'You could have just come with us'.*

My eyes flicker toward her and narrow in the direction of the four figures I now notice standing behind her. Was she serious? Is *this* how she was going to play it?

I peer back at her, her eyes searching again for my reaction. Did she think I would be upset or angry? Feel uncomfortable or show misery like I used to?

But she could think what she liked; they all could. Whatever I said would be twisted to her liking anyway. She would blacken my character so easily with just a few simple words and all the while pretending to worry about me.

I try to hold back the heavy sigh that wants to fall from my lips. Instead, I take a deep breath and pull my hand from between hers. Her gaze darkens before she quickly schools it.

"She's only saying all this because she cares." Xander steps up beside her, wrapping his arm around her, his voice matching the hardness of his gaze toward me.

Seria looks at him, a sweet grin stretching her lips before she gazes back toward Knox and Anders. Kane suddenly moves forward, placing himself in front of her like the knight in shining dickhead he is. He glowers in my direction, like I'm some sort of threat to his partner.

I roll my eyes, and the reaction is caught by Xander, who thinks it's an affront to Seria.

"What's your problem, Micai?" Xander grits out. "Can't you at least be civil when Seria shows you so much care? Or are you just *that* sad and bitter?"

"Xander," Knox calls, a warning tone in his voice. "I'm sure Micai didn't mean it that way." He glances toward me with a strange look before Kane scoffs.

"Sure she didn't. Not like it's been proven time and again how she treats Seria. She's just manipulative and spiteful." The angry bite in his tone and the cold gaze he gives me have my brows raising and a scoff leaving my lips.

"Kane–" Anders calls before I cut him off.

"Manipulative?" I chuckle, the sound dark and humourless. They could call me many things, and I wouldn't pay it any heed, but manipulative? They have a master of the craft beside them, and they call *me* that?

"When have I ever *manipulated* you, Kane?"

His dark brows pinch together as Seria calls his name from behind him, but he ignores it, his stern gaze set on me.

"Give me an example, one incident?" I push, gazing into his darkening eyes.

His brows furrow deeper, his eyes flickering to remember and pulling down further.

"When have I ever had any influence over your actions? When we were kids? 'Cause I don't remember you ever being the type to do something you didn't want to."

His eyes flicker back to me, a strange look forming in them the longer I stare. "Or are you talking about when you and your *other friends* like to mess with me?" He flinches slightly, his hard look falling. "Tripping me up, calling me names, destroying my stuff, knocking me into lockers...did you feel *manipulated* by me then,

Kane?" Kane's eyes widen, his mouth opening, but before he can speak, Xander chuckles, a cold humourless laugh peeling from his lips.

"And you've just proven it. Manipulation at its finest." He waves a hand toward me. "A perfect act. I'd almost believe it myself..." His chuckle cuts off, his lip curling up as he sneers at me, "If I didn't know you better."

And just like that, Kane's face hardens again. Any doubt wiped away with Xander's cold words.

"Xander, Micai's not–" Knox starts before he's cut off.

"Not what, Knox? You don't know the real Micai–"

"And you do?" I couldn't stand to listen to another one of Xander's insults. He acted like he knew me when he knew nothing at all.

"I know enough."

"You know nothing–"

He takes a step closer, his eyes dark and tone threatening. "You're the worst kind of–"

A large hand slides between us before a body stands in front of me, blocking me from Xander's harsh gaze.

"Why don't you all calm down? There's no need for all of this. Whatever happened, just put it behind you." Ezra's turquoise eyes flicker back to me and then toward Xander, a grin on his lips that doesn't quite meet his eyes as he stares at him.

"What's it got to do with you?" Xander scowls.

Ezra smiles playfully but clenches his fist beside me before quickly releasing it again.

"Well, I'm also a part of this class," he shrugs, "and you're disrupting the atmosphere. It's so sombre and dark now." He peers around the class, the room silent and the mood bleak. "That, and..." He flicks his gaze to me, our eyes briefly meeting before he turns away again. "Five against one isn't exactly fair, especially when four of them are guys...and against *one* girl."

Kane scoffs. "As if we were going to do anything–".

"If that's how you normally act, then maybe I should give you a few lessons on properly treating a girl," Ezra chides playfully. "Because getting into her face and threatening her, isn't it." He smiles, meeting each of their gazes one by one.

"We weren't–" Anders starts before Seria gently pushes her way beside Xander. Her eyes quickly flicker down Ezra's front before focusing fully on his face. A slight blush coats her cheeks the longer she stares, and a glint forms in her eyes as her smile widens.

"There seems to have been a misunderstanding. Micai is my sister, and the boys are my partners. They're just very protective." She brushes a strand of hair behind her ear as Ezra's smile grows tight, his knuckles going white the longer she stares at him.

"A misunderstanding?" He gives me a slight glance before turning his gaze to Xander, the large dickhead still scowling. "It didn't look that way."

Xander scoffs. "You don't know her or any of us. So why even get involved?" He glances back at me before his scowl twists into a sneer. "Or are you trying to be some white knight?" He turns back toward Ezra, his gaze bold and mocking as he continues, flickering between us. "Well, let me warn you. Micai's no damsel. She's the demon lurking in the shadows, and my suggestion is to run before she tries to get her claws in you. She likes to pretend to be good, but there's nothing *good* about some weak, bitter–"

Knox yanks Xander's shoulder, making him stumble back slightly and cutting him off.

The look they share is hard and cutting, the room falling pin-drop silent with their darkening expressions and stand-off.

Knox opens his mouth, but before he can speak, Seria slides in between him and Xander, placing her hands on each of their chests and sweetly calling their names. They both twist to her, Xander's gaze softening instantly and Knox's dark expression lightly seeping from him.

They both give her a small nod as I turn away.

Stopping before I head back to my seat, I turn back and whisper my thanks to Ezra.

He may have done it for the class or the atmosphere. But for whatever reason, he tried to help me, and that didn't happen often to me.

He turns toward me, ignoring the annoying hallmark scene playing out behind us and gives me a slight nod and smile.

Just as I'm going over to my seat I hear my name. Her voice is affectionate and soft as she calls me. "*Micai?*"

I ignore it and take my seat.

Just as I hear my name again, Mrs. Fleur bursts into the room. She's holding a sizeable, unsteady stack of sheets in her hand as she rushes over to her desk to put them down. A large grin plays on her lips as she makes it there without them tumbling over.

Ezra takes his usual seat in front of me. He sits down

briefly, glancing at the rest of the class, who whisper and glare at me as Seria and the rest take their seats together.

He turns back toward me, his eyes bearing a hint of sympathy.

"You okay?" he whispers.

I meet his turquoise eyes that are flecked with lilac swirls, the colours always dazzling and bright. The gaze he gives me seems sincere enough, so I nod.

"Always," I mutter.

An unreadable look flickers across his features as a small smile spreads across his lips. He leans slightly closer to me, his scent surrounding me as he whispers. "Let them look and talk but take no shit. *Ever*." A darker grin cuts across his face, a coldness appearing in his eyes as he glances at the rest of the room. No one else notices his change in expression. "Don't ever let them see you stumble. There's strength in a smile. Even if it's forced." His gaze meets mine, and whatever he sees has his expression softening. "You seem like a fighter anyway, little sea star."

"Sea star?" My brows scrunch together. Wasn't that a starfish?

What kind of nickname was that? And why would he even give me one when we didn't even know each other? "Why–" I begin to ask, but he just gives me a small smirk and wink before turning back in his chair to face the front.

It was right in time as Mrs. Fleur called for everyone's attention and started the class.

A silent sigh falls from my lips, my shoulders drooping as I lean further back in my seat. Couldn't I go at least one class or day without any drama or stress? Or was that just too much to ask for?

I glance around the class. Most of the second—and third-years are staring daggers at me, while the fourth-years around me seem uninterested.

Bright lilac and brown tones mix together in front of me as the sun catches them, pulling my attention back toward my front. And toward Ezra.

Maybe *everyone* wasn't bad here.

CHAPTER TWENTY-TWO

I skipped Defence class, hoping to avoid the keen eyes of the owner whose elven daggers I had yet to return.

Those beautifully crafted daggers cut like silk and felt light to the touch. I had never felt this kind of want for a weapon before. I knew I had to return them *eventually...* but I had to give them at least one last whirl before returning them.

I will make sure to spend my time with them tonight while training. However, right now, I have a crisis of a different kind to deal with.

Fajitas or Lasagne?

My eyes dart from the spicy, colourful dish to the creamy layered meal, both sitting on the counter. Maybe I could ask Finn to put whatever I didn't get now away for later?

I nod to the lasagne; the female server tonight gives me a small, knowing smile before passing over the creamy dish. One with extra cheese on it.

I've learnt that some of the nicest people in this academy were the cafeteria staff. There were no judgments if a girl wanted an extra big slice or second serving, and a simple '*Thank you*' went a long way here.

I thank her and head to my usual spot before digging in. This time, I wouldn't let anyone ruin or disturb my delicious, layered meal. They would get the tip of my metal fork in the centre of their meaty hands if they tried.

A small moan leaves my lips at the first bite. The tender pasta and creamy sauces mixed with cheese hit all the right notes and warm me from the inside.

As I continue my meal, I notice a shift in the room's atmosphere. The laughter and talking quickly turn into quiet hushes and whispers as I fall into my own delectable world.

I'm enjoying my next bite when suddenly, four large shadows fall over the table.

I pull my plate towards me and grip my fork.

What asshole was starting on me today?

I lift my head and am met with a pair of dark golden amber eyes, their cold glare aimed solely toward me.

For a split second my eyes widen, glancing at the figure towering over me.

He looked like he belonged on the front spread of GQ magazine, or the male muse for some famous fashion designer or artist. This boy was...captivatingly gorgeous.

I shake my head, pulling myself out of whatever daze he's put me under and remind myself of the cutting glare I'm currently receiving.

The boy in question had raven-black hair framing his

model-esque features and amber-gold eyes. It's a *pity about the scowl he's currently wearing.*

"Move," he grits out, the word carrying more power than it should.

I flinch; with his six-foot-plus frame and darkening expression, I'm sure anyone else would have already fled by now or at least peed themselves. Even the group nearest this table grab their trays and quickly leave with his cutting tone.

But no one could make me leave my favourite spot or creamy lasagne again. Not even the huge hot guy who looks like he's planning my murder.

I grip my fork and stab it into my lasagne.

"I'm not moving, so find somewhere else to sit." I scoop a forkful into my mouth, my eyes never leaving his as I swallow and lick the corner of my lip.

The air becomes tight as a heavy weight floods the room with his darkening expression. His eyes flare, something dark about to break loose as he takes a step toward me.

"If you don't move, I'll-"

He's cut off mid-threat as a familiar voice chuckles, popping himself down on the seat opposite me.

"It's okay, Creed. Red's with me."

The other three figures whip their heads toward Annex, their eyes slightly widening as the crazy ass in question takes a bite of his fajitas.

Another small chuckle sounds beside Annex before the figure sits down, and I'm met with two familiar turquoise eyes.

"How do you know this crazy asshole?" Ezra slaps

Annex on the shoulder, a broad grin on his face. "I knew you had a fighter's spirit, little sea star, but I didn't know you ran *toward* the trouble."

Annex stops his next bite–fajita mid-air–to turn to Ezra. His brows are drawn together as he flickers his gaze between Ezra and me. "How do *you* know Red?"

"Music class," Ezra grins as his eyes find mine.

Annex shakes his head, mumbling something about *'not hacking people singing and shit'* before turning back toward me. A wide grin stretches his lips before he takes a bite of his food.

"And Red's got her own brand of crazy, Ez." Annex chuckles through a mouthful of food.

"I don't think anyone could reach your level." I narrow my eyes toward Annex, a wider grin splitting his lips.

"We met in World History class." I glance toward Ezra. "He wanted my seat, going blade happy on me trying to take it." I take another bite of my lasagne as Annex chuckles.

"A fond memory for you too, Red?"

Ezra flickers his gaze between me and Annex. "And you didn't run for the hills?" He slowly leans closer, his smile growing mischievous. "If you need help...blink three times–" Annex elbows him in the side, cutting him off as they both grin playfully.

"You *both* know her?" The one Annex calls *Creed* scowls. His glare never leaves my face as he slowly takes his seat a couple of spaces from Ezra.

I twist away and look toward the fourth and final figure as he sits down, taking the furthest seat from me at the end of the table. He wears a black hoodie under his academy blazer. His hood pulled up partway as a slight tuft of his hair peeks out from under it. It's almost white in colour, and I'm met–*for a brief second*–with a set of grey-blue eyes that turn away from me almost instantly.

A heavy sigh falls from beside Ezra as Creed looks at me. His glare is gone, but his expression is still sour and lacking even a speck of warmth.

"If you both want a plaything, you should find it *outside* of the academy..." He looks me up and down, *and if the lasagne wasn't keeping me busy,* I would jump across this table and land my fork square in his–

"It's too messy dealing with some clingy junior because you both gave her a little attention." He looks around the room, watching all the bent heads and hushed voices, nobody daring to turn this way. "No doubt she's already using it to her advantage." He glances back at me as if I'm some speck of dirt who's messing up his tidy space and polluting his clean air.

"They're all the same."

Whose *they*? And what stick shoved itself so far up his ass that he felt the need to spew shit?

This asshole didn't know me, but then why would he ever try to? Why listen when you can form your own opinion anyway, right?

Power and status were all that mattered in this school, and clearly, this dickhead embodied that. He was just like all the other morons before him. *And I've dealt with enough of them today.*

"Plaything–"

"She's not like that, Creed," Ezra cuts me off, giving

me an apologetic smile before turning back toward the asshole. "We met in group Music class, and I sat in front of her. She's never tried anything with me...which is more surprising." He gives me a small wink as I shake my head.

"*Right.*" Creed rolls his eyes, his tone sarcastic and mocking as Ezra opens his mouth again.

I stab my fork into my last piece of lasagne, scraping the plate intentionally and cutting Ezra off.

All their eyes fall on me, and a dark, knowing smirk spreads on Annex's lips as our eyes briefly meet.

"So let me get this straight. You think I *want* you? That any girl sitting at this table couldn't *possibly* just want to eat? They must be up to something and want your attention?" I raise a brow, shaking my head as I quickly continue. "And *you* want girls to fuck, to use, and to then throw away when you please, but *they* should have no expectations or needs themselves?" I lean a little closer toward him. "What? They should be *grateful* to get your dick?" I swing my fork in between my fingers as I pull back and sit straighter.

"What's so good about you?" I ask, "I mean, yeah, you're pretty. And maybe you've got some sort of power or high status...you may even have a huge dick," Ezra chokes on the drink he just took a sip of as I continue. "But you're a *complete* asshole. Any girl having to put up with your shit and insecurities deserves a fucking trophy the size of your ego. Or maybe they don't make them that big. I don't know." I shrug, pointing my fork toward him. "But that sounds like a *you* problem, meaning I don't have to give a shit," I say before scooping up my last bite and slowly chewing.

I look at Creed, a wicked cold sneer spreading across his lips as he opens them, but I cut the dick off after swallowing.

"If that's how your relationships really are, then that's pretty sad. But shit attracts flies, what do you expect?"

Ezra's eyes widen slightly before a grin spreads across his lips.

A small cough that sounded strangely like a chuckle rings out from the hoody boy at the end of the table as Annex breaks out laughing. The sound echoes around the room and sends the students near us to go stiff.

Creed's face darkens, his nostrils flaring as his jaw tightens.

Then something unexpected happens.

He leans back, his features relaxing as he takes a deep breath. The others around the table fall silent, their grins and snickers fading as Creed stares at me.

To any other person, they would think he's dropped it, that he was being magnanimous and moving on. However I could tell from the dark expression on his face, *those piercing amber eyes*, that he was the silent killer type. The hit you never saw coming. Murder wasn't messy or quick for this one.

He was the strategic type who liked to pull the strings and watch from the front row. The type that when he snapped, everything would burn with him. It was the look of a predator watching its prey as it planned the most painful of deaths.

But death...I'd been there, done that.

Living was harder.

And there was no point in living in fear. That wasn't living.

A slow grin spreads on his lips.

"Tomorrow, we'll be here." He points to the table, his dark gaze never leaving me. "And *you* won't. Am I clear?"

"Creed–" Calls Annex before he cuts him off.

"Shut it, Annex." Creed's tone is cold and cutting, leaving no room for compromise. Annex goes to open his mouth again as Ezra pulls his arm, shaking his head, his eyes never leaving Creed. He appears stiff and nervous.

I guess Creed meant business.

But I wasn't going to budge either. I've dealt with enough assholes in both my lifetimes to know it's not worth it to back down or give in. It's better to fight back.

I feel my features change and darken as I stare at him, a visible shift in the table's atmosphere.

"Thanks for the suggestion. Noted. But let me make one of my own." I pull myself up straighter, my gaze meeting his dark glare. "You either learn to share or get a new space 'cause this is *mine*. I'll be here tomorrow, the next day, and *every day* this week. My presence is permanent."

"Do you have a death wish–"

"Death?" A chuckle falls from my lips, surprising even me with its dark tone. "It doesn't scare me." I slowly stand, his dark gaze following my every move, seeming ready to pounce if I take one wrong step. "Nothing can anymore. So, get used to my presence, *Creed*. Because I'm not going anywhere." I turn around and leave the cafeteria, ignoring Annex's voice and Ezra's gaze as I head towards the girls' dorms.

I refuse to back down from this. As stupid as it may seem, that was my space—a small place of peace where I could rest and eat undisturbed. There weren't many in this academy as it was, so I wouldn't be giving it up for them.

But I guess now I can see why everyone else avoided it. Maybe it was *originally* theirs?

I make my way to my room, slamming the old door behind me and shaking the ancient wood.

The only other oasis for me to relax was in this old-falling-apart room. Except there was no one to talk to here, to trust, or to call my own...I guess there never was here to begin with.

I fall onto the bed, exhaustion taking over.

Even with the sun still bright in the sky, I close my eyes.

'*Micai*'...A low, gravelly voice flows into my ear as my eyes begin to flutter, a small pain and ache working its way into my chest with its memory.

My only *true* haven and home in this world was *him*.

The only person I could trust, the only one I could truly be at ease with...

My world, my ally, my strength...*my mate.*

CHAPTER TWENTY-THREE

I make my way toward the old, abandoned building about half a mile back behind the academy and training grounds.

I found this place during one of my runs. Apparently, it was the first training area when the academy was established, but after a bad fire and the deaths of a couple of students, the place was abandoned. In only a few decades, the building now resembled something you would see in a haunted movie.

I make my way through the new area of forest, feeling fresher from the nap I had earlier and ready for a good training session tonight.

I needed to work off some of the agitations from today, and what better way than feeling the cold metal of two beautiful elven daggers beneath my fingers.

I was going to miss my little clearing, but after the attack during the Halloween dance, there were more people making their way into the forest and getting nearer to it.

At first, I thought it was just some students looking for a thrill, though they didn't stick to just one area. It was almost as if they were searching for something.

My instinct told me after the second day that I'd better move if I didn't want to be caught training. I came all the way to the forest behind the defence training grounds, and to the opposite side of the academy. It takes a while longer sticking to the shadows and sneaking behind the academy and current training grounds to get here but so far, I've seen and heard no-one. It was worth the time if I could train in peace again.

I push past the overgrown bushes and make my way down the broken pathway.

The closer I get, the more features of the old building I can see. Overgrown ivy climbs its derelict walls with grey brick peeking out from beneath it, scorch marks running the length of one side of the building, and small curved windows with tree leaves crawling from their now empty panes.

I make my way through its front entrance, an open space where only rusted hinges covered in ivy and moss are any indication that a door once stood here before.

The space inside is entirely open; most of the old walls decayed with time or were destroyed by the fire. The moon sits above me, and a sizeable crumbling hole is now where part of the roof once stood. Trees sprout from every corner with moss and green bushes covering most of the floor. Only little parts of grey brick or old black tiles are still visible where nature hasn't fully taken over. Ivy and moss also climb up the remaining walls, with tiny flecks of brick peeking through here and there.

On the left side of the building—*which is still partially intact*–there stands a strange broken cabinet that lines half of its wall. It has hooks and clasps of varying sizes that seem to have once held the weapons. Below it sits an old broken board with strange black marks hanging from the wall. The shape on it looks vaguely familiar; maybe it's some sort of magical symbol I'd seen before or some old family crest?

But I can't fully make it out as the rest of the board is burned and charred with the wood cracked and large chunks missing from it.

There's a stairway still whole on the far-right side of the building where the roof is still intact. There are fewer burn marks there than in the other half of the building. However, time and neglect have taken their toll as the decayed wood and bricks slowly crumble while nature reclaims it with large trees and shrubbery.

The floorboards creak as I make my way over the old decaying wood to the centre of the room with the sturdiest-looking boards.

Pulling my hoody off, I place it on a nearby hanging tree branch before pulling out the beautiful silver daggers. I flip them back and forth in my hands.

I know I have to return them soon, but just for tonight, I could train to my heart's content with them in my palms. After today's drama, I deserved it.

Gripping the dagger, I shift forward in one swift movement, slicing through the air, as a 'shing' sound echoes out around the area. Then I switch to rapid thrusts, the sound of the blade turning to a tune almost like a whistle as it echoes throughout the open space.

I push harder, throwing a few bends and twists into my movements, battling all the memories from today: of those blue eyes, Xander's glare, and Kane's cold voice. With the breeze running through the room, I move back and forth, my movements growing fiercer with each strike.

Everything around me fades away as I lose myself to the rhythm I've created. The only sound I hear is the beating of my heart as I go to a place solely for me.

Gadriel's POV

I watch on, mesmerised by the small lithe figure in the near distance, a familiar face yet with a speed and agility I had not seen before.

Her small hand holds the daggers I've been searching for since I noticed them missing last Friday.

I had sworn I would make the thief pay heavily for taking them, but as I watch her with them now, I'm overtaken by a new feeling, one far from anger or retribution.

Her movements are nimble but swift. She was more skilled in combat than one her age should be.

The first time my eyes met those endlessly blue irises, I could tell that they held more than the years she carried. That they had seen and fought things her lips would never let free.

She twirls around before twisting into a backflip while thrusting the daggers outward mid-air. Her form and execution are near-perfect.

Her rosy gold-toned hair flutters with her quick

movements, brushing back and forth about her cheeks as she moves.

Her piercing blue eyes are fixed on an unknown enemy before her, so focused, unnervingly so.

What was she seeing? What, or who was she fighting?

And why did the thought make me want to pick up my own blades and join her?

My brows furrow, my gaze still fixated solely on the small figure whose movements held so much strength.

With some help and some more training, she could become a threat greater than whatever darkness plagues her now.

The thought has a grin stretching at my lips.

I had seen the fight in her eyes when she fought those boys during class. She was a warrior, a fighter. She would push through whatever lay ahead, no matter how dark or bloody. Her eyes were like those of someone in battle, constantly watching their back, waiting for the next attack.

But the problem with constantly being on guard is that there's no rest, no place to find comfort or peace. And she didn't seem like the type to want someone to save her.

No. She wanted to protect herself.

And I could help her with that.

Her movements were good; strong, agile, and quick, but she needed to gain experience.

She needed a strong partner—someone to spar with and help her grow to a higher level.

Looking at her movements and how she works in class, I can tell she will learn quickly.

I take a light step toward her, and then another. The nearer I get to her, a strange feeling slowly begins to build within me.

I watch her movements quicken almost to a blur as she pours everything into them. Her own rhythm forms as she loses herself to it and falls into another world.

Stalking closer, I stick to the shadows. I get as close as a few yards from her before she twists around, her gaze narrowed to the shadows where I lay with the blades flicked in my direction.

Never before had someone so quickly noticed my presence when I did not want them to.

I step out of the shadows and enjoy the way her eyes widen. The fierce glare she wore just seconds before now filled with surprise and...worry?

Her gaze flickers to her hands.

Ah, my daggers.

She palms them, a hesitancy in her as she clutches them tighter. I can tell she doesn't want to part with them. *It seems she also has good taste in weapons.*

She quickly straightens herself and meets my stare.

I take another step closer when suddenly she speaks up.

"I know how this looks..." Her gaze shifts from me to the daggers still clutched in her small hands. "I didn't–I mean..." She sighs before shaking her head, "I had my reasons for taking them, but I know it still wasn't right. I'm sorry, sir." Micai slowly lifts the daggers, hesitating as she extends them toward me, her blue eyes never leaving my elven daggers as she hands them over.

I take them from her, holding back the grin wanting

to stretch across my lips at the minor slump to her shoulders and slight pout to her rosy lips.

"I'll take whatever punishment you deem fit." Her chin tilts down, a small frown lacing her lips.

I flip the daggers in my hands, my movements bringing a wistful look into her gaze. *She must really like them.*

I twist them back around and hand one to her, keeping the other.

"Show me how you use it."

Her eyes widen slightly before a warm smile takes hold of her.

I freeze, the image before me catching me off guard.

Her face lights up, a sparkle shining in those deep blue eyes that pulls me slightly closer. Her full, rosy lips curve upwards, a smile of genuine happiness pulling at her cheeks as her face transforms. It becomes so bright and captivating I have to stop myself from moving closer.

I shake my head and pull myself straighter to turn away for a moment.

It was just the excitement in her eyes that caught me. The pure joy and warmth in her smile and the feeling of camaraderie. An appreciation of similar interests ...that's all.

I shove away the unfamiliar feelings and thoughts as I turn back toward her.

And we begin.

I lunge forward, trying to catch her off guard, but she sidesteps me, twisting as she does to then lash out at me. I rotate, catching her blade with my own as we clash, sparks flying with the force of the metal blades hitting each other.

Her attacks are strong, and she has no hesitation in aiming for my vital points, but she still lacks precision.

We break apart, taking a step back from one another as we take our time to size each other up, both waiting for the next attack to come.

Her eyes search for an opening. And this time, I can't stop the grin forming on my lips.

She was like a tiger prowling around her prey, waiting and watching as she slowly stalked closer.

She suddenly strikes from my left, noticing the old injury on that side. *I see she's also observant.*

Unfortunately for her, that's exactly what I wanted her to see.

Our blades clash again, and she quickly retreats.

She noticed, even though slightly late, that it was a trap.

Her reactions and observations are quick, and her ability to adapt even quicker—a rare feature for someone her age.

She would make a worthy partner.

A new sound plays in my ears as we clash, a symphony playing in the background of my mind as we spar. Our movements quicken, our blades swift, and our bodies nimble as we almost dance back and forth through the old desolate building around us. Neither of us gives in or slows as our breaths begin to quicken, the night air growing cold and sharp around our now-tiring forms.

I haven't felt this kind of exhilaration in many years.

Time passes as we become lost in our own world. There is a fevered gleam in her narrowed blue eyes as we move together—one I'm sure I, too, *mirror*.

Suddenly, movement from beside us pulls us to a halt.

I grip my blade, stepping toward the overgrown bush, when a large grey owl suddenly flies from its green leaves, carrying a tiny mouse between its claws.

A light chuckle rings out behind me.

"Be careful, I hear they scratch." A gentle smile spreads across her lips, her eyes curving into crescents as she watches the owl fly into the distance. She now wears a more relaxed expression, as if something heavy had been removed from whatever burden she's been carrying.

Her eyes meet mine, and for a brief moment, she stills with whatever she sees before quickly turning her gaze away, a slight pinkness coating her cheeks.

Something unfamiliar stirs in my chest with the look before I push it away.

"It's late. You should get some sleep."

She whips her head back, opening her mouth slightly before closing it again. "You can't be late for your day classes."

"I always attend-" she begins.

"Good. Then get some rest in between because I won't go easy on you, even if it's late at night." I peer around the old building, for even in the dark of night I could see its broken and decaying features. Even abandoned, there's great beauty in the nature that consumed it, bringing new life to what was once burned and broken. It seems the perfect place for us to train.

I twist back to her, her eyes wide with a slightly surprised expression pulling at her small features.

"You need a sparring partner, don't you?"

She quickly nods her head as a grin tilts my lips.

"Then we'll continue again tomorrow. Be prepared...*Micai*." I turn away and head toward the old entrance as she grabs her hoody and joins me.

We walk back to the academy in silence, surrounded only by the sounds of nature and our own contemplation.

A peaceful moment I haven't had in a long time.

We slowly make our way through the shadows toward the girls' dormitory, where I stay as I watch her enter through the back door.

A small laugh leaves my lips as I watch her make light work of the door lock and head inside.

I couldn't wait to see what else this small one could do.

CHAPTER TWENTY-FOUR

MICAI

$\mathcal{I}$t's been over a week and a half since Mr. Valor caught me in the old, abandoned training grounds with his daggers. We train together there every other day now, and he teaches me more advanced techniques than he would show us in class.

We take to sparring for most of the sessions, and with each one, I feel like I'm improving and learning more and adapting swiftly.

When we spar, I notice his forest green eyes shining in a way I've never seen during class. It changes him.

He also doesn't treat me like a student during our sessions but more like an opponent or equal, and he doesn't hold back or let up when we spar. But I prefer it that way.

I've begun to look forward to our lessons.

If I had it my way, I would train with him every night, but he believes I need a break in between our sessions and doesn't want me to fall behind in other classes.

But even without him, I still train every night, finding

a sense of peace when I'm pushing myself, my mind solely focused on moving forward. And then the relief that follows when I'm done, drained of all the frustration and stress from that day with each drop of sweat I've shed.

In the short time that we have trained together, I've also grown used to his company. I have learned more with him in just a few days than I have in the past couple of months of training alone.

That's why I was a little disappointed when he had to postpone our next session due to a faculty meeting this Friday.

I head toward the cafeteria, having just daydreamed my way through *'Modern Language and Ideology'* class. An hour and a half is too long to listen to quotes from Macbeth and not fall asleep.

Ms. Cheron seemed like a nice teacher, though. Her shoulder-length strawberry blonde hair and five-foot-two frame made her look petite. Her casual style of jeans and baggy jumpers also made you think she was more relaxed and laid-back about lessons. But she even gave Mrs. Brunswick a run for her money if you messed around in her class. And her ability as a seer made it so no one could get away with anything.

I make my way over to the cafeteria doors, a delicious paradise just feet away, when suddenly, two girls slide in front of me, blocking my way.

"Where do you think you're going?" The brunette on the right sneers as the girl beside her shoves her hand in front of me, stopping me from entering.

The two girls scowl toward me, both wearing the

same disgruntled look. That's when I realise they're mirror images of each other—t*wins*.

Each has matching green eyes and long, pin-straight mousy brown hair. They both wear emerald ties and have a cluster of faint freckles on their cheeks.

"Right..." says the twin to the left, her eyes sliding up and down me. "You think you're *special*. Were you planning on sitting with them again?" Her eyes flare, her lips twisting upward as she watches me.

"Of course she was." The right twin scoffs, her grin turning mocking. "She thinks the Infernal Four actually *want* her."

My brows scrunch together. The Infernal Four? What was that?

They both share a look, a venomous glint forming in their eyes.

"But *we* know better. They're just using you. A pathetic nobody like you could never get a boy's attention around here, let alone one of *those* four."

"So harsh, girls." A cold chuckle falls from behind me as a third brunette shows up.

She circles around me; this girl is shorter in stature and clearly not related to the twins. Her brown hair is darker, her eyes an ashy grey, and her face is covered in one too many layers of makeup.

"They probably felt some sort of pity, throwing the stray bitch a bone." She joins her friends, blocking my way as they continue to keep me from my meal. And my patience is beginning to wear thin.

Oblivious to my building anger, they continue to prattle on.

"I wonder what kind of tricks she used to stay beside them." the right twin sneers. "Bet it involved an open mouth and some bruised knees. That's all she'd be good for."

"Makes sense," Adds the left twin, "I heard she even went after her younger sister's boyfriends."

The newest addition to Tweedledum and Tweedledee drags her eyes down my front before her gaze meets mine.

"You're nothing. Not even worth the tip of Seria's fingernails." She spits. "How dare you even *think* of going after someone else's partners, let alone your own sisters." She shakes her head, a mocking laugh leaving her lips. "And now you think you can go after the Infernal Four?"

She takes a step closer to me, a vicious look taking over her expression as she gets in my face.

"Don't even think about it. Just because they let you eat with them once, doesn't mean you're important. Don't get lost in your delusions, thinking you're more than the weak bitch you are." Her grin widens. "They probably pitied you, a speck of dirt with no place, a stray bitch with no bark, an easy set of spread legs–"

Before she can finish, I reach out, wrapping a hand around her mouth and cutting off her words before I tighten my grip. Then, her eyes widen with surprise.

"My ears would *bleed* with all the trash I have to listen to these days. More and more morons thinking I'm easy, that they can say and do what they want, and I'll just allow it." I tighten my grip further on her face. "Well, not anymore."

She flinches as she stares at my expression before I feel movement to my side.

The twin on my left suddenly shifts forward, her fist aiming toward me. I let go of the brunette's face in my hand, pushing her back into the other twin behind her before twisting around and catching the hand coming at me.

She opens her mouth, her teeth gritted, and her eyes narrowed before her gaze flickers behind me. Her face falls as she pulls her hand quickly back from mine.

"What's going on here?" The familiar deep tenor of his voice beside my ear sends a slight shiver down my spine. *Ezra.* He takes a step forward, stepping beside me as he glances from one girl to the next. "Nobody?"

Suddenly, the brunette jumps forward, slight tears forming in her eyes as she cups her red face.

"She put her hands on me, Ezra." She flickers her gaze toward me, shaking her head before turning back toward him. "She was talking about you and the boys...*bragging* about how she has you all wrapped around her finger, and telling people you all give her special treatment."

The twins behind her nod, agreeing with everything as they stare daggers at me.

I roll my eyes. *Special treatment?*

We haven't even spent much time together. Anyone with eyes could see that Creed hates me, Hoody Boy ignores me, Ezra tolerates me, and Annex... just enjoys annoying me. But if that's special, then yeah, they give me the *good* stuff.

"Although *everyone* knows she has a reputation. Maybe you and the boys didn't know, but she–"

"Lillith," Ezra cuts her off. The playful smile he normally wears no longer lacing his lips as he meets her eyes. "I don't care about any of that." A slight, weary sigh leaves his lips before he schools it and smiles.

She's taken aback for only a fraction of a second before quickly sliding closer to him.

"That makes sense." She gives him a small nod. "Why would you need to listen to crap about *her*?" Her gaze finds mine, the fake charade dropped as her lips twist back into a sneer. "She's not even worth wasting breath on."

She turns back toward Ezra, a hooded look filling her eyes as she drags them up his large frame and toward his face. A slight blush coats her cheeks as she takes another step closer.

His fist clenches tightly beside me, his brows creasing as the smile he wears becomes stiffer.

Lillith quickly closes the distance between them, taking his silence as some sort of agreement. She trails a finger along his chest, trying to look seductive as she bites her lips. *But she looks more constipated than captivating.*

"Just because you were kind to her, she thought she was special. A little attention can do crazy things to stupid people."

I glance toward Ezra. The smile on his lips doesn't reach his eyes, and his jaw is tight, hardening further as Lillith pushes herself into his side.

Tweedledum and Tweedledee giggle behind her, their eyes and smiles smug as they watch me.

THE BLACKENED BLADE | 265

"Well, I do agree with that last part." Ezra's normally playful smile grows a little darker as he places his hand on Lillith's shoulder.

I think I'm the only one to notice the annoyance in his tone and the darker glint in his eyes as Lillith's grin widens with his words.

But all too quickly her smile drops as she stumbles a step backward into the twins.

Ezra wipes his hand over his blazer. "A little *attention* and people go crazy."

He meets the eyes of the three girls in front of him, their smug expressions falling. "I appreciate your...*intentions,* but I can make my own mind up about who I spend my time with." By the time he finishes his words there's no longer a smile of any type on his face. The warm and playful persona he wears like a mask faltering and replaced by someone colder and cutting.

He gently pushes past them toward the cafeteria door, their faces paling further as he ignores their calls. He stops at the door and turns back, "You coming?" His turquoise eyes meet mine. I give him a small nod and quickly make my way toward him.

Lillith's hand snakes out, trying to stop me.

I grab her by the wrist and stand mere inches from her face, staring her dead in the eyes.

"Be glad he came...if he hadn't, you wouldn't be walking away in one piece." I yank her wrist, a pained whimper falling from her lips as I whisper in her ear. "And if you call me a bitch again, I'll make it so you can never utter another word."

Her hand trembles as I let her go and head over to Ezra, the two twins flinching as I pass them.

Lillith's gaze turns to Ezra, but he ignores her.

"Lillith, you're not gonna let her–" begins one of the twins before she's cut off.

"Shut up!" Lillith barks.

She gives Ezra one last look before turning away and leaving, her two annoying sidekicks huffing before following after her.

Ezra gives me a knowing smile before it quickly falls into a frown, an almost exhausted sigh leaving his lips.

"I'm sorry about all of that..." He rubs a hand down the back of his neck. "You shouldn't have to deal with crap like that."

"It's not your fault you're favoured by rabid animals." I shrug, and he chuckles, a genuine smile stretching his lips this time.

"You know...I don't know if you've heard anything but some...unsavoury rumours are going around about you." He bites his lower lip, a slightly hesitant tone to his usually happy voice as he continues. "They say you want your sister's men. And that you treat her horribly because of it." He shakes his head. "I mean, I know it's bullshit, but I thought you should still know."

Similar rumours existed in my previous life as well, ones I'm now sure were spread by Seria and her cronies. Everyone believed them, so I expected as much this time, but why is he different? Why doesn't *he* believe them?

I didn't know Ezra that well, and he certainly couldn't know much about me. Eating beside each other and sharing a class didn't make us close or make me a credible source. So why help me?

Why believe me when no one else did?

"Why do you think it's bullshit?" I ask.

His brows furrow, an expression of 'it's obvious' written all over his face.

His hand gestures toward his body. "If you wanted to drool over a hot guy, clearly, I would win over anyone else. You've also eaten with me and the guys, and you haven't thrown yourself at us...*yet.*" He wriggles his eyebrows, eliciting a small chuckle from me. He shrugs, shaking his head. "Why would you want a milk dud, when you can have the whole goddamn bar that's sitting *right* in front of you?" He lets out an exaggerated sigh. "Make it make sense, Micai."

So, the reason he believes me is because he knows he's hotter?

I try to bite my lip to stop the laugh that wants to fall from them. *And fail.*

A small chuckle breaks free, and then another until I'm clutching my waist and wiping the tears from my eyes. A genuine laugh flows from my lips, the sound strange even to my own ears.

I meet his gaze, a soft smile spreading on his lips as he watches me.

I clear my throat, a wide grin stretching my lips.

"So, basically, you believe me because it's obvious I would choose the rib-eye over ground beef?"

He chuckles, "Ground beef? More like dog scraps. Trust me, even with Annex's craziness, Creed's alpha-holeness, or Mallyn's gloomy silence; we would still beat every other guy in every way: strength, looks, *and* loyalty."

He opens the cafeteria door for me and leans down as I pass him. "And I don't believe in baseless rumours or sweet lies, little sea star. I know what's what, I can see it better than most. I can see the good from the bad, and *everything* in between." His eyes become a little unfocused as he steps closer, his breath brushing down my neck as he whispers in my ear. "I don't know everything about you...*yet*, but a little voice inside me tells me you're not the bad guy here." He turns to meet my eyes, a gentle expression taking over his features. "You look so small and frail on the outside, and yet you handle yourself like you're bigger than me, Micai." A soft chuckle leaves his lips. "You don't back down, even when faced with something much bigger or badder. You seem soft on the outside but actually have spikes." His grin grows mischievous. "Though I don't mind getting pricked."

His brows instantly furrow as the words leave his lips. He has a questioning look on his face as he mumbles, '*Why did I...*' except I can't make out the rest of his words. Just as I'm about to ask what he means, loud laughter rings out from behind us as Ezra pulls away and straightens himself.

Right, the cafeteria. And as if on cue to remind me, my stomach growls.

A blush creeps into my cheeks as a small chuckle falls from Ezra's lips.

He pulls the door open wider for me. "Why don't you go get something to eat?"

I turn back to him as I head inside. "Are you not coming?"

A dazzling smile stretches his lips. "Can't get enough of the ribeye?"

I give him my best deadpan look as he chuckles.

"I've got to meet up with Creed, but I'll catch you later." He gives me a wink, his usual playful smile plastered back on before he turns and heads off.

Shaking my head, I make my way toward the food queue. The smell of steak hits my nose as I point to the striploin and chuckle at our little analogy a moment ago. I add an extra-large portion of crispy fries to my dish and get some bottled water.

My eyes are glued to my plate as I move toward my seat on autopilot, the growling from my stomach now playing out its own symphony as I sit down.

I start to dig in, a little moan leaving my lips as I take the first bite of the tender steak.

A deep laugh rings from opposite me, pulling me from my delicious meal toward two piercing blue eyes. They continue to watch as I take another bite, glued to my mouth as I continue to eat.

"Enjoying that, Red?" Annex shifts in his seat slightly, his eyes never leaving me.

I swallow before taking another piece into my mouth savouring every bite.

I nod, not caring to form words or retort back since this tender piece of meat is tasting better with every new bite I take.

I wrap my mouth around my next forkful, pulling the steak off of it and licking the juice from my lips.

I continue to eat as he shifts again in his seat, a slight, almost groan-like noise falling from his lips.

"Watching you makes me hungry, Red."

I freeze, my eyes narrowing at his empty plate and back toward my half-eaten steak. I grip my fork and gesture back toward the food queue.

"Then go get some."

A wicked smile spreads on his lips. "What I want isn't on the menu."

This couldn't have been the last steak, but if it was, he would have to fight me for it. *My odds aren't too bad.*

My eyes meet his, a dark glint in them as he leans in nearer, closing the distance between us. He lowers his voice to a deep whisper so only I can hear him.

"I wasn't talking about the food, Red." His gaze trails down to my mouth, his tongue darting out to lick his bottom lip as he watches me before his gaze meets my own again. The look he gives me is dark and feral, with something else in his eyes that sends a shiver down my lower spine and a heat burning at my cheeks.

He takes the fork from my hand and pierces my last piece of steak. Before I can tell him it's mine, he lifts the fork to my lips and waits for me to open them.

"I'm a giver, Red." My eyes slightly widen, his grin growing as he raises a brow. "Don't get me wrong, I'll take what I want as well." His tongue snakes out again, licking his top lip. "*Most definitely.*"

I open my mouth, my body on autopilot when it comes to food, as he pushes the fork in. I pull the meat off with my teeth as a small growl leaves his lips, a dark and satisfied look in his eyes. "*Good girl.*"

He puts the fork down and leans back, a wicked smirk still on his lips with a more dazed look in his eyes as he watches me chew.

"Any plans for Friday night, Red?"

My brows draw together. *Tomorrow?*

Other than a quick run and the usual training, there was nothing. I didn't usually have *plans*.

"I have a place I go every Friday. It helps me relieve some *stress*," he continues.

"I'm not into group therapy, thanks."

His grin widens, "I'm more of a doer, not a talker, Red."

"Funny, every time we meet, you don't stop talking."

He freezes, his brows furrowing, an odd look forming in his eyes as he stares at me.

"That so?" A slow smile spreads across his lips as he casually shrugs. "Guess you're the exception then." Before I can ask him what he means, he stands up and leans toward me, whispering in my ear. "Fight Night in *Bellevere*. Meet me tomorrow night at ten, down past the gates." He straightens up with a giant smile stretching his cheeks. "What's the worst that can happen? And at the very least, you can get away from this dump for a couple of hours." He snickers before turning and making his way out of the cafeteria, knocking into a couple of guys who were laughing and sending them flying to the ground. They scurry along the tiled floor to get away from him, but he doesn't even spare them a second glance.

A fight night. *With Annex.*

Sounds like it would be a bloody mess if he's involved.

And do I really want to go to some shady fighting ring that Annex frequents?

A heavy sigh leaves my lips. But a night away from the academy? I have to admit, it was a tempting offer.

I look around the room at the other students chatting and laughing, some of them openly glaring at me with looks of contempt or annoyance twisting their expressions.

I guess one night away wouldn't hurt me.

CHAPTER TWENTY-FIVE

MALLYN

The full moon shines above, and the cold winter air seeps out around me.

I hear small prey moving about the forest floor in the distance, and *he* itches to come out and play. His idea of fun being the bloodbath kind; bodies ripped to shreds and unidentifiable.

The monster inside me makes Annex's crazy look like a toddler at playtime.

He rolls about under my skin, his murderous thoughts and primal needs flowing through me like waves. He whispers in my ear with each move and breath I take, trying to push me, *control* me.

That's how it's been ever since I had my awakening, when the beast began lurking within me.

"...*lyn*...Mallyn." Creed's voice pulls me from my darkening thoughts and back to the present.

"What?" I answer, hoping he doesn't read too much into my slow response.

Creed could always tell when I was in my own head, always reading me too well.

He was like the leader of our little group and the reins that kept us all steady and close.

They call us 'The Infernal Four', and with good reason. Even Hell wouldn't be able to stop us if we wanted something. Chaos and pain were our pleasure, our only sanity, and the demons that drove us to keep moving forward.

These boys surrounding me were more than friends; they were brothers, accepting even the darkest part of me as their own.

"Annex wants to bring his little toy to Fight Night and apparently Ezra agrees." Creed sighs, his brows permanently furrowed as he glares at our two brothers.

The '*toy*' he was referring to was the girl Annex always talks about. *Micai.*

A small blue-eyed girl with rosy-gold hair and a fierce glare.

She sits at our table, not budging even when Creed tries to intimidate her. Very few men have been able to withstand his glare, let alone a tiny thing like her.

It's strange for Annex to even be interested in someone, unless it involves broken bones or a bloody mess. And she was the *opposite* of all that.

She was just so *small* and *frail*, with a body that looked like it could break with one touch.

And yet still, my eyes would follow her, watching her slight movements and listening intently as she spoke, drawn toward her small features and alluring soft scent.

Her small, rosy lips flash in my mind, her hair

brushing across her shoulders as she leaned in to eat, and her blue eyes...they seemed so familiar, but why?

I shift to the side, the beast growling under my skin, almost laughing at me.

It's strange, usually he would go on a rampage every other night, calling for blood and carnage. I had to go hunting every two or three nights just to appease his thirst; otherwise, it would consume me. Except lately, he's been...calm.

I can feel him, watching in the background, listening, waiting for something...I just don't know what or why.

I shake my head. I wouldn't lose it tonight.

It was 'Fight Night', which meant releasing a little bit of our pent-up stress and enjoying the chaos and blood in our own domain, and under *our* control.

It was also one of our sources of finance and the best way to collect information. What better place for all that than an illegal fighting ring?

"She can handle herself, Creed. She's no toy," Annex adds, leaning against the gate, grinning as he picks his nails with a seven-inch bowie blade.

"What makes you so sure? What makes *her* so fucking special? What if she can't handle your level of crazy Annex?"

Annex pauses, the small smile momentarily faltering on his face before turning toward Creed.

And I can tell by the look in his eyes that she's different for him. There's something more about this girl that makes him feel *something* more than what he's used to feeling.

And he's never been interested in, let alone gotten

attached to, any of the girls or women Creed or Ezra bring around. He doesn't even blink their way. *We both don't.*

Only this is different.

I can see the hesitation, the slight worry of whether she can accept him fully.

Creed continues, knowing he's pushing our brother.

"You're bringing an unknown into our group and around our family–"

Annex pulls himself straighter, his eyes narrowed as his face darkens.

"So, it's okay for you to bring who *you* want around, but I can't bring who I want because she's not a plaything or quick fuck?"

Ezra tries to place a hand on Annex, but he shrugs it off.

"What, 'cause you fucked them a couple of times before so they became *'known'* and are okay?" He takes a step closer to Creed. "Who are you kidding? You're pissed because she's not like your little whores who want your money or power. She's different. You can't control her. You can't read her, and you can't rein her in. And *that's* what bothers you, Creed."

Creed's face hardens. "If she's a threat in any way, I *will* kill her." His eyes darken, his power pouring from him, emphasising its truth.

Annex shakes his head placing his bowie away, a sadness to his smile I'd not seen in a long time.

"She's different, and one day soon, Brother, you'll regret saying that."

The words echo in my head, a loud growling noise

falling from the beast inside me, an agreement of some sort from the monster under my skin with Annex's words.

Just when Creed is about to open his mouth and argue again, a shuffling sound from behind the gates pulls our attention.

We all stop, turning toward whatever is coming our way, when her scent hits me: a soft floral scent like wild-flowers mixed with sweet vanilla, with a slight metallic undertone. It instantly tickles my nose and draws my eyes straight toward her.

She's clad in black jeans and an oversized grey hoodie. It's pulled up over her head as she makes her way toward us, with a small soft lock of her hair falling from the hood's fabric as she moves closer.

Annex passes me and Creed, a large grin forming on his face before he quickly schools it.

"Little late, aren't we, Red?" He taps an invisible watch on his wrist.

"It's two minutes past ten, but I'm more surprised you can even tell time." She raises her hands and gives him two thumbs up. "Good job."

Ezra breaks out laughing, and I try to school the chuckle wanting to leave my lips.

She's different alright.

Clearly, she has no fear when it comes to Annex, and he's a straight-up psychopath. One look or smile from him could literally have men three times her size pissing themselves.

"I love it when you flirt with me, Red." Annex winks and I almost choke. I've never seen that bastard *wink*.

"If sarcasm is flirting, I better be careful with my

insults."

Ezra's brows cinch together as he stares at her. "Why?"

She points to Annex. "He'd probably think it's foreplay."

Ezra and Annex chuckle, before he takes a step closer to Micai.

"We can skip the foreplay and head straight to–"

"Enough!" Creed barks, glaring at all of us. But he turns his coldest glare toward Micai, who meets his fierce gaze with her own.

Different. *Definitely* different

"Let's go," he grits out.

We head down to the small, narrow road outside the academy's gates to where our rides are parked. The town is around ten miles out, so walking would take too long. Plus, any reason to take my Ducati for a spin was good enough for me.

The feel of cold, heavy metal beneath me with nothing in my way—even the beast fell silent as the world around me blurred —was a feeling unlike any other. The feeling of being alive and truly free.

I throw my leg over the silver metal and flick the ignition key, my engine thundering to life as I hear Annex's laughter sound out behind me.

He's sitting on his own Ducati, having opted for a custom crimson red instead of my ice silver tones. He pats the space behind him as he takes his seat.

"Hop on, Red, and hold me tight." His grin grows wider than the Cheshire cat's.

"Why does she have to go with you?" Ezra stands behind Micai while she gazes at Annex's bike as if in some brief daze. "She might prefer to ride with me and Creed in the Dodge Charger."

My gaze flickers to Creed's face. His expression says it all.

My stubborn friend loves his sleek black Dodger, almost treating it as if it were his firstborn. He never let anyone drive it, not even us. It was his pride and joy.

Just as he's about to open his mouth to argue, Micai speaks first.

"I'm good." She grips Annex's shoulder and throws her leg over the bike, steadying herself with ease.

She turns back to Ezra and Creed, meeting Creed's narrowed eyes, "Let's go."

He grits his teeth and heads to his car.

My brother did not like being told what to do, especially when his own words were being thrown back at him. It would be an interesting night, if nothing else.

Ezra follows Creed, shouting over his shoulder, "See you there!" before he hops in the car.

"Not if we get there first!" Annex chuckles before his engine roars to life and he quickly takes off down the road.

I follow after them, swerving and twisting down the old stone roads and making chase. *They weren't the only ones here who knew how to ride.*

My beast's voice roars in my ears. The only thing we ever agree on is this—the speed and thrill of the ride.

I catch up to them, our bikes going back and forth,

each only gaining an inch or two on the other. Time passes as we twist and turn around the bending roads, our speed never slowing as we race back and forth between each other.

But before we know it, we're nearing town and our destination.

I speed up, pushing my bike to its limits and skid into the abandoned parking lot in front of our building. The noise of it screeches out around me as I come to a halt.

Smoke and dust flow from the ground below me as Annex follows in just seconds behind me, laughing. "And they call *me* the crazy one."

Micai jumps off the bike and comes straight at me. She stops only a couple of feet from me, her eyes searching me for something.

My beast falls silent. Calm. Watching and listening as she stands before us.

Her petite frame and deep blue eyes trailing up and down me.

Her scent hits my nose, and my heartbeat picks up. A light growl rumbles at the back of my head as she leans slightly toward me.

Suddenly she pulls back, a small sigh leaving her lips before her eyes meet mine.

"Do you have a death wish? Or do you just enjoy pain?" Her blue eyes narrow, searching my face for something. She shakes her head and sighs, turning back toward Creed and Ezra as they pull into the parking lot.

I clench my fist, halting the hand that wanted to reach out and drag her back to me. To have those deep blue eyes gazing at me with that strange look of hers.

Was it... worry? Did she think I would hurt myself? Why would she even care?

And why did the thought of whether she did, matter to me?

We had barely talked. *I* had barely talked to her. Only watching and listening from a distance as she ate and glared at Annex or gave some sort of snappy or funny line to shut him down.

She didn't seem to be afraid of us like the others, or care about our families or our power. She didn't drool over my brothers or try to cling to them like other girls.

I could tell she knew there was something different about us, but unlike everyone else, it didn't seem to faze her. She stares us down, stands her ground against Creed, keeps up with Annex's crazy, and gives Ezra some peace.

My brothers didn't realise they'd already changed even in our few encounters with her. There's a calm and comfort in her presence that seems to soothe some of their darkness without them even knowing it.

But I was different.

The darkness in me would never yield.

Only my brothers could handle me and understand what moved inside me. *And why I had to be this way.*

Anyone else that got too close would only get hurt.

I clench my fist, pulling it to my side. She would be no exception.

No one could *truly* understand or accept what I was.

"Mallyn." Ezra pulls me from my thoughts as he and the others approach the entrance.

The old slaughterhouse was our domain. The old

factory had been abandoned two decades before and was rotting until we found it.

We had claimed it not long after entering the academy as a form of amusement and to gather information and easy cash.

It also helped being able to jump into the ring and vent our frustrations from time to time.

The beast rolls under my skin with the thought before her voice catches my ear, and he calms again. Tonight, the newest member of our group stands just feet from me.

I don't think she would be able to handle seeing me let loose in the ring. I never left my opponent without a few broken bones and bloodied up beyond recognition.

I shake my head. Why did I even care what she thought?

We head into the large open warehouse, making our way through the crowds as people move out of our way. This was our territory, our operation, and everyone here knew who we were.

Cheers and shouts ring out from the crowd circling around the centre of the room. They watch on around the makeshift fighting cage as one large shifter knocks his opponent to the ground. The crowd cheers again, shouting *Kill him*, *Go for his eyes* or *Take him out*.

The larger shifter partially shifts his hand, claws extending from the tips of his fingers before he lunges forward and thrusts them into his opponent's chest. Blood splatters from the smaller shifter as laughter rings out around the cage.

The smaller guy sags to the ground as the final bell

rings, calling an end to the fight. The bigger guy grins maniacally as the crowd cheers around him.

These fights had no rules, but we did try to minimise the deaths as much as possible though. It wasn't good for business or having to constantly clean up dead bodies.

I narrow my eyes at the large idiot in the cage. None of us liked to be disrespected. Here, our word was law; if you mess with that, you mess with us.

The large shifter raises his fists, shouting into the crowd, "Anyone else?" while laughing.

I take a step forward, but before I can go any further, I notice Annex already making his way to the cage. He stops before pulling off his black leather jacket and top and throwing them towards Micai. The dark grin on his face tells me it's gonna be a really bloody fight.

He then opens the cage door and heads in, closing it behind him.

The large idiot begins laughing as he looks at my brother. He must be from out of town because everyone here knows Annex's face.

"You? This *tiny* thing?" Fuck, he really wanted a painful death, didn't he?

No matter how built he was or whether he stood a foot taller than my brother, he would fall and bleed like the rest of them. And now Annex would make it as painful as possible.

My brother found joy in watching other people in agony, more so if he was the one inflicting it.

The crowd falls quiet as the shifter chuckles, some of their faces even going pale as they watch Annex begin to make his way toward the shifter.

I glance back toward the small blue-eyed girl holding Annex's favourite jacket. Her eyes are narrowed but focused fully on him.

Another growl rings in my ears.

I shake it away and look back towards the cage.

Let's see how she does with a taste of what our darkness looks like unleashed.

CHAPTER TWENTY-SIX

MICAI

J catch Annex's black leather jacket and top as he heads into the fighters' ring and get a few narrowed looks from a few scantily dressed women around the ring before they turn back toward the fight.

I get the jealousy...his body was a lot more built and toned than even *I* thought.

He has a perfect six-pack laced with tattoos. They stretch and swirl around each ab and taut muscle, etched from the top of his neck down to his hips and then further dipping into his low-slung black trousers.

There are skulls, snakes, black roses, and wisps of shapes trailing down every inch of his bare skin; the look is as dark and intimidating as much as it is striking. Match that with his piercing blue eyes and bad boy aura, and even I pull his top closer.

A shiver runs up my spine, so I throw the jacket on. I was probably still cold from the bike ride over here.

Who knew I'd be riding the back of a motorbike tonight. I had never been on one before, previous life included. But I had always wondered what it would feel like. And hell if it wasn't fun.

It was more freeing than I'd ever thought it would be. A kind of rush I'd never felt before and something I definitely wanted to feel again.

Even if I had to 'borrow' Annex's bike from him to do it.

As I pull on the leather jacket, a smoky scent hits my nose. It smells like the embers of a dwindling fire, with a hint of a deep caramel scent lingering behind it.

I look around, noticing lights flickering overhead in the large warehouse. Huge metal machinery and large rusted grey chains with hooks fall from the metal beams above us. The beams and roof are rusting into a reddish-brown hue as the wall's grey paint below it fades and peels away. A large, battered blue signboard catches my eyes. The words *'Bellevere Abattoir' are* written in a greying-white script on the old decaying wood.

The crowd around me begins cheering loudly again, pulling my attention back to the ring just as the bell sounds and the fight starts. Some people in the crowd push up against the cage in their excitement, shaking it as they continue to shout and cheer.

"You sure you're okay here, little sea star?" Ezra stands beside me, a small, awkward smile gracing his lips as he watches me.

He flickers his gaze toward the bustling crowd around us as they become rowdier, his brow furrowing as people push past us and closer to the ring. He pulls me into his side as a large man shoulders into me, trying to get a closer look at the fight.

Ezra releases me, taking a step closer toward the man

with a dark look in his eyes. I grab his hand and he whips around quickly. His gaze flicks to his hand in mine.

"I'm good, Ezra." I give him a little squeeze, his eyes slightly softening as a small smile tilts his lips. "Let's watch Annex. Do you think he'll win?"

Ezra chuckles before looking behind me. "What're his odds again, Creed?"

I turn around, having yet to notice him behind me.

The silent hoody boy that I now know is *Mallyn*, makes his way over to us, and stands on the other side of Creed. The ass in question narrows his eyes at me before answering Ezra.

"*Obviously*, there's no competition." He scowls down at me. "Don't wet yourself or run away crying when it gets bloody, *Micai*." He says my name as if he's pronouncing some slur, a sharp bite to every syllable that rolls off his tongue.

Except blood doesn't scare me, and I don't run from fights. Not anymore.

I give him a smile so big it stretches my cheeks.

"No need to worry, *Creed*. I can handle myself. You just worry about you." I turn back toward the fight just as the host shouts 'Begin' and watch as the large shifter and Annex circle each other.

The shifter's eyes begin to glow, preparing for whatever attack he has planned. Annex just smiles mockingly at the massive tank of muscle.

I glance back and forth between the two. Was this a fair fight?

I had never seen Annex fight before, so I didn't know what to expect.

I know students and teachers in the academy fear him, but that's different from a huge shifter that quite literally just killed someone a few minutes ago.

Would he be okay? What if he got hurt?

I know he likes to annoy me most days and can be a bit of a psycho, but there was something about Annex. He was different from all the preppy or pompous asses in the academy. He acted the way he wanted and bowed to no one, not caring about status or other people's thoughts.

The large shifter lunges at him, but Annex doesn't even try to dodge; he takes the hit, falling to the ground with the big guy on top of him. I unconsciously step closer to the ring as I watch him fall.

A deranged laugh falls from his lips as he twists around easily and wraps the guy in a headlock from behind, stopping his movements with his legs tightening around his waist.

The giant shifter picks him up and slams back into the ground with Annex wrapped behind him, but the psycho's laugh only grows louder.

The shifter slams his elbows back into Annex's side as Annex tightens his grip around him. The crazed, glossy look in Annex's eyes tells me all he sees now is the prey below him. His grip tightens further as another laugh peels from his lips.

A small sigh of relief leaves me. If he had a look like that in his eyes, then this wasn't his first or second fight. How he looks and moves with such surety and strength shows me he knew what he was doing. Probably more than he should.

And now I feel bad for the asshole he's against.

The shifter's movements become more desperate realising Annex's grip isn't going to loosen. He begins to lash out, extending the claws from earlier again, ones I now recognise as bears.

He slashes them back toward him, trying to catch Annex with them. Thankfully, Annex notices, and before the bear shifter can catch him, he flips their positions. His movement is so quick and powerful that it leaves the shifter no time to react. Annex now sits on top of the shifter with his knee to the man's throat. He stares down at him with the most deranged expression I've ever seen.

The shifter tries to growl and that's all it takes for Annex to start his onslaught.

His fists slam into the shifter's face, the force of it instantly breaking his nose, the sound of cracking bone heard even from where I stand as blood splatters all over the shifter and Annex.

It sprays over Annex's face and drips down his chin, but he doesn't stop. Again and again, his fist meets the shifter's bloodied face. Until all I can see is the blood pouring from the man as small groans and whimpers leave his mangled mouth.

Annex's face is frozen in a demented smile, a look in his eyes that tells me he's not here anymore. Lost in a world of his own and dealing with something other than the bleeding shifter in front of him.

And that shifter would have happily killed Annex if he hadn't gotten the better of him first. Annex was surviving in the way he knew how, even if it was a bit bloodier than necessary.

It was a kill-or-be-killed world. And who was I to judge him?

What I had planned for my own demons wouldn't be noble or heroic either. It would be bloody and painful, and nobody but me would understand the carnage or darkness that would be unleashed on those who had wronged me.

I watch as Annex's fists continue to pummel the shifter, his face resembling a chunk of meat more and more. If this is what he needed to fight *his* darkness, then so be it.

"I heard you're only nineteen..." a sultry voice calls from behind me, pulling me from my thoughts and the fight.

I peer back to see a group of scantily clad women. They avoid Mallyn, keeping their distance from him as they slide closer to Ezra and Creed.

"But that's a lie, right?" A busty blonde woman slides next to Creed, pushing her chest into his side as her already skimpy red bodycon dress rides further up her thighs.

She giggles, brushing a red fingernail up his chest. "Either way, I don't mind younger guys." She bites her pink-tinted lips as she leans in further. "I'm sure I could even teach you a thing or two."

Creed shifts his gaze from the fight to the blonde. "Is that so?"

I hear giggles from the other side of me and watch as two honey blonde-haired girls, both wearing matching black mini-dresses, pull Ezra toward a small room across the warehouse.

My brows furrow as he heads away from the crowd and readily goes with them. They head into the room, their gazes hooded and their arms linked with his as they enter. Does he know them? Or were they together?

I guess Ezra *was* really attractive. And with such a sociable personality and *those* looks, why wouldn't he have girls throwing themselves at him?

The blonde behind me lets out a little hum, drawing my attention back to her as she leans further into Creed as his gaze flickers toward me, their lips meeting in a searing kiss as his hand wraps around her waist, her tiny dress pulling up toward her ass.

His eyes stay on me as small, exaggerated moans leave her lips. His hand then reaches down to her ass and squeezes it, pulling her even further against his front.

I roll my eyes and turn away from them, and back toward the fight.

Whatever little voyeurism kink he has, he can show to the rest of the crowd.

I was no naive virgin...well, not in my previous life, anyway.

After I had graduated from the academy, I had a couple of one-night stands, wanting to shed my inexperience. It was before I was taken by The Facility. They were shitty and short-lived, but *experiences,* nonetheless.

The crowd's cheers pull me from my thoughts as I take a couple of steps closer, making my way through the crowd and nearer to the cage. A hand suddenly slides down my lower back and grabs my ass from behind.

The asshole in question places himself beside me, his

dark hair slicked back and his beady eyes pretending to watch the fight as his hand gropes me.

I take a slow breath as his grin grows wider, a sleazy satisfied look spreading across his face as if he thinks I'm enjoying his old greasy fingers fondling my ass.

Then suddenly, his grin falls, his face twisting in pain.

He spins toward me as I tighten my grip on his hand, and with another flick of my wrist, I snap another of his fingers. He groans in pain before gritting his teeth. His other hand lashes out, trying to grab me, but quickly falls when I snap a third finger.

"*Bitch,*" he spits out between whimpers.

I yank his hand forward, twisting it behind his back as his knees give way. He tries again to hit me as we move, but I dodge it, swiping his nearest knee and snapping his wrist as he falls forward.

"Fucking whor–" His words are cut short as his eyes widen in terror. Black marks quickly form around his neck and look almost like smoke coiling around him like a noose. He begins to gasp and struggle for air as a large shadow falls over us.

"Who do you think you are, causing shit in my domain?" Creed's face is like stone, with a fury and rage I hadn't seen before.

A dark energy forms around him, emanating power and dominance. My eyes instinctively fall to the floor briefly before I remind myself that I no longer fear anyone or anything.

The crowd has fallen silent, their heads turned away or turned down. I twist back toward Creed and am met with two black swirling orbs with silver irises.

A shiver runs down my spine. My instincts screaming to turn away, but a louder voice in my head tells me to stare him down.

Creed's brow furrows as his dark eyes continue to gaze right at me, only shifting away when a gurgling noise rings out beside us.

Right, the sleazeball.

I watch the black coils tighten around his neck with Creed's fierce gaze set on him.

Was this Creed's ability, his power...these black coils?

I hear a rattling nearby and the clang of metal, followed by a few gasps before a huge dark figure jumps toward the man choking on the floor. I watch as a foot kicks the man in the face and sends him tumbling into the people around us, all of them falling like bowling pins with the force of it.

Annex turns to me, his eyes scanning my body before narrowing toward the man gasping on the ground just mere metres from us.

"Annex?"

He whips back around to me, his face is a mess, with blood dripping down his torso and fists. He looks as if he just walked off a horror set, except I know the blood isn't fake. *Or his own.*

"Yeah, Red?" His brows are still drawn downward, yet his expression slightly softens as he gazes at me.

I hear a shuffling sound and a low whimper and try to peer around Annex's bloodied body to where the sleaze-ball fell, but he's gone.

Mallyn heads over to us from that direction, giving Creed a small nod.

Creed's stony face begins to relax, his black and silver eyes fading into his usual golden amber shade.

A warmth surrounds me from behind, and a sweet, calming scent instantly hits me, like honey and lavender mixed with a slightly salty undertone. It tickles my nose as an arm wraps around me and turns me toward it.

Ezra's brows are cinched together, his face wearing a strange expression as his gaze trails up and down me. The longer I stare at him, I notice he now wears lipstick stains on his shirt, his hair is dishevelled, and a new unnaturally sweet scent is mixing with his own. It makes me feel sick the longer I smell it.

I shake his hands off and take a step back from him. "I'm okay."

His face slightly pales as I move away from the sickly smell and twist back toward Annex.

"...make it slow," is all I hear from Annex's conversation with Creed, before he notices my gaze.

"Red, it's never a dull moment with you around." The smirk he wears is almost contagious. *Almost.*

"Where's the asshole gone?" I hope he hasn't gotten away. Assholes like that needed a little more than just a few broken fingers to learn a lesson.

The sickening look in his eyes had my hackles up. It was a perverse look I'd grown too used to from the guards in The Facility and from the creeps like Adam Manser and Dean Phillips. Boys who thought they were above you and could take what they wanted with no repercussions.

And I didn't want some young girl getting caught in the crossfire later on.

I'm looking around the room, when I hear Annex chuckling.

"What, did you want to finish him off, Red?"

"...Maybe."

Annex's laugh cuts off, his gaze unreadable for just a brief moment before a wicked grin stretches his lips.

The others fall silent around us, too. And I could feel each of their gazes on me.

Did they think I was crazy? That I was taking it *too far*?

"We're going back," Creed barks as he turns toward me, "Fights over."

"Pity," I say.

"You wanted in, Red?" Annex steps closer, a dark glint in his eyes as they trail down my body. "Or do you just like the idea of being locked in a cage with me?"

A smirk stretches my lips.

Annex was crazy, unpredictable, and the *complete* opposite of Mr. Valor, so I would be lying if I said the thought of sparring with him didn't excite me a little.

"Who needs a cage, or even a reason..." I take a step closer, the tips of my shoes hitting his as I stare into his eyes. "I'll take you anytime."

A slight tremor works its way down Annex as he closes his eyes before slowly opening them again. He shakes his head before gazing down at me, a grin that screams *sin* growing on his lips.

He leans in closer, his lips brushing against my ear as he whispers, "Don't make promises you can't keep–"

"I don't." I meet his gaze as he tilts his head toward

me, his lips just a fraction from mine as our breaths begin to mingle.

A throat clears behind us as Ezra awkwardly rubs the back of his neck, his gaze flickering back and forth between Annex and me.

"Creeds waiting." His eyes land on me, his mouth slightly open before quickly closing again. A questioning look forms in his eyes before he quickly schools it. He shakes his head before turning around and walking in Creed's direction.

I pull away from Annex and follow behind Mallyn and Ezra as we make our way to the now-empty parking lot.

We head over to the bikes when Annex suddenly starts chuckling.

"Damn, Red, you look hot in leather. How the fuck did I not notice it before?"

Ah. I was still wearing his jacket. With everything going on, I had forgotten.

I pull it off as he raises his hand, a frown pulling at his lips.

"I wasn't asking for it back...it suits you."

I take it off and throw it to him. "You look like you need it more."

He was covered in blood, his torso and face splattered in the red crimson liquid with only his bare, inked skin beneath it. He slides a hand down his bare and bloodied torso before meeting my eyes again.

"*Ah*, the jealous type...I like it. I'll cover up *for now*." He gives me a wink and puts on his jacket with a mischievous grin. Suddenly he freezes, pulling the collar toward his face and taking a deep breath in, a small groan leaving his lips. "...*Fuckin' hell.*"

"Annex!" Creed shouts from the Dodge charger, his expression back to its familiar cold and stony glare.

Ezra jumps in beside him as he calls, "Let's move!" while Creed revs his engine.

"Fine, fine." Annex reaches into his jacket pocket, his brows furrowing before he checks the other one.

I take the keys out of my trouser pocket, twirling them around my fingers as I approach his crimson Ducati. I slide my hand over the cold metal before throwing my leg over and straddling the bike. All eyes are on me as I lean forward, put the keys in the engine, and let it roar to life beneath me.

A large grin pulls at my cheeks as I grip the handles, letting its rumble ring out again around us. I turn back towards Annex. "Let's go."

Annex breaks out laughing before quickly walking towards me.

"Wait," calls Ezra. "Do you know how to drive that?" He nods toward the Ducati purring under me.

I turn to him and stony-faced Creed, "I'm a quick learner."

"Fuck no!" Creed yells from his car.

"Fuck *yesss!*" Annex shouts as he climbs on the back behind me.

He wraps his arms around my waist and leans further into me until he's flush against me, with something very hard and very large hitting my lower back.

"Be gentle, Red..." His lips hum in my ear, his grin growing against my neck as his hands tighten around my waist. "I'm not used to someone else taking the reins."

I shake my head as he chuckles.

Gripping the handles, I rev the engine again and go over the route we took here in my head. Slowly, I begin to make my turn out of the parking lot just as Mallyn pulls up beside me, his pace matching my own as I quickly get the hang of it. He stays beside me as we pass the closed shops and dimly lit roads. And just as we're turning out of town and getting on the road to the academy, a car pulls out in front of us.

I hit the brakes a little too quickly and Annex and I jostle forward just as Creed and Ezra drive up beside us. If looks could kill...Creed would have me dead and buried twice over.

Annex just chuckles. "If I die, at least it's by your sexy hands, Red." He fixes himself against me. "I'm not scared to—"

"Thanks for the support," I grumble.

"But dying—"

I shift myself back into him, my ass hitting his already hard dick as a guttural grunt falls from his lips and cuts off his words. "Quiet. I need to focus."

A throaty hum rings from his lips in response as he tightens his grip around me, his fingers lacing around my front as a warmth floods each area he touches.

I push down the strange thoughts and start driving again, the roads to the academy emptier as we leave town.

Speeding up, Annex chuckles behind me while I bend and swerve down the curving roads, enjoying the ride and the feel of power between my thighs.

Mallyn stays beside me for the most part. His bike jumps back and forth, circling around us as we move with ease together. And I swear I see a small grin playing on his face as we ride side by side.

Creed and Ezra keep behind us the whole way, but at a small distance. *Probably worried I'd scratch his precious car.*

We ride towards the academy, the grey brick building and large black gates now looming in the distance, and a strange new feeling comes over me. One wishing this night and this ride would last just a bit longer.

CHAPTER TWENTY-SEVEN

CREED

*S*ince the Fight Night last week, I've been watching the girl Annex seems to favour. *Micai.*

Annex is anything but normal, *none of us really were.* However, he wore his darkness like a badge of honour for all to see. He kept his distance from other people, only ever interested in inflicting pain or watching others bleed.

So why change now...why *her*?

I'll admit, she was different. Stubborn, annoying and *uncontrollable.* Not good traits I liked in the women around my brothers.

At first, I thought she was just another groupie-type wanting to brag about being bedded by one of us, or someone trying to use us to climb some social ladder. Another girl who would soon run like the rest, if she was in any way smart.

But she surprised me.

At the fight, she had snapped that pathetic excuse of a warlock's fingers with no hesitation or remorse. She didn't whine or ask us for help, handling it with a swiftness and brutality I'd not seen in a woman before.

A small chuckle leaves my lips with the memory. The asshole had been almost twice her size, but she hadn't hesitated for a second. Her small hand broke his fingers like she was snapping a twig. And all while wearing a dark expression I never expected to see on that tiny, soft face.

I lost a little reason when I saw him trying to hit her and let my power loose. I even pushed the busty blonde, who was a definite for the night, away to maim the bastard. She had come in with *us,* and he thought he could touch her?

For disrespecting us in our domain, he left without the appendages he used against her, and would be a good example to anyone in the future who would try the same.

If Annex hadn't intervened earlier, I would have drained the life from him right then and there. Maybe her seeing a bit of what's buried inside me would have been for the best; maybe she wouldn't be so stubborn or even want to be around us anymore if I had.

And the sooner she left, the better.

It would happen eventually, either when she got what she wanted or when she realised what we really were.

I lean back in my seat, watching as students enter and leave the cafeteria. Their eyes only glimpsed briefly toward me before either blushing or turning away quickly.

I watch as Ezra and Annex enter and stand on either side of Micai as she drools over the food the server hands her. She acts like she was deprived of food...

My brows scrunch together before I shake the thought away.

She's from a prestigious family. Even if she lacked power or favour, she still carried the 'Bane' name.

My eyes trail down her petite body. Her figure seems quite toned; even with the academy's uniform, I could make out the dips and curves sitting in all the right places. She snaps her free hand out, slapping Annex's fingers away from her food as he laughs.

Was he really serious about this, about her?

I shake my head, a heavy sigh leaving my lips. He couldn't be.

It was *Annex*. And the only thing he was serious about was blood and carnage. This was a phase. Something to pass the time. He would realise it soon, and everything would go back to how it was before.

I look outside the bay window near our table and out toward the dormitories in the distance.

I never found the person from the night of Morgan's attack.

Annex and Mallyn had scoured the forest every night for a week, with Ezra pulling every bit of information he could from everyone around him. Except there was still nothing.

No one saw or even heard anything that night. Like the guy didn't even exist.

Mallyn makes his way over, taking a seat in his now *normal* spot. Even *he* couldn't get a trace on them, and his beast was...something else.

Morgan also confirmed that they had actually helped her that night, though she couldn't recall many details.

She said it was too dark and to drop it, that they helped her, and that's all that mattered. But I think she knew more than she was telling.

Even though I was grateful for them helping her, I still wanted answers.

And this *assassin,* or 'ninja' as Annex liked to say, must have some.

And what I want, I always get my hands on, one way or another.

Micai's POV

I make my way past Annex and Ezra and towards my seat, ignoring Creed and his usual cold stare. *And the distance Mallyn chooses to sit from me.*

I notice the pointed stares and whispers as I walk over. More and more people have been paying attention to me, even more than usual.

Were they really *that* jealous I was spending time with their 'Infernal Four'?

I stifle a chuckle. It was a terrible name. Imagine one small spelling error, and they become 'The Internal Four.'

It also sounded like some hell-bound quartet or demonic boy band.

I skim my gaze between the four boys, an image of them wearing matching boy band costumes taking over my thoughts and it has a stupid grin stretching my cheeks.

I sit down and start to dig into my dinner: three extra-large slices of pepperoni pizza. Over the past week, eating together has become more normal; even Creed has made more of an appearance since the fight night.

Annex, Mallyn, and I would meet in class, sharing more of them than I had thought. I guess they just never showed up before. Then we head to the cafeteria together for lunch or dinner, sitting with Ezra and Mr. Sunshine over here.

"Lovely little message you left for me in class, Red." Annex grins, piquing Ezra's interest as Mallyn displays a rare smirk.

"What message?" Asks Ezra as he grabs a slice of his chicken barbeque pizza and starts eating, his eyes flickering between Annex and me.

I take a giant bite of my own slice, the crispy dough and melt-in-your-mouth mozzarella making me hum happily, his question now forgotten as I eat.

Annex chuckles as he watches me, his own lips making their way around a huge meat-lovers slice as Mallyn opens his mouth.

"She made a little addition to Annex's name on her seat in World History Class. *Annex eats dick.*"

I stop eating for a moment, looking at Mallyn. He spoke more today with that one sentence, than I've heard him speak since we met.

I'm staring at him, my eyes a little wide as a muffled laugh breaks out behind me.

"Annex eats dick..." Ezra puts his half-eaten slice down and wipes his lips through his laughter.

The psycho in question leans in toward me, his gaze flickering between my eyes and the food I'm eating.

"I'd prefer to wrap my lips around something a little sweeter, Red."

The table falls silent.

Ezra whips around to Annex, his eyes widening. Mallyn's mouth opens slightly, and Creed's gaze seems to be burrowing a large hole in Annex's face.

A strange feeling wraps itself around me, a shiver working its way down my lower abdomen with the dark gaze Annex is giving me. I don't think he was talking about dessert, at least not the edible kind, anyway.

I shake my head, shoving the thought away. No, he meant the food. He *had* to.

"Then go get some." I grab my last slice and take a huge bite as his grin grows more wicked.

"Is that an invitation, Red?" His eyes drop to my lips as I finish off my last bite, licking a little sauce from my lip. *"Fuck,"* he mumbles as he shifts in his seat.

He moves closer, bending closer towards me with an almost feral look in his eyes just as a hand reaches out and smacks the back of his head.

Annex whips around, a widened look in his eyes before they narrow at Ezra.

Ezra shrugs, a small smirk stretching his cheeks. "Gotta treat a girl with respect, Bro."

"Girl?" Annex almost chokes on the word, his brows reaching his hairline as he stares at Ezra before he turns toward me.

A sinful expression quickly takes over his face as he watches me. His eyes slowly trailing down me before finally landing on my lips. "I don't see a *girl*, Ez."

A heat begins to creep up my neck and into my

cheeks with his words. The dark gleam in his eyes catches me off guard, wrapping me in its intense thrall. *Maybe we weren't talking about food after all.*

A throat clears from my left and pulls our attention back. *Creed.*

"Funny," he calls, leaning further back in his seat and propping his feet on the nearest chair. "All I see is an annoying chick who has issues sharing..." He flicks his gaze toward my empty plate and then to the chair below me. "And is a little psychotic about where she sits."

I scoff, turning toward the smug asshole.

"As if you can talk. Obviously, your *sharing* issues are worse than mine." I flick my gaze between him and the table we're all sitting at.

Annex chuckles while Ezra bites back a laugh, his gaze falling on Creed before he schools his features.

"*And*, if I'm psychotic...and he's clearly demented," I point to Annex. "What does that make the three of you?" I glance towards Mallyn, then Ezra, and finally land on Creed.

Ezra's grin returns as he points toward Mallyn.

"He'd be the berserker, and I'd be..." He taps his lips, a playful smile spreading on them as he gives a casual shrug, "The loveable romantic?"

Annex chokes on a chuckle, "More like *obsessive*."

Ezra's smile falters, and he turns toward Annex as a scoff leaves his lips. "As if *you* can talk."

Annex follows Ezra's gaze as it flicks towards me, a strange expression forming in his eyes before he shrugs and grins. "I didn't say it was a bad thing."

I shake away the unreadable look they're both giving

me and turn back to Creed, who seems completely bored with their conversation.

"What about him?" I point toward Creed.

"What about me?" Creed calls, his interest now piqued as a small scowl darkens his expression.

"What are *you*?"

"What do you think I would be?" A dark amused look spreads in his eyes as the other guys fall silent around us.

"Major Asshole?" I reply, tapping my chin as Annex and Ezra snicker, "Patronising Prince...Harbinger of Glares..." I shrug. "There's plenty more, but we only get such a short break to eat."

Creed's feet drop to the floor as he leans towards me, a dark gleam in his eyes. "Patronising Prince?"

I mock gasp, shaking my head before slightly bowing it. "My apologies, my dark *Lord*...how could there be anyone more patronising than *you*."

After a second's beat, I lift my head, waiting for the angry glare to split me in two or rage-filled words to be thrown at me, but I freeze instead.

Creed's dark brows are drawn together, but there's no anger in his gaze. His lips slowly tilt up as he slowly pulls back, a slight roll to his eyes as he leans further back in his chair again.

The others break out into chuckles around me.

"You look like a deer in headlights, Red."

Even Mallyn is chuckling.

"What were you expecting?" Ezra laughs.

"Probably to be split in two." Annex grins.

"Yeah," I answer, looking back at Creed. "I wasn't

expecting *that*." I point toward Creed's face. "It's way more terrifying."

Creed's grin grows broader and smugger with my words as he leans a fraction closer to me.

"Good that you–" Creed's words are cut off by his ringtone.

He glances down at the screen, his brows furrowing before he quickly taps out a response. Then he turns toward the guys, all playfulness now gone from his face as he straightens himself and stands. "We've got business to deal with."

He gives them each a pointed stare before turning and heading out of the cafeteria. Mallyn gives me a quick glance before he follows straight after him. Ezra sighs, pulling himself up from his seat.

He gives me a small grin, telling me he'll '*Catch me later*' before he joins Creed and Mallyn.

Annex grumbles as he looks after his friends before turning back to me. A small smile spreads on his lips as our eyes meet.

"Don't miss me too much, Red. I've gotta go play for a bit, but I'll be back soon."

"Play?" I ask.

"Nothing too fun, just business stuff." He pulls himself from his seat, rolling his eyes before he soon freezes. A dark twinkle growing in them with whatever crazy idea probably formed in his head. "Maybe, someday, you can come and give me a hand." A wicked grin spreads on his lips as his eyes become a little dazed, lost in his own thoughts. "You would look so beautiful wielding a blade covered in blood..." His voice lowers to a throaty hum as he bites his bottom lip, his gaze returning to me. "And then afterwards, you and me can have some *proper* playtime." He gives me a devilish grin, one full of sinful dreams and dark promises, before turning and following the others out.

A familiar heat creeps into my cheeks and up my neck with his words.

Crazy bastard. Who wanted to '*play*' with him? His idea of fun probably ended with multiple corpses and a few hefty wanted posters.

But he did get one thing right...I *do* look pretty cool with a blade in my hand.

CHAPTER TWENTY-EIGHT

*H*ow the hell did I let this happen? How did they even manage to get the better of me?

I should have known it was too quiet. And that one of those dickheads would do something.

It's my own fault.

I had grown too complacent, too comfortable with the guys around and being in their company that, for a brief moment, I forgot this was never a place to relax in. There was no such thing as '*safe*' here for me.

I attempt to shake off whatever they had drugged me with, the drowsiness still pulling at my eyes as I seek to make out my surroundings. But even with being dizzy and my vision blurred, I can tell that everything's pitch black around me.

I try to stand, a tremor running down my body with the slight movement, and then I quickly realise my hands and legs are restricted. *I've been tied up.*

This was not what I was expecting when I woke up this morning and headed to class.

Whatever bastard did this, even waited until *after* I had attended all my classes before they drugged me. *They could have at least spared me from the day's lessons.*

At least one thing was to my benefit...they had underestimated me.

I feel the restraints wrapped around my wrists and legs. Thankfully, they weren't metal cuffs or chains, just rope. I tug at them and wait. No backlash from a spell or tightened restriction either.

For once, the rumours circulating about me actually helped. My kidnappers thought I was still completely useless with no power or strength, so why should they waste magic on me?

I shake my head again, the room or wherever I was, slightly spinning with the sudden movement.

I try to pull myself up, sitting straight as I try to work on the restraints around my wrists. But the darkness around me has an eerie feeling sliding up my back as I move.

I pull at them once, then twice, my brows furrowing at the weakness running through me and the lack of movement from the rope. Something like this should have fallen off with one pull.

What had they given me? And how did they even manage to drug me? I had been so careful around everyone.

The last thing I remember is making my way out of the cafeteria after eating...The server, she looked kind of new and seemed a little...off.

Fuck, they drugged my food. It's the one thing I don't

hesitate to touch, and the only time I feel a little less guarded.

What had they even given me? A spelled potion or some drugged concoction?

I gaze around the dark space, a slight panic beginning to unfurl in me.

What if I was powerless again? What if I was trapped here like I was in The Facility?

I keep trying to look around, my heart racing as my eyes search the dark for *anything*.

What if I was locked away alone again? Where no one can find me.

What if I couldn't get out, if I died–

No. I wouldn't go there. This wasn't The Facility. And these weren't those shackles.

I was also a different person and stronger than ever before. I just needed to stay calm and think.

If they used some magic drug on me and it was a student, then it couldn't be something that potent. It had to be temporary. Or if it was a drug from humans, it would also wear off after a while. How long had I even been unconscious?

By the feel of it, whatever they gave me was already trickling out of my system as the haze in my head was slightly receding and the drowsiness fading.

I release the breath I didn't even know I was holding.

In the meantime, I couldn't just wait for someone to save me.

I wasn't that weak young girl anymore, and even without my strength or speed right now, I could still do *something*.

My racing heart calms down as I think things through, and the panic slowly subsides as I pull at the rope again. Over and over, I tug and pull at them until I feel something give. I keep at it until my wrists feel sore and my skin feels raw, but I continue. *I wouldn't give up until I was free.*

After a few more painful tugs, I finally feel the rope give way and loosen so I can free my hands. I reach for my legs and fumble, working to untie them as quickly as I can, still slightly dizzy from whatever spell or drug they gave me.

I finally free my feet and stand up, stumbling as a wave of dizziness hits me again.

Shakily moving forward, I feel around in the dark trying to find my way around.

Was it night or still day? And how long had I been out? Minutes, hours...*days?*

A bitter laugh leaves my lips. It's not like anyone would come looking for me or even notice I was gone anyway...so what did it matter?

Annex, Ezra, Mallyn, and Creed hadn't appeared in school all week, not since the little call they got in the cafeteria. Even Mr. Valor had been busy after school with other work, so we hadn't been able to train together the past few days. He was also my last class, and since I had attended, he wouldn't even know I was missing.

I freeze. Why did I think of *them?*

Had I become too used to their company?

Did I think they'd actually *notice* if I wasn't there?

They would probably be happy I was gone, especially Creed. He might even be *smiling* right now.

But Annex...would *he* notice?

Or maybe Ezra?

I give myself a slight shake, the room spinning again when I do.

Why would they care about me anyway? We hadn't even known each other that long. Plus, faith and trust in another person wasn't exactly something I gave so easily anymore. I could only depend on myself. Letting my guard down just a little already put me in this predicament as it was.

My hand catches on what I assume is the wall. When I hit it, it's cold and makes a slight 'clanging' noise. *Metal.*

Metal was a strange choice for a wall in the academy, especially since they were mostly made of brick, stone, or wood. It didn't fit in with the old aesthetic vibe they usually go for there.

But where am I, if not inside the academy? Where else is there?

I take a deep breath, trying to calm my racing thoughts. And then it hits me.

The smell.

A smell so foul, I question how I didn't notice it before.

The stench trickles into my lungs, turning my stomach and making me want to wretch. What is that? And where the hell am I?

I start moving as quickly as my body will allow, a new panic setting in with the foul scent flooding my senses. Something dark and familiar about the smell sets alarm bells ringing in my head and has my instincts telling me to run, to get as far away from it as possible.

My hand catches on a latch, and feeling around, I quickly find a handle.

I unbolt the latch and push against the door with all my might, praying it wasn't locked or, worse, *spelled.*

It slowly creaks open, the weight hard and heavy as I continue to push.

The large metal door only moves a few inches, but the fact that it isn't locked gives me relief and spurs me on to keep moving.

Shoving the door harder, I throw every ounce of my energy and the complete weight of my body against it. It slowly screeches open, dragging across what sounds like rocks or gravel. I continue pushing against it until there's enough space in the gap I've made for me to squeeze through.

The ground crunches beneath my feet, the jagged rocks stabbing into my bare flesh, the fact that I'm shoe-less only dawning on me now. The bastards had taken my shoes and didn't even let me keep my socks.

Glancing up, I see a crescent moon above me and the dark night surrounding it. I guess that answered at least one question.

I turn toward the area surrounding me. An ocean of trees and dark forest were spread out around me and as far as the eye could see. The dark green trees reach toward the night sky in every direction with the academy nowhere in sight.

I take a deep breath, closing my eyes, and try to shake off the nausea rushing through me as strange images hit me.

Ivy Harris.

Jeremy Colton.
Jake Andrews.
And Alice Parker.

Their faces flash before me, and I can make them out even blurry and shaky. Their voices and laughter sound out around me like an echo as I feel my body being stirred back and forth in the quick memory.

So they were behind this.

I should have known. Most of the time, it was always them. Why do they continue to bother with this crap?

The effort to do this alone was baffling me. Did they not have anything better to do?

What did they even hope to get out of this? To see me cry, to break my spirit a little more? To teach me where my '*place*' was?

Or did they just plan to leave me here?

I look out to the forest in front of me. There are rows upon rows of dark trees and bushes as far as my eyes can see.

I turn back from where I came, and that's when I see it. The dark place I've just escaped from.

It's a giant metal shed of sorts with dark warning signs and sealing spells all over it. But they're now torn and broken.

And that's when it all clicks.

This was the detainment shelter for the sixth-year Defence class. This was where they kept wild, magical beasts for training. It was only for final-year students with the magical capacity to take on these kinds of creatures. Usually, they would take them on in groups or teams.

The school didn't want to risk injury or danger to other students, so they placed them at the back of the academy, through the forest, and up toward the mountain, which was one of the furthest points from the academy.

And now I was here...and the spells keeping the beasts in place were gone.

They weren't inside. If they had been, I wouldn't have made it out, especially having been drugged and unconscious.

Quickly turning around, I watch the treeline, flicking my gaze in every direction. How many of them did they have in there?

Did these assholes truly want me *dead*? This was beyond some cruel prank.

I'm thrown into the forest—*at night*—with wild, magical beasts set loose to hunt me. All while weakened by whatever drug or potion they've fed me with.

I knew they were sick and twisted, that they enjoyed the pain and misery they inflicted on me...but *this*?

They had never gone as far as to actually try to *kill* me before.

This wasn't a game. This was life or death now. And I needed to get out of here as quickly as I could.

Just as I step toward the treeline in front of me, I hear a rustle in the trees to my right.

I freeze. What are the chances of it being a cute little lost squirrel?

The growl that follows is anything but *cute*. It grows louder as two large yellow eyes appear from the forest, focused entirely on me.

A large form slowly stalks out of the treeline. The creature's body is like a combination between a horse and a wingless wyvern. Its eyes were sharp slits, with a long face and crooked sharp teeth. And a strange foam-like substance clings to its mouth, like some rabid beast. It's too dark to make out the skin shade, but its texture seemed coarse and scaly even from this far.

Its mouth opens, and a strange howl and rattling sound fall from it as strange black saliva drips from its razor-sharp teeth.

It growls again, its yellow eyes falling back on me, and I take that as my sign to start running.

My feet bleed as I race through the forest, rocks and tree roots scraping and stabbing into my soles as I try to keep as much distance from whatever creature is now chasing me.

Pushing my legs harder, my strength not fully returned, I will my body to keep moving and not fall. I wouldn't give the beast or those bastards the satisfaction of an easy kill.

My anger spurs me on, remembering the blurry faces laughing and smirking above me as I fall unconscious.

Never again will I fall so easily. Never again will I let my guard down and so stupidly lose to small fish like them. If I wanted to face and destroy The Facility in the future, I had to be stronger than this and much better than I am now.

I force my legs to keep running, my anger and will to live giving me more strength as an eerie growl rumbles behind me.

I see a cliff in the near distance. If I didn't have my full strength or any weapon to kill it with, then I would have to be smarter than it.

Pushing myself harder, my legs and lungs burning with the force as I try to shove the dizziness behind me to keep moving towards the cliff.

I'm nearing the cliff a few minutes later and racing toward its edge. Then, I run to the large trees sitting on top of it when suddenly I feel a heavy force slam into the side of me and throw me to the ground. I tumble and roll before slamming straight into the tree, pain searing from my waist and back. There were unquestionably a few fractured–*if not broken*–bones there now.

Turning towards the nearing feral beast, I reach around for anything to use against it.

It lunges toward me as I reach for a fallen branch.

The creature's sharp teeth meet with the wood just inches from my face as it pushes further into the bark, closing the distance between us. Its foul breath hits my face, like sewage mixed with something that smells like it's been decomposing for days.

I'm jerked back from my thoughts as the beast suddenly rears back, still gripping the branch in its mouth, trying to pull me with it. Digging my feet in, I try to stop it from taking me with it, glancing to the tree above me and to the cliff just a few feet beyond that.

I peer back at the beast.

Gathering the remainder of my strength, I quickly release the branch, letting the creature stumble back as I use the tree behind me to kick off. I jump up, reaching for a low-hanging branch. Catching it, I swing forward, leaning my full weight into it as I push out and toward the creature now rushing at me.

My feet connect with the beast, and the force of my body causes it to tumble back sideways and towards the cliff's edge.

I drop from the tree and run at it, jumping into a fly kick to finish the creature off.

It shrieks and howls before tumbling back and falling off the cliff. The steep drop and jagged rocks below kill it instantly.

Stumbling backwards into the tree, my legs grow weaker and I'm no longer able to stand. I sag down to the ground, a heavy breath leaving my chest. That was too close.

This feeling of being weak and almost helpless again...I refuse to allow this to happen a second time.

I take a few deep breaths, calming my racing heart as I look out beyond the cliff.

After resting for a few minutes, I straighten as a loud rattling howl rings out from the treeline in front of me, where two familiar yellow eyes appear.

No. I had killed it and watched it die, so how?

Before I can move, the creature rushes towards me. Its razor-sharp teeth are bared and almost a foot from my face when suddenly it's knocked to the ground and sent tumbling past me.

A huge beast stands where the creature had been just seconds before—a huge, *familiar* blue-eye beast.

Its frame dwarfs the other creature, its body massive and dark as it roared at the now trembling beast on the ground.

The creature shakes while picking itself up and begins to snap and froth at the mouth, with more strange dark saliva dripping from its jaw as it lunges at the larger beast.

The blue-eyed beast swipes a claw at the smaller creature, slicing its side open and making it howl in pain. The bigger beast then lunges toward it, teeth bared and claws ready. With one swift move, it rips out its neck.

The smaller, yellow-eyed creature falls limply to the ground, its eyes now lulling to the back of its head, as its last breath seeps from its lungs.

The huge blue-eyed beast then turns to me, blood dripping from its jaw as the creature's darkened eyes lock on mine.

My breath catches in my chest. Is it going to kill me? Finish off what it didn't last time?

It takes a slow step toward me, its eyes never leaving mine as it moves.

Suddenly, another rattling howl echoes out in the distance.

A low snarl leaves the giant beast's mouth as it gazes toward the sound and then back to me.

It is definitely contemplating something. Maybe it will eat me first and then go after the new creature in the distance? Or to let me live so that it can hunt me another day?

It seemed like the type to enjoy the hunt more than the kill anyway.

"You could always...catch me later?" *Stupid.* What was I even saying? Was I really trying to persuade a beast to let me live? It was a *beast*.

I know it's smart, but who knows if it even understood me.

The beast chuffs, its eyes a little lighter as our gazes meet, and I swear it seems almost *amused* by my words.

Before I can open my mouth again, it runs off in the direction of the rattling howl and the creature it had come from.

It probably went with option two, then.

And it *would* be safer for me in the forest if it killed those things, too. I just have to make sure I get out of here before he's finished and decides he wants a smaller snack.

Steadying myself against the tree, my legs shook, still weak from the attack and having run so much. But thankfully, I was feeling less dizzy and drowsy now, sure the drugs from earlier were leaving my system.

I skim the trees surrounding me.

A heavy sigh falls from my lips.

Now I just need to make my way through the forest with what little strength I had left and without knowing which direction to go...Never mind the enormous intellectual-homicidal beast roaming around...which knows my scent.

CHAPTER TWENTY-NINE

$\mathcal{I}$ had walked for God knows how long or how far with my feet now raw and bloody. My body felt heavy and tired, with every inch begging me to rest. Yet the thoughts of a warm bed, a hot meal, and wiping the smug faces off the bastards who did this had me taking each step forward until I found my way here.

Wherever 'here' was.

I slowly make my way over some jagged gravel when suddenly I hear a familiar voice calling my name.

I peer up and into Mr. Valor's green eyes as they widen. His features slowly darken as he takes in my current state, my torn and dirty clothes, my messy hair, and my bleeding and bare feet.

"Micai." He rushes over to me just as I stumble, lifting me up to carry me in his arms.

His hands pull me closer to him, but the feel of his body heat has me leaning in further, hoping to soak up the warmth and rid myself of the cold that's seeped into my bones.

A slight tremor works its way down his body, his hands clutching me tighter as he carries me like I weigh nothing. He turns his gaze to the forest in front of us and slowly begins walking. He doesn't ask me anything or push me to talk right away. Instead, he simply allows me to take a moment to relax and feel the relief of being safe.

His gaze is cold and stern, his brows are cinched downward, and his jaw is tight. His lips pull into a straight line as he looks ahead and makes his way through the forest.

Everything about his expression at this moment is a complete contrast to his slow, careful movements and his soft hold on me, or the warmth that seeps into my skin with his gentle touch.

"How did you..." I start. Only he answers as if he already knows my question.

"I had finished my duties earlier than expected and figured you would be training, as you usually do." He gives me a knowing look, breaking his cold and dark gaze, turning it into something smoother as he glances down at me.

"When you weren't there..." He hesitates, observing the trees ahead of us as his steps grow slower, his eyes slightly glossy as he continues. "I felt that something was wrong. So, I began to check the surrounding area. I heard a noise in the distance..." His grip tightens around me and I wince. He catches the minor shift in me, quickly loosening his grasp, and gives me an apologetic look.

He stops walking and glances down at me, the iciness in his eyes wholly thawed as he meets my own. "What happened, Micai?"

His deep green eyes search mine for answers, a strange expression pulling at his features as he watches me.

But what do I tell him? That I was drugged by a group of students that hate me?

That they tied me up and let wild, magical beasts loose to hurt me?

That I killed one of them but was attacked by another one soon after?

And that I was then saved by a much bigger and more terrifying beast that I'd fought before?

There were too many strings attached to everything, too many stories and explanations that would have to be told to understand how I got to this point. And even if I did tell him everything, he couldn't help me, not really.

Even if he tried, it wouldn't stop them or change their minds.

Sometimes, violence had to be met with violence. And I had every intention of showing them they made a mistake by messing with me.

"Micai…" He places his hand over mine, one I had put on his chest and tightened without realising it. "Tell me so I can help." His forest green eyes plead with me, a look of genuine worry seeping through his gaze as he awaits my answer.

And something prickles at my chest with the look. I could see the concern in his features, the anguish in his eyes, and something else: an anger or fear waiting patiently behind it all…but this was for me to deal with.

And I had been holding myself back in the academy for too long.

I let all those pretentious assholes get away with too much and let them believe I was still the same girl as before.

Maybe a part of me had convinced myself that they were all just nasty pranks and things that I should tolerate. And that it wasn't real torture, or that they hadn't really hurt me...that it wasn't like The Facility.

But that was the problem.

The Facility was *literally* a prison and a place of true nightmares and Hell. Nothing could compare to that.

I had gone easy on them, thinking they were still 'kids'. But I too was once a kid, and they spared me no mercy then, or now.

I had been put through enough. But not anymore.

"Micai, you need to–" He sighs before stopping and taking a breath. He closes his eyes before opening them again, his gaze now firmer and more resolute. "I can help. Whoever did this to you...will pay." His eyes darken, his gaze returning forward before he begins walking again. "Give me their names or their years... *anything.*" He grits out, a slight tick forming in his jaw as his brows pinch downward.

I follow his hardened glare and spot the academy's grey roofing in the distance. My limbs stiffen as a slight chill works its way up my back at the thought of heading into the academy.

I couldn't go there. Not like *this.*

I wouldn't give them all the satisfaction.

"Micai–" He continues, but I cut him off, twisting around and trying to break free from his embrace. His grip tightens as he tries to stop my movements, a confused expression drawn across his face.

"Not the academy." I shake my head, my narrowed gaze meeting his.

"You need to be treated–" His brows pull together, a sterner expression taking over his features before I cut him off again.

"No."

"There's no '*No*', Micai. You need to be–"

"Not there." My voice breaks a little, a vulnerable crack appearing in the armour I wear. One I didn't even realise was there.

He stares at me, his gaze penetrating as he searches my face for something. They slowly soften once they find it and then flick to the academy again as a new conflict creeps into his gaze.

Maybe we could go somewhere else. Somewhere where we wouldn't be seen. But where?

Then, a thought hits me. "I'll go to the abandoned training building where we–"

"It doesn't have what you need to be treated," he counters before I can even finish, his features gentle yet voice firm.

"It's either there or my room. And I'd say it's a longer walk to the girl's dormitory than to the old training building from here." I flicker my gaze around us.

"Why–" He starts, but his words cut off when I place my hand back on his chest. His muscles tense below my touch as a slight breath escapes his lips. His eyes meet mine again and I let a bit of how tired and weak I feel seep into my expression.

"I don't want anyone to see me like this." I look down at my torn and dirt-ridden uniform with blood dripping from my legs and feet. And then toward the cuts and scrapes that coat every bit of my exposed skin. "Please, Mr. Valor..."

I'm not entirely sure what he sees when he looks at me or how much he understands, but he gives me a slight nod.

"*Gadriel...*" His voice is low, and his brows are slightly pinched as he speaks, a strange look forming in his eyes before raising his voice again. "You can call me Gadriel."

He begins walking again but veers away from the main academy building and toward our training spot.

"*Gadriel,*" I mumble, the name falling from my lips without thought.

Gadriel pulls me in close with the call of his name, his eyes glancing down to me for a brief second as a small grin tilts his lips. His green eyes twinkle as the moon above us shines on him, his hair like white golden silk against its light. The little smile he wears, for just a brief moment, changes his features into something warmer and...captivating.

But then, all too soon, it's gone, his usual serious look reappearing as his gaze falls back toward the forest in front of us.

After a few more minutes of walking, we finally reach it—the old training building.

He takes me inside, finding a small old wooden bench beside the dilapidated stairway, and gently places me down.

He glances back and forth between me and something in the direction of the academy.

"I'll get some supplies...will you be okay?" His eyes watch me for some kind of reaction, though I simply give him a smile and a nod, trying to reassure him.

"I'll be fine."

He quickly makes his way to the entrance, then stops and turns around for a moment to peer back at me. "I'll be back soon."

He's gone in seconds, in a blur of movements and matching the speed I would have had at my normal strength. However his steps are so silent that if I hadn't seen him leave, I would have thought he had just disappeared.

I'll have to get him to show me how to do that someday.

A couple of minutes pass as I stare down at the rips and holes in my uniform and at the dirt and dry streaks of blood on my body.

I notice a small cut on my leg slowly closing up and healing. I guess my power was gradually recovering.

I try to stand but wince from both the sting from my feet and the pain searing up my side. *Right, fractured or broken bones.*

Hopefully, whatever was in my system would fade fast and allow these injuries to be properly healed by the morning.

Just as I'm thinking that, Gadriel shows up holding a large black duffel bag.

He kneels before me and pulls out wipes, ointment, and lots of gauze. Did he think I needed that much? That amount would probably wrap the torso of a guy twice my size and still have some to spare.

He leans towards me but then suddenly stops, an awkward look on his face as he flicks his gaze to the medical supplies in his hands before meeting my eyes.

"I need to...touch you to help. Is that okay?" His nose scrunches slightly with his words, and the small expression has a smile stretching my cheeks. It was an expression I'm sure he would never show in class. Something more casual, *cute* even.

I stifle a laugh and give him a slight nod, his own face softening with my grin.

He wipes away the dried blood and dirt around my legs, cleaning them with some disinfectant. His touch is slow, careful, and gentle to not hurt me. But concern pinches at his brows with each new mark and wound he discovers.

He takes my hands in his, cleaning the minor scratches around them, but his movements quickly freeze when he reaches my wrists.

Tension radiates from every pore on his body as he goes rigid. His eyes turn cold and hard with a darker look in them than when he first found me.

He gently pulls my cuffs up further, and I flinch.

I had forgotten about the rope marks and how raw my skin was from them. They appeared almost blistered now, with small parts of my skin peeling from the friction of forcing myself free.

I try to pull my hands away, but he takes them to gently cradle them in his own large hands. His fingers gently hover above the raw skin before his gaze turns up toward me. His forest green eyes turn a darker shade as he grits out, "*Who?*"

The anger in that one word sends a shiver rolling down my spine. He must notice because a moment later, he releases my hand, his chest slightly swelling and deflating as a look of conflict wars within his gaze. He turns back toward me with a look of almost desperation etched in them as he opens his mouth again, but I cut him off.

"I'll be fine. By tomorrow there won't even be a mark." His brows furrow with my words before quickly straightening out again. His stare falls to my wrists and feet again as I continue. "Everything will be okay–"

"No." His face hardens again as he shakes his head. "Whoever did this to you can't be let off." He leans into me again as his fingers gently brush along my wrists. The contact sends a small tingle down my back. "Anything...*anything* could have happened to you..."

The thought seems to take a little breath from his chest as his eyes close briefly before opening once again.

"I'll never go down without a fight. And I'll make sure they can never do this to me again." I meet his deep green eyes. "You may not want to hear this as a teacher..."

He gently takes my wrists and shifts his gaze to the forest beyond us. "With what I feel right now, I would do things a teacher shouldn't...and not regret them." He turns his gaze back to me and freezes.

I hadn't realised I had leaned in closer when he turned away, our faces now sitting just inches apart.

I feel the slight inhale of breath he takes as our eyes

meet; something quickly flits across his face before he twists away.

"I'll help." Before I can protest his words, he pulls himself away and stands. "I'll train you so that no one will ever be able to touch you, let alone hurt you like this again."

Gadriel wasn't kidding about the training. If I thought he was pushing me before, I was wrong. It was like he was in constant battle mode with endless sparring sessions, only stopping to eat or sleep.

He also stayed at the academy over the weekend, training with me all day and even having meals together. I think he might have been worried about the chance of another attack and was keeping an eye on me, too.

Truthfully, I enjoyed his company. There was more to him than just the *'Defence teacher'* or the *'Elven instructor from the Valor clan'*. And with each training session and meal, he showed me a new expression in the form of a small smile, a slight chuckle, or a soft gaze. Things I'd never thought I'd see on his face or directed towards me.

A small smile stretches my lips at remembering I have Defence class as my last lesson today.

I stroll through the corridor as more glares and whispers are directed my way. You would think they would get bored of this shit already, but it only seems to have gotten worse lately.

I meet each glare with a smile of my own, and by the change in their expression it's not a pleasant one. But I wouldn't be holding back anymore, even for those who just look or glower at me.

I head to the Music room after just finishing *World History* with Mr. Finch. He had been harping on about 'student conduct' and 'proper education', his narrowing gaze locking on me repeatedly in class.

Since Annex and Mallyn stopped showing up to his class last week, the ego-ridden fart seems to have a larger pep in his step and a boost to his annoying voice.

I walk into the classroom, a minor headache worsening as I go to my seat and take notice of silence falling from around half the room.

"No shame at all," one of the girls states to the back of the second-year seats, while another beside her stifles a laugh.

I stop, twisting back to the familiar voice holding their laughter. *Alice Parker.*

I narrow my eyes at the small black-haired girl and she flinches.

This little witch was one of my kidnappers.

I remembered every face from the flashes of memory I had and of those involved in my little kidnapping. I had resolved that each and every one of them would pay me a hefty price when they least expected it.

"W-what?" the petite witch stutters, her mock bravado failing her without her accomplices around.

A taller, sandy-haired girl places herself in front, covering the petite witch from my eyes and her own glare at me.

Her lips pursed together before curling upward. "So,

334 | ISLA DAVON

bullying your little sister isn't enough for you. Now you're trying to start on Alice?"

Alice tugs at the girl's sleeve, her eyes flicking between me and the tall girl beside her. "It's fine, Sylvia, I–"

"What's fine? Her throwing her weight around acting like she's something she's not?" A mocking scoff leaves her lips. "And all because she got a little bit of attention from guys who probably don't even know her name."

This again.

Her eyes trail down my front, a familiar look twisting her features as she mirrors so many others before her. "They could only ever want her for one thing anyway."

They were really put out by this, weren't they? That I spent time with their 'Infernal Four'. The guys must have a bigger reputation than I thought. Or did they just want their attention *that* bad?

When I don't immediately respond, she glares at me. All her anger and vitriol pull at her features as the rest of the class falls pin-drop quiet.

"You're an outcast for a reason. Someone so pathetic and weak with absolutely no magic shouldn't even be here. This academy isn't for you. You should slink back into the gutter and shadows where you belong." She raises her hand mockingly as if shooing some animal away before continuing on with her rant. "Know your place and be grateful that you are even allowed to attend classes here...And that's *only* because of your name. How *blessed* you are to be born a Bane and have family like Seria who tolerates you. But you..." Her lips curl upward, a look of pure disgust scrunching her brows before she shakes her head. "You're such a bitter, ungrateful bitch who doesn't know the grace she's been shown." A mocking laugh falls from her throat before she continues, "And now you're trying to bed the Infernal Four. Except they'll throw you away when they realise how *disgusting* you truly are."

All her words fade away as she keeps on her one-woman show with a single sentence replaying in my mind. *'The grace she's been shown'*...by who?

Who has shown me grace or even mercy here? Was it when I was attacked and almost assaulted by Dean and his group? Or the time I had to fight against Jeremy and Jake before defence class with the rest of the boys cheering them on?

Or was it when I woke up after being drugged and placed in a beast detainment shelter in the forest and left to die?

A strange noise escapes my lips, something low and dark and utterly unrecognisable to my ears flowing out. And then another follows until I realise, I'm laughing. The whole room turns to me, their faces and expressions questioning before either turning pale or shifting away completely.

"Why are you laughing–" Sylvia's words cut off, her features turning colourless with whatever expression she sees on me.

"Don't people usually laugh when they find something funny?" I take my seat and lean back in my chair, my gaze never leaving the stiff, sandy-haired *Sylvia.* "It's *so* funny how people think they know everything about me. Like they're the sword and hammer of justice ready to punish me for whatever they think I've done wrong." My gaze flicks to Alice, still standing beside Sylvia. She flinches again and takes a step back, her gaze falling to the floor. "You call me pathetic, weak and magicless, and then in the same breath say that I'm the big bad villain picking on her little sister." I scoff, "How does that even make sense? Especially for someone as *powerful* as Seria? Are you all blind or just that dumb?" I glance around the room, noticing some furrowed brows and questioning stares, though I ignore them all and continue.

"As for the Infernal Four, well...it's not worth my time or breath explaining it all to you. People like you don't use their heads anyway. You only listen to what you want to hear, to the sweet lies whispered and spread around for fun. You only follow along like cattle to the slaughter."

Sylvia's cheeks flush a bright red, her brows scrunched and her mouth opening, only I cut her off with a wave of my hand. "You *want* me to be the bad guy because then it makes all the shit you've done to me okay. But if I'm going to be treated like the bad guy..." I look around the room, meeting each set of eyes watching me, "I might as well become one."

And I mean it. No more of the pathetic or weak schoolgirl they've known. It's time they meet the new Micai and realise they shouldn't have fucked with her.

I give Alice one last look, a promise in my gaze of things yet to come for the part she played. A small tremor works its way into her hands as she gawks at me before I glance back toward Sylvia.

"Whatever." Her voice is low, almost whispered, as she shakes her head and moves a step back, bumping into Alice behind her. She takes her seat with Alice scurrying alongside her, their gazes unable to meet mine again.

I turn toward the board just as the door bursts open, and Seria, Knox, Xander, Kane, and Anders walk in, laughing and giggling. They soon freeze when they notice the hush of the room and the heavy atmosphere.

Their gazes flick around the room before falling on me.

Seria opens her mouth, "What's going on–" except she is soon interrupted by Mrs. Fleur scurrying into the class. They take their seats as she begins to talk about the next two singers for the class-based assignment.

"Micai Bane and George Harrison. You'll both be doing your solo songs today." She beams toward the class, utterly oblivious to the atmosphere.

Wait. She wants me to sing?

That isn't going to be happening, and not just because of the little showdown a moment ago.

I promised myself I wouldn't sing for anyone ever again. Only *him.*

My voice was *only* for him.

"Ms. Bane," Mrs. Fleur calls. "You're first and–"

"I won't be singing." I shake my head, ignoring everything and everyone else as I meet her furrowed gaze.

"Don't be silly, Ms. Bane. It's worth forty percent of your overall grade. You–"

"No," I cut her off, my tone much colder than intended.

She flinches before fixing herself hastily, shirking it

off as her regular smile turns into a frown, disappointment etched into her features.

"You could fail, Ms. Bane. Are you sure about this?"

I give her a curt nod but try to soften my hardened features. I didn't want to take my emotions out on the wrong person; she had nothing to do with the ache building in my chest or the lump in my throat trying to choke me.

"Fine." Her shoulders sag slightly as she bites her bottom lip, clearly seeing this isn't a battle she'll win right now. "But come to me after your next class to discuss this further." She gives me her best 'serious look', but it instead appears more comedic and like a child scolding another child. "I won't take no for an answer."

I nod again. I would just have to be very clear about my decision. I wouldn't sing for anyone, especially the people in this school.

She sighs and calls the next person up to sing.

I wasn't trying to be difficult, and I actually quite like her as a teacher. She isn't patronising or boring and doesn't seem to listen or care about the rumours going around.

As far as teaching went, other than being late and a little unorganised at times, she was quite good.

However, singing in front of other people, and specifically *these people*...I refuse.

It reminded me too much of *him* and of my past life. The time we spent together singing was ours, and ours alone.

He had taught me how to sing properly, how to pour every drop of pain and emotion I felt into each lyrical word. It was our escape, our freedom, and something just for him and me. It was our way of pulling through the more challenging days in The Facility together. It was how we would communicate with each other, escape to our own world away from it all, and be free...when we were anything but.

He was the reason I sang, the melody to my words, the soul and heart of my songs, and the reason I survived so long in that hell hole...My beautifully lost siren, *Zrael.*

CHAPTER THIRTY

$\mathcal{I}$ was on autopilot for the next class. Thankfully, Gadriel had kept it simple in his defence lesson with some light obstacle work and a quick jog.

However even in my dazed state, I could feel his gaze flicking towards me throughout the lesson. He wanted to talk to me when we finished, but I grabbed my stuff, rambled on about meeting Mrs. Fleur, and then headed quickly to her class.

I didn't want to talk to anyone, not with how I felt right now. And this wasn't a *'spill your emotions and feel better'* kind of feeling. Nothing could stop the ache seeking to consume me.

And I couldn't rid myself of the thoughts of Zrael. It had been a battle just getting through class. Every second seemed longer, every breath like it was catching in my throat. And as much as I struggled to push the memories down, they now seemed to be overflowing in me.

Wanting to pour out and drag every painful thought and emotion with them.

I had tried to keep busy and not think of him too much. Except reality has a cruel way of hitting you. It waits for just the right moment to strike and break you down when you least expect it.

I make it to the music room and look around the class. Mrs. Fleur wasn't here.

I had hoped she would be at least on time for this, though given her track record, I should have known better.

I just needed to make it clear to her that I wouldn't be singing and leave just as quickly as I came.

Right now, I needed my own space, to be able to bury myself in my blanket, and to allow what was trying to break out of me to flow naturally. I couldn't fight it any longer.

I take a deep breath, trying to steady the tremor working its way down my body, and look around the dimly lit room. It looked much bigger now that it was empty. The lights were off and the rays from the sun now gone as dusk quickly covered the skies.

I sit down on a chair near the window, my body sagging down a little further as the weight of the emotions I have been holding back all day slowly begins to seep through.

A cold chill from an open window at the back of the room fills the air as my eyes slowly close, a memory instantly hitting me: his gravelly, pained voice, my name on his lips, and then...*silence*. An unending and infinite silence that will haunt my dreams with an agony so searing and destructive it pierces my soul to its depths. It's followed by screams so unearthly and pain-ridden that it's hard to believe they're my own.

I'm pulled back through my memories and to *him*.

We met in The Facility. I say 'met' but we never actually saw each other.

I was placed in the cell next to his, with large old cement blocks separating us and a massive metal door holding us each prisoner.

It was after my first week and first *'test'* in The Facility and after all the tears and screams had left my throat and eyes raw, it I had finally fallen silent in my cell.

That's when I first heard him. A low hum that slowly rang out from the cement bricks behind me.

I limply sit against the cold grey wall after their first little 'test', my body bleeding and aching all over. Suddenly I hear a noise behind me, a low voice humming on the other side of the thick cement wall. It rings out around me in my cell as I sit listening to it.

With no contact or communication of any kind—other than the twisted guards here—it was strange to hear a voice other than my own around me.

But that's all I hear. There's no voice, no words, just a low melancholy humming that fades after a while.

A few days later, and after another 'test,' I hear it again. And then again, the day after that. It becomes consistent and I realise whoever it is would hum their sad melodies when I would return from another 'test'. It was almost as if they were trying to help me in some way. To soothe some of the pain I felt with their gentle humming.

It started as a light hum, but over time, it slowly grew into a low, soothing song.

When the first words flowed from his mouth, I felt my breath catch in my lungs, my heart picked up pace and something small pulled from the depths of tender emotions I thought I had very little of left.

I didn't even realise I was singing along with him until he had stopped. The voice that then called out to me was nothing like the beautiful, melodious one from when he sang. It was low and coarse and so fractured. And almost sounded like he was in pain trying to even speak.

"Ho...w? No...o not h...ere..." His words were rough and his voice so broken, it was hard to determine what he was saying.

What did he mean? Was he telling me not to sing?

It wasn't something I had intended on doing either. I don't even like singing, especially in front of others.

Or did he mean he wouldn't sing for me again?

A small ache works its way into my chest with the thought. His voice and light melancholy hums had been the only reprieve from this nightmare, from the months of torture, pain, and silence.

It was the only comfort in this dark and cold room that made me feel like I wasn't alone. That even with a wall between us, I had someone here to come back to.

"I...it won't happen again," I call to him, "I won't sing again, so please..." I didn't even know him, not even his name, and yet I felt almost desperate not to lose this small contact with him. "I won't—"

"No...N..oo!" he shouts, his voice like gravel as he raises it, sounding more pained than before as it cracks on the broken vowels. "Don..t st...op sing...ing. Beau...ti...ful."

Beautiful? He thought it was beautiful?

Was he joking?

I don't think I had ever been complimented on my voice before. Even when I had to sing in music class in the academy, my voice was low and feeble, and I'd always fumble the song's words. The rest of the class would laugh or whisper to each other. I hated every second of it.

"Z...rael..." he murmurs after a moment of silence.

"What?" I lean closer to the wall, trying to hear him better.

"My n...ame is Zrael."

"Zrael," I mumble, gazing at the cold grey wall before leaning closer to it. At least I knew his name.

"I'm Micai."

I hear a slight intake of breath and a slight shift in movement beyond the wall. I realise I have my ear pressed against it. I guess being starved of any proper human contact or conversation for months will do that to a person.

I can hear the rattling of keys and heavy footsteps at my door; the guards were probably coming for another 'testing' session. They were becoming increasingly frequent lately, each time pushing me that bit further.

They had also started bringing in strange-looking beasts for me to fight, trying to push me harder and almost to the brink of death. But I was learning, becoming faster and stronger.

But just as quickly as I grew, they halted it, shackling me with their metal cuffs and throwing me in here to heal at a snail's pace. They only ever allowed me to recover so much before another 'test' would take place. Never giving me enough time to properly heal and fight at my best.

But each 'session' would take more and more from me

mentally. I wondered just how long it would be until what was left finally shattered...

I'm pulled from my thoughts as the guard opens my door and calls for me to move.

I pull myself up and approach them when I suddenly hear banging from the wall next to me. Zrael.

He shouts as high as his broken voice allows, "No! L..eave her! T...ake me!"

The guard pushes me out and past Zrael's door, ignoring the yelling as he continues to bang on his walls and shout as loud as his broken voice will allow him.

Zrael's voice slowly fades in the distance as I head down the dark corridor and to one of the testing rooms, wondering what they have in store for me this time.

I wake up in my cell after another one of their 'tests'. In the last session, I had broken too many bones to stand without pain cutting through me and had lost enough blood on my cell's floor to fill a bucket.

They didn't care too much for prisoner hygiene here, throwing only a dirty bucket of water in to clean up the drying blood and an old rag for me to 'tidy up'.

Healing was a slow process with their shackles on me, and I wasn't quite sure how long I had been unconscious for or when they had placed me back in here.

If the meals thrown on the floor were anything to go by, then three days had passed while I was unconscious. The small buns they gave us had grown even harder, and green mould was already starting to form. Not that they had ever really been fresh to begin with.

I pull myself over toward the wall and to where I would hear Zrael best. It had become our little spot.

But there had been no humming since I woke up, and no songs.

It took me a while to conclude that he wasn't in his room. Then, a day passed with no return, and then another, and I quickly began to panic.

They usually don't hold us for testing for more than a day. What if they moved him somewhere else?

What if they had gotten annoyed with all his yelling and had decided to punish him?

What if one of their 'tests' were too much for him?

What if he's...gone.

Panic begins to spread through me, an ache building in my chest with the thought of losing him. My thoughts race to all the 'what if's'. Worry and fear were taking hold of me like a tightening vice.

Maybe it was because we shared a similar fate or a similar type of pain, but a connection formed between us, a bond that had slowly grown with each hummed note, each lyrical word, and each gravelly broken sentence. To me, he had become a balm to my battered soul, a small glimmer of light in this otherwise dark nightmare of a prison.

A shuffling noise rings out in the empty hall outside, then a couple of grunts and a heavy bang against the wall in Zrael's cell. It's followed by the sadistic laughter of a couple of the guards before they head back down the corridor.

I press myself flush against the wall separating me and Zrael, hoping and praying it's him.

I hear a faint, familiar, broken groan and some laboured breaths.

"Zrael?" I hoped he was okay, that whatever they did wasn't too bad. But who was I kidding? They didn't exactly hold back here.

A sharp pain splits my chest with a feeling of being completely helpless and useless, consuming me.

I call his name louder, but there are only more low-laboured breaths.

My panic begins to resurface, my voice sounding more desperate and frantic.

"Zrael? Are you okay? Please..." I hear slight movement. It's slow and light but gets closer until I can hear him against the other side of the wall.

His breathing sounds weak...and pained.

I rub my chest, and the helpless feeling cuts me there. I wish I could help him...What had they even done to him? Was it like what they put me through? A shudder runs down my body with the thought.

"I wish I could help you, or do something for you..." I shake my head, stopping before my voice cracks and shows him how weak I really am.

"Pl...ease..." His voice is so low I have to hold my breath as I place my ear against the wall to hear him.

"What can I do?" I say, placing my hands against the cold cement and wishing with all my might that it wasn't there so I could go to him. So that I could help him the way his songs had helped me through my pain.

"...ing.." His voice was so low, I struggled to make it out. It was almost like it could fade or disappear at any moment.

"What?" I ask, praying I could hear him more clearly.

"S..ing."

Sing? He wanted to sing? With the way he was right now?

And then I understood what he meant. He wanted me to sing. For him.

But my voice wasn't like his, and I hadn't had the best experience singing for others. Nobody even liked my voice.

"P..lea..se." A pained groan follows his broken words, his voice cracking more as his breathing becomes more strained. It pulls me from my insecure thoughts.

Even if I sounded horrible, if that's what he needed and wanted right now, then I could do it.

I close my eyes and take a deep breath before beginning. The first few words are a little shaky and low as I sing my favourite song, *Giants* by Dermot Kennedy, but gradually I grow in volume as I continue.

I can feel myself slightly swaying as I sing, pouring all the emotions into every word as I grow louder, not even recognizing the powerful voice echoing around the room as I reach the final line.

I'm panting slightly as silence stretches between the two rooms, with not even his laboured breathing heard.

I place a shaky hand back against the wall. "Zrael? Zrae—"

"Beau...tiful. So beau...t...iful...Mate." His voice is still broken and coarse but sounds less pained with his breathing steadier.

Wait. Did he call me 'Mate'?

He couldn't mean that kind of mate, right?

I mean, we hadn't even seen each other so how would he even know?

I had heard that different supernaturals had distinctive

ways of knowing if they were fated mates. Some involved scent or blood, but even then, it was so rare.

Had he meant as a friend or companion?

"Mate?" I call, "Do you mean like fri–"

"Fat..ed." He cuts me off, his voice slightly deeper, a more steady and sure tone with each syllable. "Your voi...ce. I ca...n te...ll. You..r my m...ate, Micai."

He says my name with such warmth and tender affection, and an unmistakable surety in his tone that leaves no room for compromise, even with his broken voice.

No words leave my lips as my mind tries to process his words. I try to think back to all the times we've talked and the strange and warm feeling that would well up inside me simply hearing his voice. Could it be possible?

...A mate.

A fated mate.

A bond stronger than any other in this world.

I twist back around to his voice, a smile stretching my lips before my shoulders quickly fall again; the elation leaves me as I stare at the grey cement bricks in front of me. And a weight of sadness blankets me.

Even though my soul wants to sing with joy at finding its other piece, I'm overtaken by the reality of our situation.

I have a mate. A piece of my soul probably just inches from where I sit...except we're stuck here. Trapped in this never-ending nightmare.

I can hear his voice and listen to him sing...but will I ever see him or be able to touch him?

My face falls into my hands as a sob begs to break free from my chest, but I try to hold it in. As much as I wanted to, I couldn't cry.

He would hear me, and I couldn't do that to him. He needed me now, and I had to be strong. Whatever I felt, I'm sure he did too.

We suffered enough in here. At the very least, when we were together, we could be each other's strength and comfort.

I lean the back of my head against the wall as silent tears stream down my cheeks.

A little hum begins to play from Zrael's cell, the tune flowing into my ears as I listen with a sad smile tilting my lips.

My mate and me. What did we ever do to deserve this?

Zrael slowly explained over the following days how he had known I was his mate. That from the first time I had sung along with him, he had known.

He told me he was a Siren, one of the very few of his kind left, and that they could find their mates through singing.

Over time, he told me how he had been brought here after a fight trying to protect a friend of his. He had been here around a year before I arrived, and that his voice hadn't always been so broken and hoarse. It was once like velvet. He made a small broken chuckling sound at this.

He said the only time his voice sounded 'normal' was when he sang because it was a Siren's voice, and their songs were laced with pure magic.

When I asked why I hadn't been entranced, he chuckled, telling me not all of his songs had to use powerful magic and that it was also different with a mate.

When I asked how his voice had become the way it was, he said it was what they did to him. They tried to exploit his ability and power, and it left him like this. He fell quiet after saying it, a heavy atmosphere falling over us both as I remembered my own sessions.

For almost five years, we sang to each other and talked about a place of our own together, far away from here. A dream away from all the pain and hell we lived each day in The Facility.

He pulled me through my darkest days. It was only with his *voice*, his *songs*, and his support that I lasted as long as I did here. He built up a strength in me I never knew I could have and showed me a love so pure and unconditional that I knew anything I felt before wasn't real love.

Our bond was stronger than anything I had ever felt...or ever would again.

That day...the day they took him from me...will be a memory and pain that will forever be etched into my soul.

The only sounds that day were my screams, my sobs, and my pleading with him not to leave me. They took a part of me away that will never be whole again without him.

My beautiful soul and lost siren. My Zrael.

I'm pulled from my memory and thoughts as an ache splits my chest, tears trickling down my cheeks as his voice calls my name.

How I managed to exist without him for almost a whole year after that, I don't know.

All I recall was my raw screams, trying to take out as many guards as I could when they came to me, and a lot of bloody fights.

Each day, I woke up cursing my existence, cursing The Facility, and wondering why death would keep eluding me. I wanted to join him and leave this hell. I didn't want to breathe another day in a world where he no longer existed.

But each time I came close, I would hear his broken voice in my head telling me to fight. And to live for him and the dream we had together.

I try to take a deep breath and pull myself back to the present, rubbing my palm against my chest and the pain promising to split me in half.

I had another chance.

In this life, I could do more than just get my revenge. I could find Zrael.

I don't know how or where to look, but I had time.

I would find him. And when I do, I'll never let him be taken from me again.

I take another breath, this one steadier, as I slowly calm myself.

I remember one of his favourite songs, the sweet melody forming into a hum before falling from my lips, words soon following.

I hear his voice singing in my ears, joining me as I close my eyes in the dark room, surrounded only by his memory and my echoing voice.

CHAPTER THIRTY-ONE

EZRA

*T*he lights flicker above me as I walk down the hallway, the silence a peaceful reprieve as I pass the empty classrooms and lockers.

All the other students had left as soon as their final classes ended, and the corridors were now void of any life or noise. *Thankfully.*

I drag a weary hand down my face. It had already been a tiring week, what with the attack on our operations out of town and some dumb lone shifter pack trying to take over our territory here. It was solved as it always is: a lot of broken bones and Annex bloodying up.

But it had been annoying nonetheless and an unwelcome trouble I didn't want to deal with right now.

We had been kept so busy that we couldn't even come to the academy or attend classes. Usually, I'd be happy to escape it all, but lately, it had been a bit different...a little fun even.

I push the unfamiliar thoughts away and head down

the dimly lit corridor, thinking back over the past few days.

A disturbance that should have taken a day or two to handle became more meddlesome, pulling our attention away for far too long. I could see it in Creed's face that something else was up.

I'll have to set my feelers out again tomorrow, slapping on my usual friendly facade and finding out what information I can relay back to Creed. His mind worked on a different level, seeing some bigger picture. It's one of the reasons why we always turn to him, the grumpy leader of our little group. Our *'Patronising Prince'*.

I chuckle when I remember Creed's face when Micai called him that. He wasn't happy, but he wasn't exactly angry either.

He didn't know it yet, but he was already warming up to the little sea star.

Another chuckle leaves my lips with the memory of her little scrunched nose and drawn brows when I gave her the nickname. It had left my lips before I could think, fitting more naturally to her the more I thought about it.

A sea star, something so soft and pretty in appearance but with a thicker skin to protect itself from others. A creature bright and beautiful but also strong and resilient.

There was something special about Micai. Something that kept drawing my attention back to wherever she was and always wondering what she would say or do next.

And she was also completely different from every other girl I'd met before.

She didn't look at me with glossy or dazed eyes or the

usual lust-filled look every girl and woman gives me when they see me. They want a taste of what they think I am; some Fae, Elf, or halfling...little do they know.

Their carnal gazes twisted my stomach into knots and made me feel like throwing up. Thankfully, it's something I've managed to master and hide behind the mask they see. But Micai, she doesn't look at me like that.

My brows pull downward...why *didn't* she want me like that?

Why was Micai any different? Why wasn't she lured in like all the others by my appearance? Why did my fake facade and sweet smile not work with her?

I pass by another empty classroom, the dark sky flooding in through the open windows as the first few stars begin to flicker and wake.

How had she been without us? She clearly wasn't well-liked in her class. *Or even in the years below her.*

People were never short of ill words or looks toward her, but all that was bullshit. She wasn't anything like what they made her out to be, and if anyone spent just five minutes with her, they would see that.

They were all fucking idiots.

I clench my fists with the thought. Something just didn't sit right with me about it all.

Why were so many people against her? Who was orchestrating all this aggression and isolation? And why?

I could read people better than most, and I could tell she was genuine. She didn't want anything from me and my brothers, and she might have even *enjoyed* our company, even Annex's.

A small smile stretches my lips with the thought of Annex.

He had been moaning all week about seeing his 'little Red'. Even covered from head to toe in blood, he would grin like some maniac saying, '*She would probably enjoy this too'.*

She would have to be as demented as him and the rest of us to be able to stomach our daily lives and darkness.

We all had demons.

Each of my brothers and I had our own special brand of dark. No one could manage even one of us, let alone all four.

A girl would have to have been made for us to be someone who could withstand the darkness that surrounded us. Someone made by the Gods and Fate themselves...*a Mate.*

A wistful smile stretches my lips. Was I still holding onto that hope? That one day I would find my own mate, the one being made for me.

I shake my head as a small sigh leaves my lips. It's just a young boy's dream; one told by their mother when they're small and naive and believe in fairy tales and true love. I, out of everyone, should know better.

A fated mate was almost as impossible as bringing someone back from the dead or travelling through time. It was a miracle in and of itself. And those blessed were so far and few between, with just a tiny handful in the supernatural world being gifted with one.

Who was I to think I would be blessed with such grace?

I turn the corner and head toward the music room.

I had heard some new unsavoury rumours about Micai while we were gone. They had been slowly dying down with our presence before we left, but I guess in our absence the assholes spreading shit got bolder. Annex would want to go on a killing spree if he heard this bullshit.

Even I was getting pissed.

I would have to find the source of these rumours soon and make whoever spread them unable to spew any more bullshit.

What did Micai ever do to deserve such crap?

From the little time I had already spent with her over the past month, I could tell she was the complete opposite of what everyone believed.

If she had a problem, she wouldn't bite you behind your back; she would call you out and face you head-on and have some cute, snappy retort to throw back at you for every one sentence you had for her.

She was a cute little pit bull, alright. One with bright blue eyes and plump, rosy lips that make you wanna lean in and see what they taste like.

I stop walking.

Did I just think that? I want Micai...like *that*?

I shake my head, my brows pinching together.

I had never wanted to kiss any of the girls around me before. It was always them making the first move, and I just went with it. But it had never crossed my mind to want to do it myself, not with anyone before, anyway.

Micai...she was different.

I'm pulled from my thoughts with the sound of music...no, a *voice*.

Someone was singing.

I take a step closer before freezing.

My feet are glued to the spot I stand on as a tremor works its way through my body and down to my very core.

A warm and tender feeling spreads in me, flowing through every vein and bone and filling me with it as it quickly consumes me whole. It takes even the air from my lungs as it moves.

A voice rings in my head, a feeling of surety joining it with a single word.

Mate.

A bond and connection intertwine and unravel within me, beckoning for the one whose voice floods my ears and calls to my soul. My breath comes back and catches in my throat, my heart racing faster than any adrenaline spike.

I take a step closer to the music room's unused back door. It's slightly ajar as I get closer. The voice inside the room rises higher, words flowing seamlessly in perfect rhythm to her song.

A song filled with so much love and pain, it pulls at something inside me, willing my own voice to join her and to soothe and embrace her with my own melody.

I stop myself before I pull the door open, trying to rein in the overwhelming feeling of running to the girl inside the room and holding her. *My fated mate.*

Who is she? Have we met before?

Is that why her voice sounded sort of familiar?

Except that voice...if I had heard such a beautiful and soulful voice like that before I would have remembered. You couldn't forget something like this. Something so mesmerising, so heart-wrenching, so captivating...I take another trembling step closer to the door, her voice luring me in before my movements still once again.

There, sitting across the room and singing that heart-breakingly beautiful song, is Micai.

My fated mate, the one made for me by Fate and the Gods themselves...was *Micai*.

A shaky breath falls from my stretched lips. I knew there was something about her, something different and special. I could already *feel* a connection with her...I just didn't want to admit it to myself.

I bite my bottom lip, trying to stop the laugh that wants to leave my lips, as an unexplainable emotion wells up from within me.

It was Micai. My little sea star was my mate and the other half of my soul.

I peer back at her dimly lit silhouette as her voice echoes around the room, seeping out to where I stand.

Should I wait until she finishes and then tell her? Should I explain to her what we are and what she means to me?

Would she even believe me? I mean, fated mates are really rare.

And how would she feel? Would she feel the bond on her end or...I push the thoughts from my head.

Thank god we got to know each other a little before this. Hopefully, she doesn't believe all those playboy rumours about me.

I ruffle my hair as a slither of panic slides over me thinking about all of them. And then the image of her at the fight hits me and I curse myself.

She saw me with those women.

It was just to get information for Creed, and we didn't do anything more than some light kissing, and I sure as hell didn't enjoy any of it, but...*Fuck*.

I'm not like that. It was just for work, and they meant nothing.

But what would Micai think?

I drag my hand through my now messy hair, giving it a pull.

I'll have to explain everything. I was never interested in any of the girls or women, none of them. It was always information collecting for Creed. *And that's done now.*

I'll tell her everything.

That no other girl ever made me feel anything. That there's only her, now and until our last breath together.

I look over at her; her hair is slightly swaying with the air flowing in from a nearby window. *Gods she was beautiful.*

Would she feel it too...the bond? She would have to eventually, right? Over time, at least.

I'll have to make sure I spend every minute I can with her.

Fuck, I wish I was a year younger, then we could have at least been in the same year. Maybe I could drop down a year? Failing a few classes could work.

I'm about to step into the room when I notice something that has me stopping again.

Tears.

The small, tiny droplets fall down her cheeks as she continues to sing.

And that's when I realise...this isn't just some song. She isn't just singing for the sake of it. This *meant* something.

I rub my chest, feeling the pain and emotion bleeding through with each word. The song was about love, but I could also feel...*loss*.

How could I have missed that? So blinded by my own happiness, I missed her misery.

My gut twists, my fingers twitching at my sides, wanting to reach for her. Except I pull them back.

She had lost something, or *someone,* and this was her way of dealing with the pain.

I take a slow step back. Now isn't the time to go in grinning from ear to ear and telling her we were meant for each other. She is in pain, and as much as my hands itch to reach out to her, to take her in my arms and tell her it will be okay...I can't.

Because I could feel it. That kind of loss wasn't something that I could kiss away. It would take time to heal, and only when she was ready could I help her.

Right now, she doesn't need me to be lost in blissful thoughts of us being mates or me trying to push my feelings on to her. She deserves more than that.

I watch on as the tiny clear droplets fall from her cheeks, her beautiful soulful voice trailing off and echoing around the large music room as her song comes to an end.

My mate has a deep pain inside her, one that needs time to heal. And time, I have plenty of. In fact, every moment from now was hers; every second to have and every day to decide what's next.

Suddenly, a clap rings out from the other door at the top of the class, pulling both of our attention.

Mrs. Fleur bursts into the room from the main classroom door, a huge, oblivious smile on her face as she approaches Micai.

Micai turns toward the window, wiping away her tears with her sleeve, and I clench my fists. There was nothing to be embarrassed about.

I shift my gaze to the woman making her way toward my mate. Couldn't that stupid teacher read the room? Micai couldn't even have this moment.

I narrow my eyes on the annoyingly ignorant woman beaming from ear to ear and talking so fast that I can barely make out her words.

'Beautiful voice' and *'Perfection'* are all I catch. But that's *obvious*. Anyone with ears would say the same.

Micai's voice could make an Angel weep and any Siren green with envy.

And she was mine.

A feeling wells up inside my chest with the thought.

I watch Micai as she grows a little flustered and I, in turn, become more angered at the presence of Mrs. Fleur.

I never had a problem with the music teacher before, although this was a different story. How could she be so blind? Clearly, anyone could see Micai was uncomfortable.

The overly enthusiastic teacher rambles on and Micai's anguished expression from earlier creases out. It's now overtaken with a slight look of annoyance; her cute brows are pulled down, and her plump, kissable lips are slightly pursed. It has a grin pulling at my cheeks.

She rolls her eyes when the teacher turns away and a small, relieved sigh leaves my lips. At least she doesn't look in pain anymore.

But I'll have to help her deal with whatever she's going through. Hopefully, over time, she'll open up to me more.

I take one last glance at her, ensuring her expression looks better, before turning around to leave.

There was a lot to do, and I'd have to make sure I sorted out as much as I could to get every minute possible with her from now on.

Those rumours would have to be dealt with first. I'll make sure no one even thinks a bad thought about her from now on, let alone spew any more shit.

And I know a certain deranged psycho who would be more than happy to help me with the clean-up.

I crack my knuckles and make my way down the dark corridors. Annex wasn't the only one who had a dark streak.

I wasn't afraid to get bloody, I just never had a reason. *Until now.*

It's time the people around here remember why I'm a part of The Infernal Four.

CHAPTER THIRTY-TWO

MICAI

I t was an exhausting evening spent talking with Mrs. Fleur, who wouldn't stop praising me and ranting about how I should show my 'gift' to others.

I declined, making it clear that I would never sing in front of anyone else. And that her hearing me wasn't something that I had planned.

After a lot of debate and disappointed looks, she eventually gave in. But she told me I should reconsider it in the future and that she would help me in any way I needed.

She also told me that she would take the song I sang as my class assessment and grade me on that while also heavily hinting that I would be getting full marks. *Not that any of that mattered.*

She kept me there until the curfew bell rang, a sad pout puckering her lips as she watched me pack up and leave and head to my dorm.

I sunk into my bed as soon as I got into my room. The

day's activities and memories had taken an emotional toll, draining me and sending me quickly to sleep.

The next thing I know, I'm being woken up by a knock at my door. It feels like I've only slept for a few moments, yet the annoyingly bright sun shining in through my window tells me otherwise.

The knock rings out again, and I roll over, pulling the blanket over my head.

I wasn't in the mood to deal with anyone today. And who would even knock at my door? No one and nothing good, I'm sure.

The knock rings out again, followed by a soft, angel-like voice.

"Micai, are you awake?" I go stiff, her sickly sweet voice sending goosebumps down my arms. "Micai?" Seria knocks again, her voice growing louder with my lack of reply.

What was so important that she came to me herself? What scheme was she planning now? After last night I didn't have the energy this morning to deal with her manipulative crap.

She knocks again, clearly determined to pester me until I answer her.

With her next knock, I sigh, pull myself out of bed, and make my way to my door. Pulling it open, she freezes, her hand mid-air and about to knock again.

Her eyes turn upward, her lips parting on a soft smile as she opens her mouth. "Micai, you're awak–" I yawn loudly, cutting her off. Her smile falters for the briefest of seconds before quickly reappearing again. "I'm glad you're okay. I heard about the rumours going around..."

She looks at me, searching my expression before she continues. Whatever she sees on my tired face must give her the answer she wants as a dark glint grows in her eyes. She shakes her head, her blonde hair fluttering side to side with the slight movement. "Some people can be unsavoury and say things they shouldn't. But it'll all die down soon. Just don't react or pay them any attention. We can't have it affect the Bane reputation." She glances my way as the words leave her lips, "We know the truth anyway."

Of course, that was what she was here for: to make sure I didn't react and to keep me weak and in check by using the family name. It was something I used to bend over backward for, but now...*the Bane's reputation?* Don't make me laugh.

I couldn't care if it went up in flames. I would happily pour the fuel and light the match to watch it burn even brighter.

"Can we talk?" She glances behind me, her eyes trying to peer into my tiny room as she steps closer.

I slam my hand into the doorpost, stopping her movements and blocking her way in.

"Let's talk here." If she thought I would let her take one step into my room, she had another thing coming. It was bad enough just being near her, let alone allowing her into my personal space and where I rest. I watch as her eyes widen a fraction before they meet my gaze. "It's messy and small. And there's nowhere for you to sit." I give her a small smile. But don't budge an inch as her mouth slightly opens before quickly closing.

She takes a small step back as her smile returns.

"Right. I did hear about your new room." She glances behind me again. "It may be a bit smaller, but the academy has limited spaces. It's just unfortunate what happened to your old one. I'm sure whoever did it will get what they deserve in time." *Oh, they will.*

A small smirk stretches my cheeks with the thought. Because I'm sure she was the one behind it, moving her little pawns to do her bidding like the puppeteer she is. And she most certainly will pay for it in this life. "But... there were some *other* rumours going around." She pauses for a brief moment before shaking her head. "They say you've been spending time with The Infernal Four. But anyone with sense knows who they are and not to mess with them. They're...unhinged. And even if they look the way they do..." A strange, glossy gaze takes over her eyes as the words leave her mouth, and a peculiar feeling slithers across my chest with the look.

She shakes her head again. "But they don't care about girls here or proper relationships. They don't want a girl-friend, just easy girls to..." She stops speaking, a fake look of worry taking over her expression as she glances back at me. She leans in closer, her voice lowered as she continues. "I don't want you being one of their many numbers. Bane's have more strength and self-respect than to throw themselves at boys just because they have some power or good looks." She reaches for my hand, taking it between her soft flesh as goosebumps make their way down my body. "As your sister, I wanted to warn you. They only want one thing, Micai, and it's not your company." Her eyes burrow into mine, trying to drill her unspoken words into my head. *'They don't want you.'*

A laugh wants to bubble up from inside me with her words. Her *'tender and concern-ridden'* words, ones laced with pure manipulation and condescension.

I hold my laughter back, wearing an unreadable expression as she awaits my reaction.

But she'll get none.

Two things I know she loathes the most are indifference to her words and being interrupted.

When I show no reaction or sign of responding, her smile becomes tight as a slight tick forms in her jaw.

She clears her throat and schools her stiff smile. "Well, let's put that aside for now and discuss something else." She takes another step back, her voice raising to its average volume as a grin splits her cheeks. "I planned a trip to a well-known boutique for the two of us. We'll spend some sister time together like we used to." She claps her hands in a seemingly playful manner as her smile widens. "And we'll help each other pick out our dresses for the Winter ball, too."

As soon as the words leave her mouth I'm reminded of this day and memory of my old life. Today was my eighteenth birthday. And Seria, like in my last life, had come in a similar fashion and woke me on this day. The conversation was a bit different back then, but it still ended with her inviting me out, saying she had *'planned a trip for us to choose our Winter ball dresses'.*

The naive younger me thought she remembered my birthday and was secretly planning something to celebrate. But instead, the day was spent catering to Seria's every whim and choosing dresses and accessories that would suit her for the ball.

At the end of the day, she picked out a dress for me, saying I would look beautiful in it. It was a fuchsia pink halter neck gown, one that seemed to mirror her blush pink dress in every way except for its absurdly bright colour. And stupidly, I had agreed. *And had played right into her hands.*

When the Winter ball was held, the dark glares and sneers I received for *'Trying to copy Seria'* were enough to make the younger me shrivel up and cry. It was a night filled solely with taunts, tears, and terrible memories.

Seria calls my name, pulling me from my memories. She turns around and starts to make her way toward the staircase, oblivious to my change in mood.

"So, throw on some clothes and meet me downstairs in a few minutes, and we'll head out." She places her foot on the step just as I call to her.

"I won't be going shopping, Seria."

She whips her head around, but before she can speak, I hold up my hand and continue. "I'm not going to the Winter ball, so I won't be needing a dress. But you enjoy yourself." *While you can.*

"But Micai, why would you not—"

"I'm not interested in going." I shrug, cutting her off and watching as her brows pull together.

She turns around fully and takes a step closer. "If it's because you don't have anyone to go with, I can help find someone that would be willing—"

"Like Adam?" I shake my head as her lips form into a straight line at the mention of his name. "I'm not interested."

370 | ISLA DAVON

"I didn't mean him; we're not even friends, Micai. I could–"

"I'm not going, but thanks for the offer anyway." I watch her eyes darken, her smile slightly falling at the constant interruptions and rejection.

"Now I need to get ready for class, so you should head off. You have an appointment to make, after all. *Enjoy.*" I turn around, ignoring her questions that follow, asking *'If I'm sure?'* as she tries to take another step closer. But before she can reach me, I close my door.

I hear her footsteps at the entrance of my room. They stand there for another minute or two before I hear her turn and walk away and head down the dormitory stairs. As if I would let her waste another minute of my time, let alone a whole day. *And my birthday at that.*

That was probably her plan all along last time: to make sure I didn't have a minute to do anything I wanted and spend it chasing after her instead.

And if I didn't go to the ball in this life, then I wouldn't have to deal with her bullshit or be surrounded by all those morons either. The night would be better spent training or maybe looking into a few unanswered questions I had.

I wash up and get dressed, and a few minutes later, I head toward the main academy building.

I forgo the cafeteria, not having much of an appetite after seeing Seria so early. It's never a good start to the day, dealing with bullshit and bad memories.

I head to the stairway and toward my first class. Even if it was my birthday, I would choose dealing with a grumpy teacher and a boring lecture over a day shopping with Seria. *Even the thought of her has goosebumps forming on my arms.*

Birthdays didn't mean anything to me anyway. It was the day I was born and the day my mother died...so I never celebrated it. I wasn't allowed to.

I try to shake the bad memories and mood Seria had put me in as I head to class.

I'm making my way up the stairs when I bump into something solid. A deep, familiar laugh rings out from the figure I've just bumped into as his large hands hold me up and stop me from falling back down the stairs.

"What's the rush, Red? Something chasing you or..." Annex's blue eyes curl upwards, "Were you looking for me?" A playful grin stretches his lips as another familiar voice joins him from behind.

"Why would she look for *you*?" Ezra throws an arm around Annex's shoulder as his gaze meets mine. "She could have been looking for me."

Ezra chuckles before giving me a wink. But his smile is different from the usual one he wears. And there's a strange look in his eyes, which seems warmer and more tender than before.

But maybe I was overthinking it.

"The fuck she was. Tell him, Red..." Annex flicks his gaze between Ezra and me, and he has an almost comical look on his face. "It was me, right?"

I hold back a chuckle as he narrows his eyes at Ezra, but there's no anger in his glare.

Then I notice flecks of red on his face. The small red splotches trail down his neck and continue onto his sleeves and arms. His knuckles are also dyed a pinky-red hue and there are small red marks on his trousers and covering the tops of his shoes.

My brows scrunch together.

"Were you fighting this morning?" Had he been in the fighting ring this early in the day? I guess I wouldn't put it past him. It was Annex we were talking about.

Or did some poor, unfortunate soul try to mess with him, not knowing who he was or how crazy he could be?

Ezra puts his hands in his pockets, his grin seeming sheepish. And there on *his* white shirt collar are red stains matching Annex's.

What had happened for even Ezra to get involved? He didn't seem like the type to fight without a good reason.

"Let's just say some dickheads got on my bad side and got what they deserved." Annex chuckles darkly, a sinister gleam in his eye as he remembers something.

"It's nothing for you to worry about, Micai. Where were you off to anyway?"

I could see Ezra was avoiding my question, though if he didn't want to draw attention to it, then they should clean themselves up better. But I wouldn't pry any further. Their business wasn't mine to know.

"I was just heading to class." I pull myself from Annex's hold and begin to make my way around them. Until a familiar large hand reaches out toward me, taking my hand in his. His piercing blue eyes meet mine as a playful grin traces his lips.

"On a day like this?" He shakes his head, his brown hair waving side to side with the movement. "Red, you can't go to shitty classes when the weather is *this* good."

I peer out the window nearest us. There was no rain

or heavy winds, and the skies were clearer than I've seen all week. I guess for a November day, it *was* quite good.

But why did that even matter?

"But–"

"No buts," Ezra adds as he slides beside me and takes my other hand in his. "We're taking you to town to have some fun."

"Hell yeah." Annex grins.

Fun. I guess it would be better than going to classes. And after this morning, I could use a break from the assholes in this academy, even if it was just for a few hours.

"I never really spent much time in town. Where are we going?" I flick my gaze between Annex and Ezra.

"Never?" Ezra's eyes widen slightly as Annex chuckles. "Was the Fight Night your first time?"

Annex's grin grows mischievous. "Guess I'll take this first from you too, Red."

"What first?" I ask, my brows pinching together with his dark cocky grin.

"The first of many firsts I'll take." The look he gives me is almost feral and has a strange heat prickling my cheeks. His eyes begin to slowly trail down my front before Ezra reaches to his side and slaps Annex on the back of his head.

Annex just grins as he rubs the spot. "Don't get it twisted, brother, I can share...a little."

Ezra rolls his eyes, a scoff leaving his lips before they both share a strange look. Something unspoken yet quickly accepted between them.

Annex turns his gaze back to me. "I'll need a check-list, Red. I wanna take em' all."

A checklist? For what? But before I can open my mouth to ask what he means, Ezra moves closer to me.

He fixes his hold on my hand, lacing our fingers together. His gaze meets mine, and that strange new look takes hold of me as he opens his mouth.

"I want in on that." A genuine smile stretches his cheeks, his turquoise eyes bright and alluring. "Count me in."

"So, what have you done?" Annex asks.

I really couldn't understand the way their minds work. But I presume they mean in town?

I shrug, "I guess I haven't done much. I mainly just stayed in the academy and trained or studied."

They look back and forth between each other, their grins becoming more wicked.

"That means we get the lot, right?" Annex's smile couldn't grow any bigger or darker. Except the matching grin Ezra wears is the most surprising as he nods a reply.

Maybe I should be a little worried?

CHAPTER THIRTY-THREE

ANNEX

*R*ed's eyes glimpse from shop to shop as we stroll down the small avenue in town.

She had seemed off earlier, like something was bothering her. Her eyes had been a little darker and drained, like she'd been dealing with something probably best left forgotten. Or for me and my nine-inch bowie and brass knuckles to deal with.

A grin pulls at my lips. *Later.* Right now, it was about spending time with Red and driving away any of those bad thoughts from that pretty, rosy-haired head of hers.

We'd hopped on a bus that runs by the academy once every hour or two and headed into town. I could already see her brightening up. All she needed was to escape that shitty academy and all those dumb fucks.

I walk behind her like a loose shadow, edging closer as she moves down the pathway.

Red had grown on me. And more than I ever thought any chick could. She seemed to crawl under my skin and carve out a place somewhere in me just for her. And fuck if some bigger part of me didn't love it.

I missed her this past week while we were gone, and even tried to sneak away from the boys to see her at night. But fucking *Mal* caught me and ratted me out to Creed.

I only wanted to watch her sleep for a few hours and get my little Red fix, but Creed said I was being more demented than usual. He kept harping on about her being an 'unknown' and a 'liability'.

But fuck was he wrong. Micai was special.

From the very first day we met, I knew she was different. From how she sat beside me to how she stared me down with those pretty blue eyes of hers...And the moment she leaned into my blade like the badass she was, I *knew* she would be one of us.

But these boys...they were my brothers not by blood but by choice, and our dark pain and blackened pasts brought us together.

They were always secretly worrying about the darkness inside them, about it spilling out and burning everything around them down.

Me, though? I couldn't care less.

I'd happily pull up a chair to watch the show. *And what a show it would be.*

Unfortunately, none of them wanted to reign down hell on the academy, or the world, just yet.

But none of us could have ever seen her coming—a girl who could weather our storms and stand beside us. And Red was the one.

Even if the rest of them didn't know it yet, I did. I knew it as much as I knew that pain was fleeting and that if I were cut down right now, I'd rise to kill again tomorrow.

I could tell every time I looked into her endless blue eyes that she had a darkness of her own buried deep inside her. It called to my own like a beacon.

She'd been through shit and made it out the other side, just like we did. She was one of us. Mal and Creed just didn't know it yet.

Ezra laughs, pulling me from my thoughts with whatever Red's said to him.

But that was another thing. *Ezra.*

His eyes are glued to Red like she's his salvation and the fresh breath of air he's always been looking for. The dopey expression on his face when she's not looking is almost *comical.*

Just last week, he was the same guarded asshole with the nice guy act. Always smiling yet never happy, and now...look at him. What had happened for him to change so much?

I narrow my eyes as I watch him try to get a few inches closer to her as they walk together. There's a strange expression on his face as he listens to her, a look he's never worn before with any other girl I've seen him with.

I shrug. Guess the why's or how's didn't matter anyway. He was another ally for the cause. *The one to make Red ours.*

And she will be; she just doesn't know it yet.

I make my way to the other side of her just as some dipshit starts in our direction. His eyes trail down Red as she talks to Ezra, who is oblivious to the asshole now ogling her.

Hope the dipshit enjoyed the view 'cause it'll be his last. His eyes wouldn't be the first I'd ripped from their sockets. *Or the last.*

As he nears, I shift in front of Red, fingering the blade in my back pocket.

He flinches when he notices me, his greasy smile falling and face paling as he freezes on the spot. Too late dickhead. You eyed the wrong girl.

She was *ours.*

Just as I move toward him, a small hand grabs me from behind.

"No blood and carnage today. Just fun, remember?" Red gives me a knowing look, a small grin tilting her perfectly plump, rosy lips. *So fucking biteable.*

"But what's *fun* without a little bit of blood?" I argue, glancing back at the asshat who looks like he wants to piss his pants.

"Another time," she says, her small grip tightening on my hand carrying my blade. I hadn't even realised I had taken it out.

The guy sees his chance and bolts. Just as I'm about to follow and take my tiny trophies, Red gives me a harder tug. Her cute little brow is raised with a knowing tilt to her lips. There's a look in her eyes telling me I'll pay if I don't listen. And *fuck,* if I didn't wanna see what she'd do to me if I didn't.

She gives me another hard tug, and I remember her tight little ass pushing back against me on my bike after the fight night. Her voice telling me to be quiet as the engine revved beneath us. I adjust my pants and the growing boner in them.

Red notices the movement and shakes her head, mumbling 'crazy' as she lets go of my hand. Except I can see the small blush creeping into her cheeks and the slight grin stretching her lips.

Ezra flicks his gaze to Red before turning toward me, his brows furrowing before he notices the tent pitching in my pants.

He rolls his eyes. "You need a minute?"

"I need a hand." I eye Red, her gaze meeting mine as I grin back. "Any volunteers?"

"Not into you like that, man." Ezra pats me on the shoulder before stepping beside Red.

"I prefer the small, soft kind anyway, not your rough, scaly fingers. How about it, Red? I mean, this *is* your fault. You should take a little responsibility, right?"

A light chuckle falls from her lips, the sounds sweet and seductive, and making my dick just that much harder. Her smile grows, stretching those blushing cheeks as she shakes her head. "I think you can handle it yourself."

"But where's the fun in that? I'll be thinking about you anyway, so–"

Ezra slaps the back of my head, cutting me off. "Watch it."

He has a cute little glare going on as I shrug and adjust myself.

I turn back to Red, but she's already making her way to the next shop. She moves quickly from one place to the next, never lingering for long. Her eyes constantly flicking back and forth to each shop as if she were a kid seeing new things for the first time.

Guess she really had spent too much time in that shitty academy, not having any fun. But I'm here now.

She walks over to a small little bakery near the corner. It has some sort of multi-layered cake in the front with long gold candles sticking out the top. Her eyes go a little dazed for just a split second before she snaps out of it.

"You want some cake, Micai?" Ezra calls, his brows drawn as he watches her expression shift. But she shakes her head.

"I'm good." She takes off toward the next shop, not even glancing back as she moves. Maybe she's hungry.

I swipe a fresh chocolate muffin from some douche's table. He opens his mouth and tries to stand up but sits straight back down when he sees my face. *Wimp.*

After several strides, I'm back with Red, handing her my gift.

Her brows scrunch cutely together as she takes it from my hand, "How?"

Her eyes glance at me and back at the shop before a small, soft smile appears on her lips. She takes a small bite, her eyes widening slightly with a tiny twinkle growing in them as she goes in for another bite. A tender look spreads on her face, a mix of awe and pure joy. *Fuck I needed to feed her more.*

If something so small could make her give me an expression like that, then I needed to rob the whole fucking bakery. And Ezra looks like he's thinking the same.

We spend the next few minutes window shopping

with Red only ever stopping for a minute or two before moving on. That is until we reach a small dress shop.

Her little blue eyes gaze at a silky teal number on the mannequin in the window. And fuck would she look *edible* in that. It'd cling to every delicious curve she had, and with such a thin slip of fabric, it would be so easy to–

"Do you want to go in?" Ezra asks, cutting off my train of thought and growing semi. But he was probably thinking something similar from the heated look in his eyes.

Red shakes her head before turning away, glancing back at the window only once before she quickly moves on.

Ezra quickly claims her right side as we make our way over to her and head to the next place.

We head onto a couple more shops, talking and joking until we reach a small metal trinket shop. It's got odd, fancy metal pieces hanging in its window and has captured Red's full attention. We stroll in, looking at all the large and small metal decorations and ornaments. They have a lot of different shit here; some look old, while others seem brand new. Yet everything was made from various types of metal.

I wonder if they have any blades.

Red and Ezra head over to the jewellery as I find the old weapons section. Or the *'Antiques'* as Ezra pointed out. But even being old, these blades looked like they could slice into flesh and bone with ease. Looks like I'll be adding to my collection today.

Flipping a bronze dagger between my fingers, I glance

back at Ezra as he tries his best to talk Red into letting him buy her something. But she flat-out refuses.

My brows pull down, something slithering at the back of my mind from the expression on her face as I try to place it. There was a strange look in her eyes, something that went beyond stubbornness or someone being guarded...but what? And why did it have me clenching my fists and feeling so angry?

What did my little Red have to face to make her so unwilling to receive anything from others? And for her to be so happy with something as tiny as a robbed muffin?

I know she's like us; she has her own pain...but how deep does it run?

Has someone hurt her? The thought has me instantly clenching my fists harder, the force of it drawing blood as it drips down my fingers and creates a trail to the path below.

No. I shake my head. She couldn't smile so beautifully every day and be as strong as she is if she had suffered like that.

Me and my brothers were different. We only survived our pain because we had each other and even then, we're still broken. Our cracks show.

Whereas someone like Red, if she had suffered anything like that and alone...a heavy breath leaves my chest as I rub the spot there, a strange feeling making its way beneath my hand as I look toward her.

If anyone *had* hurt her–even so much as a papercut–I would gut the fucker.

I'd rip the flesh from their bones and burn them alive. And then rinse and repeat that shit every day until there was nothing left. Not even a speck of dust would survive what I'd do.

Red was one of us now, and no one gets to hurt her.

She was mine, ours, and she deserved the world. Every blade, every diamond, and every chocolate muffin.

My woman wouldn't just eat crumbs, she would have the whole fucking cake and everyone else's too. If I had to threaten, rob, and maim, I would.

What's life without a bit of fun anyway?

I watch as Ezra tries to talk her around again, but she just shakes her head.

My Red didn't know how to treat herself. Guess that was our job from now on, and making her smile would be our number one priority.

I notice my brother's frustration and give him a nod before making my way over to the shop owner.

Apparently, they do custom metalwork here and I've got something perfect in mind for Red. Something with a bit of me and Ezra written all over it. That way, anyone who saw it knows she's taken.

And *ours*.

Micai's POV

It starts to get dark as we make our way out of the small metal trinket shop called *Ellies*. Such a strange name for a shop that sold metalwork—but maybe it was a family name?

Either way, the metalwork, antique weapons, and jewellery were beautiful. So many pieces caught my eye, and I think we spent a good part of an hour just browsing through them all.

I peer up just as the streetlights flicker on. Maybe it was time to head back? Classes would also be over by now, and the frustration from this morning and the weight of last night had already been eased. Just as I'm about to say as much, Ezra grabs my hand and pulls me hurriedly across the road. There's a grin so wide and full of genuine glee on his face that I forget what I was about to say.

We stop in front of an old building at the end of the avenue, further away from all the other shops. This building looks older and more run-down than any of the others in town. *Well, other than the boy's slaughterhouse.*

The once dark green paint on its walls is chipped and falling off, and all its windows are boarded up with planks of thick brown wood. A faded sign sits above us with dull pink painted letters making out the words 'The Roller-Room' behind broken neon light bulbs.

This place couldn't possibly still be in business being in this state. So why were we here?

Ezra whips out a set of keys and opens the large rusty doors in front of us. Before I can open my mouth, he gently takes my hand in his again and tugs me inside as Annex follows closely behind us.

The place is completely empty inside and exactly what you would imagine an abandoned roller rink from the 1980s to look like.

Ezra gives my hand a small squeeze and grins before letting me go and heading to a booth across the room. After a couple of minutes—and the sound of him tinkering with something–the lights around the room come on, giving us a better view of the space around us.

I make my way further in and notice the enormous roller rink covering two-thirds of the room. Its red flooring is discoloured with three large, pale black stars printed through its middle. To one side of the rink are a couple of large booths with large stereos or racks of dusty rollerblades. And to the far right are some benches, some old arcade games, and a small kiosk-like stall that seemed like it once held sweets or hot food.

The largest booth–where Ezra went—is at the very back of the room. It has large, brightly coloured lights above it and two huge speakers at each end.

I look around the vast space and the large roller rink just as the music starts to play around the room. Colourful strobe lights begin to come to life and flash above the rink to the rhythm of the song that's playing, giving the whole room a different atmosphere.

Ezra makes his way back to us with a massive grin on his lips, carrying a bundle of rollerblades in his hands.

"What is this shit?" Annex laughs as he grabs a pair of skates and points to the large speakers around the room.

"It has all 80s tracks." Ezra shrugs. "And I love a bit of Toto."

Ezra chuckles as the song "Africa" plays around us before handing me a pair of old rollerblades. Taking the white and purple shoes from him, my mind goes blank.

Did they actually want me to skate?

I probably should have put two and two together, being in a roller rink and all, but I had never even put *on* a pair of rollerblades before, let alone *moved* in them.

They must notice my hesitation as we make our way over to a bench to put on our skates.

"Don't tell me you've never skated before?" Grins Annex as he throws on his red and white rollerblades with ease. Great, something else for the crazy asshole to poke at.

Ezra drops to his knees in front of me, a softer smile on his face as he holds up the rollerblades. "Don't worry, Micai. If you haven't, it's not a problem. I can always teach you." He leans in closer, his voice a little lower. "And I would never let you fall or get hurt. I promise." The look he gives me seems so serious and resolute, combined with a slightly sharper expression like he would never allow such a thing to happen. It has a small grin pulling at my cheeks, and with that, his expression softens again.

I give the skates he's holding another weary look. Would I even be able to stand properly in those things?

He raises a brow, a smirk tilting his lips as he shakes the skates. "I didn't take you for the type who gives up easily though, little sea star."

"Nah, definitely not." Annex grins as he laces his skates. "Hurry up, Red. I wanna see how you look when you fall on that perfectly plump ass."

I could see what they were doing: trying to appeal to my stubborn and competitive nature or using reverse psychology to motivate me to push past whatever block I had.

And as much as I hate to admit it–with Annex's smug grin and Ezra's eyes full of challenge–it was working.

I also didn't want to give up without even trying. *Who knows, I might even be good at it.*

I throw on the skates and take my school blazer off, chucking it on top of the bench.

Annex is already on the rink, and Ezra is waiting for me by the entrance.

I take a deep breath. I could do this. It was just one foot after the other, right? It couldn't be that hard.

I was wrong.

Ezra's hands wrap around me, catching me as I fall forward, my legs wanting to go in opposite directions.

Annex comes speeding toward me from the opposite side of the rink like some seasoned professional, his chuckle echoing throughout the rink.

"Didn't know I was watching a rerun of Bambi." His laugh grows louder with whatever annoyed expression he sees on my face.

"It's her first time, dickhead," Ezra calls, as he steadies me.

He turns me around, placing himself behind me with his hands gently gripping my hips. "Take your time. I'll move when you're ready, and we'll go slow."

His breath brushes across my neck, the deep, rich tones of his voice ringing in my ear as he leans in closer. I feel a slight blush creep into my cheeks as his hands shift on my hips, with a strange heat spreading wherever his fingertips graze.

My chest feels strange; my heart drumming a new rhythm of its own the longer we stand here together. Was Ezra always this tall? Were his hands always this big and steady?

"Micai?" he says, snapping me out of my thoughts.

"Yeah? Right..." I shake my head, trying to shove the strange thoughts away. "So, what do I do?"

"Push one foot forward at a time and just take it slow. Move your hips slightly as you move, and don't worry..." He gives my hips a small squeeze, and the smouldering heat from earlier flares up, sliding lower down my back before unfurling in my lower abdomen. "I'm right here with you."

His voice only adds to the heat twisting and curling within me as he leans in closer, his scent instantly hitting me and wrapping itself around me, like lavender and sweet honey. I lean back toward him, his scent pulling me closer and wanting to feel more, wanting a small taste... until Annex races by breaking me out of whatever strange trance I was falling into.

I feel my cheeks flame and my breath catch as I try to rationalise what is happening to me. What is all this?

Why am I behaving like this around Ezra? We're just friends, right? And we haven't even known each other for that long either...What is happening here?

I wasn't naive or stupid. I knew how my body was reacting, what it wanted...but from Ezra?

I mean, *clearly,* Ezra is attractive. Was that all this was?

Then what about Annex?

I watch as the tall smirking asshole in question passes me again, his dark brown hair swaying as he glides back and forth the rink with ease. The muscles in his arms flex as he waves to us while skating, moving the dark tattoos covering every inch of visible skin on his biceps.

The heat in my cheeks flames as I remember them

wrapped around my waist on his motorbike, with the feel of each muscle and ab flush against me...with something even *harder* poking lower into my back.

I continue watching him as he does another lap around the rink. And even with the smug, shit-eating grin he is wearing, there is no denying my physical reaction. *From either of them.*

There is no denying that Annex and Ezra are attractive. I'd have to be blind and deaf not to be swayed by their looks or the deep and smouldering voices they have.

It was obvious why 'The Infernal Four' were famous and why people tried to flock to them. Their power and strength weren't the only thing. Their looks were what had even the most terrified of students sneaking double glances. They were all...breath-taking.

But how could I feel this way about them? I had Zrael. He was my mate. I couldn't...

I know that it's normal in our world to take multiple male partners, though I'd never even had *one* before Zrael. And Zrael and I weren't physical in any way. Our love was soul-deep. All I ever needed before was him; he was the one who helped me survive, who pulled me through everything, and who showed me what unconditional love was...So why?

Why was I reacting like this to Annex and Ezra?

I shake my head. No, I had to be wrong.

Maybe it was because Annex and Ezra were around me a lot these days and treated me like they actually *liked* being with me. It was just because they were affectionate and attentive; something I wasn't used to.

It was also probably because it had been so long since I had someone touch me in any kind of way; all of my sexual experiences were quick and lacklustre as well. They never had any kind of emotion involved, and foreplay was an afterthought or not a thought at all.

Annex and Ezra were very touchy. It was normal for them to act this way. I was just overthinking it.

I push the thoughts away and focus on the task before me.

Ezra calls my name again, and we start to move slowly together. I stumble here and there as we make our way around the rink, but I soon start to get the hang of it with Ezra at my back keeping me steady.

I get into my own rhythm, swaying to the music as I make my way around the rink. I feel Ezra drop his hands from me as I pick up speed, enjoying the quicker pace now.

I'm swaying with the song "Like a Prayer" by Madonna and enjoying the rhythm as I move with it, when suddenly Ezra comes up beside me. He takes my hand in his and gently spins us around together.

We're both laughing as Annex comes up behind me and whispers in a low, husky voice. "You *do* know this song is about giving a blow job, right, Red?"

I twist around too quickly and almost fall again. But two sets of hands reach for me, landing on my waist and hips, steadying me.

Pulling myself up straighter, I'm met with two hooded blue eyes to my front and Ezra's turquoise and lilac pair behind me.

A beat passes between us, and neither of us moves

away or laughs at the moment we seem to be having. Instead, their gazes intensify even more.

A quick look flickers between Annex and Ezra before the hands on my waist gently slide down my sides and the pair on my hips tighten. Both bodies lean further into me, caging me in between them as the heat from earlier begins to unfurl again within me.

Ezra's lips brush across my neck from behind as he leans in closer. A tremor works down my neck and back with the minor contact. His large hands then slowly slide back up my waist, his fingertips spanning out and grazing against the bottom of my breasts as they move. I feel my heart rate pick up with each slight movement and my breath coming out in quick little rasps as his body becomes flush against mine from behind. Every inch of him leans further into me as something large and thick grows harder against me.

A deep, husky chuckle falls from Annex's plump lips, pulling my attention back to him. But there's no humour in his gaze, only a dark heated look. One so wicked and sinful it has me clenching my thighs and trying to stop the ache quickly growing there.

He pulls his bottom lip into his mouth, my eyes glued to the movement before he bends down closer to me with his face just a couple of inches from mine. His breath skips across my face as his lips lower slowly toward mine, his grip growing bruising on my hips.

"*Red...*" He says my name so softly, it almost sounds like a prayer leaving his lips. His mouth inches closer toward mine as his eyes watch me, the piercing blue of his irises turning into a darker hue with a hunger growing in them that makes a shiver run up my spine.

I'm lost, my mind in a daze, and my heart beating out of my chest as I feel each graze and trail of both their hands and each hard dip and curve of their bodies against mine as they lock me between them.

Each touch and heated look stirs something new inside me, almost burning me in their wake and leaving me wanting more of them—of their hands and bodies against me and on me and of their lips. My gaze flits to Annex's plump lips...I lean in closer as desire and instinct take over, my lips gently meeting Annex's in a kiss I'm sure will burn me from the inside out.

But just as our lips meet a bang echo's out around the room and startles us. We turn around to find Creed standing on the other side of the rink. His eyes are narrowed in a cutting stare toward us. *Mainly me.*

And like an ice bath, the hard glare wakes me from whatever heated dreamworld I was in. I quickly pull myself from Ezra and Annex's embrace, my body already missing the warmth from the both of them as I move away.

Except it was for the best.

What had I been thinking? What were Annex and Ezra to me?

I guess it was something I needed to think more about from now on.

I look back as Ezra sighs, an annoyed look coating his expression as he peers over at Creed. Annex grumbles something about *'killjoy'* while openly glaring at Creed.

I slowly skate toward the rink entrance, where Creed

stands, looking like a bull seeing red. Then, I quickly change back into my shoes. Annex and Ezra skate over and whisper with Creed in hushed tones.

I'm about to get up and head back to the academy when Ezra steps in front of me with his hand out to help me up.

"I'll put them back." He takes the skates from me. "And we'll head back together, okay?"

"No," Creed barks. "You're needed here. She can make her own way back."

His glare is more cutting than usual, with something darker swirling in his eyes as he stares at me.

Ezra stands in front of me, blocking my view of Creed.

"There's no '*No*', Creed. I'm taking her back myself." Ezra's voice drops lower, a harder grit to his tone as he continues. "And don't look at her like that. She doesn't deserve your anger."

Annex's eyes widen before curving upward, a small smirk lacing his lips as he nods his head and takes his place beside Ezra.

I can't see Creed's face from behind Ezra and Annex, though I can hear the hostility in his tone.

"You're serious...both of you? For *her*?" He scoffs. "You don't even *know* her." A beat of silence falls between them. "Have you both lost your minds?" His voice is steely, a harder edge to his tone as they continue their standoff.

"It's been gone a long time, Brother." Annex shrugs, grinning playfully as Ezra lightly chuckles.

"...*Fucking stupid*." I hear another bang as the bench beside us falls over.

"Be quick," Creed growls, his voice rougher than I've ever heard before. "We have enough to do without adding this shit to the list."

Annex shakes his head. "Not shit, Brother." His hand reaches toward what I can assume is Creed. "You'll understand soon enough."

"The fuck I will," he grits out before I hear a shuffle and some footsteps followed by a door slamming.

"Don't mind him, Micai," Ezra sighs as he changes into his shoes. "Creed can be a bit rough around the edges. And it takes a bit longer for him to trust people."

"Also, sometimes he's just a stubborn *dick*," Annex adds as he pulls me up, already ready to go as he slings his arm around my shoulder.

"Let's head back, it's getting cold here," Ezra calls as he glances around the rink.

"It's fine, Ez. I'll keep Red warm." Annex tugs me closer, a wicked smirk growing on his lips. "I have *many* ways to heat her up."

Ezra's hand reaches out toward Annex's head to smack him, but he catches it.

A smug smirk stretches his lips. "Thought you had me, bro, but–"

Ezra's other hand whips out at Annex, his fist connecting with his side.

"*Fuck*." Annex bends over, slightly winded for a moment before a grin stretches his cheeks. *The demented ass.*

I spin to Ezra, my mouth slightly open from surprise. I didn't think he would be that strong. But maybe that was an unfair judgement. He *was* a part of their 'Infernal Four' as well.

My gaze flicks between them but there's not an ounce of anger or annoyance in their gazes to one another.

"I've always got you, Brother." Ezra places himself on my other side, wrapping a hand gently around my waist.

Annex straightens up, his arm reappearing around my shoulder as he nods slightly to Ezra. They both look down at me, now sitting in between them.

"Let's get you back before you get eaten, Red."

"Eaten?" My gaze flicks back and forth between them as they chuckle.

Heat creeps up my neck with their words, the memory from moments ago, of their hands on me, their bodies pushing closer into mine and Annex's lips...I shake my head and heated thoughts away as we leave the Roller-Room.

We head toward the bus stop just as the last bus arrives. Ezra takes the seat beside me, and Annex takes the one in front, as I watch the scenery from the window.

There's a gentle and comfortable silence that sits between the three of us as I watch the town's shops fade into the distance. And then follow the winding grey roads that turn into dark green forests as we head back up toward the familiar grey bricks of the academy.

They walk me to my dorm, chatting and laughing playfully, and wait until they see my room's light flick on before leaving.

And as I lay down to sleep, a single thought crosses my mind...*It was a much better birthday this time around.*

CHAPTER THIRTY-FOUR

*I*t's been a week and a half since my little day trip with Annex and Ezra.

Gadriel had come to find me and see how I was the night after his Defence class, and when I wasn't around, he thought something bad had happened again.

The following morning, he found me leaving the girls' dorm. His expression was filled with worry before quickly turning to relief at my appearance.

I told him I went into town because I needed some time away from the academy. Thankfully, I think he understood because he didn't push for more answers, only asking that I tell him next time, so he doesn't have to scour the forest for me.

After that, we spent every other night training together in the old training building.

We had moved on from daggers and swords to spears, and I think I mastered most of them after ten days.

Gadriel seemed impressed with my ability to grasp and master techniques and new skills so naturally.

But even *I* was surprised by my quick learning pace and adaptability.

Was this a new ability in itself and connected to all my other new skills?

I know I have a good memory and have adapted quite well, but this...this was something else entirely.

I make my way through the academy corridors, which are now fully lined with decorations in preparation for the Winter Ball. The hallways are covered with large crystal snowflakes and icicles hanging from the ceiling. The windows shimmer with what looks to be some pearlescent magic, giving the illusion of an opulent snow scene outside them. The walls were coated in hues of iridescent whites and blues matching the wintery snow theme. And large holographic-looking posters float neatly between the crystal decorations. 'Winter Ball' is spelt out with a magical shimmering countdown sitting at two days beneath it, with the words *This Friday* below that.

I pass the groups of students near the posters, laughing and talking about their dresses and partners. One benefit for me with all this Winter Ball stuff happening is that everyone has been too preoccupied with it to annoy me. In fact, they didn't even glance my way these days and even gave me a wide berth in classes *and* the cafeteria.

I also hadn't been getting any hassle from the usual dickhead shifters and warlocks who liked to harass me. Apparently, they hadn't been showing up to their classes or even been seen around the academy either. *Not that I cared.*

Annex and Ezra were back and kept me preoccupied most days. We ate together and hung out between classes, and Mallyn and Creed even joined us in eating and talking. I guess whatever business they had that kept them away had been dealt with.

A couple of girls giggle across the classroom, lost in their conversation, as I make my way in and take my seat. I usually enjoy and pay attention in the *Dark Beasts and Creatures class*. However, Mr. Heinley was absent, so it became self-study, allowing the rest of the students in the room to chat and giggle away about the upcoming Ball.

A light blush creeps into the girl's cheeks as two boys chuckle beside her, one wrapping his arms around her and the other taking her hand. They were probably her dates for the Ball.

The thought has my mind wandering to the guys. Were they going to the Ball?

They hadn't mentioned anything, and I hadn't seen them with anyone.

Did Ezra and Annex have dates, or would they go with the same girl? The thought has my stomach slightly twisting with the image of another girl between them...I shake my head.

Why did it bother me so much?

What even were we? Friends? Classmates?

I don't know...but they weren't mine. We weren't together like that...*So why did I care?*

After a very slow hour of contemplation, the class bell rings, signalling the end of my only class today.

The '*Modern Calculus and Geometry*' lecture had been

cancelled due to Mr. Aldeir helping with the Ball's preparation.

I walk out into the hallway, thinking I should go outside and get some fresh air to try and ease the knots twisting my stomach, and smack straight into something hard. A low grunt huffs out above me as I steady myself.

"*Micai.*" My name falls from her sickly-sweet voice and instantly has me wincing, almost like I was just hit.

"Are you okay?" Seria stands beside Xander, her hand on his arm as he glares down toward me.

So that's what I smacked into. This stupid asshole. I instantly wish I had knocked the dickhead down.

"What's with the stop?" Anders calls as he comes to Seria's side, his smile falling a little as our eyes meet. Knox and Kane are next to appear, both surprised by my appearance. *Unfortunately,* we go to the same school and share a few classes.

Morons.

I shake the hit and the contact off like a bug bite. I'm about to leave when a hand snakes out, grabbing me.

"I wanted to talk to you, Micai." Seria takes a step closer to me, a small frown tilting her small pink lips. "I know you've been a bit distant lately...I just hope it wasn't because of the talk we had before. I only want what's best for you." Her hand drops from my arm, her eyes slightly sorrowful as she watches me. And I wonder what she's plotting now.

Xander wraps his hand around her shoulder.

"What talk?" he asks her, his voice soft and gaze gentle, before turning to me with a cold tone and stony glare. "What did you say?"

Always Seria's knight in shining dickhead. How did I ever like such a pathetic moron? One so blind, with no sense of his own?

"Xander, Seria never said Micai did anything–" Knox states, stepping beside him and slightly between us.

"She doesn't need to. Just look at her." He glances back at Seria before turning his glare back at me. "And either way, we all know what Micai is like–"

"Do you?" I cut the dickhead off, his voice already grating on my ears as a headache begins to form. I wasn't in the mood for their bullshit today. And how did he think he knew anything about me? He didn't know shit, and I was tired of him acting like he did.

"What do you know, Xander? I would love to hear it." I look directly into his narrowed eyes. "Because last time I checked, we hadn't shared more than a couple of words with your ass glaring at me and being an asshole for gods knows what. But..." I shrug as Seria calls my name, trying to get my attention. I ignore her and continue. "I don't care anymore. All this bullshit going around that I want you all." I meet each set of eyes as a humourless chuckle falls from my lips. "I have better taste these days. I don't need someone else's leftovers."

"Micai, we–" Knox starts, but I cut him off.

"It's funny that you think I'd pine over you like some love-lost girl. Do you honestly think I'm the same girl you abandoned all those years ago?"

Anders' brows knit together while Kane's face wears a deeper scowl than usual. Knox opens his mouth trying to take a step towards me, but Seria cuts him off, stepping closer to me and blocking their view.

"Micai, you need to—" Seria says, a strange dark twinkle in her eyes as she tries to reach for me. Only I ignore it and dodge her hand making her stumble forward in the process.

Xander jumps forward and catches her before she reaches the floor, his face hardening as her hand clutches onto him.

His glare turns dark with pure venom. "Exactly the same as all those years ago." He spits out between gritted teeth. "Always trying to hurt Seria. Your jealousy and manipulation know no bounds. Even when she tries so hard for you, you still treat her like shit. You don't deserve her love..." His face contorts, his lip curling upward as Anders calls beside him.

"Hey Xander, you—"

"Don't—" Knox calls, trying to position himself in front of me, but Xander pushes him to the side and into Kane.

"No one could ever love someone like you. We were lucky to get away from you back then. You're nothing but a—"

A hand flies from the side, catching Xander straight in the face.

He's frozen for a second as Morgan passes him and places herself in front of me.

"You kiss your mother with that disgusting mouth? She'd have to bleach her cheeks from all the shit stains if you did." Her two large partners flank her on both sides, covering my view completely of Xander and company as she continues. "I knew you were stupid, but who knew you were so vile?"

"Morgan," Seria says, "Xander was just defending me–"

"From what?" Morgan snaps, and they all fall silent.

"What happened for you to need to be saved?" She laughs darkly as she meets each frozen stare. "What? From a little fall?" She scoffs. "Fuck, you're *precious*. How is your two left feet her fault?" Her head whips back to Xander. "Is she so precious that you become a witless dickhead with no eyes or ears?" There's no room for compromise with her tone, her voice cutting and cold as she continues. "Only a sloppy tongue wagging at the wrong one."

Her head turns back to me, her amber eyes narrowed. "Want me to get the other side?" She hitches her thumb toward Xander, a small red mark appearing on his left cheek as she points to the right.

I meet his gaze, surprise etched across his features as he watches Morgan and her two partners.

"No," I reply as his eyes flick to me, "he's not worth it..."

"Micai," Seria calls. "You know Xander didn't mean it, he just thought–"

"None of them are worth it." I step around Morgan's partners, their focus entirely on the boys and Seria, as I place myself between Morgan and Xander.

His words struck a chord in me, finalising and severing the friendship we had in the past, or whatever scrap of it was left in me.

There was no space for them or the memories we used to share anymore. They made their choice in my past life and in this one, too.

I glance at Morgan. I was treated better by a stranger I had met only a couple of times, than them.

Like a switch finally flipped in me, I realised they never deserved me.

The friendship of the past was dead.

They were only a dream that had once helped to give me comfort when I was young and alone, but no more. Now, I would let those memories and feelings go.

A small grin tilts my lips, a strange feeling of almost relief falling over me.

"I'm nothing to you–"

"Micai—" Knox calls from Morgan's side. My gaze is solely on Xander and his returned cold glare.

"The feeling's mutual." I take a step towards Xander, his eyes widening slightly with the proximity. "So, when you see me...don't even *look* my way." I peer at the other sets of eyes on me, making sure they know I mean every word. "Let's stop pretending like we ever really knew each other."

Clearly, what I thought I had with them in the past was all an illusion or some sort of dream of mine. And even if it wasn't, none of it mattered...they weren't the boys I knew as a kid anymore.

I take a step back, turn to Morgan, and nod as I call over my shoulder. "And don't come near me again. Because I won't take your shit anymore."

I head to the girls' dormitory, wanting to change and go for a quick run or sparring session to release some stress. I make it to the courtyard before a hand grabs me from behind. *Morgan.*

Had she been following me this whole time? Why?

And why had she even helped me back there in the first place? We only shared one class and hadn't even spoken before, so why would she care about me? Why get involved?

I had heard she and Seria didn't get along, and from my past memories, I do remember Seria complaining about her. But would she have really helped me because of that? Or because of some hostility toward Seria and her puppets?

"Seems like you're overthinking things." Morgan gently pulls me over to a nearby bench, the area quickly emptying out of the couple of students sitting there as we make our way over.

Morgan sits down, pulling me with her and waving her entourage away. They look back and forth between Morgan and me, but don't budge an inch.

"I'll be fine, Grey. Go take Ash for a walk." The one I'm presuming is Ash raises a brow, his green eyes filled with an amused glint as he slides a hand through his short, wavy dark-brown hair. The taller, ash-brown-haired boy standing beside him, *Grey,* gives her a tiny smirk.

But neither of them moves.

"Overprotective dickheads." She turns back to me, a sigh leaving her lips. "I can't even go to the bathroom without them checking if anyone's had a whiz before me."

She sighs while rolling her eyes at them as I try to school the small grin trying to spread on my lips.

Morgan seemed like the honest and blunt type. She would rather say something to your face than talk behind your back or play little mind games. Maybe that's why she and Seria didn't get along.

Either way, it was refreshing. And a complete change from how the majority of the girls in this academy treat me. Which usually involved dirty glares and smug smiles with either hateful or degrading words spit at me for fun.

She gives me a small smile and a softer expression as she leans in closer.

"Although we both know I'm safe with you."

My brows draw down together as she continues.

"After all, you already saved me once." Her smile widens as a knowing gleam grows in her gaze. I open my mouth to ask her what she means, but she quickly cuts me off. "I have a question, though." She taps a slender finger against her lips. "How did you manage to pull off all those moves in that tight black assassin outfit?" A large smirk stretches her lips as her eyes curve up into crescents. "'Cause you looked *badass.*"

I feel my facial features fall at the certainty in her gaze.

How did she know it was me?

How was that even possible? I had been covered from head to toe and it had been the dead of night.

Or was this some guess of hers? Some suspicion or theory she wanted to test out.

But why me? The rumours around the academy alone should have dissuaded her from thinking it was me. *Weak, magicless Micai and all.*

"I don't know what you're talking about." I shake my head as Ash and Grey whip around toward Morgan.

"Morgan," Ash says as his gaze flicks to me, a look of

406 | ISLA DAVON

confusion taking over his expression as he looks at my more petite frame. "She's the one..."

His words fade off as she gives him a smile and curt nod. The boy beside her, Grey, narrows his blue eyes at me. They seem to be searching for something before widening with some realisation.

Then it dawns on me. He was the boy on the ground in the forest during the beast attack. I flick my gaze to the other boy named Ash. His tall frame and dark brown hair seemed to match the other one that night too.

I shake my head again. They have no proof it was me.

Then why was Morgan so sure?

"My ability–" Morgan starts before Grey cuts her off, his face stiffening.

"You don't know her well enough."

Morgan raises a perfectly shaped brow. "There was a time when I didn't know *you*, Grey Aston, but I took a chance..." Her features soften a fraction, a slight warmth flooding her amber eyes as she continues, "And I don't regret it."

His gaze meets hers, and a stoic and serious look flows from his eyes as they share a moment.

"Besides," she grins, turning back toward me, "she's worth the risk."

Morgan shifts closer to me as Grey and Ash turn away. They continue to watch the surrounding area like sentinels while never leaving our side.

Morgan's eyes turn an iridescent hue as a light glimmer forms around us, casting a transparent cover over the area around us. Her eyes change back, and she gives me a small, sheepish smile.

"Everyone knows I have this psychic power to cast shields." She waves her hand at the light barrier covering us as I nod.

I didn't know much about Morgan other than what I'd heard from other students whispering. She was a second-year student and didn't have a good relationship with Seria or the girls in her year; she was only known to stick to the two boys around her.

Morgan also had a very blunt and fierce nature, but she was still known throughout the academy for her talent and aptitude for shields and barriers. Even the faculty was impressed by her skills.

But it wasn't just her strong ability that kept others away. She also apparently had a strong family backing, one that no one wanted to mess with.

"The truth is, I have another power...one I can't let others know about." Her expression turns a little sombre, the confident smile fading as a strange look of worry enters her gaze. She turns to Ash and Grey, a slight hesitation holding onto her gaze before she finally speaks again.

"It's not some amazingly strong power, though." She shrugs as a humourless laugh leaves her lips before they pull down into a frown. "...it's not even an attack type." A shaky sigh leaves her throat while she takes a moment before continuing. "But it's one I have to keep secret because there are people who would want to use me for it." Her eyes meet mine as a flicker of worry crosses them. However, whatever she sees makes the creases around her eyes smooth out, and the weariness in her gaze fades. "I can read people's auras..."

Was that it? I don't understand why that was such a big deal. I guess it wasn't a common thing, but some witches could do it, right? I'm about to say just as much when she starts talking again.

"I can tell when people and supernaturals lie. I can tell what their powers and abilities are and their personalities...I can read beneath the layers they try to hide, right down to their very core—souls and all." The hesitancy in her gaze returns as I feel my mouth slightly open.

That was different, alright.

She was basically a walking lie detector machine with the ability to see through everything and everyone, the good *and* the bad. Imagine knowing the true personality of every head in the founding families of the supernatural world. What abilities they were hiding, if and when they were lying, and if the smiles on their faces were only masks covering something darker beneath...Is that why she didn't get along with Seria? Could she actually *see* and *hear* the bullshit?

"So, *Micai*..." she says, pulling me from my thoughts. "I *know* you're the one who saved me because of this ability." She glances briefly at Ash and Grey. "Only I don't know how you did it, or even why– not that I'm not grateful," she rushes out. "...But," A slight frown coats her lips, her brows creasing. "How did you manage to fight off that beast by yourself? Why were you even there that night? Were you... involved in some way?"

There's a slight stiffness that works its way into Ash's shoulders with Morgan's words and a slight tremor that makes its way into Grey's clenched fists.

I meet her clear amber eyes as a heavy sigh leaves my lips. If she really thought I was involved, she wouldn't have helped me earlier with Xander and Seria, and she most certainly wouldn't have told me about her secret ability...Maybe she's wondering how someone who was supposed to have no power was able to fight and kill a beast that she couldn't? Or how I knew where she was that night? Or maybe why I even helped her to begin with?

Either way, there was no longer any point in hiding the fact that it was me.

Whether it was because I helped her that night or our tragic fates in our previous lives, I felt a slight connection with her. A part of me *wants* to trust her.

"No, I wasn't involved, and how I could fight...well," I shrug. "I've been training."

Even though a part of me wanted to open up, another part screamed that not even the walking lie detector would believe I came back into the past after dying.

"Training? You took out that thing with ease, Miss-weak-with-no-magic-Bane." She taps my shoulder with hers, a small smile tilting her lips.

I mirror her expression. "Doesn't mean things can't change. What do you see when you use your ability?" I ask, wondering if perhaps she could see something different or off about me.

Her eyes change into their iridescent colour before a slight gold shimmer slides over them. She trails her eyes down my body and slowly backs up again. She stops at my chest for a brief moment before meeting my eyes, the hue in her own changing back to her normal amber.

"You're something different." Her brows crease, "And you weren't like that at the start of the year, I'm sure of it."

She gives her head a small shake, a slight look of confusion overtaking her expression. "I just don't understand how that's possible...or what you are." She looks back at my chest. "*That colour...*" she mumbles before shaking her head again. "What are you?"

"Hell if I know." I shrug. I thought she might have some answers since I still don't.

She takes in my expression, her own softening before she chuckles. "I think you're my kinda girl, Micai."

"Careful." Chuckles Ash as the transparent shield fades and he steps closer.

Morgan rolls her eyes. "She's okay–"

"I was talking to her." Ash smirks, turning his green eyes to me, "She's a wild one." He gestures to Morgan, his grin growing wider.

She slaps his side, "Asshole."

"Don't pretend like you don't love it." Ash takes her hand in his before she can pull it away and places a kiss along her fingers.

Grey looks on from beside them, a softer look briefly crossing his stoic expression before he schools it.

"Ah!" Morgan whips back around to me. "A certain fish told me you've tamed the psycho reaper we call Annex."

"What?!" Ash shouts, drawing the eyes of a few students passing in the courtyard. "*She's* with Annex?"

He peers around at the mention of Annex's name,

twisting and turning in every direction as if waiting for him to appear from thin air like Beetlejuice.

"I'm not with Annex, or anyone. We just hang out." I shrug. I wasn't sure what we were or even how I felt about him or Ezra. Although I'm pretty sure we weren't *like that.*

A slight frown pulls at my lips as a small pang tries to work its way into my chest with the thought, but I push it down just as quickly.

Ash and Grey share a look as Morgan grins.

"Annex doesn't *hang out* with anyone other than my brother and their friends, and he certainly doesn't spend time with girls." A weird smirk pulls at her cheeks as my brows cinch together.

Brother? Annex hangs out with Morgan's brother?

"Who's your brother?"

I had seen her with Ezra before during Music class, but they didn't resemble each other. But then, who am I to talk? Seria and I don't look anything alike. *Thank the Gods.*

"Creed," she replies and I almost have to steady myself with the shock.

Creed, as in Captain Asshole, Mr. Stubborn Incarnate, and the Dark Lord himself?

How was he related to someone so beautiful, genuine, and funny?

I lean in, peering closer. I guess there were some physical resemblances: their model-esque features, dark raven hair, and amber eyes–although Morgan's were slightly brighter in colour.

Even though they looked similar, they couldn't be more different. Morgan may be blunt, but she isn't mean or arrogant like Creed. Even with her fierce personality, she had a warmer side. I could see it in the soft and gentle gazes she gave me or Ash and Grey. She wasn't rude or overbearing either. Clearly, she got all the good personality traits in the womb. How was Creed so lucky to get her as a younger sister? *While I got Seria.*

"Like what you see?" She wiggles her brows comically before shaking her head and sighing. "Sorry, Micai, I'm already taken." She hitches her thumb toward Ash and Grey. "These assholes can be really possessive."

The boys in question roll their eyes, a small grin stretching their cheeks as they watch her joke around.

A group starts to gather on the other side of the court-yard: a couple of first-year girls and a few second-year boys, all laughing and talking about the Winter Ball.

"Time to go," Grey calls as Ash nods, a more serious look in their eyes as they don the roles of Morgan's personal bodyguards again.

Morgan sighs, taking her turn to roll her eyes.

"As I said before, *overprotective.*" But I can see the warmth that bleeds into her gaze as she glances their way. She gets up, dusting off her skirt before making her way towards them. And then, with one final wave, they're gone.

I wait until they are out of sight before heading up to my room. Except once inside, I freeze.

There was a different scent drifting around my room. Scents that felt strangely familiar...sweet and salty, and then smoky. It reminded me instantly of Ezra and Annex.

I go over to my bed and notice a large white box with

a silky black ribbon and bow across it. There's a small card too.

It has two different writing styles on it. The first says: *'Micai, Will you be our partner for the Ball?'*

It has Ezra's name underneath it. Below that, in messier script, it reads:

'Wear this Red, you'll look hot as hell.' It's finished with a large *'A'*.

I'm guessing that must be Annex.

Something warm builds in my chest as my hand traces their handwriting, a grin painfully pulling at my cheeks with their words. I place the card down carefully on my dresser and make my way back over to the box. Slowly, I begin to open it.

Inside sits black tissue paper wrapped neatly over a small bundle.

I gently pull the black paper off, and a dark teal bundle slips out. I catch the rich, silky fabric before it reaches the floor, and my breath catches in my chest with the beauty of what I'm now holding.

It's a floor-length dark teal dress with a bias cut. It looks decadent and breathtaking and somehow...familiar.

Then it hit me: the small dress shop in town. I had only looked at it for a moment, but they noticed. And they bought it for me.

How had they known in just mere seconds that I had wanted this dress? And made it their mission to get it for me? We hadn't even known each other for long and yet they seemed to be able to read me so well.

These two boys...how did they always manage to surprise me and make me smile like this?

I pull the dress to my chest and turn to the mirror.

I hadn't planned on going to the Winter Ball. I wanted to avoid another bad memory and the morons that made up the majority of the student body.

But why should I?

Why should I miss out or hold back for them anymore?

With Annex and Ezra, I was sure to have a good night. *Maybe even more than that.*

I smooth the dress down my front, gazing at the reflection that's smiling from the mirror.

Guess I was going to the Ball.

CHAPTER THIRTY-FIVE

*C*lasses had been cancelled the day before the Winter Ball. I guess prestige and money spoke louder in the academy than the actual education of its students. It seemed the students getting their hair and nails done was of more importance than actually attending class or learning something.

But why it would take up so much time–even needing its own day–I still had no clue. A quick shower and a bit of mascara and I'd be done.

I shrug, watching from my room's window as groups of students make their way out of the gates and to readied cars for their primping and preening. And probably a few towns over.

The town nearest here and those around it weren't known for their trendy boutiques or spa facilities.

I grab my black hoodie and head to the forest and old training building.

I pat my stomach as I zip my hoodie up. I ate too many pancakes doused with syrup and strawberries for breakfast this morning. I'll be lucky if I don't have any issues fitting into the dress Ezra and Annex bought me.

I had awkwardly thanked them through a mouthful of pancakes, which had them both chuckling and saying, 'They would take that as a yes, then'.

They seemed even more enthusiastic than I thought they would be about a school ball, spending most of breakfast talking about 'coordinating' and 'matching styles'.

We all agreed to meet in the courtyard in front of my dorm just before the Ball started.

It was a peaceful breakfast until Annex and I got into a debate over who could eat the most pancakes...I obviously won. Nine pancakes to his seven, but the grin on his face looked nothing like a loss. He even called me *cute*.

I'm pretty sure there was nothing cute about me munching down nine pancakes, but Ezra actually *agreed* with him. I guess their idea of cute was a little warped but what could I expect from guys nicknamed the Infernal Four.

I make my way through the forest and down the old, abandoned path. I would have to do some heavier training and add a quick run to be able to burn through all those pancake calories.

Still worth every fluffy bite.

I head into the old building, the place I've claimed as my personal gym, and am met with two deep forest-green eyes.

Gadriel flips two daggers between his fingers as a grin tilts his lips.

"I thought you would come."

I pull off my hoodie and throw it on a nearby tree branch as he throws me one of the daggers in his hands. I twist the blade between my fingers, a small smile stretching my lips as I sprint towards him. His stance quickly changes to a defensive one.

Just what I had expected.

I drop to the ground, sliding beneath him and aiming to kick his feet out from under him. But he quickly twists into a flip and lands behind me. His blade lashes out towards me with the movement, but I swivel, dodging it and thrusting my own blade out to meet his. Our blades collide as they meet time and time again, sparks flying in every direction as we move around the old building.

We go back and forth in what has become our regular routine every other day. We would jump straight into sparring, our fists or weapons clashing against one another for hours, losing track of time and becoming lost in our own little world here.

I didn't need to restrain myself with Gadriel. I could spar with him and not have to hold back my strength. It benefited me more to give our sessions my everything, and he, in return, did so as well.

I had seen the surprise in his eyes the first time I let loose before it quickly turned into something else: a look of anticipation and excitement with a small glimmer of something else I couldn't quite read.

The academy bell rings in the distance, pulling us from our own world. The sky above us is now falling to dusk, and the laughter and chatter of returning students are clearer in the distance.

I wipe the sweat dripping down my neck as Gadriel

puts his dagger away in a large black duffel bag he'd brought.

I flip the dagger in my hand before heading over to him and handing it back. He takes it but flicks his gaze between me and the blade. He opens his mouth but closes it quickly again, his brows furrowing before he finally begins to speak.

"Micai, are you...going to the Winter Ball?"

My brows raise a fraction. Why was he asking? Had there been more rumours about me going around? I had thought it had been too quiet lately.

But I'm sure no one knew I was going with Annex and Ezra, and they both didn't seem like the type to talk about it with others so easily.

Annex just had to look at someone for them to turn tail and run. And even Ezra had been acting differently lately. He wasn't wearing his signature smile around people anymore or spending time with girls who were trying to be overly nice to him, even going so far as to outright ignore them at times.

"Here." Gadriel takes out a small black bundle, pulling me from my thoughts.

He hands it to me with a hesitant look as he watches me open it.

"I thought it best if you had something with you...just in case."

I unfold the tiny bundle. Inside sits a black strap attached to a small black sheath with a silver handle poking out.

I pull it out, my eyes going wide at the beautiful, curved blade.

I grip its handle in my palm. It is so small and light, but its blade appears razor sharp. On the blade itself sat a small ornate and delicate carving...*in Elvish.*

My eyes go wide. This couldn't be.

I shake my head, my eyes flitting back and forth between the blade and Gadriel.

"Is this...an *Elven* blade?"

The responding smile he gives me is breathtaking, light humour bleeding into his gaze as he opens his mouth. "I had hoped you would like it."

How could I *not* like it?

The smile I give him must answer any questions he has because the slight tension in his shoulders instantly seeps from them when he sees it.

He points to the small black sheath and strap.

"You place this on your thigh and make sure no one sees it. It makes for a better surprise if anything were to happen. And should you need it, don't be afraid to use it."

My brows scrunch together, this wasn't for sparring.

Then it hits me. He had asked about the dance.

He must take my expression for confusion over the sheath and how to put it on instead because, in the next moment, he's taking it from my hands and kneeling in front of me.

He opens the strap, places it loosely around my calf, and starts to slide it up my thigh. His movements slow until they stiffen the further up my thigh he gets.

I'm wearing black leggings so I can feel each touch and graze of his large fingers, a slight shiver making its way up my body with each small contact and a small heat creeping into my cheeks.

His eyes slowly look up, reaching mine as he tightens the strap, but whatever he sees freezes him for a slight moment before quickly shaking his head. He pulls away from me and straightens himself, pausing for a brief moment before turning back to me.

"Hopefully, you won't need to use it, but...it's better to have it with you anyway." His expression becomes more serious, and his tone slightly colder as he continues. "Don't let anyone hurt you. I know it's a Ball and not a battlefield, but..." His eyes flick to my feet and then my wrists. "You can never be too careful."

Now I understand. He was worried that something like before might happen again.

I gently brush my hand across the sheath and blade's handle before looking back at him. "I'll use it well. Thank you."

He gives me a nod. "Hopefully, you won't have a need to. And...make sure you have fun, Micai. I'll be around if you need me."

His gaze lingers for another brief moment before he turns away and heads through the old forest trail. He had told me before that he had to leave and help the other faculty members check the barriers around the academy for the Ball.

I unstrap my beautiful little Elven blade and tuck it under my hoodie after putting it back on. No need to explain what it is to the dorm's head or anyone else if they saw me.

I don't think they would be as impressed with it as I am. And if anyone tried to touch it or take it from me, I might have to take a note from Annex's book and get all stabby.

After all, it was an *Elven blade.*

I head over to the cafeteria, grabbing an apple and a cold ham and cheese baguette, having already missed dinner time.

I'm making my way out of the empty cafeteria when I come to a sudden stop.

There's a group of students in front of the exit: Ivy Harris, Aiden Hopps, Pearse Mattews, and Cody Dalton, all first-year warlocks.

They were blocking the exit as they surrounded Ivy. Aiden's hand was on her thigh, sliding higher as her lips locked with Cody beside her. Pearse is to her other side, his hand sliding back and forth his front pants and...*gross.*

A bit of bile makes its way up my throat. I'll have to bleach my eyes when I get back to my room.

I clear my throat loudly just as Aiden's hand slides under Ivy's skirt. *Not on my watch.*

I didn't need to see how monkeys copulated. That's probably a bit harsh...on the monkeys.

Ivy flinches, pulling her skirt down and pushing away from Cody, but none of the assholes around her budged. Well, other than Pearse, who thankfully removed his hand from his pants.

All three boys turn, glaring at the interruption as Ivy tidied herself before turning and freezing. Her worried face turning into annoyance.

"What, so now you're a perv watching people? Enjoying the show Mic–"

"If I wanted to see animals fuck, I'd go to the zoo, Ivy." I give her my best deadpan look. "But I probably wouldn't feel as nauseous...normal animals don't disgust me." I spin to look at the three pairs of eyes slightly widening. "Besides," I turn back to Ivy, taking a step closer, "I'm not the one blocking the cafeteria exit with my body. You should probably take your little show somewhere else..." Her small nose scrunches up, her eyes narrowing and her lip flattening into a thin line. "Unless you *want* people to see you." I pull back, shrugging. "I mean...whatever you're into, I guess."

Her mouth opens, her nostrils flaring, as a large hand lands on my shoulder. "You asking for an in, Micai?" Cody smirks before I shove his hand away.

How did he come to that conclusion from what I just said?

Ivy's eyes narrow at the boy who, moments before, had his lips all over her. He notices her scowl and moves back from me, his hands raised in a pacifying manner.

Then she shifts her rage at me, a vicious expression coating her small features as a bitter chuckle leaves her lips. "Can't get your own man, so you throw yourself at other girls' partners? Just like you did with your sister." She sneers, "Or did the Infernal Four finally see you for what you really are?" She looks me up and down, a scoff falling from her mouth as she trails her gaze up my over-sized hoodie to my messy hair. She smiles, but it's anything but pretty. "It makes sense, the Infernal Four have taste. They also *never* go to dances or balls...or did you think you were the exception?" She laughs, an annoyingly high-pitched sound falling from her thin lips that quickly grates on my ears. *"Poor Micai.* Of course, you're no exception. I'm sure they had their fun with you, but hopefully, now you can find some self-respect and realise you're not up to standard. Not theirs. And not ours." She smirks as I squeeze the baguette in my hand, probably ruining it beyond repair. She sneers again, stepping toward me, "It's *sad,* really. All you are worth is your basic looks and what's in between your legs–"

I slam my hand against the door behind her, pinning her against it.

"Unlike you, I wouldn't fuck trash, and my worth... can't be measured by the likes of you."

A hand grips my shoulder again, trying to pull me back as another reaches from my side.

I easily shirk off the hand gripping me and dodge the other incoming one.

I kick the door behind Ivy open sending her falling backwards and onto her ass. She knocks over a trash can as she falls, all the garbage falling out and on top of her as I make my way past.

I head to my dorm, hearing her screams even as I walk inside.

I trudge to my room with my now squashed baguette and my apple now missing. It's probably rolling in the cafeteria hallway somewhere.

The image of Ivy's shocked face and her sprawled on the ground replays in my mind as a small chuckle leaves my lips.

She was exactly where she belonged, *with the rest of the trash.*

CHAPTER THIRTY-SIX

MALLYN

The leaves from the forest trees brush against me as I make my way towards the academy's beast detainment shelter.

Creed's contacts had found out that there were some strange movements made around here a couple of weeks back, around the time we were kept busy. It might have some connection to our own attacks, so he wanted me to check it out. See if I sensed anything off.

Why had they even come to our town and our domain? And why bother with the academy?

Who were they? And what were they planning? There were too many unanswered questions.

And Creed was on edge more than usual, especially after Morgan's attack. He thinks the two might be connected. And if it was...Hell hath no fury like my brother. You don't mess with one of our people and walk away breathing.

I make my way up to the shelter. I heard some of the beasts had gotten loose back then, or that some of the students might have released them as a prank. Highly unlikely, though. Even a low-ranked creature would be hard for them to handle around here, unless they were fighting it in a group.

The beast runs along under my skin, a feeling of familiarity as I near the shelter.

It had definitely been tampered with. The containment spells were gone, and the shed was still wide open with no creatures to be seen.

It's cordoned off with restrictive spells, probably from the academy's staff, but I brush past it. I feel a small static prickle against my skin, but there wasn't much that could hold my beast or its power back.

I head into the shelter and look for anything off or unusual.

The stench instantly hits me. Whatever had been in here was foul. My beast growls beneath me in agreement. But whatever it was, it was well gone.

The space is darkly lit, with no magical fuse or electricity running through it; only the glow of the sun from outside puts any sort of light into the shelter.

I narrow my eyes, my beast's abilities allowing me to see even in the darkest of places and showing me it almost as clear as day.

I look around, other than a few broken ropes in the centre of the floor, I see nothing unusual.

I pick up the ropes, my beast pushing me forward. I bring them to my nose, hoping to pick up someone's scent, maybe one of the people behind all this, but instead, I am met with a slightly familiar scent. A sweet floral scent instantly tickles my nose and wraps itself around me.

I take another deep inhale wondering if my senses have gone haywire. Why would she have been here? And in these ropes?

Then I notice some dried blood on them...a tremor makes its way through my body as the beast rolls under my skin. A dark growl floods my ears and rings in my head before I shake him off, reminding myself she had been with Ezra and Annex all week.

She was fine.

If she had been hurt or in any danger, they would have said so.

I place the ropes down and leave the shelter, trying to shake the thoughts from my head and the growing, growling noises ringing in my ears.

But why would she have been here? Only the sixth-year students were allowed to train here. But that was definitely her scent...

Another tremor works its way down my body, his voice growing louder inside me. I make it outside, the cold evening breeze hitting me as I take a slow, deep breath.

I wouldn't allow him to take control. Taking a deep breath again, I push him down and to the back of me. There was no threat, not here or to any of my brothers. *Or her.*

My mind goes back to the shelter, running through the images of the frayed rope and then to Micai.

She was a complete mystery to me. How could something so small be so resilient and fearless?

Others can't even meet our eyes, but she faced us head-on, meeting our gazes and glares with her own. And for some strange reason her presence seemed to calm parts of me.

The beast didn't roar beneath me, and there was no feeling of bloodlust or rage when she was near. He would listen to her, watching attentively behind me, his interest piqued and thirst for carnage calmed. That in itself was more terrifying than anything else, for me... and for her.

What did he want with her? What was he planning, and why *her*?

I had tried to stay away from her, keeping as much distance as I could. But I found myself slowly edging nearer and before I knew it, my eyes would unconsciously search for her, for her scent, her voice, and those deep blue eyes that would stray my way when she thought I wasn't looking.

But she didn't know about the monster dwelling inside of me. *One that watches her too intently.*

I should keep away from her.

She could get hurt because of me. She would be no exception to his carnage or cruelty. Only another innocent casualty.

I had to keep my distance before she found out what I was and before she got hurt.

I know that I should, that I *needed* to, but the peace her presence gave me...I hadn't felt that way in years. Even after my beast has his *'fun'*, when he is calm and placated, there is no peace or reprieve. I would wake up in the forest wondering whose or what blood I was covered in. Only riddled with guilt and questions as to what he'd done...to what *we had* done now.

Except with her, *Micai*, it all fades away. Her scent, her voice, her smile, they do something to me that nothing and no one else ever could...

Her soft smiles and gentle laughs make my breath catch in my throat, while my eyes watch and wait for each new expression she gives me. There's this sweet scent and warmth that flows around her and calls to me, pulling me a little closer each day.

I have to stop myself from laughing with her and hold back the words that want to leave my lips when she's talking to us.

I have to stop my hands from reaching for her, or my fingers from brushing through her silky soft strands as she sits just feet from me.

My fingers twitch by my sides with the thought.

I shake my head. No, it was too dangerous, for her *and* for me.

As long as he was inside me, she wasn't safe. No-one was.

But would I be able to push her away...ignore her?

Annex and Ezra were bringing her to the Winter Ball tonight, and if I'm completely honest with myself...I wish it was me.

I drag a hand down my face, a slow sigh leaving my lips.

Now wasn't the time for this. I had to look for any clues or scents that would help Creed find out who or what was messing with our territory.

I open my senses, allowing my beast's power to filter through and help.

I hear animals and smaller prey shuffling through trees and bushes around me, a small brook trickling in the distance, and birds flying overhead, but nothing unusual is happening, and no people are wandering nearby.

I close my eyes and take in the scents around me. The smell of pinewood and oak instantly hits me, as does the scent of deer, rabbits, and other small prey, and...something else. Something slight and faint tickles my nose. It scratches at my senses and has my beast rolling warily beneath me.

He growls under my skin–his warning–as I push him down. What was there to be wary of?

I open my eyes and move in the direction of the strange scent. It becomes stronger the nearer I get to the brook I heard just moments ago.

I get closer to the scent until it becomes so strong that I can't smell anything else around me. It's a sickly sweet scent, one filled with magic and malice.

I look down at the widening brook, but it's not water that's trickling down through it. There's a pure black liquid, one so dark you couldn't see your reflection in it, with just an endless stream of darkness.

It also reeked of magic—the kind you didn't want to mess with.

I get closer to the brook, trying to get a better look at the black substance, just as my beast begins to howl in my ears. He tries to push me back, fighting for control as his roar rings painfully in my ears.

I push him back down again, a little more shakily, as I take out my phone and try to call Creed. He would need to know about this.

Suddenly, I feel a sharp pain in the back of my head.

I fall forward, my eyes hazing over from whatever hit I've taken from behind...and fall straight into the black flowing liquid.

CHAPTER THIRTY-SEVEN

MICAI

J smooth the teal fabric down my chest, the silk soft and light against my skin, as Morgan pulls the zip up my back. A low whistle leaves her lips as she takes a step back after finishing.

She had come to my room a couple of hours ago, saying we should get ready together. But had been shocked by my lack of 'preparation supplies' as she called it. She made a quick call, one that had Ash arriving at my door a mere ten minutes later with a large silver case filled to the brim with almost every known makeup brand and hair piece available.

An hour and a half later, after some heavy nagging and fixing from Morgan, we were both finally ready. And I had even found some time to sneak into the bathroom and slip on the sheath and dagger Gadriel had given me without her noticing.

I walk over to the mirror, my mouth slightly parting at my reflection. The dark teal dress slides across my body, hugging and accentuating every dip and curve. It sits tightly around my breasts, dipping at my small waist and clinging to my curvy hips.

A couple of inches from there sits a slit that parts the fabric all the way to its hem. It shows a slight bit of thigh when I move and flares out in gentle waves down to my feet with the teal silk fabric feeling light and flowy against my skin.

I lean closer to the mirror and brush a hand over my cheek and out towards my hair. My short strands fall to one side of my face in a loose finger wave framing and complimenting my natural features, making me look more feminine and mature. It also gives my whole look a 1940s feel.

Morgan had gone with what she called 'a glamour look' with a more modern and glamorous makeup style. While I had opted for a more classic and natural look and a dark mulberry lip.

Morgan slips into her strapless navy dress, the beads swaying and shimmering down her dress as she moves. The colour compliments her raven black hair and porcelain skin, making her look even more like some foreign princess or a model from a Vogue magazine.

She gives me a knowing smile, throwing a pair of black suede cut-out stiletto heels at me.

"Thankfully, I brought a spare pair." She winks, gesturing toward my bare feet.

I give her a sheepish grin and my thanks before slipping them on.

We make our way slowly down the dormitory stairs in our heels. Morgan tries and fails to stifle her laugh as I stumble several times. However, by the time we reach the front door, I'm much steadier.

That is, until I see *them.*

Ezra and Annex stand at the doorway; Annex leaning against the wall as Ezra chats nonchalantly to Grey and Ash. Ezra's brown and lilac wavy hair is styled in a quiff, his sun-kissed skin a contrast against the dark charcoal grey suit he's wearing. There's a deep teal shirt under his suit jacket that he's unbuttoned at the neck. And that's where I see a slight bit of dark ink trailing down his chest.

I didn't think Ezra would have any tattoos.

My eyes trail down his front and to where his teal shirt tucks into his suit pants, the fabric looking just a fraction darker than the colour of my dress.

A heat creeps into my cheeks the longer I stare, thoughts of us in the Roller-Room flashing in my mind and of his body flush against mine.

I turn my gaze away, trying to push the memories down. But my eyes instinctively fall on the tall, dark figure beside him who screams danger and sin. *Annex.*

He leans against the wall with an almost bored look as he listens to Ezra and Ash talk. His dark brown hair is loosely slicked back, showing off every ear piercing and tattoo. A thick black chain sits on his neck matching the metal colour of his drop dagger earring, while black ink flows down his neck and onto his chest. His shirt is loosely open down to his waist and shows little snippets of daggers and skulls inked on his torsos skin.

Where Ezra wears a dark charcoal suit, Annex has opted for a pure black combo, except for a small snip of

434 | ISLA DAVON

dark teal fabric peeking out of his jacket. *Which looks exactly like the fabric I'm wearing.*

A blush coats my cheeks as I trail my eyes up their physiques.

Both of them look drool-worthy, their suits fitting and hugging them in all the right places. *And tonight, they were all mine.*

A small smile tugs at my lips with the thought as I follow behind Morgan. She opens the door and pulls their attention straight to us.

And they all fall silent.

Ezra's smile drops, his eyes slightly widening as they trail down my body.

Annex stiffens, mumbling *'Fuck'* as he follows Ezra's burning trail. Their eyes slowly meet mine after their perusal with a look of almost awe in them before they quickly turn hooded.

A grin stretches my lips, a small chuckle tumbling out at their dumbstruck faces. It pulls them from their little trance.

"Fuck, Red," Annex groans as he adjusts his trousers. "I knew you'd look hot, but...that's fucking criminal." He pulls out a blade and palms it in his hands.

"Annex." Ezra narrows his eyes at the blade as Annex points a finger toward me.

"If anyone tries to eye fuck her while she's looking like *that*...I'll be taking souvenirs and starting a collection, Brother." His gaze turns heated as he trails his eyes back over me. "Don't blame me, Red. It's damn near sinful what you're doing to me." His grin turns wicked. "Thankfully, I'm more on the morally grey side of life and enjoy committing a few sins." He leans in closer, his eyes burning a trail up my front before they land on my lips. "How about we forget the Ball and go commit some sins together?"

A hand from the side slides in between us and pushes him aside. Ezra shakes his head at Annex before turning to me. He leans in, his breath tickling my neck and ear as he whispers, "He is right, though..." His lips graze my ear as a shiver works its way down my spine with the dark timbre of his voice. "You look absolutely *devourable*."

Heat creeps into my cheeks as he pulls back, his eyes dark and hooded with a wicked grin stretching his lips. There seemed to be a lot more to Ezra than I thought. And with each new day we spent together, he seemed to show me more of him, and a different side that I don't think he let others see easily.

A slight warmth flickers in my chest with the thought.

A throat clears behind us as Morgan narrows her eyes playfully at Ezra.

"We'll be late for the Ball if we just stand here watching you two slathering like dogs over Micai's hot ass. So, let's get moving!"

"Slathering?" Ash chuckles as he wraps an arm around her waist. "Just say drooling, Babe." His chuckle dies off, his face falling as his eyes meet Annex's. Annex gives him one of his signature smiles–meaning it looks almost demented–and Ash starts shaking.

"S-sorry." His face pales slightly before he quickly turns away.

Grey slaps Ash on the back and wraps an arm around

Morgan, his gaze focused fully on her as he gently pulls her along toward the main academy building.

"How about we head in first?" He turns slightly to Ezra, giving him a nod before heading off with Ash and Morgan.

I feel two burning gazes on me as I watch Morgan leave, a small giggle leaving her lips as Ash whispers in her ear.

"Red," Annex calls just as I'm about to follow after them.

He slides a hand over my right arm as Ezra takes my left hand in his, entwining our fingers together. He pulls them to his lips, placing a light kiss along my fingers, just as Annex pulls my right hand toward his lips.

But he doesn't kiss them...he *bites* them. Not hard enough to hurt or break my skin but enough to distract me from Ezra's tender touch and gaze.

I go to pull my hand back from Annex, but his grip is like steel. He leans down and licks the marks he's just left, an expression the complete opposite of Ezra's on his face.

A shiver runs down my spine and straight to my lower abdomen, a new heat beginning to unfurl with all of their heated gazes and light touches.

"Enough playing, Annex...it's time." Ezra gives Annex a look, the both of them sharing a brief moment before Ezra nods and slowly pulls his hand back. Almost reluctantly.

Ezra takes out a small black box and places it in my hand. Annex gives me a slight squeeze before releasing my hand.

I look at the small box in my palm and then back toward them. What was it?

And why did the thought of them giving me something have my breath catching in my throat?

Their gazes flick between me and the box as I stand there, slightly frozen, not quite knowing what to do or say. Between the dress and now this, they had given me more than I had ever received from someone. And simply because they wanted to.

Ezra rubs the back of his neck. "We hope you like it."

"It'll definitely suit you, Red," Annex adds, his eyes a little narrowed toward the box as he bites his bottom lip.

I gaze between the two of them. They were both acting strange.

They looked almost nervous. But why?

Was it because of what was in the box? I guess there was only one way of knowing.

I slowly open it, half expecting something to pop out at me or for it to be empty as some kind of prank.

But it wasn't.

My eyes widen at the sight of the small silver necklace.

I lift it in my hand. And in the centre of the chain sits a small glinting dagger. It instantly reminds me of Annex's drop earring, except this was all silver with a slightly longer blade.

Small markings on the metal dagger catch my attention and have me leaning in closer. Along the tip of the blade, delicate music notes are carved all the way to the hilt. They look so small and ornate and must have taken a lot of effort to carve.

A knot catches in my throat. It is so beautiful, but... somehow, it feels like I was receiving more than just jewellery from them.

I look at the two boys whose eyes haven't left me, their own growing more anxious with my silence.

"Do you like it?" Asks Ezra, his eyes searching mine as he tries to read my expression.

"We should have gotten one with a bigger looking blade, or maybe an actual blade," Annex mutters, his brows furrowed and focused on the delicate metal glinting between my fingers.

"I *love* it." And I do. I lift the necklace up between them, their expressions instantly relaxing with my words. "Put it on me?"

I don't know who I'm asking, but they both jump forward, reaching for my hand.

I chuckle, hearing them scuffle as I turn around.

"Just as fucking sexy from the back." Annex groans.

Ezra's hand takes my necklace, having won the scuffle. He leans in closer and places the chain around my neck.

"You look so beautiful, Micai." He places a soft kiss against my shoulder, mumbling, "I'll end up joining Annex if they stare too long."

"What–"

"Nothing." Ezra spins me around, a soft smile on his lips as our eyes meet.

He and Annex then give me an arm to link, and their gazes turn tender as I place an arm in each of theirs.

We head to the Ball. The expressions and widened gazes are almost comical as we make our way in. There were some open mouths, bitter glares, and quick glances directed my way as we made our way inside. But tonight, I couldn't care one bit about any of it.

We make our way further into the room, and I'm met with two slightly widened blue eyes and a rigid expression that quickly schools itself into its usual fake smile.

"Micai." Seria steps forward in her long, hot pink halter neck gown, her blonde hair loose and falling down her chest in curls.

Suddenly, my view is blocked by Ezra's frame as we pass her and the group around her and head to the dance floor. He turns to me, a small grin on his face. "There's no need to waste time with the past. Tonight's about you and us, no one else."

Annex flicks out his blade, glaring at anyone who stares our way too long and quickly narrows in on a group of boys across the room looking this way. "Guess I'll be starting my collection early–"

I grab his shoulder before he can finish and pull him and Ezra to the dance floor with me. "You can be stab-happy another night, but right now you're both mine."

His eyes slightly widen before growing hooded, a groan leaving his lips as I pull them both closer and start swaying to the music.

"I knew you always wanted me," his smirk grows, turning into something sinful, "I could see it in the cute little glare you'd give me."

I chuckle as Annex leans further into me, his hands reaching for my hips as Ezra's reach for my waist, that familiar heat building inside me as Ezra's body sits flush against my back and Annex to my front.

The music thrums throughout the room, the white

and blue crystals glistening like stars on the ceiling as we become lost in our own world and the feeling of each other.

We slowly sway with the music, our bodies completely in tune. Their hands slide slowly up and down me, reminding me of our time in the Roller-Room. And I realise that I want this; I want *them*.

I place my right hand over Annex's fingers on my hip and slide up his arm until I reach his shoulder. While my left hand reaches behind me for Ezra, his head falls onto my shoulder to meet it. I brush my hand through his hair, eliciting a low hum while my fingers trace the ink along Annex's neck. His eyes turn slightly dazed and heated. I can feel my heart beating like a drum in my chest as our touches become more fevered.

"Fuck, Red..." Annex grins, a more tender look in his eyes as he leans his head against mine. "You're too fucking perfect." His nose brushes softly against mine as his voice lowers to a whisper, "I never knew I was missing something until you came along."

The look that follows pulls the breath from my chest as he leans down further and kisses me. It's a kiss so sweet and soft and so unexpected from Annex that I lean further into him, wanting more. Annex lets out a low growl before deepening the kiss. His lips and tongue explore mine, capturing and consuming every seam of my lips. It's a kiss that's both punishing and pleasurable, and *all* Annex.

His grip on my hips tightens as he pushes further into me, each hard edge, muscle, and ab laying flush against my front as our tongues slowly battle for dominance. And with each twist and stroke of his tongue and lips on mine, he stokes the heat that's quickly building in me.

A hand on my waist slides up my side, its fingers spanning out and brushing gently across my chest before quickly sliding down again. He repeats it again, and the slight movement sends flutters to my core.

Ezra's lips leave a trail of soft kisses down my neck while his fingers brush up and down my waist.

I become lost in the feel of the two of them.

"*My turn.*" Ezra's lips brush across my neck once more as his deep voice rings in my ears. Then I'm gently pulled from Annex and twirled around.

A small, annoyed noise leaves Annex's lips with the sudden movement before he schools it and pushes flush against my back. One hand goes to my hip, and the other falls to my waist. He then takes over Ezra's heated trail up my shoulder. A shiver works its way up my back as his teeth graze across my skin, his tongue licking a path up my neck as he moves.

Then, two heated turquoise eyes quickly draw me in, his lilac flecks swirling as he leans toward me. His fingers brush along my cheek before he captures my lips with his.

If Annex's kiss was passionate and dominant, then Ezra's was intense, loving, and all-encompassing. The feathery strokes and soft twists of his tongue have a small moan leaving my throat as our tongues dance and entwine, quickly becoming lost in the taste of each other.

A slight sting on my shoulder has me pulling apart from Ezra. Annex chuckles, his tongue sucking and kissing the spot on my shoulder he's just bitten.

Ezra leans in again, his lips brushing across my cheek and drawing me back toward him.

My breath comes out in small gasps, the heat between my thighs building to new heights with each touch and kiss.

"Micai–" Ezra groans low in my ear before he's suddenly pushed forward and cut off.

"The fuck!" Annex barks as he steadies Ezra and me, his dark glare cutting toward the group behind us.

"I'm so sorry." Seria tries to place a hand on Ezra, but he shirks her off, wrapping his arm around my waist, completely ignoring her as he checks me over.

"I didn't mean to bump into you..." She frowns, her gaze sympathetic before they flicker to Ezra for his reaction. "I just lost my footing in these new shoes."

She tries to give him a warm smile, but he doesn't even look her way. So, she turns her attention back toward me.

"Micai, you look..." Her eyes trail down my dress, and her jaw stiffens slightly. "...Really pretty."

Her gaze flickers from Annex to Ezra. "Who are your–"

"Pretty?" Annex's eyes narrow toward Seria, a demented, incredulous look slashed across his face. "She's fucking *breath-taking*."

His grip on my hip tightens, pulling me into his side as he glares at a speechless Seria. I have to school the grin trying to spread on my lips with her look of surprise. I don't think anyone's ever been so outright hostile toward her. "You don't need to know us, and we *sure as fuck* don't care about you and your fucking shoes." He bares his teeth, "The next time you act like some thick clutz, I'll cut your fucking feet off."

"Hey! What the hell do you think you're saying to her?!" Xander steps up in front of Seria, his typical dickhead glare set on Annex.

"Her future, if she keeps fucking breathing near us." A slow, demented grin spreads across Annex's lips as his gaze shifts to Xander.

By the look on his face, I bet he's imagining all the ways he would make Xander bleed. Xander's slight flinch tells me he sees it, too.

I watch Annex reach for the blade he always keeps tucked into his back trousers. I squeeze the hand still holding my hip, trying to pull his focus to me, just as Knox, Kane, and Anders come up beside Seria and Xander.

Seria takes a step closer, her hand gently falling onto Xander's chest, and she smiles at him. Then she turns to Ezra again.

"I'm not sure what Micai has told you about me...but I–"

Ezra looks at Seria, but the expression on his face is so hard and cold that she flinches with just one glance toward him.

His expression is more cutting than I've ever seen it before, his jaw tight and eyes narrowed as he looks back and forth between her and the boys behind her.

"Why do you think you're so important?" He gives her a smile Annex would approve of, his voice stony and cold. "Micai has never mentioned you, not once...and now I can see why."

Her brows furrow, "There must be some misunder-standing. I'm her sister–"

Annex chuckles darkly, a humourless tone laced in his voice, sending even a shiver down *my* spine with the sound of it. He notices and takes my hand in his, lifting it up to his lips as he places a kiss along each finger. His piercing blue gaze meets mine as he opens his mouth, "She doesn't need you or anyone else now. She has us."

Ezra follows suit, entwining our fingers together. "She's a part of *our* family now." He places a slow kiss along my knuckles, "We take care of our own."

Seria's gaze flicks between both boys before falling on me, her mouth slightly opening as she steps toward me. Annex shifts forward, placing himself to my front, and Seria quickly freezes. His eyes narrow in a dark glare, daring her to take another step closer.

"Back the fuck off," Xander barks as he pulls Seria behind him. "She's only worried about her sister..." His eyes move to me behind Annex, "Not that she's worth worrying about."

"What the fuck did you just say?!" Annex takes a step towards Xander, his frame a fraction taller as they go toe to toe with each other. Ezra tightens his grip on my hand as if trying to hold himself back.

"Let's all calm down." Anders steps in between Xander and Annex, trying to push them apart but only moving Xander as Annex doesn't budge an inch. "There's no need for a fight."

He looks at Ezra and me, his face slightly paling at Ezra's glare before moving to me.

"Seria didn't mean any harm. She would never hurt you, Micai. You know that–"

"Fuck, are you *blind* as well as deaf?" Annex grits out, his eyes more maniacal than before.

"Calm down, Annex," Ezra calls as he takes a deep breath, his eyes still dark and menacing. "There's no point in wasting your breath on them. Let them stay in their little delusion."

"Delusion?" Xander scoffs, a vicious sneer twisting his lips. "You're the delusional ones, thinking she's something she's not."

"*Xander–*" Seria calls as she tugs at his sleeve, but he pulls away, too engrossed in his own anger to listen to anyone anymore.

"We also used to believe all the lies she told us and the fake little '*act*' she put on. But the truth came out, and we realised what she truly was..." He glares at me, disgust dripping from each vitriol word thrown my way, "A horrible, lying, bitter–"

Something finally snaps inside me. Like the end of a rope pulled too tight and stretched for too long past its limits.

I move in a flash, grabbing the blade from Annex's hand as he takes it out, and reach Xander in a fraction of a second. I kick his feet out from under him and place the blade to his throat. His words cut off, his eyes widening in shock as he stares up at me.

"I remember warning you before..." I push the blade a little closer to his neck, a small cut forming on his skin as a few gasps sound around me. "Not to start shit with me."

"Micai–" Knox shouts, his voice a little shaky as Anders echoes him.

"Gut him, Red." Annex grins, coming up behind me. "If you don't, I fucking will."

"Don't, Mic–" Knox reaches for me, but Ezra steps forward blocking him.

"She'll do whatever the hell she wants, and not you or anyone else will get in her way."

Kane gently slides Seria to Anders and steps up beside Knox, a stand-off starting between them and Ezra, as Annex chuckles darkly behind me.

Kane's eyes flash gold as Knox raises a hand, a slight static forming around his fingers. "We don't want to fight, Micai, please–"

"Shut the fuck up," Annex growls before his lips reach my ear. "Make sure you hit the right artery, babe. If you get the wrong one, your sexy dress will get blood all over it..." His gaze slides down my dress, a heated look taking over his eyes. "Scratch that, you'd look *even hotter*."

I grip the blade's hilt, and even with the tension spreading throughout the room, I feel calm and quickly realise it's because of Ezra and Annex. I wasn't planning on killing Xander, but knowing they had my back and were giving me the option to...it had a warm feeling spreading throughout my body.

Just as Kane attempts to take a step toward me, Ezra's deep voice lowers to a dark timbre. "Don't even think about it."

"Who do you think you–" Kane starts before I become tired of all this bullshit.

I lean closer to Xander, staring into his shaking eyes

as the blade nips his skin further.

"There won't be a second time, Xander. I'm not putting up with any more shit. Stay away...*All* of you." I look at Kane, Knox, and Anders before I pull the blade away and straighten myself before handing it back to Annex.

I turn back to Xander and watch as Knox helps him up.

Ezra's hand reaches for me, pulling my attention back to him. I place my hand in his, and Annex's arm slides around my waist.

And the growing warmth settles in my chest as I look at them both.

They flick their eyes to Xander and Knox, a look telling me this is far from over with them. And a single thought crosses my mind...They didn't care what others thought or said, they had *my* back.

Seria calls my name, but a blood-curdling scream drowns it out.

Everyone turns toward the doors as a female student in a bloodied grey gown falls to her knees.

"Beasts!" She shrieks, "Magical beasts are attacking the academy." She falls to the ground limply as blood pours from a large wound on her side.

Was this some sick joke? This never happened in my previous life.

A resounding roar filters into the room from outside, pulling me from my thoughts. Screams and shouting soon follow.

Ezra and Annex grab me and place themselves around me just as the area turns into chaos.

$\mathcal{W}$e make our way through the panicked crowd and to the grounds outside.

Annex leads the way, punching anyone who comes near and promising to gut anyone else who pushes against us. Ezra wraps his arms around me from behind, making sure no-one jostles or touches me as we move.

We head through the doors and freeze, like all the students in front of us.

It was pure chaos.

Everywhere we looked, beasts were fighting teachers or attacking students. Spells were being thrown at them from every direction, but nothing seemed to stop them. Even attacks that inflicted heavy wounds couldn't stop the ceaseless attacks. The beasts seemed completely feral and crazed, attacking everything and everyone that moved.

A scream from my right pulls my attention. A small first-year female falls to the ground as a large, deformed, tiger-like beast stalks closer to her. Its irises are like pins, and a foam-like substance dribbles from its mouth as blood drips from its face and claws. With no visible wounds of its own on its face.

Just as the creature pounces, a figure jumps in front of it, slicing the creature's extended claw. Gadriel grips two large daggers in his hands as the creature growls before lunging toward them again. He pushes the beast back with a swift slice from his dagger, this time taking the whole creature's limb off.

The creature stills, a strained howl leaving its mouth before it suddenly begins to shake. A loud roar bellows from it before it charges toward Gadriel again. He nimbly flips over the creature, slashing his daggers outward before landing behind the beast. The creature's head rolls to the ground as Gadriel rushes to aid another group of students shouting for help.

Mr. Heinley, Mr. Hampton, Mrs. Brunswick, and Mr. Aldeir, with a few sixth years, are spread out in groups trying to stop the beasts. But there are too many with some higher-grade creatures mixed in, and their magic does not hold them for long.

Suddenly, Ezra pulls me to the side, a worried look in his eyes. "Stay here, Micai. Please." He turns back to Annex, a look shared between the two as he takes off his jacket to place around me. "We'll lend a hand and be back in no time."

Annex cracks his knuckles, a small scowl taking over his face before he flickers his gaze back to me, his grin reappearing. "I'll fuck 'em all up, Red, and be back to claim my reward for being a good scout."

"Who said I give out rewards?" I grin, enjoying his nonchalant thoughts in the midst of all this chaos.

Annex's smile straightens out, his expression turning more serious as he steps closer to me. His nose gently grazes my cheek as he leans down before placing a soft kiss there. "You are the reward, Red."

He meets my gaze, a look of pure resolve and something new and unreadable passing across his face before he schools it, giving me one of his playful grins. "I'll even get you a present if you're a good girl." He looks out toward the beasts as he rolls up his jacket and shirt sleeves, taking out his blade and tapping it on his lips. "Which head would be best?" He narrows his eyes in the distance, his gaze moving across the beasts attacking students like he was browsing a catalogue. "A coat made from *that* thing's skin would look hot as hell on you..." He points to a large creature fighting Mr. Aldeir's group. Its body is ostrich-like in shape except for the enormous razor-like claws on its legs and snake-like scales on its head. It has small black and blue shimmering feathers falling down its back and legs, which is what I think Annex is referring to.

Annex looks back at me and nods. "Yep, you'd look sexy as fuck," He narrows his eyes menacingly at the beast, "And it won't be needing its skin if it's dead." He chuckles darkly before darting towards it.

I watch as he makes his way over, clutching his blade. He lunges at the beast without hesitation and starts hacking away, effortlessly dodging the beast's attacks as he mercilessly attacks its weaker spots. This is just what I would expect from Annex. He didn't get the nickname '*Psycho*' for nothing.

I take a step towards him, wanting to join in. I couldn't stay on the sidelines and just watch. I was more than capable of handling myself and these beasts.

But before I can take another step, Ezra blocks my way.

"Ezra–" My brows cinch together as I try to move around him, but he blocks me again.

"*Please,* Micai." His gaze is pleading, his eyes filled with worry and...fear? "I know you don't want to watch. I can tell by your eyes that you want to help, but..." His shoulders drop slightly, and he has a tremor in his hand as he reaches toward me, brushing it softly across my cheek. "If anything happened to you..." His brows furrow, his eyes closing for a brief moment as his voice falls to a whisper, "I couldn't...not when I've finally found you."

He leans his forehead against mine as he opens his eyes, the turquoise tones swirling with lilac as he watches me, begging me with his gaze to listen to him just this once.

I open my mouth to tell him I'm stronger–stronger than any of them know or can imagine. That I'd fought beasts before and could do this. That I could help.

But before I can tell him, he starts talking again. "I'm not the nice guy everyone thinks I am Micai...I couldn't care less about anyone else. Only my family matters, and that includes you now." He quickly leans down, slamming his lips to mine in a bruising kiss. One so intense it has me leaning further into him. Our lips meld together as he pulls me flush against him, his tongue taking possession of mine with each lick and stroke and quickly building a heat in my core. But all too soon, he pulls back, a reluctant but heated look in his eyes as his tongue darts out, licking his lips as he watches me.

"We're continuing this when we get back." His gaze darkens as his eyes trail down my front and flow back up to my mouth, a promise lacing his lips in the wicked grin stretching them.

He looks at the area around us, his eyes resting on the two teachers nearest us, Ms. Cheron and Mr. Finch. They're both casting spells and chanting, forming a more substantial barrier around the academy and protecting the students nearest it. A few sixth-year students beside them are calling out to people to come over and make their way into the academy for safety.

"Stay and help the others here if you want, but don't leave. *Please.* I'll be back with Annex soon." He places a soft kiss on my forehead before reluctantly pulling back and dashing off in Annex's direction.

He joins Annex who is sitting on top of a strange dark green furry creature with large talons and razor-sharp teeth. He's laughing like some crazed maniac as he wrangles the creature like a bull, slicing into its sides as it tries to flip him off.

Ezra grabs a large, discarded blade and stabs it into the creature's chest. It falls limply to the ground as Annex jumps off its back.

I can't make out what he's saying from here. The teacher's barrier is blocking my heightened senses, but by the look on Annex's face, I see he's annoyed at the assistance.

They dart towards another nearing beast just as a familiar navy gown catches my eye.

Morgan.

Her face is slightly pale, but her eyes are focused as she runs in the direction of the courtyard near the girl's dormitories. She's clutching something to her chest, something large and metallic. They look like large chains.

I call out to her, but she doesn't even look back. Where the hell were Ash and Grey?

I look at the students and teachers fighting but don't see either of them. Turning back to her, I watch just as she disappears from sight.

I couldn't let her go off on her own, not when she looked like that. Who knows what would happen if she went somewhere alone? She didn't exactly fare well against the last beast she went up against.

Gripping the skirt of my dress, I kick off my heels and start chasing after her, ignoring the calls from Ms. Cheron to '*Stay*'.

I dash towards the courtyard, their voices now faded as I get closer to the dormitories. And that's when I see it.

Morgan must be crazier than Annex to run *towards* this thing.

Just in front of the dorms is a huge creature that seems to be battling two large animals—shifters, I presume—a huge white and grey polar bear and a golden-eyed leopard.

The massive creature roars, shaking the area around us. Its face reminds me of a bull, but its body mirrors that of a lion and goat. It has four hooves and two arm-like appendages and is covered in black and brown fur up until its torso and face. Its size towers over the two shifters trying to fight it.

The leopard shifter's side is wounded from the fight, blood slowly dripping from the injury as it continues to battle the beast.

The creature roars again, lashing out just as the polar bear tries to strike it. They both clash as the leopard strikes at the creature's lower limbs, trying to weaken or unbalance it. But its attacks only agitate the large creature further. It strikes a heavy hoof out, catching the wounded leopard and sending him flying into a nearby wall. He sags limply to the ground as Morgan screams 'Ash' and dashes toward him.

Ash was a leopard shifter. Then was the polar bear, Grey?

I watch as he struggles against the strength of the feral beast before him, unable to even glance back at his friend. He needed help, and quick.

I rip my dress at its slit and sprint toward the metal chains Morgan had dropped on her dash to Ash. Grabbing them, I head into the fight.

The beast was huge and clearly as crazed as the others. Even when attacked or wounded, it wouldn't back off. These magical beasts were usually fierce and wild, but not like this. It's as if they lacked any sense or instinct, only wanting to cause carnage and attack whatever came their way.

But that could also work in my favour. A crazed beast was a mindless one. It wasn't thinking about its next move or meal or wanting to survive. This wasn't a beast with intelligence trying to hunt me for fun. I could handle this creature.

Grey's polar bear looks like it's struggling, as he's being pushed back by the creature's large limbs and overwhelming strength.

I move quickly, using the distraction Grey gives me by tackling the beast. Gripping the large, heavy chain in my hand, I throw it over my shoulder and leap onto Grey's back. Using his shoulders as leverage, I leap towards the beast and land on its back.

"Hold him!" I shout to Grey as I wrap the chains over the beast's neck and pull, gripping each end of the heavy metal chain with each hand.

The beast begins to thrash and throw its head back toward me. It tries to reach for me, but Grey grabs its limbs, holding them in place as I wrap my legs around the creature's large torso and pull tighter on the chains.

It bucks its hind legs and stomps its front pair down, its movements more frantic as I jostle back and forth, pulling as tight as I can while Grey tries to stop its movements. He grabs its arm-like limbs, holding them tightly with his sharp bear claws and allowing me to pull the chains with my full strength.

It begins to make what sounds like a low rasping sound as its movements begin to slow. Hearing the metal creak and crack beneath my hands, I give the chain one final yank.

The beast's hooves give way, dropping to the ground as Grey takes a step back. Its head falls back towards me, its eyes going still as its last breath falls from its mouth.

Grey's polar bear gives me a slight nod before I let go

of the chains, the clang of them hitting the ground rings out around us as I slide from the creature's back.

I'm making my way over to Grey when a voice shouts from the treeline.

"Morgan!" Creed runs to a sobbing Morgan, who's holding a now-human Ash. His body is bloody with a large wound down his left side. Morgan's holding her gown against it, trying to stop the bleeding. Grey shifts back and makes his way to Morgan, quickly wrapping an arm around her.

"It's okay, Morgan. He's already healing. Look..." He points to Ash's wound, the ends slowly knitting themselves back together as he kisses her forehead. "He'll be back to annoying us in no time."

"Morgan!" Creed comes up behind Morgan, pulling her into him as he calls her name again. He checks her over, a small sigh of relief leaving his lips as he notices the blood on her dress isn't from her. Then he turns toward Ash and Grey.

"What the fuck happened?" he grits out, his eyes darkening quickly.

"The academy is under attack." I step up beside Grey, the poor shifter shrinking back with Creed's dark glare. "There's more over by the main building. Ezra and Annex are helping out over there." *Shit.* Ezra and Annex. They won't be happy I left.

Creed stares at me, his brows furrowed and his eyes narrowed as he looks me up and down. There's an unreadable look in his eyes. His gaze falls behind me to the downed beast and back before glancing at Morgan.

He opens his mouth just as Annex and Ezra call my name.

"Micai!" they shout, running through the courtyard and jumping over the creature's corpse. "What the fucks that–"

"I told you to stay there–"

"Red, you can't just leave us like that–"

I'm about to open my mouth to answer their calls and to tell them I can take care of myself until I'm met with their anguish-filled eyes.

"Were you hurt?" Ezra asks, an uneasiness to his voice as he and Annex surround me, scanning every inch of me, checking for any kind of injury or wound. Annex walks around me as I tell them I'm okay. He slides a hand down my back and places it on my ass before giving it a slap.

I turn and glare at the asshole as he grins.

"You deserve more than that for not listening," He trails his eyes up and down my body, his grin turning wicked as he bites his lip. "But we'll settle that later... when it's just us."

He rubs his hand over the spot he just hit before giving it a light squeeze. I'm about to slap it away when Ezra suddenly pulls me toward him, sliding his arms down mine as he pulls me closer.

"Micai..." His tone is tight, his brows drawn together as his gaze meets mine. He was clearly upset that I broke our promise to stay put.

But how could I? Morgan needed me, and I wasn't some weak damsel. I could fight...But any anger or annoyance I have fades the longer I stare at him. Seeing the real worry and fear etched across his features. It's in the slight tremor of his hands on my arms and the flickering of his eyes as they repeatedly search up and down me for reassurance that I was really okay.

How could I be angry at him? Even if he might be with me, I couldn't be with him. Not when his anger came from a place of genuine concern and care.

A small ache begins to spread in my chest the longer I look at him.

I reach up to his face, cupping his cheek in my hand as my fingertips brush the strands of hair falling onto his face.

I couldn't apologise for leaving. Morgan, Ash, and Grey needed me, and I knew I could handle myself. But I guess *they* didn't know that.

They thought I was still the weak-magicless Micai.

I was stronger now, but how would I even begin to explain it? On how I came to be like this or what I am now? When I myself didn't know or understand it all.

He leans into my hand, pulling me from my thoughts as a gentle smile stretches his lips.

And a slight prickling sensation spread in my chest with his expression, one filled with so much affection and warmth. Maybe he was different.

I glance at Annex. Maybe *they* were different.

Maybe one day...when I have the answers I need, I can tell them the truth. But for now, my words will have to do.

"I'm stronger than you think, Ezra. You'll have to learn to trust me on this."

"But–"

"She's fine," Creed calls, glancing at me. "She handled *that* with Grey."

He nods at the dead creature as Ezra's eyes widen.

"How?" he asks, his brows drawn down in confusion.

"Fuck, babe, I knew you were made for us," Annex murmurs as he wraps his arms around me from behind, leaning his head on my shoulder. "Pity I missed it, though."

"We've got bigger problems." Creed sighs, shifting his gaze to Annex and Ezra. "Mallyn's missing."

A shiver runs up my arm with his words. Mallyn was gone? Where?

Had he come into contact with one of those creatures? Had something gotten to him–I shake the darkening thoughts from my mind. I didn't even know Mallyn that well. But from the little time we did spend together, he seemed quiet and reserved, only ever close when needed and keeping a firm distance from everyone else as much as he could.

But there was something about him—something familiar about those grey-blue eyes—that seemed to draw me in and make me want to close some of the distance between us.

"What?" Ezra shouts, pulling me from my thoughts as he turns to stare wide-eyed at Creed. "How?!"

"How the fuck did anyone even get close to that asshole?" Annex shakes his head before grinning. "Well, whoever it is will soon be dead...the problem will be the clean-up."

"No jokes, Annex. He's been missing since this morning. I tracked his phone and found it by a dried-up brook in the forest..." He narrows his gaze at them. "With his clothes torn apart."

"During the day?" Ezra asks as Creed gives him a curt nod.

"*Fuck.*" Ezra drags a weary hand down his face as Annex whistles.

What was I missing here? What had happened to Mallyn? And why were all their expressions like *that*? They didn't seem worried or fearful for Mallyn, it seemed like there was something else going on here.

"Is Mallyn–"

I'm cut off by a loud roar, followed by another and then another. Then I feel a pair of hands pull me behind them.

Annex positions me beside a wide-eyed Morgan. Her eyes jump from the two beasts in front of us, and the one making its way near us from the other side.

The two creatures in front of us are similar to the yellow-eyed beasts I fought during my little kidnapping incident, while the magical beast on our other side was new.

It was pure black, its body as sleek and shiny as a snake but without any scales of its own. It crawls on all fours with small limbs like a crocodile, but its head is shorter and round with jagged teeth that are already bloodied.

A chunk of flesh falls from its mouth and I almost retch.

Morgan turns to Creed, her shaky hands clutching an unconscious Ash as she calms her breathing and closes her eyes. When they open again, her eyes are iridescent, and a shield begins to form around us.

"I don't know if I can hold it against multiple magic beasts if they attack together." She pulls Ash closer, cradling him against her as he heals slowly. Creed gives her a nod before turning to me and opening his mouth.

Suddenly, a high-pitched screech bellows from the courtyard. Another beast, the strange-looking ostrich from earlier, appears. Four beasts now surround us, two to our front and another to each side.

"You take the bird, Ez," Annex yells as he palms his blade. "Make sure you don't damage the skin too much, though...I promised Red a present." He gives me a wink before he points his blade at the two creatures in front of us. "I bagsy these freaks."

"Annex," Creed calls, and it's enough to make him halt his next step. "Let Grey help."

Annex sighs as Grey makes his way over.

"No!" Shouts Morgan as he leaves her side.

"He'll be fine." Creed pats Morgan's shoulder before he turns toward the black croc beast. "This will only take a few minutes."

"I can help." I take a step towards him, but he puts his hand out to stop me.

"Stay beside Morgan and Ash."

"I can help, Creed–"

He turns back to me, his eyes beginning to turn an obsidian black.

"Keep her safe then. *Both* of them. If any of them get past us...protect them." He gives me a look, one different from his normal glares or stubborn asshole expressions.

I glance at Morgan and Ash, still laying on the ground. I would prefer to fight instead of staying back. But looking at how Morgan clutches Ash, I suddenly realise I can't leave her like this. Not when she had helped me before, and not when she now looks so vulnerable.

I give Creed a small nod. I'll just bide my time and be ready for when I'm needed.

I remember the blade Gadriel gave me and pull my dress to the side to unsheathe it from my thigh.

I grip it in my hands as a groan sounds out in front of me. Annex adjusts his pants with his free hand, his eyes glued to my thighs and the blade strap.

"Focus, Annex," Ezra shouts as he narrows his gaze toward the beast in the courtyard.

"Easy for you to say, you didn't just see the hottest fucking thing ever." He turns back to me, pointing to my blade as a serious expression takes over his face. "We're playing with *that* later."

"If you survive." Ezra chuckles.

"Oh, I will, Brother, and I might even let you watch."

Ezra glances my way, a heated glint in his eyes. "I won't be just watching."

"Both of you focus!" Creed barks.

"Easy for you to say, you don't have to fight with a fucking boner." Grumbles Annex.

The two beasts in front of us let out a rattling howl, pulling our attention back to them. With that, all four beasts start to make their move on us.

I grip my blade, ready for whatever will come, when suddenly, a thunderous roar echoes out from the forest.

Then out bursts a familiar enormous beast, its body huge and eyes burning an unusual deathly blue. It charges toward the black croc beast and tears it apart in one bite before the creature can even move.

The beast then leaps at the two creatures in front of us. It takes a swipe with its large claws and rips the first creature's side apart. The yellow-eyed beast falls to the ground, blood pouring from the wound as the large beast lunges at the other creature beside it. This one tries to put up a fight but lasts only seconds longer than the previous one. The smaller creature soon drops to the ground, joining its comrade with its neck now torn out and shredded by the beast standing over it.

The beast roars, shaking the ground around us, the last creature in the courtyard turning around and quickly fleeing.

"Shit," Ezra curses as he drags a slow hand down his face.

"This is bad," Annex mumbles, gripping the blade in his hand.

Creed takes slow and quiet steps until he's beside Annex. He raises both hands as he steps towards the blue-eyed beast in front of them but freezes when their eyes meet.

The beast growls, a gravelly-deep warning ringing out.

"I'll stop you if I have to," Creed states.

My brows cinch together with his words. What was he doing? Was he trying to pacify it or reason with it? It did seem more intelligent than your average beast. And it sure as hell was quicker and stronger. But something wasn't right this time.

Its eyes were like pins, its mouth foaming and bloody. The intelligence I had seen before in its eyes of a predator and hunter was gone.

It was similar to the creatures here now: a primal, crazed, and mindless look in its eyes. There was no reasoning or talking to it now.

Creed narrows his gaze, taking a step closer as the beast bares its sharp teeth.

"Don't make me hurt you." Black shadows begin to coil around Creed and the area around him.

The beast's snarl grows louder as he gnashes his teeth at Creed.

I don't know about Creed's ability or how strong those black shadows were, but I *do* know that beast. It was strong and powerful, and I'm not sure if Creed could take it out before it made its move. It was quick. *Too quick.*

I should know, it had chased me more than once.

Then it hits me. Maybe it would follow me?

Maybe it would remember its favourite little snack that kept getting away?

Maybe I could lure the beast away from everyone?

I had gotten a lot quicker and stronger since our last fight.

But how would I get its attention? And how could I get it to follow me?

I grip the blade in one hand and slide my other hand over it, wincing slightly with the sting. Blood begins to drip through my fingers as I place the blade back into its sheath on my thigh. And squeezing my hand, I allow the blood to drip to the ground.

The beast stills, its snarling and growling stopped as its nostrils flare. Its eyes meet mine, a lower growl falling from its mouth as I dash to the treeline.

"Micai!"

I hear my name but don't respond or turn around. I need to focus on moving as quickly as my feet will take me.

I run, ignoring the rocks cutting into my feet as I move, trying to put as much distance between me and the beast as possible.

I could tell it was following me, its heavy steps sounding too close for my liking.

I reach the forest with the beast's growl growing closer in my ear.

Let's hope I can outrun it.

CHAPTER THIRTY-NINE

I dash through the forest, my dress tearing and ripping from the trees and the branches catching it as I move.

The beast growls behind me, but I'm not the same girl it had fought before. I quicken my pace, pushing my legs to move faster as the forest around me begins to blur, creating more distance between me and it. Scrapes and cuts form on my arms and legs from branches and rocks catching me, tiny droplets forming a trail down my arm, mirroring the one on my cut palm.

The beast bellows, picking up pace to match me and closing the distance between us again.

We move together through the forest, heading deeper inside and further away from the academy.

I slow slightly as the beast nears and lunges from behind. Twisting around, I whip my blade out and take a swipe at its torso as I tumble beneath it. It lands in front of me, turning around quickly as I grip my Elven blade.

Its unearthly blue eyes narrow at my hands. It growls

again before moving towards me. It reaches me just as I kick off a tree behind me, thrusting my blade at it.

It dodges, and I land behind it, twisting back around and jumping towards its unguarded back again. However, it quickly dodges me, and my blade catches on a thick tree root below it.

I try pulling the blade out, but the beast lunges for me again, and I have to dive to get out of its path. I swiftly twirl around but am just a second too late as the beast is upon me.

It hovers over me, its cold, icy breath brushing against my skin as its teeth fall inches from my face. Would this be my end? Would the beast finally take its meal? Or would it somehow spare me again for its own cat-and-mouse amusement?

It leans down at me, its eyes in line with mine. And never before have I seen such luminous blue eyes, so huge and monstrous yet so deep and endless. It's then that I notice its eyes are no longer pinpoints. No longer crazed or mindless.

It had become the beast I had first met, one of intelligence and of the enormous predator I knew before.

It bares its teeth at me, a low growl pouring from its mouth as it sits face-to-face with me. It opens its jaw and I instinctively close my eyes.

I didn't want to die again, I couldn't...I had too much to do in this life: my revenge and freedom and...Annex and Ezra.

No. I promised myself I would never give up and that I would always fight.

I open my eyes, ready to give this bastard the fight it

never expected from me, when I suddenly feel something warm and wet on my hand.

The beast leans down, lapping at the wound on my palm. Did the bastard want a little taste first?

I try to move my hand, but he growls and I freeze. He continues licking my hand until all the blood is gone and the wound is fully clean and...*healing?*

The skin was slowly closing, the cut healing rapidly on my hands.

I narrow my eyes at my hand and then at the beast who has moved to the scratches on my arms and legs, doing the same to them.

What the hell was happening?

Was it helping me? But why?

Or was this another one of its games, wanting to heal me and lull me into some sense of security before shredding me up like noodles?

I try to move away, but the beast growls again, this time nuzzling at my arms. Its black and white-tipped fur tickles against my skin as it shifts closer to me.

Its eyes meet mine again and my breath catches in my throat, something small tugging deep inside me. These eyes weren't the eyes of some animal or wild beast. They had a depth to them, an intelligence of a higher level and an anger and anguish I would recognise with ease.

I reach my hand towards its face, and this time, it doesn't stop me. I brush my fingers through its fur, the feeling soft and warm against my hands.

A noise vibrates from its chest, not a snarl or a growl, more like a chuffing noise.

My hand reaches above its jaw and its eyes slowly close, a small breath leaving its lips with my touch.

Suddenly, the beast begins to tremble and shake, its figure convulsing above me as my eyes flicker back and forth between its head and body as it changes.

What was happening, why–

My thoughts are cut off as its body begins to shrink, its arms and legs slowly shifting from the massive beast's shape into something else.

This was a transformation I'd seen before...by shifters.

The *murderous beast* was a shifter?! But I'd never seen or heard of something so big and powerful being a shifter before.

I look at the body forming above me...a very *naked* body. My gaze trails up his toned legs to his *very* large...*package*...I move quickly up to his torso and the tight six-pack there before trailing up the muscular arms sitting to each side of my head. And that's when we meet. Two grey-blue eyes.

A very familiar pair of grey-blue eyes.

Mallyn's.

His face is now fully visible and not hidden by a hood. His white hair shines almost silver above me, his skin almost a porcelain shade as his eyes swirl with grey and bright blue hues. But it's his face that captures the air from my lungs.

It's a face that could rival even Creed's model-esque features. But where Creed had a classic Grecian God kind of beauty, Mallyn's looks were a mix of light and dark, of

470 | ISLA DAVON

soft and sculpted. Looking at him was like seeing a Fallen Angel. Something truly breathtaking and untouchable.

He sits above me, his eyes glued to me with my hand still cupping his cheek.

I move to take it back when he suddenly shifts forward, leaning further into my palm with his eyes never leaving mine.

A strange look pulls at his features as he gazes at me, his eyes slightly widening before they soften almost just as instantly. His mouth parts, "*Micai, I–*"

"Micai!"

"Red!"

Ezra and Annex's voices echo out behind us with their footsteps following soon after.

"Mic–" Ezra's voice cuts off. His shoes are now at my eye level before he moves to help Mallyn up off me.

"What are you–" Annex shouts as he comes up beside them. "Oh."

Ezra tells Annex to give Mallyn his jacket to wrap around him, while he takes off his own. He pulls me up and wraps his teal shirt around me.

I meet his turquoise eyes, a shaky sigh falling from his lips as he pulls me closer and leans his forehead against mine.

"Never again, Micai. Never do that to me again." He kisses the tip of my nose as his hands slide around my waist, a slight tremor in his fingers as he pulls me into his bare torso. "Don't ever do something so dangerous again, and don't ever leave without me. I'll always follow you, no matter what." He pulls back, his eyes narrowing, "Lead the way...but never leave me behind again."

THE BLACKENED BLADE | 471

Annex wraps an arm around Ezra, his eyes meeting mine in a mock glare before grinning.

"I told you she was my kind of crazy." He places his hand on my cheek, brushing his rough fingers along my skin before his grin fades into a more serious look. "But Ez is right. *This...*" He gestures between us all. "This isn't negotiable. We go where you go and vice versa, Red. Never leave us behind again." His gaze softens slightly as a warm smile stretches his lips. "It's too late to run from us...you're ours now."

Ezra nods as a grey-blue pair of eyes gleam behind him—a strange look forming on Mallyn's face as he takes a step closer to us.

Mallyn had always been an enigma, but now a piece of that had come undone. He was the beast and predator I had come to know and fear, my forest rival and foe.

Is that why he always kept his distance from me?

The eyes I'm gazing into now don't seem like the same creature from moments ago, though...

A plethora of questions flood my mind, racing back and forth, when suddenly, a shout rings out around me.

A set of hands grab me before I can think, throwing me to the ground, sending me tumbling to the forest floor.

I pick myself up, my vision slightly blurry and my head ringing as voices sound out around me.

I rub my aching head and scratched arms before pulling myself up straight. Turning back, I see Mallyn snapping the neck of a large grey beast. Blood runs down a huge curved black horn on its head as it falls limply to the ground. Green liquid oozes from its mouth. But if that was its blood, then the red blood on its horn...

"Stay with me, Annex." Ezra's voice is shaky as I peer over to him...and to where I had just been standing.

Ezra's crouches over Annex's body, his hands pushing down on a large gaping wound in his chest. Blood seeps through the gaps in his fingers as he tries his best to stop the bleeding.

I rush over as Ezra shouts to Mallyn, telling him to get Creed, to get help...but everything fades to white noise in my ears as I edge closer to Annex's side.

My heart comes to a screeching stop as I stare down at him. *Annex....*

A pool of blood seeps out below him, his eyes fluttering open and shut, his face falling paler by the second as his breathing grows raspy and gurgled.

I slowly crouch down beside him, my hands fumbling to take his in my own. His cold fingers grip weakly onto my hand as his head turns slightly to meet me.

He tries to open his mouth and give me a smile but starts coughing instead, blood spluttering from his mouth with each painful bark.

I grip his hand tighter, squeezing it as I feel a vice wrap around my chest and my throat feeling narrow.

"Stay with us, Annex," Ezra pleads, his hands pushing down harder on the wound. "We still have to punish Micai for not listening. You don't want to miss out on that, do you?"

A small gurgling noise falls from Annex's bloodied lips as a weak smile stretches them. A feeble sound follows from his throat, but it lacks any of his normal dark, playful tones.

"No...ca...n't mi...ss that." His voice sounds frail and shaky, growing weaker with each syllable.

But I shake the thought from my head. I had to focus.

Annex would be fine. Nothing could kill this psycho. I just had to help him until someone came.

But what could I do? My eyes flicker toward the shirt draped over my shoulders.

I pull Ezra's teal shirt off and place it on Annex's wound. Ezra nods, taking it from me and using it to help stop the bleeding.

"Red..." Annex calls weakly. I take his hand in mine and lean down closer, thinking about what I could do to help keep him conscious and here with us until help arrives.

His eyes flutter as a trickle of blood drips from the side of his mouth and a panic like no other slices through me as I watch his complexion darken.

I grip his hand, pulling it toward me as nonsensical words fall from my mouth.

"You always call me *Red*. Red this and Red that...why, it makes no sense!" My voice is a little higher pitched than I'd like, and some of my panic seeps through as Ezra tries to call for help.

A small, feeble grin embraces his blood-stained lips. "Closer Red..."

I bend in closer, his voice almost like a whisper in my ear as he beckons me to him. A gurgling sound falls from his lips as he tries to chuckle again, his eyes fluttering a little as I squeeze his hand.

"It's because...you're everything that colour stands for...and more. Dangerous. Fearless...And a temptation... I shouldn't touch or want...but can't help coming back to...You're the salvation I never knew I needed. *My Red.*"

"Annex..." I pull back slightly, my face mere inches from his, as his fingers twitch in my hand. I take his hand and place it on my cheek, his feeble smile growing a little. He coughs again, more blood seeping from his mouth and down his neck, as my mind goes blank. The sound of his breathing grows weaker with each passing moment and panic lances up my back and splinters through my chest.

This couldn't be it.

Annex *couldn't* die.

Not him, not the demented psycho who was blood-mad, who annoyed me to no end, who tried to take my food, and who...made me laugh and smile.

The ache in my chest starts to grow, spreading to each limb, my fingertips feeling weak as I clutch his hand and watch as his eyes turn hazy and dark. My throat dries up, my breath coming out in small gasps trying to pull whatever air I can into my lungs.

My hands tremble as the memories of the day I lost Zrael flood my mind. I couldn't lose another person I loved...I wasn't strong enough. The grief and pain almost killed me the first time.

Life wasn't worth living when Zrael left me, only my pain and revenge spurred me on.

But Annex and Ezra...they brought back a part of me I thought I'd never have again. They filled a part of the gaping hole, trying to consume my heart and soul, and made me smile again. They made me feel like there could be more to this life than I thought if maybe they were in it with me. They gave me *hope*.

Tears trickle down my face as I hear Ezra's voice somewhere nearby.

The fingers on my cheek brush weakly along my skin before instantly loosening. I grip his hand, the weight becoming heavier in my grasp as I lift it to my lips. I place a shaky kiss along his fingers, praying to whatever Gods there are that they help, that they save him, and that *they don't take him from me.*

Our eyes meet, and I watch as the glint from those piercing blue eyes darkens, his hand now limp in mine as I clutch it.

Everything around me darkens, each sound and feeling falling numb as the broken pieces inside me further crack and splinter.

A part of me leaving with his last breath as death takes another piece of my soul with him.

ABOUT THE AUTHOR

Isla Davon is an Irish author who loves reading. Especially Paranormal Romance and Why Choose books. She enjoys creating stories with magic, strong female characters, and as many love interests as her mind can handle.

When she is not writing, she is spending time with her family and three Jack Russells. Or snuggling down to a good movie or Netflix binge with as much chocolate as she can eat.

Keep up to date on future books by following Isla on her Facebook group; Davons Shadows~Isla Davon's Reader group, or on her Tik Tok and Instagram; Author.is-ladavon.